PRAISE FOR TRACY CLARK

Hide

"Tracy Clark's not-so-hidden talent is for conjuring characters who are engaging and achingly real. Detective Harri Foster is a stellar recruit to her new team and to our crime fiction shelves. *Hide* is a page-turner with heart."

—Lori Rader-Day, Agatha Award–winning author of *Death at Greenway*

Runner

"You know those books that are wonderful, but that envy, the worm in the bud, makes you shy away from praising because you wish you'd created that prose or those insights? *Runner* by Tracy Clark. She understands the streets, kids, the way a PI and a cop really work. Kudos."

—Sara Paretsky, *New York Times* bestselling author of the V.I. Warshawski series and cofounder of Sisters in Crime

"Clark writes with purpose, her sense of social justice never venturing into dogma but remaining fully rooted in Raines's actions and personality. She saves, but is no savior, because she operates in a world where survival is the benchmark, and pain remains in the aftermath."

—*The New York Times*

"Clark has a unique voice in the PI genre, one that is articulate, daring, and ultimately hopeful."

—S.A. Cosby, Anthony and ITW award-winner, *The Washington Post*

Broken Places

Engrossing and superbly written—I can't say enough good things about *Broken Places!*"

 —Lisa Black, New York Times bestselling author of *That Darkness* and
Unpunished

"Unforgettable . . . Distinctive, vividly written characters lift this promising debut. Readers will be eager for the sequel."
—Publishers Weekly (starred review)

"Clark's compelling, suspenseful, and action-packed debut introduces a dogged, tough African American woman investigator who is complex and courageous and surrounded by a family of fascinating misfits. Fans of Sue Grafton's Kinsey Millhone or Sara Paretsky's V.I. Warshawski will welcome Cass Raines to their ranks."
—Library Journal (starred review)

"This street-smart first mystery boasts great characterization and a terrific new protagonist. Get this writer on your radar now."
—Booklist

Chicago Mystery Series

"A potent mix of empathy and rage fuels Sue Grafton Award winner Clark's exceptional fourth Chicago mystery. The action builds to an exciting showdown. Those who like their crime novels with a social conscience will be amply rewarded."
—Publishers Weekly (starred review)

"Clark has a unique voice in the PI genre, one that is articulate, daring, and ultimately hopeful."

—*The Washington Post*

HIDE

OTHER TITLES BY TRACY CLARK

HIDE

A DETECTIVE HARRIET FOSTER THRILLER

TRACY CLARK

THOMAS & MERCER

Text copyright © 2023 by Tracy Clark
All rights reserved.

No part of this book may be reproduced, or stored in a retrieval system, or transmitted in any form or by any means, electronic, mechanical, photocopying, recording, or otherwise, without express written permission of the publisher.

Published by Thomas & Mercer, Seattle

www.apub.com

Amazon, the Amazon logo, and Thomas & Mercer are trademarks of Amazon.com, Inc., or its affiliates.

ISBN-13: 9781542037570
ISBN-10: 1542037573

Cover design by Damon Freeman

Printed in the United States of America

HIDE

CHAPTER 1

Elyse Pratt hated Mondays on principle. She hated running on a Monday even more, but at thirty-eight she knew time was not on her side, and she was determined to stay in a size six if it killed her.

She jogged her way along the Riverwalk, heading east, sweaty, huffing, resigned. She'd win no marathon or speed record, but she was out here, she was doing it, and her reward would be gotten on the scale. One hundred and twelve solid pounds was her sweet spot, give or take a tofu salad.

She passed the City Winery and another unhappy jogger going the opposite direction. They exchanged a head nod and a slight smile. Ariana Grande wafted out of Elyse's earbuds, the beat of the up-tempo pop fluff just lively enough to keep her toned legs moving and her mind off the early hour and the fact that she would allow herself nothing for breakfast but a kale smoothie and half a mandarin orange.

She flicked a look at the clouds overhead and filled her lungs with fall air, breathing in earthy algae from the green-gray river running along her left, mixed, strangely, with the aroma of coffee and chocolate chip cookies—Satan's temptations.

Elyse picked up the pace, Michigan Avenue and the DuSable Bridge just ahead. She'd stop at the underpass leading to the marina and then turn around and complete her route. Three miles. Then the smoothie. She ticked off the landmarks as they loomed over her from street level—the Merchandise Mart, the Jewelers and Wrigley Buildings, the Tribune Tower, and, on the site of the old *Sun-Times*, the building Elyse let her eyes sweep right past, its name emblazoned on the side so large that she would swear astronauts could see it from space. She picked up her pace.

As she jogged past the bridge, the underpass in sight, something off the path caught her eye. She squinted, slowed. It looked like a pile of leaves. Odd. There weren't that many trees down here, not enough certainly to account for so big a mound. It was curious but not alarming. There were leaves. It was autumn. Some city worker had likely raked them up and left them there to scatter again. But as she got closer, she saw something sticking out of the pile. A foot, though it didn't look real. Some idiot's sick joke. It was probably a mannequin underneath, someone's idea of starting Halloween weeks too early.

Elyse slowed as she got nearer, then stopped right where the path abutted the pile. She padded forward, pulling the earbuds free, letting Grande sing on. The foot was ghostly white, almost blue. There was toenail polish on the toes. Not a joke. Not a mannequin.

Her scream tore through the morning like the screech of a thousand crows. Elyse backed away, her heart pounding, and then she ran back along the path the way she'd come, every alarm in her body clanging as panic overtook her. Her phone. She stopped and fumbled for it in her pocket but dropped it on the path when her trembling fingers couldn't work the keypad.

"Damn it."

She finally managed to scoop the cell up and ran for the stairs that led up to the street, but there was someone there right at the base of the steps. A man. A Black man sitting on the ground, his head on his chest, a spot of blood on his jacket. She screamed again, this time losing every ounce of composure. Fast, as though the man might leap up and grab her, Elyse backed away, no thought in her head following any logical pattern. Blood. Foot. Leaves. Man. *Blood.* Dead. *Dead.*

Her third scream was otherworldly in its desperation. Birds scattered at the sound, and foot traffic along the bridge stopped. She fell to her knees, unable to stop herself from trembling. She needed to get away, flee, but couldn't get to her feet.

"Call 911," she screeched, tears streaking down her face. "Please, somebody, call the police. They're dead."

CHAPTER 2

Monday. 0800 hours. Eight a.m. Detective Harriet Foster couldn't get her legs to move as she stood on the sidewalk in front of CPD's District One building at Seventeenth and State. She was expected inside. Now. But she couldn't get past the sidewalk. Instead, she stood facing the door, cars whizzing past along the wide street at her back, firmly rooted in the in-between.

This was her first day back from leave, the first day on a new team. There would be a new boss, a new desk, a new . . . partner. Nothing she felt gave her any indication that she was ready, not one single thing. Only eight weeks had passed since it happened, eight weeks that felt more like eight seconds.

She inhaled deeply and held the breath for a time before letting it out slowly, but the building was still there, cops and noncops going in and out. Through the windows on the ground floor, she could see the uniformed cop standing at the metal detector just inside. He was watching her, definitely assessing her threat level. Weird Black woman standing on the sidewalk watching the building—friend or foe? Nothing in his level stare indicated that he was taking his assessment lightly.

Cop entry was around the side on Eighteenth Street, accessed through the lot for staff and official vehicles, but she had circled the building at least six times, unable to pull her car in. She knew it was ridiculous, something that she'd have to get over *today*, but right now the bigger issue was deciding to get inside the building. Her star was in her hand, hard metal pressed to her sweating palm. She held it up so the cop could see it. He took one last sweep, and they exchanged a look. Then he nodded and went back to his morning. Friend, not foe. She was one of them.

Two months. Not long enough and yet interminable since the day her partner, Detective Glynnis Thompson, had woken up on a Tuesday, fed her kids, kissed her husband, Mike, goodbye, then driven to work and blown her brains out in the CPD parking lot. A PO walking through the lot heard the shot and found her. Glynnis would have been forty-three on Christmas Day.

Signs. There had to have been signs. There almost always were. But Foster had missed every single one, even though she had been trained to lock in, to be observant, intuitive even, to always see three moves ahead. Where had she failed? She had replayed that day over in her head for weeks, eight weeks, but the picking didn't change anything. Dead was forever. A chance missed to say just the right thing or do the right thing would never come around again.

Glynnis had been a good cop, a decorated cop, and they had worked eleven years together like well-oiled gears in a high-performance machine. After Foster had lost her only son, Reg, to a thug with a gun who'd demanded his bike, a painful divorce had followed. Amid all the pain, Glynnis had helped her stay sane.

Foster was godmother to Glynnis's youngest son, Todd. There had been nothing unusual about the marriage as far as she could see. Mike and Glynnis had been married more than fifteen years. There had been ups and downs, of course, but nothing that might explain what had happened. The kids, though . . . Foster always came back to them. The Glynnis she knew, the one she trusted with her life, wouldn't have done that to her kids. To Mike. To her. But she had.

With a nod and an unconvincing half smile, she moved past the cop at the detector and flashed her star to the cop sitting at the desk in the lobby before heading up to homicide, every step reining in fear and self-doubt and resentment. By rote, the mask went up, her shoulders went back a little farther, and the cop returned. Eight weeks. Eight seconds. She held her breath, kept her dark eyes steady, and put the hardness in them.

"Here we go," she muttered to herself. "Here. We. Go."

Foster stood at the office door, peering in. Just another cop squat—scarred desks, CPD insignia everywhere, the stench of burnt coffee, and sweaty cops who'd seen more than any human should have the misfortune of seeing.

She squeezed her eyes shut, breathing, remembering who she used to be, needing that woman back like yesterday. She'd lost fifteen pounds off her five-foot-seven frame since Glynnis's funeral. The shirt, pants, and jacket she had on today were new. Fresh start and all that. Even her hair was different. She'd gone short and natural, short twists ringing her thin, serious face. Less bother. Less interest. Primping her hair and planning her wardrobe were the least of her worries. Jacket, shirt, slacks, gun, badge, and shoes with a low heel were all she needed. Cop. The job. The rest of her lay buried.

A white cop, tall, thin, brushed by her, flicked her a look. "You're the transfer? Foster, right?"

She nodded. "Harriet Foster. Don't tell me they made an announcement." She glanced at the cop room again, panic rising, her heart fluttering like butterfly wings. If there was a welcoming committee hiding somewhere or cops with prying eyes, she was out of here. "Please, don't."

He chuckled. "Relax. There's no brass band. I just saw your paperwork on the boss's desk." He held out his hand for a shake. Foster took it. "Kelley. Matt." His dark-blue eyes were filled with understanding and a tinge of pity. He looked to be in his late forties, wiry, about six feet, built like a runner instead of a stevedore. "Sorry about . . . you know. That's tough."

Foster stiffened. It was the pity she couldn't take. It felt like it burned her skin and set her insides on fire. Mask on. Eyes ahead. "Thanks. Everybody knows, I guess."

He nodded. "You know the cop grapevine, but it's cool. We get it. Here, let me show you where to go."

She followed Kelley through the office, feeling the looks at her back. She was the oddity, the cop whose partner had killed herself. Foster could just imagine what they were thinking. Where had she been when it all happened? Why hadn't she stopped it, intervened? What kind of partner was she? Could they trust her? She kept her eyes on the back of Kelley's shirt. They were right. She had asked those same questions of herself every single hour of every single day since that day. What kind of partner was she? What kind of cop? What kind of friend? What kind of mother? The last thought, random but not, caught in her throat, and she pushed forward, a tiny fear and a tiny sorrow stabbing at her core. Today, she thought. She just had to get through today. Once today was past her, everyone would turn away, the cop bullshitting would take over, and there would be no great attentiveness shown to her. After today, she could ease back into the routine of the job and fill her days with the misery of others.

Kelley pointed at a corner office. The door was closed. "The boss is there. What do you go by? Harriet? Harri?"

"Either's fine."

He smiled. "Got it. See ya around, Harri."

She nodded, eyed the door, and then remembered her manners, catching him halfway down the hall.

"Hey, Matt? Thanks."

He tipped an imaginary hat as Foster walked to the door, knocked, and waited to be invited in.

"Yeah, get in here."

Sergeant Sharon Griffin sat at her cluttered desk, jacket off, white blouse spotless. She checked her watch, then looked up, stern of face, giving Foster a quick once-over. She pointed to a chair. "Detective Foster. Sit." Griffin's posture was as straight as a ruler, her face implacable, blue eyes sharp as Arctic ice. She folded her hands on the desk. Foster couldn't miss the wedding ring.

Midfifties, maybe. Griffin's ash-blonde hair was sprinkled with strands of gray and cut short, easy to tuck under a uniform cap. Simple makeup, a little lip coloring, mascara, nothing more. Just female enough to identify, the rest all career cop. Proudly Irish, too, Foster divined from the shamrocks on Griffin's coffee mug, the dusty Saint Patrick's Day fedora sitting on a side table, and the photo on her desk with three pale, freckled teens.

"I've just been going over your personnel file again. Solid career, which is why you're here and not out in the boondocks answering nuisance calls about rabid squirrels. Commendations. Solid leadership skills. Impressive clearance rate." She looked Foster over again. "I intend to tap those leadership skills. I want you out in front." She paused. "How're you doing?"

Foster had no idea how to answer the question. How *was* she doing? She was here. She'd gotten through the front door. Her mask was on. She was almost sure she could be a cop today.

"Fine," Foster said.

Griffin sat back to study her. "Maybe. Tough thing losing a partner that way. Losing a partner period. I'm sorry for your loss." She flicked another look at the personnel file. "Detective Glynnis Thompson. Family and everything. Jeez. This job . . . sometimes . . . it just breaks you." She looked up and saw the stricken look on Foster's face along with the beginnings of a cold sweat. "The elephant in the room." Griffin laced her hands together in her lap. "Your first day back. Are you all here?"

Foster let a beat pass. This was the moment, one of several over the last weeks when she had a decision to make, a side to take, in or out, as she'd had to do five years ago after losing Reg. "Yes, boss."

Griffin didn't miss the pause. "I talked to Sergeant Traynor. He told me you and Thompson were a star team. A real buddy act. It's a loss . . . but not the only one you've suffered." She flicked a look at the photograph on her desk. "Losing a kid. I can't imagine anything tougher than that. I can see from your face you don't want to talk about it. I respect that. It's not common knowledge out there with the team. Up to you what you share."

Foster heard Griffin, her words made sense, but she'd detached, distanced herself from the pain behind the wall she'd built for just that purpose. She watched Griffin's mouth move, heard the words, but she was elsewhere, somewhere safe.

"Foster?" she heard Griffin say. "Harriet, you all right?"

She cleared her throat and dialed back in. "Yes. Sorry. Slight headache."

Griffin reached into her top desk drawer, pulled out a bottle of aspirin, and slid it across the desk to Foster. "Take two."

Foster grabbed the bottle and watched as Griffin rolled her chair back, reached into a tiny fridge behind her desk, and pulled out a squat bottle of spring water, which she offered to her. She swallowed two tablets and washed them down. Foster started to push the aspirin bottle back across the desk, but Griffin held up a hand. "Keep it."

Foster slipped the bottle into her bag and nodded thanks.

"You always this subdued?" Griffin asked.

Their eyes held. "I don't know what you're asking."

Griffin leaned forward. "I'm asking, Detective Harriet Foster, if you have your head in the game and your waders on tight. You've had two devastating gut punches. One of them would have been enough to sideline most people. I need to know that you're solidly on the beam. Traynor says you're steady. I believe him. I'll believe you, too, if you say it."

Foster's breath caught. She wanted to scream and run out of Griffin's office, out of the building. She needed air. Only pride, stubbornness, and concern that it was this job or nothing nailed her to the chair. "If I weren't ready, I wouldn't be here," Foster said. "Boss."

The women sat watching each other. This was the start of it. Foster's road back, Griffin's necessary ask. "I had a suicide on my team," Griffin began. "He'd been on the job twenty-five years. A bit of a loner. Dombrowski. One day he's the same old Dombrowski, cracking jokes, clowning around; the next day he's strung up from a pipe in the john. He hung himself with his own tie. We found his star in the toilet. You've lost a son, a marriage, now a partner. What have you got outside this building, Foster? Faith? Family?"

"A mother. A brother. A niece and nephew. Cousins, aunts, uncles."

"Close?"

Foster thought about it. Some families fractured after loss. Sometimes the fractures were slow to repair. It was complicated, too complicated to go through here and now. "Enough."

"Hmm. You couldn't see yourself staying with your old team?"

How could she stay when she couldn't bear to park in the lot? To sit at her desk? To see someone who wasn't Glynnis sitting at hers? "I needed a change. I left on good terms. Traynor can vouch for that."

"He has. He was also sorry to see you go, but he understands. As I do." Griffin smiled. "You've had your fair share, Foster, that's for sure. But you're still kicking, and that shows me what you're made of. Still, CPD can't be what you hang the rest of your life on. I'm glad to have you here, but don't bury yourself here. Understand?"

Foster nodded but said nothing.

"I'm going to need to hear it," Griffin said.

Foster cleared her throat before speaking clearly. "Yes, boss, I understand."

"Then you're in. Here's the spiel. I don't do the old boys' club here. I actively recruit women to fill my spots. In my opinion, women are smarter, faster, more intuitive. You're a woman, Foster."

"Yes, boss."

"And you're a Black woman. That doesn't go unnoticed."

"Well, how could it."

Griffin nodded. "Ah, there it is."

"Boss?"

"The steel, Foster. You're down but not out." She closed Foster's file and stood. Foster stood too. Griffin held out her hand for a shake. "Welcome, Harriet. Just promise me you won't suffer in silence. If you need help, ask for it. No dishonor. If I find you in my lot with your brains shot out, I will literally walk to the ME's office and beat your dead body to a bloody pulp. Got it?"

Foster's heart raced as she beat the image back, but she met Griffin's gaze without a flinch. "Understood."

"Good. I paired you with Jim Lonergan. Full disclosure: he's an asshole, but he's serviceable. Don't take his crap. He'll give it, guaranteed. Ignore what you can; challenge the rest. You've dealt with assholes before?"

Foster managed to grin. "Everywhere I've worked."

"Then you're ahead of the game. If it doesn't work out, I'll find you someone else. Now get out there and catch me some killers."

Dismissed, Foster stood outside Griffin's door, her eyes sweeping over the office with the strange cops milling around it. She could do this. She knew how to be a cop. Glynnis's loss hadn't stripped that away.

"Symansky."

She jumped, startled by the stumpy white guy who'd shot out of nowhere. He held out a hand, grinning. "Al." He looked like Bela Lugosi in a loud plaid blazer and a tie that cried *Father's Day 1985*. "Welcome aboard."

"Harriet Foster," she said, going in for the shake. "Thanks."

He pointed to a desk at the back of the room. "You're over there with Mr. Personality. Try not to kill him. He ain't worth the time you'll do."

Foster shook her head. Yet another warning about Lonergan. "Is he that bad?"

Symansky's bushy gray brows lifted. "Decent. No finesse. Part of the team, though." He winked. "Hang in there."

The desk was a piece of garbage facing another piece of garbage just like it. City issue. A metal, dinged-up block with half the drawer pulls loose, a desk shared by hundreds of cops over hundreds of hours of round-the-clock shifts. It was beaten down, dirty, with decades of coffee rings on its surface, foul words etched into the raggedy blotter with crude sketches of penises. Foster knew she'd find wads of old chewing gum tacked to the underside of the chair if she bothered to check.

Underwhelmed right out of the gate, she glanced over at the broad, doughy white man sitting at the other desk, leaning back in a squeaky roller chair, assessing her through squinty brown eyes. Lonergan. She scanned his desk, but there was nothing on it but paperwork, a half-eaten stromboli, and a chipped Bears mug with coffee in it. A breakfast of champions.

Lonergan's eyes never wavered as he sucked on a toothpick, the short, pointed piece of wood toggling up and down like a seesaw between dry, thin lips.

"You're Foster," he said. "Boss told me we'd be partnering up. Jim Lonergan."

Foster nodded, then ran a finger along the top of the desk. It came back sticky. She wiped her hand against her pant leg.

"They're all slobs on third watch," Lonergan explained. "You'll get used to it." He stood and stretched. "Welcome to the nuthouse. Let me show you around." He pointed at the sticky desk. "That's you." He flung his arms wide. "This is us. End of tour." He sat back down and worked the toothpick some more.

Griffin and Symansky had been right. Asshole. Foster pulled out her slouchy chair and dropped her bag into the seat. "Thanks."

"Now we'll transition to the get-to-know-you portion of our program. You married?"

Foster checked the desk drawers to see where she could eventually stow her stuff. "No," she answered absently. She looked around the office, noting the significant distance between her and Lonergan's desks and the hub of activity half a room away. She'd gotten the new-kid spot next to the blowhard no one wanted to sit next to. Great.

"Ever?" Lonergan pressed.

Foster stared at him and then decided to answer, hoping to shut his line of questioning down. "Once." She figured that would do it. Her frosty tone alone would have signaled to a normal person that more intimate details were off the table.

"Gay?"

Foster looked up, giving him another good, long sweep. The man with the twenty questions, her new partner, didn't look like he was going to be an easy fit, not like Glynnis. She hadn't yet cleared off her workspace, and already she wanted someone better than him.

"No, but would that matter to you?"

"Nah. I live and let live."

"Then why ask?"

"Just trying to get a bead on you. See what I'm working with. Got kids?"

Foster let a moment go. "Maybe we can ease into the personal details over time." She opened the top drawer on the desk, peeking inside. "Or not."

Lonergan plucked the toothpick from his mouth and chucked it into the trash basket beside his desk. "Suit yourself. But know this: I move fast, and I'm an old-school cop. Keep up, and we'll get along great."

"Do I look like a rookie to you? I've switched teams, not rank."

Lonergan smirked. "I got twenty-two under my belt."

"And I've got a solid seventeen."

He held up his hands in mock surrender. "All right. Take it easy. No offense."

Foster grabbed her bag and shoved it into the bottom drawer, then sat down. Lonergan went back to his computer screen, a satisfied smirk on his face. She glared at the top of his block head, distrustful of his buzz cut. *Old-school cop* was right. But she was sure he meant that as a badge of honor, wholly unaware it might mean something entirely different to her.

"Just know, if you're worried about it," he said, not bothering to look at her, "I know how to keep my powder dry."

"What'd you say?" Foster asked, a warning in her delivery.

"Meaning my gun is for the bad guys, not for me, in case you were worried about what kind of partner I'd be. I don't mean to pick at sore wounds—my condolences and all—but I thought I'd put it out there so we'd know where we stand right from the jump."

Slowly she rose, her fists clenched, her jaw tight. She didn't know the man, having just met him minutes ago, but what she saw so far was a problem. Callousness. That was how she'd peg it. A screw loose somewhere.

She could feel the heat rising at the back of her neck. It took everything to keep her voice neutral, professional. "You don't talk about my partner. Get it?"

Lonergan rolled his chair away from his desk but said nothing. He didn't even blink.

"You don't talk about her, and nobody here talks about her. Pass it around so they all know."

Lonergan smiled. "I never mentioned your partner, did I?"

"Not you, not anyone. We clear?"

Foster held Lonergan in her angry sights. This was her nonnegotiable. Lonergan shrugged, smiled, and let it go like it was nothing. "Whatever you say, *partner*."

She reached into the drawer and grabbed the aspirin bottle Griffin had given her from her bag, then slammed the drawer shut with great force, the sound getting the attention of the cops around her. "Bathroom?"

Lonergan jabbed a fat thumb behind him. "Down the hall. First left. Gents and gals. We don't do none of that unisex shit here. You're gonna have to choose."

He was a goddamned dinosaur. She spotted a lone paper clip on the desk, plucked it up, and slipped it into her pocket. "Anyone ever tell you you make a lousy first impression?"

Lonergan swiveled around, giving Foster his back. "Nobody I give a shit about."

She looked where he'd pointed. "I'll be back."

He turned back to watch her go. "Roger that. Oh, and Foster?" She stopped, not bothering to turn around. "Anybody ever tell you to lighten the hell up?"

She tightened her grip on the bottle. "Nobody I give a shit about."

A minute later, Foster stood at the sink in the women's bathroom, staring into the streaky mirror. Things weren't going well. She'd been in the building less than an hour, and already she'd had enough. What the hell was wrong with him? Who said things like that?

She turned away from the sink and leaned against it, taking the dim room in. It looked cleanish, the smell of industrial-strength disinfectant strong, but the porcelain toilets in the stalls and the sink looked as though they'd been there since the first Daley administration. She turned back to the tap and downed another two tablets to chase the ones she'd taken in Griffin's office. Bad for her liver long term, but she had more immediate needs at present.

"He knows how to keep his powder dry," she muttered. "Bastard."

She let the cold water run a bit before wetting her cheeks to get the heat out. Foster stared into the mirror again, past the streaks in the glass, at the strained stranger looking back.

"It's only the first day. Pull it together," she told her reflection. "You don't have to go home with him; all you have to do is work with him. Cop up." She tried a smile, but it wouldn't stick. How long had it been since she'd smiled genuinely? "Do it. Focus."

She lifted her palms off the sink and stretched her fingers, checking her hands for steadiness. Rock solid, nearly. She gave herself one final look, one final pep talk, and then went back to start again.

"About time," Lonergan said as he slipped into the rumpled blazer that had been hanging on the back of his chair. "Thought you mighta fell in. We got a body. A woman. On the Riverwalk." He grabbed his coffee and the stromboli. "I'm driving. You're last one in. Besides, women can't drive for shit."

Foster grabbed her bag, glaring at Lonergan's back as he brushed past her.

CHAPTER 3

A psych eval, probation, and a voluntary thirty-day stay at Westhaven Psychiatric Hospital. That was what his lawyer had worked out for him. What a crock. Since when was looking a crime? Since when couldn't you walk on the same street, slip into the same bar, or follow a woman home just to see where she lived? In retrospect, he could see now how following someone could have been misconstrued. He'd been curious, that was all. Now he was prohibited from making any contact. Fine. There were other women. Special ones. He'd just have to be careful from now on. Bodie stuffed the last shirt into his battered duffel and zipped it tight. Thirty days. Up today. It had been intolerable even with the ill-scheduled home pass he'd been given just the day before. It was ridiculous, he'd argued, then. Why let him go, then make him come back, only to release him for good the very next day? Was it some kind of test to see if he could handle himself? Was it the result of some bureaucratic screwup the powers that be were afraid to cop to? It didn't matter, he'd decided. He'd taken the pass, enjoyed his time, and now he was packing up and getting the hell out of here for good.

He glanced around the depressing cracker box of a room, his home away from not much, and cursed it. But that was all done now. He was clear, except for the ding on his record, and he had done the thirty days. He was as normal as the next man.

It was disheartening to be here like this at thirty-two, to still be flailing about, a good chunk of what should have been the finest time of his life behind him already, ruined by failure, self-insulation, and shame. He should be married with kids. He should have a profession, a stake, instead of an endless series of meaningless jobs. He should be out in the world setting it on fire, not pinballing his way from one slipup to another and then suffering the indignity of having his sister, Amelia, bail him out, pick up the slack, *manage* him like he was some kind of idiot who didn't have the sense to run his own life. How had his twin come out on top? He felt horrible being both angry and indebted. Westhaven would have been the perfect place to unpack all that, but he couldn't, not without telling, and he couldn't do that.

He lifted the duffel off the bed and headed for the door. At least he was out of here. No more psychiatrists like Dr. Mariana Silva with her probing questions and freaky dark eyes. He'd lied about a happy childhood with loving parents, and Silva seemed to know it. But he had to lie. He and Amelia knew that no one, *no one*, could know their truth. They'd made a family pact with their father—all for one, one for all. *Morgans stick together.* Not a single revelation escaped their quiet house. But silence was complicity, and you were only as sick as your secrets. He'd learned that in AA. Only the adage assumed that once the secrets were released, there'd be a new, fresh person left behind.

What if secrets were a cancer? What if you cut away the cancer and there was nothing healthy left?

Silva saw him, and he hated her for it. He hated the way she'd tried to smugly wheedle his darkness out of him. Every look she'd given him had been predatory, grasping, greedy. She handled him as though he were unstable, the human equivalent of a ramshackle wagon of nitro rolling over a pitted road. It just showed how much she didn't know. He knew what he was. Tainted, a creature of habits, of types. *He* was the cancer, the curse.

Smiling, he closed the door behind him and headed out, pushing through the hospital's front doors, filling his lungs with freedom, starting again at zero. At thirty-two.

He passed through the gate and down the road where he knew Amelia would be waiting. He stopped when he saw his sister leaning against a silver Mercedes convertible, her arms crossed in front of her. Even in a weathered field jacket and worn jeans, her auburn hair a messy mop, she looked like she held the world on a string, like a model on a Ralph Lauren photo shoot. No makeup because none was needed. Flawless. Even Am knew she was exceptional. Was that her power? Knowing? Bodie loved that about her, but part of him resented her too.

Am smiled and lifted off the car when she saw him coming. She ran to him, grabbed him up in a big bear hug, and kissed him on the cheek. "C'mere, Bod. You're sprung, you idiot."

Bodie leaned into the hug and squeezed his sister back. Am smelled like paint and plaster, tools of her artist trade. He wished he had a trade, something he was good at. He could have been a doctor or a dentist—or an accountant like . . .

Am gave him the once-over. It didn't look like she appreciated what she saw. "Good God, you're a bag of bones. Weren't they feeding you?"

"It's not a five-star resort," he said, sliding into the passenger seat, the smell of expensive leather snaking up his nose. "What happened to that rattletrap Land Rover you had?"

"I sold a piece. Traded up. Hungry?"

"Sure. Congratulations, by the way. On the piece."

"Thanks. Pizza?"

"Fine."

She stared at him for a moment, like she was taking inventory. "And?"

He sighed. "And I gave them nothing."

He didn't mention his pass. Am didn't need to know. He gave Westhaven's gate a final look before Am sped away.

CHAPTER 4

The presence of a half dozen squad cars parked along Upper Wacker with their lights flashing had attracted quite a crowd of curious onlookers along the bridge at Michigan Avenue. Foster ignored the heckling and jeering directed at them as she and Lonergan descended the metal steps to the Riverwalk. A few people standing up top yelled out recriminations and taunts, calling for the city to "defund the police." There'd been protests all summer, their intensity unabated in the fall. In fact, just the day before, a well-attended march had wended its way through the streets, snarling traffic as protesters made their way with banners waving and horns bleating from CPD headquarters to Daley Plaza. People were angry, frightened. It was better not to engage.

"Sure got here quick, didn't ya?" an onlooker shouted down. "Wasted no time, matter of fact."

Foster didn't look up, feeling the sting of the snide remark about their response time here off the Mag Mile compared to what it was perceived to be in neighborhoods where complexions were darker and bank accounts less robust.

"Defund the police?" Lonergan muttered. "Can you believe that? Who're they gonna call when some jackhole carjacks 'em? Streets and San?"

Foster flicked him a look. The partnership hadn't started off great, and it had been a quiet ride over in the car. The less she said, the better, she figured, at least on day one.

"You got nothing to say to that shit?" He cocked his head toward the hecklers.

Foster swept her eyes along the bridge, watching the faces of those who considered her the enemy, knowing full well how the high-profile police shootings and racially tinged arrests had gotten them here, how they had galvanized the us-versus-them battle lines. Most of the heat she could understand; some she even endorsed. No good cop stood for a bad one. So why was Lonergan, the self-proclaimed "old-school cop," taking the heckling as a personal affront? She had her theories.

"No," she said, then walked away from him.

A dead body found on the Riverwalk was unusual. Occasionally, there would be a mugging reported down here, some tourist asked to "break yourself" and hand over their wallet by an opportunist who could smell the cluelessness on them. Or there would be a drowning—some blitzed, overgrown frat boy who had tottered out of a bar at 2:00 a.m. and into the river, too drunk to save himself.

The Mag Mile was just up a level, with its high-end shops dotted along the popular ten-block stretch of prime real estate—Nordstrom, the Apple Store, Saks, the iconic Water Tower farther north, and the pricey high-rise mall that sprouted up across the street from it. The exclusivity extended down here to the Riverwalk, too—the multi-million-dollar mixed-use project combining trendy riverside bars and restaurants with public art displays, pedestrian paths, and stone steps for lounging as the water taxis and tour boats slid past under the series of bascule bridges.

Foster eyed one of the tour boats moored beside a canvas overhang and signs announcing the hours of operation and cost per passenger. The promise of festiveness was incongruent to the grim reason they'd been called here. The yellow crime scene tape marking the outer perimeter had a female patrol officer standing at it, but Foster and Lonergan moved through, their stars hanging from chain necklaces around their necks. Foster's attention slid to a bird-thin white woman in neon-pink running gear crying on a bench a few yards away. Another female PO stood beside her, trying to calm her down. Foster noted, not for the first time during her career, that women were often charged with these duties—guarding the perimeter and comforting frightened children and distraught women. "You gals are better at it," she'd had a male sergeant once tell her. "It's the estrogen." She'd bristled, then, and though things were better today, there were still those bosses, predominantly male, who made it standard practice to consider gender when assigning tasks.

"Okay. What we got?" Lonergan dug into his pocket and plucked out a package of Juicy Fruit, then popped a stick into his mouth.

Foster watched as the PO straightened up and consulted her notebook. Foster's eyes flicked over the gold nameplate on the officer's uniform blouse. Hernandez. It didn't appear Hernandez had been on the job long. She still looked fresh, clear eyed, eager. Foster knew it was only a matter of time before the streets changed that. The scarring and jadedness were accumulative, years in the making, and inevitable.

"Elyse Pratt, thirty-eight, lives across the river in Marina Towers. Out for her morning run. She's running east at about zero seven thirty hours, clears the bridge, gets to about the kayak rental hut there when she sees the leaves piled up over by the fence, then the foot sticking out. She loses it and runs. That's when she sees the young man with blood on his jacket. Her screaming got everyone's attention up top there. When we arrived, she was a mess. We couldn't get anything else out of her."

The three of them glanced over at the weeping woman. "She been doing that the whole time?" Lonergan asked.

Hernandez nodded. "Not every day you jog up on a body."

He frowned, looking around. "And the second body? Where's it at?"

"He wasn't dead, just out of it. Black male. No obvious signs of injury. We checked his pocket for ID, found his driver's license. He's Keith Ainsley, nineteen. We also found an NU student ID on him. There was a little blood on his jacket, like I said, but we didn't find a weapon. He's been transported to Northwestern. Where we found him is taped off, as you can see."

"Drunk? High? What?" Lonergan asked.

"I didn't smell alcohol on him, but we couldn't rouse him. Could be a medical issue. Could be drugs. We don't know."

"Did Pratt call it in, Hernandez?" Foster asked.

The PO gave her a slight smile and a nod, her dark eyes meeting Foster's. "She couldn't manage it, she told us." She referred again to her notes. "A passerby on the bridge, a William Sims, heard her and made the call at zero seven thirty-six. He reported he heard her yell, 'They're dead. They're dead.' He looked over the side, saw her on her knees, and called it in. Then, of course, that drew the crowd you see up there now. A couple others called in, too, after that, but we were already rolling by then."

Foster looked up at the bridge. "Nobody saw anyone else but her? No one running away? Not Ainsley?"

Hernandez shook her head. "You can't see the body from up there or where Ainsley was laying unless you're halfway down the steps or standing down here on the path. All anyone saw was Pratt screaming her head off."

Foster glanced over at the second cordon, the area at the base of the steps where Ainsley had been found. It was just a few yards from the spot where Pratt had discovered the pile of leaves. She nodded at the PO. "Thanks. We'll be back to talk to her in a bit."

Lonergan nodded. "Yeah, but see if you can get her to turn off all that drama before we get back, huh?"

He didn't wait to see how his words landed or the puzzled look on Hernandez's face. Foster sighed, nodded a thanks to the PO, and met up with him at the inner perimeter, the duo ducking under the red tape together to stand next to the leaves and the two male POs guarding them. Some of the leaves, Foster noticed, were wet with dew, while others were as desiccated as old bone. The foot was pale, slightly bluish where blood had settled, the victim's toenail polish the only sign of vibrancy. It had been cold overnight, barely out of the forties. Foster wondered how long the body had been lying here out in the open, discarded like a tossed-away paper cup.

"You sure she's dead and not sleeping one off like the other guy?" Lonergan asked the tall officer next to him.

Foster slipped into a pair of nitrile gloves, moving cautiously around the leaves, noticing where they'd been brushed away from the woman's neck and chin to reveal long red hair. The responding officer, Giannis, according to his nameplate, had likely checked for a pulse and hadn't found one. She was sure they wouldn't have gotten called up if someone here had found signs of life. No one wanted to be *that* cop. Foster had an idea what was coming and didn't have to wait long for it.

"*Detective*," Giannis said, his voice as cold as a headstone in January. "We made sure she wasn't just 'sleeping one off' before we elevated the call. Then we sealed off the area, as you see it now. The young man, who was breathing when we arrived, was taken for medical eval. The body we left in situ."

Lonergan's eyes widened. "In what?" He checked for the name. "Jaynus?"

Giannis stared at him straight faced. "Giannis. Gee-ah-nis. In situ, meaning we left the body where we found it, undisturbed, except for me checking for a pulse."

Lonergan grumbled, then moved around the body. Foster hid her smile. The other POs stood close, doing the same. So it wasn't just her, she thought. Lonergan was an equal-opportunity pain in the ass.

Foster squatted down and pressed her fingers lightly to the woman's neck to confirm. She checked her eyes, frozen, fixed, the irises blue with a grayish tint. Brushing leaves gently away as though she were lightly pushing back a wayward strand of loose hair, she found the woman's left wrist and gently felt for a pulse there, too, but again there was nothing.

She was gone. But there was something there—a red ring, paint or something—circling the wrist. She didn't dare explore further, not yet.

As the heels of her ankle boots sank into the damp grass, Foster brushed more leaves away, uncovering the woman as far as her chest. She appeared to be naked. Just past the corpse's sternum, Foster saw the uneven edges of a bloody gash and was hit by the tang of fresh blood, like rusted pipe or wet coins, mixing with the musty earthiness off the river. She pulled her hand away.

For a moment, she simply squatted there, marking the woman's passing and the loss of life. Then she stood up and backed away, mindful of where she placed her feet. She'd gone as far as she dared, just far enough to confirm that this was homicide, not a lie-down after a wild night. She looked over at Lonergan and then to the somber POs, including Giannis. "Okay. Let's get the techs in here. Find out what we've got."

This was going to be bad. She could feel it.

———

"Yep. This is bad." The ME tech, Sal Rosales, looked grim as he knelt beside the body, gently flicking back the leaves with gloved fingers.

Foster stood well back along with Lonergan and the POs, now playing the part of observers. The case started here with Rosales. He would confirm manner of death, though it only took a single look to venture a guess. An approximate time of death would also be important. It would establish their timeline. The rest she and Lonergan and the team would have to work out with shoe leather and experience over countless sleepless nights. Foster watched as Rosales went in for the body temp, then she turned away to glance up at the bridge at the people gawking, their phones recording Lord knew what. What was the communal fascination with violent death? What did they gain from watching it, filming it? Maybe if they saw the body from down here instead of up there, where they were safe and removed, they'd think differently. This woman, whoever she was, had belonged to someone. Someone would mourn her, miss her.

The evidence tech moved around, photographing the scene, circling the grim tableau to document every angle, every bit of whatever had been left behind. A solemn wind blew through as Foster listened to the lap of the river against the smelly bank. The sound of the water was a reminder that rivers never stopped, wind never ceased, and despite this horror or the next, no matter who died or when, the sun would always rise and set. Foster turned back to Rosales and watched as he did what he needed to do for someone's daughter, sister, friend, lover.

A half hour went by as they watched the tech ballet take photos, measurements, and notes. Finally, Rosales's head popped up. "These wounds are deep. Jagged edges to the cuts. You're looking for a serrated knife. Fairly big. Hunting variety. Did they find one?"

"No," Foster said.

"It's likely in the drink. Perfect dump site," Lonergan said. "He killed her and tossed it right in. Now we gotta get divers out. First killer I ever had, though, who does it, then lays down and takes a nap. How about you, Foster?"

She slid him a look out of the corner of her eye. "I'll wait and see before I start calling people killers."

Lonergan grinned. "One of those cautious types bent on takin' the long way home, huh?"

She moved carefully around the body, taking another look from all angles. "It's often the safest route."

"Great. Griffin puts me with an i dotter."

"I also cross every t," she shot back. "Lucky you."

It took more than two hours before Rosales was ready with preliminary findings. "Based on body temp and conditions, I'd put time of death somewhere between midnight and three a.m. Can't be more exact until I take her in," he said. "White, female, twenty or so, as you can see. Some of the knife strikes are very deep. I'd say that's a lot of meanness." He glanced over at Foster. "Want to step closer? Get a better look at what I'm talking about?" He slid Lonergan a look. "You too. You might want to brace for it. She's pretty sliced up."

Lonergan moved forward while Foster took another moment or two to prepare. "I've seen dead bodies before," he said. "What kind of greenhorn do you . . . holy shit!"

Foster eased forward again, standing far more calmly than Lonergan had. The woman's chest and abdominal cavities had been torn open, her organs and intestines spilled out, the guts tumbling off onto the grass beside her like a string of sausages cascading off a butcher's counter.

"Told you," Rosales said. "Once I got all the leaves off, I could see what I was dealing with. Massive blood loss. Won't know which cut was the fatal one until Grant has her on her table."

Lonergan rolled his eyes at the mention of the ME. "Of course not."

For a moment, Foster's mind sputtered as she willed herself to take it all in and not turn away. She had no idea how many seconds passed before her brain reset and her mind cleared. It was then that she noticed the red lines drawn around the young woman's ankles, similar to the red ring around her left wrist she'd discovered earlier. She squatted down beside Rosales, recognizing now a familiar waxy smell.

"Lipstick." She looked around for the photographer to make sure she'd gotten close-ups of the rings. She had.

Lonergan stood over her shoulder. "Lipstick? What's that about?"

She turned to look for Giannis. "Nobody's found her clothes, a bag?"

Giannis shook his head. "Nothing like that. We're still looking, though."

She stood and moved back, sweeping her eyes along the pedestrian path the cops had closed off from foot passage east and west, then across to the north side of the river, where restaurants and bars faced the south bank where they stood. Foster wondered if their victim had come out of one of the bars there.

"We'll wrap up now, transport her," Rosales said. "We'll know more later."

"Thanks," Foster said. "Appreciate it."

She took a small flashlight out of her bag and shone it along the grass where the body lay. "No defensive wounds. No drag marks, so she fell here or was placed." She turned to Lonergan. "The leaves have to be from someplace else."

"Yeah," Lonergan said. "These are some puny trees. For show, nothin' else. No way they account for the pile used to cover her up. So where'd he get 'em?"

Foster looked up, remembering that all crime scenes were three dimensional. Above her the bridge loomed, the hecklers still around. She turned and checked the sidewalk along Upper Wacker, but there were only uniforms up there now, keeping foot traffic moving.

She stepped onto the path, her heels slightly muddy from the spongy grass and dirt. She noticed the shoes of the others—Rosales, Lonergan, the POs—were all in the same condition. Foster found Giannis. "Did you notice if there were cuts to Ainsley's hands?" she asked him. "Blood anywhere else besides the spot on his jacket? Bruises to his face, maybe?"

Giannis consulted his notes. "Ah, he looked fine." She watched as he flipped through pages, but she had a feeling he wouldn't find a notation there. In the rush to wake Ainsley up and ID him, they'd likely failed to notice anything but him lying there and the blood on him. "No," he said, definitively.

She thanked him and turned back to the body, Rosales, and the techs.

"We sent a tech to the hospital for all that," Rosales said. "You two good for now? We need to finish up."

Foster and Lonergan moved back, and Lonergan snapped his fingers at the closest officer. "Clear that friggin' bridge? If they want to heckle, let 'em do it down at the superintendent's office." He turned to Foster. "My money's on the drunk guy. Something sets him off, and she's the first person he comes across. Wrong place, wrong time for her."

"Interesting theory. You mind if we work the case, though? Take statements, canvass, at least ID our victim? Maybe we can wait until the ME has actually had a chance to look at her?"

He scowled. "Never said we weren't gonna do all that, but we're ahead of the game here. Sometimes killers are stupid, Foster. It's okay to take the win. Stop trying to work so hard."

Lonergan walked away, heading for their witness, Pratt, leaving Foster to bring up the rear. There were things she could have said in the heat of the moment but didn't. Right now, there were more important things, like identifying their victim. She just wished they didn't have to do it in a fishbowl. The bridge was packed. News cameras and on-the-street reporters now clogged the rail, their cameras pointed right at their crime scene tape.

"We'll probably find her clothes and ID in the river too," Lonergan said when she caught up to him. He snapped his fingers again, getting the attention of the nearest officer, which made Foster cringe. "Hey, you. Take a couple of your buddies and check along the edge there, will ya? See if you see anything floating that could be hers. And do not come back here and tell me you've found another body."

Foster stopped. "Are you always like this?"

"Like what?"

"Condescending. Disrespectful."

The blank look on his face answered her question. "A by-the-book cop *and* a bleeding heart? Boy, did I hit the jackpot. Look, Foster, I can take one but not both, all right?"

An officer ran up holding a pink backpack that was dripping wet. "Found this floating a few yards east. It was caught up on debris. Could be hers."

He handed the bag to Foster, who unzipped it and peered inside, picking through the contents. Lonergan was suddenly interested. "A wallet," Foster said. "Thank God." She opened it, finding a driver's license stuck inside the clear plastic slot, the photograph matching the face under the leaves. "Margaret Ann Birch. Nineteen." Foster checked everywhere before pulling out a campus ID. "A student at DePaul." She handed the wallet to Lonergan. "That's a start."

She kept looking, rifling through the pack and plucking out a compact paisley umbrella, a handmade accessories pouch with the name Peggy stitched on the outside, and a small handmade sign with the words *JUSTICE NOW*. The black marker was still legible, though the laminated cardboard it was written on was soaked through and near pulp. Foster also slid out a waterlogged paperback copy of *Paradise Lost*. "Milton. English major, maybe? And Peggy instead of the formal Margaret." She gingerly held up the sign. "Looks like she was at yesterday's march."

Lonergan searched the wallet. "Besides the license and the school ID, there's a dorm key card; Social Security card; Starbucks rewards card, two ticks left on; a folded-up dry cleaner's ticket; and a butt load of quarters in a coin purse."

"For her laundry," Foster said. "The machines."

"Wouldn't know. Didn't go to college. I went to the Marines instead. Didn't need quarters."

Foster lifted her head out of the backpack. "No cell phone. What nineteen-year-old kid doesn't have a cell phone?"

"Ainsley probably tossed that too."

"*Maybe* it was tossed," she said, "and *maybe* it was Ainsley."

"You're complicating my life, here." Lonergan walked away, sliding his phone out of his pocket as he went. "We're going to find her clothes, her phone, and that knife at the bottom of the river," he called back to her. "Count on it."

She stared at the lonely spot where Peggy Birch had been found. They didn't know much at this point, despite Lonergan's confident pronouncements, but at least they had her name and a way to contact her people.

She called to a PO. "We need a thorough search all along here, please," she said, pointing along the riverbank, a quarter mile at least toward the lake. "We're looking for anything that could be hers. And could someone get me another update on the guy they took to the hospital? Thank you."

She gripped the pink backpack as though she were keeping it safe for Birch, who'd carried it just a few hours ago, likely giving her bag little thought or care. Just a pack, until it was everything.

Foster tilted her head up past the destruction and the mess and the work to the wide, open autumn sky. "Peggy Birch."

CHAPTER 5

Amelia breezed into her studio, peeled off her jacket, and flung it on the slouchy, catchall couch pushed against the wall. She had gotten Bodie settled back at his apartment, but that hadn't settled her. In fact, the opposite was true. Bodie was out of Westhaven and on his own again. As long as he'd been in there, she hadn't had to worry where he was or what he was doing. He'd been somewhere he couldn't harm himself or—she loathed to say—anyone else.

She looked around her place at the blank canvases leaning against the walls, the paint-splotched floors, and the unused paint—ready for her brushes—stacked in a corner. Then she stood in front of the large painting that ran almost half the length of the space, floor to ceiling. She approached it almost reverently and took in the swirls of color, the brushstrokes, the smell of the oil paint, and placed her hand on it as though feeling for a heartbeat. Hers. All of it. Bodie needed something that was his.

She rolled her sleeves up, anxious to get started, and slipped into a big shirt that served as a painter's smock. She felt restless, uneasy for the first time in a month, because Bodie was outside, where anything could happen and where whatever happened, she would have to fix it.

Following women. Stalking. That was what he was into? It was creepy, but she couldn't pretend she didn't know when he'd begun to obsess over pretty girls with big blue eyes, though he always seemed to vacillate between wanting them and fearing them. She could pinpoint it to the very day, in fact, the very moment when they discovered at twelve who their father was and what he did in the basement he'd padlocked shut. Until it wasn't. Until they ventured below . . . and saw. Bodie became awkward and sullen, disconnected afterward. She found art. She discovered that she could pour everything she felt or thought or feared into a canvas and have her world all make sense. She could bring order to chaos, perspective to the incomprehensible. Art, her art, was life and emotion, the air in her lungs, her every breath. It was alive, and it was hers, and no one could take it away.

Amelia slipped out of her shoes and socks and stood barefoot on the painter's tarp surrounded by the painter's things that saved her and fed her and made her different from her brother.

She heard a rattling from the back room and turned to see her studio mate, Joie Lenk, stroll up front, startling when she saw her.

"Oh shit! I didn't hear you come in," Joie said. "How long have you been here?"

Amelia smiled and watched Joie, her brown face dusted and smeared with plaster of Paris. She wiped her hands clean on a wet towel. Joie was artsy through and through, from the purple streak in her dark curly hair down to her plaster-splattered pink Crocs.

"Not long," Amelia said. "I didn't think you'd be here."

Joie stuffed the towel into the pocket of her dusty overalls. "I had a spark of inspiration and wanted to test it." She padded over to her work in progress, a sculpture of Winged Victory that she'd been working on for months, only Joie's Nike wore combat boots and a Wonder Woman tee. The plaster creation stood six feet tall, its wings spanning three feet across, the piece commissioned by a women's outreach center in Andersonville. "But I didn't expect to see you today. It's Monday. You never come in on Mondays."

"I needed to paint," Amelia said.

"Well, if you want the place to yourself, I can bounce. That inspiration I thought I had isn't panning out."

"No worries," Amelia said. "Stay. I don't mind the company."

The scrape of dog claws on hardwood broke their exchange. They'd woken Winston, Joie's English bulldog, whose doggy pad was in the back room.

"Uh-oh," Joie said. "You've done it now. Prepare yourself."

Amelia waited for it, grinning as Winston, a waddling meatball of a thing, ran into the room, his nails clicking against the floor, mouth open, pink tongue out. The dog made a beeline for her. Though Winston went home with Joie, Am knew he loved her best, and the feeling was mutual.

She plopped down on the dusty tarp and scratched Winston behind the ears, rubbing his belly and kissing him on the snout.

Joie peeked from behind the plaster. "You're spoiling him."

Amelia gave him one last snuggle. "He deserves to be spoiled. He's a prince."

Joie grumped. "A prince that eats like a horse."

"All right, boy." Am stood and dusted off her jeans. "Enough cuddles for now. Next time it's my turn." Winston studied her for a moment, his big head cocked to the side, then waddled away and plopped down at Joie's feet.

Joie donned protective glasses, ready to get started. "Everything okay with your sister?"

Am smiled. It was one of her many reinventions, necessary to fit who she was now. A new person who had a younger sister, not a twin brother prone to mental breakdown. This new person also had a mother in Florida and a father who'd died when Am was just eighteen. She had added in a hardscrabble upbringing in a small midwestern town far from here. It made her success now all the more impressive to people. It also made her seem interesting, industrious, relatable. The truth was, she hadn't laid eyes on Tom Morgan since he'd dropped her and Bodie off at the University of Michigan with their tuition paid and a nice nest egg set aside. Then he'd ghosted them. He was just gone, moved, without leaving a forwarding address. Bodie, she knew, was fine with that. He had feared their father and needed to believe that he was dead. But Amelia knew he wasn't dead. She could still feel him, sense him, and she wasn't afraid. Where could he be now? she often wondered. Was he in another country? Had he chosen a new name? She supposed, in the end, it didn't really matter. He'd made his mark. "She fell and broke her ankle," Amelia replied. She conveyed just the right amount of sympathy and concern. "My sis has always been a bit of a klutz. Six weeks, then out of the cast and back to her life."

Joie went back to her plaster. "I have a cousin like that. She's broken practically every bone in her body, and she's barely forty. I told her she needed to roll herself in Bubble Wrap." Joie peeked around again, this time with a devilish grin. "She told *me* to go fuck myself."

Amelia picked up a brush, letting it breathe in her hand, then she approached her canvas, deciding where to start. "Family, huh? Can't live with them—"

Joie chuckled. "Can't strangle them for the insurance money."

Amelia took a bead on her feelings, then lightly dipped her brush in gray paint. She thought about Bodie, still rudderless at their age. She thought of the old Am and their house of secrets. It was a wonder she and Bodie had survived to do as well as they were doing, but that just showed how resilient people could be. Life always found a way. Amelia painted a small padlock, then moved back to assess it. There were many locks in the painting. She gently dipped her right index finger into the paint and smeared crimson against her thumb, then stepped forward again and pressed her finger lightly to the canvas. Then she painted a door around the mark. There were also many doors.

If she closed her eyes, she knew she'd see what she always did. A woman. The basement steps. The stillest, bluest eyes and hair like fire. She hadn't been able to tear her eyes away from the unimaginable— severed feet and hands, a savaged middle, and blood snaking down the basement drain. Her father's doing. A father to whom she and Bodie were inextricably bound. A father who killed for sport. Could a healthy tree grow from a twisted root?

"Families are complicated, that's for sure," Amelia said as she wiped her fingers off against her thigh. "Some more than others."

Joie peeked around her work in progress, her eyes blinking inside the goggles. "What's that?"

"Nothing," Amelia said, sweeping her brush over the image of the door, watching the mark disappear. "Just talking to myself."

CHAPTER 6

Foster and Lonergan swept into the ER and badged their way through to the treatment area. They were feeling a bit raw, having just come from the home of Peggy Birch's parents to notify them that their daughter, their baby, was dead. Foster could still hear Peggy's mother's wailing in her ears and see the ruined look on her face. No one wanted to be the cop who relayed the news that would cripple a person forever, but it came with the job. And it had to be done delicately, with compassion. It had surprised her that Lonergan had managed to do both, that his heavy-handedness and assholery had limits. They hadn't spoken in the car, not wanting to move on from the Birches' misery quite so quickly. Instead, they'd sat in the moment, giving solemnity its due and bracing for the next hard thing.

Ainsley had been placed in a back bay as far away from other patients as the crowded, busy space would allow. There was an officer standing in front of the drawn privacy curtain when they approached. He hopped to, ready to give his report.

"The doctor's in there with him now," Officer Morton said, his hazel eyes sharp and tuned in. "Evidence techs were in gathering up his clothes, taking photos. They left about a half hour ago. Kid was slow to wake up. He was really out of it."

"You get anything out of him?" Lonergan asked.

"Not much. Don't think he was sure where he was. He obviously got a bad batch of something. I've seen a couple of these. It's not booze. It's gotta be drugs."

"That your medical opinion, Officer Morton?" Foster asked pointedly.

Morton pulled up. "He's not my first blissed-out druggie. But you're right. I'm not the doc. Could be a lot of things."

The beeps and pings and blips from the machines underscored the hurried medical inquiries from harried nurses and doctors speeding from bay to bay, trying to do fifty things at once, knowing there was a full waiting room outside.

Foster stared at Morton. "We'll see."

A Hispanic doctor stood at the bedside, shining an ophthalmoscope into the eyes of a young Black man sitting up in bed. He was wearing a mint-green hospital gown. Foster's breath caught. Ainsley was a boy, a kid, with big brown eyes, tawny beige skin, and short curly hair. For a moment, she saw her son lying there as she'd seen him countless times in similar faces on the street and in the grocery store and in sappy TV commercials. But this moment was particularly glaring. Ainsley was nineteen, as Reggie would have been in just over a week. She was acutely aware the day was approaching, that the passage of time was as steady and foreboding as the measured sweep of a metronome's needle.

Foster stepped closer to the bed and addressed the doctor. "We'd like to talk to him, if he's up to it." She glanced down at the doctor's ID hanging from a lanyard festooned with bits of tape, pens, and clips. He was Raphael Santos, the attending physician. "Dr. Santos."

Santos stepped back, peeling off his medical gloves, tossing them into the biohazard bin behind him. "He's awake but foggy. Up to him if he talks. I'll leave you to it, but I'd appreciate some efficiency here. Your techs were buzzing around here like crazy, now you guys. Last thing we need is a circus, all right?"

Lonergan, who'd eased in behind Foster, nearly growled at Santos. "It'll take what it takes, Doc. You don't see us tellin' you how long to take to yank an appendix out, do you?"

"Just keep it down," Santos said, uncowed. "It's a hospital, not the county jail. Now, if you'll excuse me, I have patients to see." He sneered at Lonergan before walking off.

Ainsley's eyes darted around the room as though he were trying to orient himself to where he was and how he'd gotten here. He looked scared, small in the bed. This was the unconscious *man* with blood on his jacket?

Lonergan moved around to stand on the opposite side. It must have been an intimidating flank to the kid, and as she looked over at Lonergan's full-on cop face, she was sure he meant it to be just that.

She cleared her throat. "Keith Ainsley? I'm Detective Foster, Chicago Police. This is my . . . partner, Detective Lonergan. We'd like to ask you a few questions. Are you okay with that?" She was aware she had stumbled over the word *partner* and looked up to see that Lonergan had noticed.

Ainsley fixed glazed eyes on her, his face a wall of confusion. "I guess. What's going on? Why am I here? Why's there a cop outside, and why were they taking my picture?"

"There's been an incident," Foster said. "We're hoping you can help us clear it up. Okay?"

He flicked a frightened look at Lonergan. "What kind of incident?"

"Where were you last night around midnight?" Lonergan asked.

"Did somebody jump me? Is that it?" Ainsley asked, his voice cracking. "Where are my clothes? Did they get my wallet? My phone?"

Lonergan frowned. "Jumped *you*?"

Foster shot Lonergan a warning look and gave a slight shake of the head. She didn't want him antagonizing the kid, shutting him down. Lonergan scowled and let her take the lead, but he didn't look happy about it. "Do you remember being on the Riverwalk?" she asked. "Maybe meeting someone there?"

Ainsley's brow furrowed, as though he was trying desperately to recall something. Anything. "The Riverwalk? No, I don't remember being there. I was . . ." He stopped. "Somewhere else."

She focused on his face. It appeared he was being truthful. "Alone?"

"And what's 'somewhere else' mean?" Lonergan asked.

"I'm a little fuzzy . . ."

"You were found unconscious on the Riverwalk," Foster said. "In close proximity to a murder victim. A young woman. She'd been stabbed."

Lonergan took a step closer to the bed. "And you had blood on your clothes. Remember anything now?"

"What? No. I . . . I . . ." Ainsley's eyes searched the walls for anything that would ground him. "That doesn't sound right. You've got the wrong guy."

"Would you mind lifting up your hands?" Foster asked.

Ainsley narrowed his eyes, suddenly suspicious. "What for?"

"Just for a moment." She followed the request with an open smile.

When he slowly lifted his hands, turning them over and back, she could clearly see there were no cuts or nicks on his fingers or palms. You would expect an injury from such a brutal assault. The knife would have been bloody, and the hand of whoever wielded it would have skidded along the slippery hilt and caught the edge of the blade unless they were wearing some really heavy-duty gloves, which they hadn't found at the scene.

"Thanks," Foster said. "You can put them down now."

"A young woman was stabbed to death not ten feet from you," Lonergan said. "What can you tell us about that?"

Ainsley looked like he wanted to cry as he scrubbed his hands across his baby face. "You're saying I killed a woman? No way."

"Her name's Peggy Birch," Lonergan continued, his voice stern. "You don't remember meeting her? Maybe you two went down there to party and somethin' went wrong? What'd you take?"

"You're wrong. I don't know anybody named Peggy."

"You seem pretty sure of that," Lonergan replied, "seeing as you can't remember much else."

Ainsley was getting agitated. Foster needed to slow things down. "Let's all take a minute." She locked eyes with Lonergan again, talking to him more than to Ainsley. "Slow things down." She gripped the bed rail. "Okay," she said gently. "You don't remember the Riverwalk? Tell me what you *do* remember."

"I . . . I don't remember last night. I . . ." He shook his head. "I think I was with my friends? Saturday?"

"Sunday's what we're interested in," Lonergan said harshly. "Midnight, so technically early this mornin'. Well past the time you shoulda been down there."

"Sunday." Ainsley repeated it. "Midnight?" He shook his head again, adamant this time. "I was with my friends, I think. Or I could have been up late studying. I don't remember going to the Riverwalk."

"You were found there this morning," Foster said. "Try to remember what you were doing. You mention your friends. Which friends?" She could see the freak-out coming as Ainsley got agitated, then frustrated. And then he broke completely down.

"I don't know. I don't know anything. I . . . I don't want to talk to you anymore. I don't feel safe," he yelled, trembling. "Where are my parents? I need to call them."

"Look, kid . . . ," Lonergan started.

"No. This isn't right. I didn't do it. I'm not saying anything else until I see my parents."

Ainsley clamped his lips shut and turned his head to the wall and closed his eyes. A child's response. This was as far as they could go for now. She and Lonergan stepped out of the bay and walked away, leaving the officer on watch at the curtain.

"What the hell?" Lonergan said. "His parents? Is he for real?"

"We might have gotten more out of him if you hadn't come down so hard."

"He's a killer. Hard's the only way to go. What, are you used to some hand-holding kumbaya crap?"

"I don't work that way. He's a scared kid. We don't know what's going on yet."

"Foster, c'mon, he's playing us with that crybaby shit."

She was aware that they had gotten the attention of the medical staff, so she lowered her voice and stepped back from Lonergan. "You're so sure about that?"

Lonergan thrust his chest out, placed his hands on his hips. "You bet I am. That scared-little-boy act doesn't fool me, but it's obviously got you goin'."

She let a moment go, then chose her words carefully. "I vote for waiting until he's fully back before we approach him again. Meanwhile, we talk to the doctor, see what we're dealing with, then call his parents. Can we at least agree on that much?"

"I been feelin' you out, Foster," Lonergan said, a sour look on his face. "So far, I'm not likin' what I'm seein'." He turned and walked away down the hall. Where to, she didn't know or care.

"Same here," she muttered. She walked over to the nurses' station and flagged someone at the desk. "Would you mind paging Dr. Santos, please?"

———

When Santos returned, he didn't look overjoyed to see them again, and he appeared even more fatigued than he had an hour earlier, his hooded eyes bloodshot and tired but still sharp, like he'd gotten used to running on empty.

Foster pulled out her notebook and searched for a pen in her bag, readying herself for as much as Santos could give them on Ainsley's status.

"So what can you tell us?" she asked.

Lonergan sniffed and adjusted his belt. "Yeah, what the hell's he on? And how soon can we drag him out of here?"

Santos frowned. "*Drag* him out?"

"You expect us to call a limo?"

Santos turned to Foster with a look of disbelief. "A quick report," she said. "A discharge, if he's ready, and then we can take it from there."

Santos begrudgingly pulled up the details on his iPad. "Keith Ainsley, nineteen. Black male, A-one condition, no seizure, no TIA. BAC 0.02, so not a factor." He looked up at Lonergan. "That's blood alcohol content, by the way."

Lonergan flushed. "Do I look like some rube to you?"

Santos opened his mouth to answer, but Foster jumped in. "Please, continue."

"The only drug we found in his system was Klonopin, which explains the unconsciousness, the grogginess, and now the confusion afterward. He told me he's premed at Feinberg. Klonopin or something like it isn't uncommon, given the workload. The stress. The kids call it K-pin. It's clonazepam. In the benzodiazepine family of drugs. Used as an antiseizure med but also prescribed for panic attacks. It calms the brain, the nerves. Highly addictive after long use." He sighed. "He denies taking it, but everybody who comes in here high on something denies taking whatever they took."

"Sounds about right," Lonergan quipped.

Santos slid him a look. "I've seen Klonopin used to combat insomnia too. Not what it was intended for, but that never stops anyone, ever. It's like Ambien or similar type drugs. But I couldn't find any reason why he'd need to take anything. Like I said, he's A-one. All tests negative for anything else." He punched the iPad, his bit done. "That's what we got. He's awake. He's coming out of his brain fog. He's all yours."

"Now was that so hard?" Lonergan poked.

Foster looked down at her shoes, at the thin layer of mud around the toes and heels, and then leveled her gaze. "Doctor, when they collected his clothes, did you notice if there was mud on his shoes?"

"I didn't see any mud."

Lonergan's eyes narrowed. "You answered pretty quick. You sure?"

"I'd remember mud if there'd been any."

She'd squatted next to Birch's body, her heels sinking into the damp earth. There was mud on her shoes now. She glanced over. And on Lonergan's. She quickly ducked back into Ainsley's bay, Lonergan right behind her. The kid's eyes were puffy. He'd been crying.

"One more question," Foster said. "Were you prescribed Klonopin, or did you take it on your own?" For a moment, it looked like he wouldn't answer, but Foster moved closer to the bed, waiting. "Keith?"

He turned his head away from her. "I don't do drugs."

"When they brought you in, there was alcohol and Klonopin in your system. How do you explain that?"

He laid his head back against the pillow, utter despair clouding his face. "I think I had a beer? I think I was at a place?" He lifted up forcefully. "But I *don't* do drugs. And I'm not saying anything else until I talk to my *parents*."

The two stepped out of the bay again, moving away from the curtain. Santos was still standing there.

"He coulda knocked the mud off his shoes," Lonergan said. "He coulda wiped them on the grass or rinsed 'em off in the river."

Foster put her notebook away. "Or he was nowhere near Birch's body."

"We'll settle it in an interview room. He's conscious; he's ours." Lonergan cocked a thumb toward Santos. "Unless the good doc here would like to run him a nice, hot shower? Bring him a cookie?"

"Unbelievable," Santos muttered as he stormed off. "Cops."

"What's *his* problem?"

Assuming the question was rhetorical, Foster ignored it and instead asked one of her own. "Can we help Peggy Birch now?"

CHAPTER 7

She plopped down into her desk chair, not liking the setup any more than she had several hours ago when she'd first laid eyes on it. The chair squeaked and was set a bit too high, so her knees bumped the underside. Not a big deal but a deal she didn't have time for now. Keith Ainsley was in an interview room waiting for them to come in, but she'd needed a moment to decompress. He'd called his parents. They were on their way in. The blood on his jacket and the lack of mud on his shoes didn't go together. Unless he'd wet the shoes? If so, maybe Lonergan, as ham fisted as he was, had pegged it right. But could Ainsley, under the influence, have had the time and wherewithal to rinse his muddy soles in the river?

She glanced around the office but didn't see Lonergan. It had been a frosty ride back from the hospital. They still hadn't found a way to connect even enough to make polite conversation, but she held a glimmer of hope that she'd find something in the man she could come to appreciate . . . or tolerate. The rest of the detectives seemed okay. She'd met Detectives Kelley and Symansky, as well as Tony Bigelow and Vera Li. All good, all fine. Bigelow, a sturdy Black man with dark hooded eyes that missed nothing, appeared to be the jokester of the group. They called him Bigs. Li looked about Foster's age and moved fast, darting around the office purposefully, like she had one hundred things to do and only five minutes to get them all done. Sharp eyes, too, Foster noted. She didn't imagine much got past Li. It wasn't her old team, but it was a solid team she was sure she could blend into. Then she thought of Lonergan.

Foster rolled her chair away from the desk and rubbed her eyes, taking a moment to focus. She had a young Black man in custody for a heinous crime, a young Black man who reminded her of her lost boy. Ainsley hadn't so much as a parking ticket and had never been in any kind of trouble before. That wasn't proof of innocence, but it was a pretty good indication of character. What was the prevailing wisdom? Past behavior was a useful marker for future behavior. But something had placed both Ainsley and Birch on that Riverwalk.

Lonergan's snap-to voice broke in. He pointed down the hall toward the interview rooms. "He's in three. You coming?"

She stood, straightening her blazer. "Can we talk first?"

He looked wary, like he expected a trick. "About?"

"Somewhere with a door?"

They ducked into a small room with boxes of office supplies and reams of paper lined up against the wall. It was as good a place as any. He stood there, poised for confrontation.

"We don't see this the same way," she began. "But I think it would be better if we at least didn't work at cross purposes in there." She kept her distance, a small, scarred table between them. She leaned her hands on the back of a folding chair tucked under it. "We need his statement, first and foremost. He'll be more willing to give us that, I think, if we don't go charging in there hot and heavy, accusing him of butchery, especially when there are still so many unknown variables . . ." Lonergan watched her but didn't speak. "I think I understand your feeling on that, but I'd like to hear it again. We should run it through and find some common ground." Lonergan said nothing. "Or if there's anything else you think we need to say to each other?"

"Seems you've been making judgments about what kind of cop you think I am," Lonergan said. "That ain't sitting well. I chalk it up to you being raw about your . . ." He stopped himself, noting the warning look on her face. "I give you some slack on that being the case." He slipped his hands into his front pockets. "I think he's good for this, for obvious reasons, and you got a differing opinion. We'll see on that. Meanwhile, we go at him and see what he gives us. We wait for the techs to give us the definitive. I know the drill, Foster. This ain't my first rodeo. *And* I never once met a smart killer. This kid's half out of his head, kills her, then doesn't have enough brain cells functionin' to get himself outta there, so he plops right there at the bridge with evidence all over him. Now he's making like he can't remember nothin'. He's runnin' a game. That's how I see it, and that's how you'll see it when the blood comes back a match to Birch."

She lifted off the chair. "You're right. If the blood matches, that'll put me in a different place. But right now, we aren't there yet. Right now, we need to go in as a team and see if we can get more out of him. Right?"

His eyes narrowed, and his square chin lifted. "I push hard."

"I've noticed. I do, too, when it's called for."

He nodded. "Who starts off?"

"It's my first day. I don't have a problem with you taking it."

He hesitated, his eyes holding hers. "Nah. You take it."

"First, let's start over. Right foot this time." Foster held out her hand for a shake. "Detective Harriet Foster. Harri."

"Like Houdini?"

"Or like Harriet, only shorter."

Lonergan looked at the hand offered before returning the shake. "Jim Lonergan. Jury's still out, my end." There was a mischievous twinkle in his eye.

She smiled. "Anybody ever tell you you're a pain in the ass?"

Lonergan grinned back. "Everyone who's ever met me, including my mother."

They walked into the tight interview room expecting to see Ainsley alone, only he wasn't. He was flanked at the table by a fierce-looking couple, both dark, well dressed, and humorless, each with a hand on Keith's shoulder, forming a human protective shield. Keith was dressed in scrubs given to him in the ER when his own clothes had been bagged and tagged and rushed off for testing.

"What the hell?" said Lonergan. "Who the hell are you two? You're not supposed to be in here."

"These are my parents," Keith said.

Lonergan stormed over to the table. "Yeah, well, they can wait outside till we talk to you."

Keith looked up, defiant. "They're also my lawyers."

Lonergan's brows lifted, and he looked from one to the other, his mouth agape. "*Both* of them?"

The man sitting next to Keith stood and handed Lonergan a business card. "George Ainsley. This is my wife, Carole. We're both partners in the law firm Scholden, Eagleton, and Ainsley. Our son, Keith, is formally represented. There'll be no questions asked without either of us present. You got a free swipe at the hospital, even after he asked for us. There'll be no more freebies." He sat again, folding his hands on the table, his eyes and those of his wife as hard as mountains. "He's aware of his rights. We agree to voluntarily submit to questioning. But we can and will end this at any time. Clock's ticking."

"He's aware, but just so we're covered . . . ," Foster said. She read Keith his rights, inwardly pleased that his parents were there.

Carole Ainsley glared at Foster, contempt in the look. "You didn't bother with that at the hospital. That how you treat all the Black boys, or is my son somehow special?"

"I asked for his cooperation; he gave it," Foster said, matching Carole's death glare. "It was just a conversation."

"A white woman is killed, and you sweep up the first Black kid you see, that it?" said George Ainsley.

"We woulda swept up Jesus if we found him passed out next to a body," Lonergan said. "Don't make this something it isn't."

Carole's wrath shifted to Lonergan. "It's *always* about what it's *really* about, isn't it? With some of you."

Foster took a seat across from them, opened her file, then rested her hands on top, letting the tension sit for a moment.

She turned to Keith. "Hopefully you've had time to clear your head. Can you tell us what you were doing on the Riverwalk last night? Where you were before midnight? Who you were with?"

It was his father who spoke. "First, what do you have?"

Lonergan sat quietly as Foster ran through the case briefly—Birch, Pratt, the officers finding Keith unconscious. She emphasized Keith's proximity to the body and the blood found on his jacket, which made his presence on the scene suspicious and worthy of further discussion.

"Her blood?" Carole asked.

Foster didn't answer. She didn't have to be a psychic to see where this was going.

"You can't say, because you don't know," the woman said. "You have a weapon? No, you don't, or you would have revealed this, and he'd be in lockup already. So you have my son in the vicinity of a murder victim and a spot of blood of unknown origin on his jacket. And he was unconscious when the police arrived, so anyone could have happened by and touched him . . . even one of them."

Lonergan leaned forward, his face growing red. "Wait. Are you sayin' *we* framed him?"

George Ainsley ignored the question and jumped in. "Then he was transported to the ER, under guard, and after inexpert questioning, during which he was confused and dazed, he's brought here for interrogation, suspected of murder." He sat back, his eyes hard, prepared to go toe to toe. "Two things. One, there are enough holes in this to drive a Mack Truck through. And two, you've picked the wrong Black boy this time. This one's got money, and he's got us. You're going to have to work a little harder." The room quieted as his words landed.

"Where'd you get the Klonopin?" Foster asked, watching Keith Ainsley sitting small in between his parents. He looked shell shocked, overloaded. How quickly a life could turn. This had to be the worst day of his young life. He didn't answer. "There was a march downtown yesterday. Did you go to that?"

Carole placed a palm over her son's hands, which he'd folded on the table. "Don't answer that."

Foster sat back, dead in the water. "Look, we're trying to figure this out."

"Really?" There was no masking the woman's skepticism. "I don't think I've ever met a detective once who was in it to 'figure it out.'" She flicked a distrustful look at Lonergan, whose face had turned to stone.

Foster slid a sheet with five photos on it toward Keith, Peggy Birch's image among them. "Do any of these women look familiar to you?"

George reached out and picked up the sheet, studying it before passing it to his son. "You can answer."

Keith took a look, then shook his head. "No."

"Do you own a hunting knife, Keith?" Foster asked.

Carole banged her fist on the table. "He does not."

Foster waited a moment. She needed an answer from the kid, not his mother. "Keith?"

He turned to his mother, then his father, checking to see if it was okay for him to answer. They each gave him a subtle nod. "No," he said. "I don't hunt."

Foster studied him for a time. "Did you go into any of the restaurants or bars along the Riverwalk yesterday? Did you drive downtown or take the bus? Which friends do you think you were with on Sunday?"

Carole tapped her son on the hand again. A signal. There was, apparently, something in the barrage of questions she would allow him to address.

"Me and some friends went to the march. I remember that. Afterward, we hung out. Maybe I had a couple beers." He slid his mother a look. Legal drinking age was twenty-one. He was in violation, though a murdered woman rather trumped the Class A misdemeanor.

Foster scribbled a note, underlining the word *march* as Keith spoke. "But not on the Riverwalk," she said. "Where then?"

His mother tapped him again. "The park," he replied. "By the boats."

"The boats?" Lonergan's tone was disbelieving. "At the marina?"

George turned on Lonergan. "That's his answer."

"And the K-pin you were conked out on," Lonergan said. "Where'd you get that?"

"I don't do drugs. Somebody must have slipped me something."

"And we'll be looking into that, believe me," Carole said. "Anything could have happened to him. He could have fallen into the river and drowned, been attacked . . ."

Lonergan's brows lifted. "Or ended up next to a dead girl? And by 'somebody' he means . . . one of his *friends*?"

Beer. Boats. Marina. Foster jotted down the details. "But you don't remember meeting anyone new? Or walking to the bridge?" She walked the route in her head. Keith could have stumbled away from the marina and gone one of two ways, either along the path south, ending up on Lake Shore Drive, or north and west along the pedestrian path through the tunnel to the Riverwalk. "You had to get back to the dorm. Were you headed to Michigan to catch an Uber or cab?" If that was the case, they could trace that.

There was a blank expression on Keith's face. It didn't look like he knew which side was up yet. "I was sitting on the grass and looking out at the boats. We talked about the march. No big deal."

Lonergan's brows rose. "The anti*police* march?"

Keith straightened, assurance returning. "We're not antipolice, we're antidying. Raising our voices so the killing stops."

Lonergan clenched his teeth. She could tell by the rippling along his jawline as he bore down. "You remembered all that well enough."

"Names?" Foster asked. "Of the friends you were with." As Keith came up with them, she wrote them down.

"No blood match, no prints," George said. "Close by, but no witnesses putting Keith together with the victim. If you had any of that, again, you would have led with it." George stood, pushing his chair in. "Okay. We're done. I'm going to make some calls. Meanwhile, not another word, Keith."

When he swept out of the room in expensive shoes, his wife's eyes narrowed as she took in Lonergan none too pleasantly; then she turned and stared at Foster, as though she'd chosen the wrong side in a righteous fight.

"I'd like to confer with my client," Carole snapped, ice in her tone. Foster wondered if the woman ever rattled, ever broke to show any emotion or hint of vulnerability.

Lonergan jabbed back, seemingly still put out by the accusation of wrongdoing on the part of the first officers on scene. "If he's so innocent, how do you explain the blood?"

"It's not my job to explain it," she said. "It's yours." She looked over at her boy. "*He's* my job. My one and only."

Foster recognized the stalemate and pushed away from the table. She stood and began gathering her papers and files along with her notebook. George Ainsley was right about one thing: The clock was ticking, only time wasn't on their side. Never was. Lonergan pushed back from the table, too, scraping the chair legs noisily along the floor. He was out of the room like a bullet without another word. So much for teamwork.

"Get you anything?" she asked Keith. "A cold pop? Water? A snack?"

He lowered his chin to his chest and shook his head, but his mother wasn't about to let up. "Unnecessary. We won't be here that long."

"Right." Foster headed for the door.

"My son didn't do this," Carole called out. "You know he didn't."

Foster turned back, her eyes moving from mother to son. Did she know? She couldn't tell innocence or guilt by looking or feeling; nobody could. She opened the door. "Sit tight."

Carole Ainsley stood. "I'll fight like hell for my kid. I won't allow you to take him from me."

Foster didn't bother turning around again. There was nothing she could say that Carole Ainsley would accept. She eased out of the room and closed the door behind her. For a moment she stood at the door, her hand on the knob. "Good."

CHAPTER 8

Restless, needing to be outside instead of in, Bodie had an Uber drop him off a mile from where he was going. He'd walk the rest of the way, down streets he knew and could likely navigate blindfolded if he had to. He'd grown up here. He knew this town and the secrets it held. They were the same ones he kept now.

His feet kicked up leaves along the sidewalk as he buried his hands in his jacket pockets. He took everything in—what was the same, what was different. Fourteen years had passed since he'd been back. There wasn't a single thing he'd once thought he needed to see ever again, and yet here he was, kicking up horrors with every step he took. He was curious, trepidatious. Even the chilly fall afternoon couldn't stop him from sweating under his fleece jacket.

He rounded the corner and saw it sitting there in the middle of the block. The white house on the quiet street. As he stood, his eyes glued to the structure, he couldn't get his feet to move or his brain to process a single coherent thought. It was as though he had suddenly forgotten everything—how to walk, talk, be.

There it stood. The two-level, white-shingled nightmare with attached garage and asphalt driveway. The American flag flying from a pole on the front porch was new. Tom Morgan hadn't been the patriotic type as far as Bodie could recall. In fact, Bodie couldn't remember that he'd been at all fervent about anything, except his compulsion to kill young women with red hair and blue eyes. That was Tom's sin, but it was his and Am's blood curse. Their father was a killer. Their basement was his killing field, and they'd known it since the age of twelve, when they'd found the basement door unpadlocked and wandered downstairs to find what remained of someone's daughter. Bodie had wet himself. Amelia had been brave, stoic. Neither of them had opened their mouths about what they'd seen, not to the police or a school counselor, not to a priest or a neighbor. Tom Morgan's infection of evil had become their shame, their secret, their family legacy.

Thank God he was dead, Bodie thought. He had to be. Bodie hadn't heard a single thing from him in almost fifteen years, and he fantasized about a painful death, a true reckoning. The man had deserved no less. One thing was certain: if Tom Morgan were still alive, still here, Bodie wouldn't be. He couldn't imagine coming anywhere near this place if Tom Morgan still walked the earth. Even now, though, as he neared the house—as his reluctant feet slapped against the concrete sidewalk, as he stirred up fallen leaves in his path, his eyes boring into the shingles—he had the very eerie sense that his father's eyes were tracking him.

Staring up at the second-floor windows, one looking out from his old bedroom and the other from Amelia's, he was back there again, in the basement, staring into the stillest, bluest eyes he'd ever seen. This was where it all started, or was it more accurate to say *ended*? This was where he could have become something different and had that chance stolen from him. This was where he'd been changed.

"Help you?"

He reeled to find a man standing at the garage in a flannel jacket and skull cap. He was holding an old rake. Bodie had been so haunted by the house, so drawn in, that he hadn't noticed that the garage door was up or that there were garbage bags of raked-up leaves sitting on the driveway. The man looked to be in his midfifties. This was his house now, obviously. For a moment, Bodie stared at him. Did the man have any idea what he'd inherited? Bodie doubted it.

He smiled. It was the smile he'd seen his father give a million times—warm, friendly, fake, well-practiced. "Sorry," Bodie said. "I used to live here as a kid. I was in the neighborhood, so I thought I'd come take a look."

"A walk down memory lane, that it?" The man tossed down the rake and leaned down for a plastic garbage bag. "When's the last time you saw it?"

Bodie scanned the house's exterior again. "Almost fifteen years." He pointed at the upstairs window on the left. "That was my room. That old hickory tree still in the back?"

"It's partly to blame for me being out here. I hit the back this morning. Perks of home ownership, right?"

Bodie chuckled. "Right. How long you been here?"

"Me and the family moved in about ten years ago. It's a great neighborhood. Not so busy. The neighbors keep to themselves." He gave Bodie a playful wink. "And the school's just up the way, but you'd know all that."

He knew about the quiet neighbors. "I went to that school," Bodie said.

"What's your name?" the man asked.

"Dan. Dan Flynn." The lie rolled off his tongue easily, but he doubted the man would check the house's provenance to see if any Flynns showed up in the search.

"Frank Gibson." Gibson gave him a good long look. Bodie was clean shaven, neat, nicely dressed. He didn't look like a thief or a criminal. He looked normal, like someone the man would know and have a beer with. Safe. "You want to take a quick look inside? For old times' sake?"

The thought alone made Bodie tense. Though the smile hid most of his unease, inside his head a Klaxon sounded. Seeing the house again was one thing, but he absolutely couldn't step inside. "No. Thanks," he said. "I remember it. Besides, what's that they say? You can't go home again?"

Bodie noted that there were flouncy yellow curtains hanging in his old room instead of the blue ones with stripes that he remembered having. He'd stood in that room on his last day, waiting for Tom Morgan to start the car. All Bodie had wanted to do was go. He and Am had lived with their basement discovery six years by that point without either of them talking about it. He couldn't fathom now how they'd accomplished such a thing, how they'd managed to appear normal, act normal, say nothing, and continue to live in the same house with a murderer. The world beyond his room had felt like a giant trap. What if he slipped up? What if he told? Worse yet, what would he become if he didn't?

That last day here, Tom Morgan stared at him with his warm brown eyes, not the cold ones Bodie had seen when Tom had discovered them in his private place, the ones that held not an ounce of humanity, the ones he feared at night. He'd wondered often which eyes his father's victims saw when they realized they were going to die. Were they still alive when he disemboweled them or cut their hands from their wrists or their feet from their ankles? Some monsters didn't look like monsters. No one would ever imagine the personable CPA who helped with homework and took his daughter to ballet class on Saturday mornings held such darkness, such a twisted soul.

There were no parting words of wisdom on that last day before they were driven off to college. He and Am just packed their things, got in the car, and were driven away. And Tom was gone. Phone number disconnected. House sold. He and Am had been on their own at eighteen. He knew Am had tried to find their father, but Bodie had never bothered. Why would he when he could finally breathe?

"You all right there?" Gibson asked.

His question brought Bodie back to the present. "What's that?"

"Looked like you got lost there for a minute."

Bodie smiled. "Guess so. Memories are funny that way. I won't hold you up any longer. I was just curious and wanted to see."

"No bother. It's a good house," Gibson said. "Feel free to stop by anytime."

Bodie backed up a bit. He wouldn't be back. "Thanks," he said, already moving away, but he turned back. "My father set up a workshop in the basement."

"That right?" Gibson said.

"He made wooden toys—little things." It was the reason he had given them for spending so much time locked below stairs. There had been toy trains for him, dollhouses for Am, but not enough to account for all his time.

"I've never been handy like that. I converted it into a family room for the kids. Pool table, TV, sofas. My daughters spend half their time down there. You ever listen to a bunch of teenage girls giggling and squealing like little magpies? It's an experience, let me tell you."

"Right." Bodie's eyes swept over the lawn. "Well, good luck with the leaves."

He could hear Gibson's rake start its steady scraping behind him as he walked away. Family room, he thought. A pool table and television set, sofas. He picked up his pace.

"And daughters," he mumbled to himself.

CHAPTER 9

"Not enough to hold him and have it stick, and you all know it," Griffin announced. "The state's attorney would have laughed in our faces." The team had gathered around her to report what they had—or, more importantly, didn't have.

"So instead, we sit on our hands and let him waltz out of here?" Lonergan said, having just watched Keith and his parents walk out the front door.

"Until we can match that blood to Birch or find that knife with his prints on it? Yeah." Griffin glanced over at Foster. "What *do* we have?"

"We have Rosales's preliminary report from the scene. We have Keith Ainsley's fuzzy recollections of Sunday night. We have two names from Birch's parents: Joe Rimmer and Wendy Stroman—her ex-boyfriend and her roommate at school. Since Peggy was living away from the house, her parents couldn't account for her time day to day, but those two might have a better idea. If we can track her movements, maybe we find a point where she and Ainsley met somewhere."

"What about Ainsley's friends from the park?" Griffin asked. "Anybody talk to them?" She got nothing but shaking heads back as a response. "Right. That's why Ainsley walked. We don't have our ducks in a row. We have less than nothing."

"Blood's not nothing," Lonergan groused.

Foster turned to him. "But he wasn't covered in it. If he killed her, he would have been. It would have been under his nails, in his hair, on his shoes, socks."

Griffin watched the two of them, still clearly assessing their viability as a team. "Right. So stop whining, Lonergan," she said. "Him walking now gives us time to build a case. If we'd kept him, that would have started the clock on our forty-eight. Smarter not to waste it until we have something more than what we've got now."

"Maybe if we'd sweated him for forty-eight hours, he'd have given something up," Lonergan pushed back.

Symansky chuckled and straightened his gaudy tie. "Doubt it. His parents were all over that. I'm with the boss. We'd have lost our shot keeping him."

Detective Tony Bigelow pushed his eyeglasses on top of his head and then swiveled in his chair. "Her and Ainsley being at the same march sounds like it might be something."

"Maybe, but there were hundreds of people marching along with them," Foster said.

"Right. She coulda met anybody," Symansky said. "Those marches are like friggin' mosh pits."

Foster consulted her notes. "Otherwise, Birch and Ainsley didn't go to the same school; they didn't come from the same neighborhood. I doubt we'll find friend groups in common. Nothing else seems to connect them."

"No way I'd let my kid sign on to that fringe mob crap," Symansky offered, leaning back in his chair. "It's likely some freak taking an opportunity."

"Fringe mob?" Detective Vera Li asked, her brows raised. "What happened to free speech? And they're not entirely wrong on some points."

"Commies," Symansky countered. "This is America. They don't like it, they can leave it."

Li lobbed a balled-up report sheet at his head, but he snagged it midair and tossed it back to her. "What decade are you in, Al? Are you really advocating for America, love it or leave it?"

He shot Li an impish grin. Apparently, he enjoyed winding her up. "I just don't like kids wet behind the ears telling me how stuff's supposed to run. They don't have the life experience, and they sure as hell don't know how things work. Give them a couple of decades after the world hits them hard, and then let's see what they're willing to march for. That's my point."

Lonergan nodded, twirling a ballpoint between his fingers. "Hear, hear."

Li smirked, then reached for her coffee mug and took a sip. "*Two* cavemen. Wonderful."

Symansky and Lonergan began a chorus of caveman grunts, which Kelley playfully joined in on. Li turned to Foster and shook her head. "*This* is what we have to put up with."

Griffin clapped her hands together to get everyone back on point. "All right. Knock it off. So we start pulling some strings, right? We find somebody who can account for Birch's time and for Ainsley's. See if anything matches up. We concentrate on the march, the route. We hit the bars, the restaurants. We pull the street cameras. Spread out. If Ainsley left his friends and found Birch, let's prove it. Foster and Lonergan, you take Birch. The rest of you grab some uniforms and get back out there before this thing blows up in our faces." No one moved. "Today, people."

———

Rimmer was a barista at a Starbucks near campus, though he wasn't a student, according to Peggy's mother, Beth. Instead, Peggy had told her that Rimmer was a singer in a rock band waiting for his big break. More talented than Bono, though Beth had confessed to not recognizing the name.

Foster walked into the Starbucks with Lonergan, her eyes tracking the twentysomething grunge type working up an order, a silver ring on every finger, sleeves of weird dragon art up and down his puny arms. He looked much like the other baristas there, but this guy's gaunt, sullen face matched Joseph Thomas Rimmer's driver's license photo. As she watched faux Bono flirt with the female customers and strut between the counter and the espresso machines as though he were God's gift, she wondered what Peggy Birch could have seen in him. Beside her, Lonergan emitted a disdainful groan. He was uncomfortable, out of his element. This wasn't his scene.

Foster stepped up to the counter, jumping the line, her ID out so Rimmer could read it. "Joseph Rimmer?" She watched as his face paled. "I'm Detective Foster. This is my . . . this is Detective Lonergan." She'd caught herself about to say *my partner, Detective Thompson*. Would she ever get used to not saying it? "We'd like to ask you a few questions, please."

Light, glassy eyes focused on the badge first before traveling up to her face. He studied Lonergan next. She could smell the weed on him. "No. Sorry. Wrong guy."

It was a nice try, and Foster couldn't fault him for the attempt. She put her badge away and stood there waiting, holding up the line, prepared to do so all afternoon. The marijuana was a nonstarter. Rimmer was over twenty-one. He was legal if he had less than thirty grams on his person, but it didn't look like he knew that. He'd begun to sweat.

"*Excuse me.* I was next. You can't just cut in front."

Foster turned around to face a dark-haired woman in business attire clutching a rhinestone-encrusted iPhone, a slender tote slung under her arm. Their eyes held. She was sure the woman had seen her present her badge. She saw Lonergan standing next to her, looking like a cop. Yet it was Foster she felt confident in challenging. She stared at the woman for a few moments, her head angled slightly, watching as the woman appeared to go from haughty and entitled to docile, deciding finally to step back from the counter to give her and Lonergan all the room and time they required. Foster turned back around.

A freckle-faced barista in her midtwenties at the other end of the counter shouted, "Joe, your Caffè Misto's up." Foster's eyebrow rose. Lonergan's too.

"Not you, huh?" Lonergan said.

Rimmer's eyes began to dart around the room. It looked like he wanted to run, but he had nowhere to go. The place was crowded, even this late in the day. "Okay. Yeah. I'm Joe. What's this about?"

"Mind if we talk for a minute?" Foster asked.

"Yeah, take a break, Frank Zappa," Lonergan added.

Away from the counter and the busy line of caffeine junkies, Foster and Lonergan snagged the world's smallest corner table to talk to the jumpy Rimmer, who slid his hands over his baggy pockets and left them there. Foster was sure Lonergan caught the move and the smell, and it looked like he was finding both hard to ignore.

"When's the last time you saw Peggy?" Lonergan asked.

Rimmer let a breath go, relief loosening the tension in his face. "Peggy? Why?"

"Answer the question," Lonergan said.

Rimmer read something in Lonergan's face he didn't want to challenge. "We broke up. Haven't seen her in weeks. What's all this about?"

"Peggy was killed last night," Foster said gently. "Her body was found on the Riverwalk."

Rimmer looked from cop face to cop face as he formed a half smile that slowly faded. "You're full of shit. Both of you. Is this a joke?"

"Unfortunately, no," Foster said. "I'm sorry." Rimmer sat stunned, unblinking, and she wondered what was running through his head. Was he thinking about Peggy? He seemed genuinely surprised at the news, but not devastated by it.

"So when'd you see her last?" Lonergan asked again.

The jumpiness was back. Rimmer eyed the counter, where his espresso machine awaited. "Couple weeks . . . or more," he said. "We didn't hang anymore, so I wouldn't know where she was or what she was doing, would I?" His eyes held Foster's. "You're solid? Peggy's *really* dead?"

"She hang out on the Riverwalk a lot?" Lonergan asked.

"Of course not. Why would she?"

"We're looking for habits," Foster said, "places she liked to frequent, people she liked to hang out with. Someone who would know why she might have been down there yesterday."

Rimmer abandoned his pockets to run his hands through his greasy hair. Foster noticed that in addition to the tattoos on his arms, he had musical notes tattooed on every finger. Good reason for Rimmer never to commit a crime. He'd be easily identifiable.

"Peg. Dead. I can't believe it." He shook his arms out as though he were an athlete loosening up for a race. "Yeah, okay. A profile. That's what cops look for, right?" Foster and Lonergan exchanged a quick look, then waited on Rimmer to get on with it, because that was what cops did. "Peg was a good kid. College. Really into it. I went for a year. It wasn't for me. I want to go after my music. Get my sound out there."

Lonergan frowned. "That why you're working in a coffee shop?"

"Temporary. As a matter of fact, I got a line on a gig right now. Touring, too, so . . ."

"Who was Peggy close to?" Foster asked, wanting to move things along. "Was there anybody she had a problem with, or they with her?"

"Enough to kill her? No way. Do you have any suspects? Did anybody see anything?"

"We can't talk about that," Foster said. "Let's stick with the names."

"Doesn't seem right," Rimmer said. "I mean, we hung out for several months. That should give me rights to some details."

"You want details, buy a paper," Lonergan said.

Rimmer rolled his eyes. "Exactly why I hate talking to cops."

Lonergan scooted his chair closer to Rimmer's, met him dead eye to glassy eye. "Maybe you want to have this little talk where *we* work . . . and maybe we bring out the drug-sniffing dogs and have them sniff your weedy pockets. How's that?"

"I'm under the limit," Rimmer said.

Lonergan grinned. "I'm bettin' not everywhere, kid. We'll check your locker, your car, wherever you flop. We'll turn you inside out."

Rimmer swallowed hard. "Stella Dean. Try her. She goes to Peg's school. They hit it off, apparently. That's when I broke things off."

Lonergan smirked. "She dumped you for a girl?"

"The breakup was mutual."

"Only you didn't see it comin'," Lonergan asserted. "Had to make you mad."

Rimmer glowered at Lonergan. "You're trying to needle me. I don't like it."

"Tough," Lonergan said.

Foster was so over Lonergan's gruff, macho posturing. He was a bull in a china shop, a dull blade where a surgical knife was needed. And he was costing them time and good favor with Rimmer, neither of which they could afford to squander. "Does Stella live in Peggy's dorm?" she asked.

Rimmer's eyes stayed on Lonergan's, as though the cop were a rattler ready to strike. "I didn't ask. She didn't tell."

"What about Wendy Stroman?" Foster asked. "Know her?"

Rimmer nodded. "I met her a couple times. She's just a kid. One of those egghead types. I couldn't tell you anything else about her."

"And she didn't have a beef with anybody you know of?" Lonergan asked.

Rimmer shook his head, suddenly somber. "Nobody who knew Peg could kill her. She was okay, you know? Sweet. That's all I can say. I'm really shredded here."

Foster closed her notebook. "One last question. Where were you last night? Around midnight."

Rimmer's eyes got wide as dinner plates. "Hold on. I told you, I couldn't hurt her. I was legit home the whole night."

"Anybody with you?" Lonergan asked.

"I was working on songs. Alone. Like I said, I got a gig set up—"

Lonergan held a hand up. "Can anybody vouch for you being home alone? You see a neighbor? Get food delivered in?"

Rimmer's eyes narrowed, and he answered through clenched teeth. "No. Don't you think if it was me, I'd have a better story? That I'd have people vouching for me wrapped around the block? God, I can't believe you people."

Foster slid a paper napkin out of the table dispenser and scribbled her name, office number, and email address on it. She had CPD cards from her last district but none yet for her new assignment. Until then, this would have to do. She would've asked Lonergan to offer his card instead, but she doubted Rimmer would have taken it. "If you think of anything else that might help us, I'd appreciate a call."

"Joe, a little help here!" It was the freckle-faced barista from the counter. The line was now halfway out the door, and the exasperated look on the young woman's face broadcast an unwillingness to wrangle hangry caffeine junkies on her own one millisecond longer.

Rimmer pushed up from the table. "I gotta go."

Lonergan smiled, looking up at him. "Duty calls, huh? We'll be in touch."

Rimmer gave the napkin a quick glance, then tucked it into his back pocket. Weed in the front, cop contact in the back. *How times change,* Foster thought. When Rimmer left the table, she stood for a moment and watched him fill orders, catching his eye just once before he turned his back and focused on his work.

"You memorizing his face?" Lonergan asked.

"He didn't ask how she was killed." She knew from experience that the how was important. In fact, survivors—family, friends, even dumped exes—almost always asked how before they asked when, where, why, and who.

Lonergan turned to stare at Rimmer. "And he's got a dog of an alibi."

They wove through the crowd toward the door. "You ever do weed, Foster?" he asked when they'd pushed out onto the sidewalk.

Was he joking? She zipped up her jacket. "No."

They headed for the car parked at the curb. "Don't you want to know if I ever did?" he asked.

She quickened her step. Lonergan sighed.

"I'll take that as a no."

CHAPTER 10

Amelia slid out of an Uber at the horseshoe at Pioneer Court and stood on the busy plaza, watching a crowd of onlookers leaning over the bridge railing, cameras out, everyone in a sideshow kind of humor. The Riverwalk had them enthralled. It also warranted the attention of three news helicopters that hovered overhead, the steady whomp-whomp of their rotor blades loud enough to drown out the heavy traffic along Michigan Avenue. There were police officers on the bridge trying to keep people moving, but many looked like they were fine staying put, at least long enough to capture the oddity below for Facebook or Twitter or Insta.

Flipping her hood up, she took up a spot along the railing and peered down at the sagging police tape and the cops and techs wrapping up below. She glanced over at the glass-encased Apple Store, but no one there appeared to care what was going on outside.

"It's something, huh?" the man next to her asked. "As though Mondays couldn't suck enough."

Amelia looked him over. The man was dressed in a tan maintenance shirt and dark pants, his name stitched into a patch above his left chest pocket. Andy. "What happened?"

He held up his cell phone. "Somebody got killed down there this morning. Drowned, I think. Somebody else got taken to the ER. Made the midday news. They've been down there ever since, but it looks like they're just now packing up the last of it. I been following it all day.

They moved the body out already. I got a shot of that on my lunch hour." He swiped through his phone and held up the image of a body bag on a stretcher being towed up the stone steps toward a waiting cop van. "They were looking for something in the water too. I got some good snaps of the police divers." Andy glanced up at the choppers. "No idea what *they're* doing up there still. Not much to see now."

An Asian woman in a short car coat, a briefcase in her hand, had been following the conversation "The guy over there said it was an overdose. Two women. One didn't make it; the other was barely breathing when they found her." She shook her head, her expression displaying a hint of disapproval. "Sounds like kids."

"Whichever it is," Andy said, "I guess we won't know for a while. They always notify the families first. How'd you like to get *that* call, huh? I know *I* wouldn't."

Amelia watched the cops below. "Two women. That's terrible."

The man moved away from the railing and turned south. "It ain't good for somebody, that's for sure." He walked away, his curiosity satisfied. "I'm going home to watch the rest of it in high def."

The woman gave the scene a final look as well before walking off with a shake of the head. "I've seen enough. What people do to themselves," she muttered in a stage whisper.

Amelia stood on the bridge with the others who were choosing to hang in until there was nothing else to see. A drowning or an overdose. It was interesting to see how a lack of definitive information could quickly lead to misinformation. But she was sure the divers weren't here for an overdose.

Amelia's body hummed as though she'd been infused by a low electric charge. The sound of the helicopters, the churning of the gray water below them, the chatty passersby, the cars and cabs and buses honking behind her, the police. What a mess. Where was Bodie? Though she knew this situation had nothing to do with him, he was her first thought whenever anything unusual or tragic happened. It was a worry, an automatic reflex, like throwing an arm out to protect a child when the car lurched to a sudden stop or gripping your bag in a panic when you thought you'd lost your cell phone. She'd figured out that fear and the anger that grew out of it were what caused him so much trouble. But Morgans didn't talk of such things.

When the nearest chopper slipped away, prepared to take another pass, Amelia plucked her cell phone from her pocket and punched in Bodie's number, just to check, plugging a finger in the opposite ear to block out everything else. She breathed a sigh of relief when he picked up.

"Hey, what's up?" He sounded chipper, relaxed.

Amelia swiped a look at the chopper as it veered off over the lake. "Why's something have to be up?"

"You're calling to check on me, Am. It hasn't even been twenty-four hours. Look, I'm good. Okay?"

He'd said the same before. Bodie was always good, always okay, until he wasn't. He'd been okay, good, when he'd busted out the windows in his high school geometry class when the teacher had berated him for not having done his homework. He'd been okay, good, when he'd dropped out of college but slashed every tire in the employee parking lot on his way off campus. And he'd been okay, good, when he'd followed that woman home from the bar and gotten arrested. Bodie's *okay, good* was untrustworthy, and no one knew that better than she did.

She knew a part of him was still stuck at twelve, his trembling hands gripping the back of her shirt as they descended dusty stairs to find the unthinkable at the bottom. She could swear she'd seen the old Bodie, the sweet Bodie, die and a new one, a wrecked one, take his place at the sight of blood and the stranger's dismembered hands and feet. It had broken him, but it hadn't broken her. Amelia had found a way to survive.

"As a matter of fact, right now, I'm doing laundry and cleaning up my place," Bodie said. "Ironing is relaxing when you get into it. Did you know that?"

"I did know, actually." She leaned against the railing, easing into the relief. "And I do know you're good, Bod. I just . . . I know you're good."

"What's all that noise in the background?"

"There's a helicopter flying away. I'm downtown . . . doing some shopping. Something happened on the Riverwalk."

"Something big by the sound of it."

"Big enough to make the news already," she said. "Few details, though."

"I'll turn on the set. It's got to be big if it's chopper worthy."

She turned her back to the river. "Hey, I thought we could do dinner or something, huh? Catch up?"

"Sure. When?"

"Tonight. You pick the time. Meanwhile, have fun ironing."

"I will," he said. "Didn't think you were much of a shopper, though. You and your boho chic."

She smiled. "You don't know everything about me, Bodie Morgan."

"Oh yeah? What don't I know?"

She paused. "Tonight then, huh?"

"I'll be there."

Amelia ended the call, then turned and took one last look below before moving along.

CHAPTER 11

Bodie dropped his phone into his messenger bag and watched from behind the tour-boat kiosk across the street as Am walked south along the bridge and then across Wacker to disappear in the crowd of pedestrians. What a game they played, he thought. How close they were and yet so very different. He crossed the street, skirting the cops trying to push people along. For a moment, he stood at the railing where Am had stood and looked down at the Riverwalk, up at the choppers. A body had been found, and he wanted to see for himself.

Had he expected to find Am here? Maybe a part of him had. They both seemed to be drawn in by the same things. Shopping. That was what Am had said she'd been doing, and he'd lied as well because he didn't want her to worry about him or feel as though she had to direct him in any way. What a pair they made. Still lying. Still ignoring the elephant in the room, the damage done. He was stronger than Am gave him credit for. He loved her, but if he was honest, he had to admit that a part of him loathed her self-assuredness. Why had Am gotten everything? Why had he gotten so little?

When he'd seen enough, he left the bridge and walked north, head down, the sounds of the city assaulting his ears, welcome music after the unnerving hush of Westhaven. He could right himself. Tom Morgan didn't have to be a yoke around his neck. He hoped the man was dead and dust. He hoped he burned. Maybe there'd come a time when he didn't see him in every face he passed in the street. Evil men couldn't last forever, could they?

CHAPTER 12

Foster stared out the window as Lonergan drove them north, watching the city pass by, noting the faces, checking to see that all was as it should be, as though crime were all the city's streets had to offer. It was what happened when you'd been at the job awhile. Your eyes slid right over the good and locked onto the problematic.

"What's with the paper clip?" Lonergan said out of the blue. "I noticed you dropped one in your pocket back at the office. It was a deliberate drop, too, not some absentminded thing. You collect 'em or something?"

Lonergan wasn't as dull a blade as she'd thought, but she wasn't up for sharing confidences with him. "It's just a clip, Lonergan." She said the words but knew the truth. Tomorrow she'd slip another clip into her pocket. The day after that, there'd be another. It was a way of marking time, getting through one day, one clip, at a time. Not his business.

"Hmm. Don't think so," he said.

She glanced out the passenger window, unwilling to go a single step further. "Hmm. Well, chew on it then."

Foster had assured Peggy's mother with all sincerity that she could survive the loss of her daughter. But there was more to living than surviving. Clocks continued to tick even though they didn't keep accurate time. Sometimes people walked, talked, breathed, and ate and could still be gone.

It was well into the afternoon, and the news of Peggy Birch's murder had well and truly broken. *Woman's Body Found along Riverwalk* was the startling headline over the radio, on newspaper sites. The news at noon had even had footage of the crime scene, choppers and all.

"It's out." Foster read the initial reports on her phone, then angled for Lonergan to take a peek. "Won't be long before they release her name."

The report didn't mention Peggy's manner of death, thankfully, but when that made the front pages, she could just imagine what the headlines would be. Media wasn't known for its subtlety. *Woman Ripped Apart on Riverwalk . . . Where's the Riverwalk Slasher? . . . CPD Stumped by Thrill Killer.* The city would take notice, and they would get the heat.

Foster closed the website's window and called the ME's office. "I'll check on the time for the autopsy." Chicago had a population of 2.7 million people. Violent death was a common occurrence. But this killing was different: it had been brutal, shocking, even to her, and Birch had been dumped right on the city's front step. Everybody from the mayor and the police superintendent on down would be on the detectives' backs to find who'd done it before fingers started pointing their way, and the ME knew that as well as she did.

Lonergan pulled into the campus lot just as Foster got the information she needed. "Autopsy's tomorrow morning, at nine." She dropped her phone into her pocket, jotted the time down in her notebook, then checked her watch. It was a little after 2:00 p.m. "Eighteen hours from now." She grabbed her bag and her files and slid out of the car. She was always laden down with paper and notes and files, never knowing what bit of information she'd need or when she'd need it. Already, after only a few short hours, it felt like she'd been on the Birch case forever.

Lonergan lifted out on the driver's side with a grunt and watched her over the roof of the car. "You write down everything in that little book of yours?"

"The important things."

"Like?"

"Details. Statements. Important things." She grew defensive as she tucked the files into her bag and slung it over her shoulder. *"Work."*

He turned to watch students hustle past, none of them bothering to pay them a bit of attention. They had classes to get to, stuff to do. "I guess you got books on top of books filed away somewhere."

She did. Every case. For seventeen years. "That a problem?"

He shook his head. "Just curious." He tapped a finger to the side of his head. "I keep my notes in here. Don't have to carry a thing." He cocked his head. "What happens if we get into a foot pursuit—you carryin' all that?"

She glowered at him, not sure he wasn't questioning her competency or her readiness if, God forbid, they got into a tough spot. "I drop the bag," she said. Foster looked around, spotted the building they needed, and started walking. "Or not," she muttered low, sure Lonergan missed it.

They waited for Wendy Stroman and Stella Dean in a small study room on the ground floor of Barnwell Hall, a five-story residence building overlooking a square, leafy courtyard. A round table with two chairs sat in the middle of the space. A saggy couch had been pushed into a corner, swooshes of blue and scarlet running the length of the wall above—the school colors proudly displayed.

They'd gotten a student escort from the registrar's office, and now the RA had gone to track down the two young women they needed to talk to. Media reports on Peggy's death were coming in fast and furious. The Birch family wouldn't get a lot of privacy from here on out.

Lonergan's judgy eyes scanned the room. "Not much to write home about, to tell the truth." He wandered over to the window overlooking the lawn and ran a finger across the dusty sill. "You'd think they'd dust the place for what they charge. And it smells like feet." He turned to face her. "You go to college, Foster?"

She flipped open her notebook as she leaned against the wall. The couch looked germy and uncomfortable, so she decided to bypass it. "Yes."

"Graduate and everything?"

"With honors."

"Why be a copper, then? You could be runnin' Google or somethin' instead of pickin' through bodies. Not sayin' we're all slouches—we got some Einsteins on the job—but you had easier options is what I'm sayin'."

Foster couldn't tell if Lonergan was being sincere or setting her up for some snide remark or patronizing condemnation. He was . . . a puzzle.

"I joined because I didn't see enough cops on the street who looked like me . . . and there needed to be," she said. "Also, because I thought I might be good at it."

"And you think you're good at it?"

"I *am* good." The look she gave Lonergan dared him to challenge her words.

He leaned against the sill, studying her, his arms folded across his chest. "You know what I learned, Foster? Most killers are dumb as cheese. You don't have to be Sherlock friggin' Holmes to catch one of 'em. Sometimes the idiots run home and hide under their mommy's bed . . . sometimes they take naps under a bridge. When we find where Ainsley hid that knife, you can write that down in your book there."

It was over. The momentary thaw in the ice between them had frozen over again, and she and Lonergan were back where they'd been. "We'll see," she said.

The door opened on Foster and Lonergan standing at opposite ends of the tight room, their physical distance a visual cue to their philosophical one. Two young white women eased in—Stroman and Dean, presumably. Foster lifted off the wall and pointed them to the couch, watching as they eased down, sitting far from one another. Lonergan stayed near the window, his arms crossed. One of the women had been crying; her face was red and puffy, her eyes too. They'd explained their purpose in the office, given the RA a heads-up, so Stroman and Dean already knew Peggy was gone.

"Who's Wendy Stroman?" Lonergan asked.

The petite brunette in the T-shirt with Mozart's image on the front raised her hand, her brown eyes peeking out from behind severe horn-rimmed glasses. By contrast, the woman next to her, Stella Dean, was blonde and less birdlike, dressed in a white T-shirt and scarlet sweatpants with the school's name down the leg.

Wendy concentrated on her hands, which lay in her lap as she picked nervously at the dry cuticles on her right thumb. Stella sniffled in a ragged breath and covered her eyes, grinding her fingertips into the sockets as though trying to erase an unpleasant image. Two different reactions to tragic news. Their body language alone, Foster thought, was a lot to think about.

She glanced over at Lonergan, but it didn't look like he was going to start. He appeared more than willing to let her deal with the emotional women, like her sergeant long ago. She turned one of the chairs around to sit facing them.

"I know how hard this is, but we'd like to ask you a few questions about Peggy." Her eyes met Wendy's. "You were her roommate?"

Wendy nodded, then looked at Stella, who now had her elbows on her knees and her head in her hands. "How did they? Kill her, I mean."

It wasn't information Foster would share, though she could see how not knowing pained Peggy's friend. Besides, everyone would know soon enough once the media had its way. "Let's focus on helping her now, all right? When's the last time you saw Peggy?"

"Early yesterday." Wendy flicked her head up and let her mangled cuticles go. "She was going to the march. A lot of kids were. It was a big thing. I couldn't go. I spend Sundays with the family. My mom expects it."

"If you're local," Lonergan asked, "why're you livin' here?"

"I wanted to be on my own. Sundays are a lot better than twenty-four seven at home."

"Why's any of this important?" Stella barked. "Some nut out there just killed Peg. What does it matter that she went home for mostaccioli night?"

"We didn't have mostaccioli," Wendy shot back. "It was pot roast."

Stella threw her hands up dramatically. "Thanks for the much-needed clarification, Wendy."

Foster turned to Stella. She knew nothing about her but didn't appreciate the overbearing vibe she gave off or the insensitivity. "Stop the nonsense." The look she gave Stella told her that she meant it. "What about you?"

"I saw her before she left," Stella said. "Around ten, maybe?"

"You askin' or tellin'?" Lonergan said.

Stella looked over at Lonergan like she'd just noticed he was there as a person and not as furniture. "It was *around* ten."

"So yesterday Peggy left for the march," Foster said. "Wendy didn't go. Did you go, Stella?"

"I was supposed to," she said, "but I'm seriously in the hole in econ. I had to study, so I begged off, told her to go ahead. She took the bus down with some other kids going. If I'd gone with her, maybe . . ." She began to sob. Foster could sense Lonergan fidgeting at the window.

"Peggy have a problem with anybody here?" he asked. "Dorm rivals. Mashers?"

Both women looked up at him, the confused looks on their faces indicating that they didn't understand the term. Foster clarified. "Anyone harassing or pressuring her," she said. "Paying her unwanted attention."

Stella wiped her eyes with the backs of her hands. "No way. Peg was cool with everybody."

Wendy glanced over at Stella, the flick out of the corner of her eye unfriendly, which Foster caught. Whatever the look meant, it was there only for a second, then gone, but she was sure it was significant. "Wendy? That true?"

Wendy startled, seemingly uncomfortable with the direct question or the solo attention. "Yeah. Peg was so great."

"Anybody she might have met off campus, online?" Foster asked.

Both shook their heads. Foster opened her file and slid out a photo array with Keith Ainsley's driver's license photo included. "Have you ever seen any of these young men with Peggy?"

Both stared down at the images and shook their heads again. Foster tucked the sheet away, relieved that they hadn't pointed out Keith Ainsley. No ID, then. It was one more element in the young man's favor. "So to be clear, the last time either of you saw Peggy, she was heading out for the march on Sunday. Wendy, you were with your parents. Stella, you were studying. You never heard from her during the day?"

"Nothing," Wendy said. Stella nodded in agreement.

"When'd you get back from your parents'?" Lonergan asked.

"Around seven," Wendy said. "My dad drove me back. I studied until about ten, then went to bed. I didn't even know Peg's bed hadn't been slept in until I woke up this morning, but I wasn't worried. I figured she maybe spent the night at her house with her folks. Sometimes she did that."

Lonergan turned to Stella. "What time were you done studyin'? And who saw you doin' it?"

"Five, maybe? I studied with Ashley. Ashley Tighe. When we were done, I ordered a pizza, then went to bed early. I was fried. Econ's not my thing."

Foster jotted the name down in her book, then waited for Lonergan to continue.

"Pizza from where?" he asked.

Stella hesitated. "Zippy's."

"Got a receipt?" he asked.

Foster knew Lonergan was looking for Stella's tells to see if she was lying. She was doing the same with both girls. She had to remember they were kids, despite Stella's forcefulness, so a certain amount of care and handling needed to be taken. Foster couldn't overlook how intimidating her and Lonergan's badges could be or how guarded people became when they spoke to the police.

"I never keep them," Stella said.

"How early did you go to bed?" Foster asked.

"About nine. A little after."

A college kid in bed at nine. Foster narrowed her eyes but let it go. For now.

"And this Ashley?" Lonergan asked. "She wasn't in on the pizza?"

"I didn't ask her," Stella said. "I just wanted to kick back alone."

Foster had been a cop a long time. She knew when someone was lying to her, and Stella was lying. She glanced over at Wendy, who sat perfectly still, her face showing no emotion. Foster was sure she knew Stella was lying too.

Birch had likely been killed, according to Rosales, around midnight. Wendy was claiming to have been in bed by ten, Stella by nine. Of the two, Foster thought, Stella seemed less truthful. "In bed by nine. Here? In the dorm?" she pressed. "And before you answer, know that we *will* check."

Stella slid back on the couch. She tried doing it subtly, like she wasn't uncomfortable with the pointed questions, but Foster hadn't missed the slide. Stella played with the hem of her shirt, twisting it, picking at it. "I was asleep in my room."

Foster gave Stella one last long, unwavering look, then let up and made a note in her book. "Joe Rimmer." She said his name and then let it sit there for a moment. "Let's talk about him."

"He's an idiot," Stella blurted out. "Peg dumped him."

"He says it was mutual," Lonergan said, "and you had a part in it." Stella smiled. "You have a problem with that?"

Lonergan lifted off the windowsill. "Look, kid . . ."

Foster interrupted him. "Rimmer seemed a bit raw over the breakup."

"He was mad, sure," Wendy said. "Called her like twenty times a day trying to get her to take him back, but she wouldn't."

Stella nodded in agreement. "All he wanted was a groupie. He thinks he's going to be the next Dave Grohl." She rolled her eyes. "Fat chance."

"He been hangin' around?" Lonergan asked.

"Too big of a wuss for that," Stella said. "He's all talk, believe me."

Wendy pushed her glasses higher up the bridge of her nose, and her mouth clamped shut. She was definitely not saying something. She obviously found Stella intimidating. Foster could see how she would. Wendy was meek, a shy little mouse. Stella looked to be the kind of person who sucked up all the oxygen in a room, the kind you noticed and shied away from for fear of being swept into her vortex.

Foster stood, sliding the chair back under the table. "Wendy, would you mind showing me your room?" She looked over at Lonergan, whose mouth was hanging open in shock. "Maybe Stella can continue with Detective Lonergan." She smiled. "We won't be long." She looked down at Stella. "We'll talk again."

Lonergan walked over and pulled Foster gently by the arm away from the girls, out of earshot, both turning their backs to them for privacy. "Ah, what gives?" he whispered.

"I think Wendy has more to add," Foster whispered back. "But she's not going to talk with Stella sitting next to her."

"But I get the snippy bulldozer?"

Foster peeked behind him, noting that Stella had composed herself. "She's a kid. You can't handle a kid?" She could tell Lonergan wanted to say more, and loudly, but she didn't give him the chance. "I'll be back."

Lonergan turned around to face his misery. "I'll count the friggin' minutes."

CHAPTER 13

Wendy and Peggy's room wasn't much to write home about. It was small, crammed with personal things, and barely big enough to fit everything Peggy and Wendy had brought from home, let alone themselves. The space was stuffed with clothes, shoes, bags, makeup, hair dryers, and styling irons. The posters taped to the walls were for bands Foster had never heard of, and they held pride of place beside a collage of personal photos, presumably of the girls' families and friends. She identified Peggy's side by her wall of photos. Foster spotted several of Peggy and her parents taken at Christmas and birthdays and family vacations. Many of the photos were of Peggy with her friends—a lot of friends. It was true, then, that she'd been friendly, well liked. Looking, Foster could find no photos of Joe Rimmer. Either Peggy didn't have any, or she'd taken them all down after the break. There were no photos of Keith Ainsley either.

"Did Peggy wear lipstick?" Foster asked, recalling the troubling discovery of lipstick around Birch's wrists and ankles. If the lipstick wasn't Peggy's, that meant the sick SOB they were looking for had brought it with him. That meant he'd planned to kill, had prepared for it. Foster's stomach turned.

Wendy eased down onto her bed. "No. Why?"

"How about you?"

Wendy shook her head. "Just tinted gloss, maybe, if I'm going somewhere nice."

Foster lifted a sweatshirt off Peggy's bed, folded it, and laid it on the side of her messy desk. She straightened the textbooks sitting there, noting the yellow pencil tucked between the pages of the abnormal psychology textbook on top. Peggy would never come back to her stopping point. Wendy's desk was neater, her laptop sitting in the center. There was no laptop on Peggy's desk. There hadn't been one found in her backpack either. "Where's Peggy's laptop?" Foster asked.

"She took it with her. She was going to work on her paper on the bus. It's due . . ." Wendy stopped, stricken anew. "I guess it doesn't matter now."

So in addition to her missing phone, there was a missing laptop. Were they looking at a robbery gone bad? Foster peeked out the window, but there wasn't much to see beyond a small courtyard with stone benches. She turned back to Wendy. "Okay. Tell me about Peggy and Stella."

Wendy's eyes widened, and her guard went up. "What do you mean?"

There was a tennis ball on Peggy's desk. Foster picked it up, squeezed it, and rolled it around in her hands, giving the young woman a moment. After a time, Wendy's head fell to her chest, and she began rubbing her hands against her thighs. Nerves. Foster put the ball back where she'd gotten it.

"You asked if Peg had any trouble with anybody. Well, yesterday, she and Stella argued over the phone. It was nothing new. They were always fighting about something. I mean *always*. Stella feeds off drama."

"You know what they argued about?"

"Stella was mad Peg was going to the march without her. She thought because *she* couldn't go, Peg shouldn't. But if it hadn't been the march, it would have been something else. Honestly, Stella's a . . ."

"Bully," Foster offered when Wendy couldn't come up with the right word.

Wendy looked up, giving her a slight smile. "And clingy, possessive . . . and so intense. You saw her. She has to be the center of attention. When we heard about Peg . . . right away she started in, like it only affected her." She looked up and found Foster's eyes. "I think Stella's feeling guilty about something."

"Like?"

Wendy shrugged. "Don't know, but Stella lies. I don't think she can help herself. Peg was just realizing that about her."

"So you don't believe she was studying Sunday afternoon and eating pizza alone."

Wendy bit her lower lip and went back to picking at her cuticles, which were red and on the verge of bleeding. "Like I said, Stella lies."

"Did Peggy tell Rimmer she was dumping him for Stella?"

Wendy shook her head. "She just stopped being there for him. When he finally noticed, she made it official." Wendy reached over and grabbed a bedraggled bear off her pillow and held it tight. "This is what I know. Peg was a good person. She got along with everybody. She was excited about the march. She believed in what it was about. I don't know who those guys in the photos are, but I've never seen any of them around here." She nuzzled the bear. "She was my best friend. And the only problem she had, as far as I know, was Stella."

———

Back downstairs, Lonergan looked desperate enough to leap into Foster's arms when she walked back into the room alone. Stella's tears were gone. Foster saw something else in her eyes this time—defiance, cunning.

Foster walked over to the table, tore a blank page from her notebook, and handed it to Stella along with her pen. "Write down the names of the people you spent time with yesterday, please. Full names. Phone numbers, email, dorm addresses. Whatever you have."

Stella took the pad and pen. "Why? I told you I—"

"Just being thorough," Foster said. "Thank you for your cooperation." Foster watched as Stella jotted down the information she requested, then handed the paper back, looking far less confident as she did it. "Did you speak at all with Peggy yesterday afternoon?"

"No, like I said . . ."

"Did you try calling or texting her later in the evening?" Foster asked.

Stella shifted in her seat. "Maybe once or twice."

Foster held her hand out. "Show me?"

Stella's eyes widened. "You mean my phone?" It was as if Foster had asked for one of Stella's kidneys. A kid and their phone weren't easily parted.

"I'm not going anywhere with it," Foster assured her. "You'll get it right back. Unless you're refusing to show me?"

Stella hesitated before lifting her phone out of her pocket. She held on to it for a moment, clutching the device in her hands. "Don't you need a warrant or something?"

"Not if you voluntarily comply with my *polite* request," Foster answered.

Stella handed the phone to Foster, who quickly thumbed through her outgoing-call logs and text messages. She looked up at Stella when she was done and handed the phone back, as she'd promised. "Four calls. Twelve text messages. The last one at four this morning. A little more than once or twice."

"I wanted to make sure she was safe," Stella replied. "You know how dangerous this city is."

"What'd you think when you got no response?"

Stella dropped her head to her chest. "That she was avoiding me."

"So you got worried," Foster said. "Did you come down to her room to check to see if she made it back?"

"No."

"Why not?"

"Because I didn't, okay?"

Foster let things sit. "That's it for now. We'll be in touch."

She and Lonergan watched as Stella got up and rushed out of the room. Foster closed her file, the paper with the names on it tucked inside, then turned to Lonergan. "Did you get anything else from her?"

"We spent most of the time in a stare-off. She's one tough cookie, that one. What's with the stalker texts? What'd you get out of the other one?"

"That Peggy and Stella didn't exactly have an easy relationship. Stella's controlling and has a temper. Also, according to Wendy, Peggy never told Rimmer she was dumping him for Stella. She just stopped answering his calls."

"So how'd he know?" Lonergan asked.

"Good question."

They walked out of the room and back to the car. "Four a.m.," Lonergan said, jangling the car keys in his pocket. "Birch was dead by then. Stella didn't know it. She was just bein' a pain in the ass."

"Or she did know, and that's why she sent it."

"You distrust everybody, Foster?"

She thought about the question as she walked. She'd heard so many outright lies and shaded half-truths in her career. Everybody lied about something, even to themselves. Add murder to that, and the lies multiplied because now self-preservation was in play. Would a person lie to save themselves from a life behind bars? You bet they would, so Foster had long ago adopted the old standard of *trust but verify*. It worked for her on the job, and it worked for her when she laid the badge down at night. *Trust but verify* was somehow safer, cleaner. It protected the soul and the heart.

Foster put more distance between them, needing some space, suddenly in a gloomy frame of mind. "Yeah," she finally said.

CHAPTER 14

Bodie looked around, taking in the lakefront park and the marina beyond. If he turned south, he could see the iconic Chicago skyline glistening in the late-afternoon sun. It'd be dark soon, and then a million lights would twinkle like fairy lights in each of the tiny skyscraper windows. He often wondered what went on behind all those windows. Who lived or worked inside? Were they happy? Did they have fantastic careers and kids and dreams? Were they sick and twisted with friendly smiles? He liked to imagine they were happy, normal, and that he might fit in their world if only he didn't know what he knew—that where there was light there was also darkness.

He kicked up dried leaves as he walked along the pedestrian path, his hands in his pockets, breathing. No Dr. Silva. Not even Am, who pitied him for his weakness. Am didn't have to say the words. Bodie could feel it, see it in the way she looked at him, as though he were some poor unfortunate clod she had to steer this way or that. *Hide the scissors—here comes Bodie*, he often imagined her saying. But he knew exactly what he was doing and why. All he needed was a moment to get his thoughts together, to make a life plan. It wasn't his fault things kept getting in the way. He was strong, capable. He would prove that he was just as smart, just as talented, as Am . . . at something.

A yappy little terrier bolted out of the doggy park and ran for Bodie, trailing a glittery leash behind it. He froze as the dog raced around him, tangling the leash around his legs. His first impulse was to punt the little rat, but just a half second before he did so, a woman's voice called out.

"Gus! Oh my God." She ran over and reached for the dog, unwinding the leash from around Bodie's legs. "I'm so sorry. He just took off."

Bodie, a moment ago angry enough to strike, stood down, even managing a polite smile. She was pretty. Young. Nice smile. How long had it been since a woman so young and pretty had stood this close to him? She grabbed the rat and the leash, pushing her dark hair back from her face.

"He doesn't usually do that. I'm so sorry. Did he get you dirty?"

"No problem. Gus, is it?"

She chuckled, her brown eyes dancing. "Short for Augustus. Seriously, he didn't scratch you or anything?"

Bodie held his arms out, turned around in a circle playfully. "No damage."

"Good." She put the dog down and turned to go. "Well, have a good one."

Bodie watched her stroll up the path to whatever wonderful world awaited her. There would be friends there, he knew, maybe a boyfriend. A full life that included Gus, short for Augustus. She'd been nice, he thought. As the dog trotted along at her side, she talked on her cell phone. She was likely making plans for the night, Bodie thought. Dinner out, maybe, or a meetup at a favorite bar. That was what life was like for people not raised on evil secrets.

Should he have asked her out? Their chance meeting could have been one of those meet-cute encounters normal people always talked about. No ring on her finger; Bodie had slipped a look. He turned and walked away. He might have, he thought, if only her eyes had been blue.

CHAPTER 15

Teddy's Bar was outfitted in dark wood and brass fittings, swinging for upscale, trying really hard to look like an old English pub, only it felt a little too forced and fake, too stiff. It was just after four when Foster and Lonergan walked in to find the place all but empty. The nine-to-fivers had yet to clock out and wander over from the office buildings off Michigan. Just a few of the tables were occupied by early birds having a quick meal. The big-screen sets mounted to the wall were tuned to an English rugby match, and the sound was muted, but no one seemed to be paying any attention to the game. Foster clocked the slightly built white man behind the bar as he dried glasses with a towel—gearing up, apparently, for the happy hour rush to come.

When the bartender looked up to see them, his face devolved into a contemptuous scowl, and he rolled his ferret-like eyes. "Cops. Great."

It had been a long day made longer by her push and pull with Detective Jim Lonergan. The eye roll and contempt from the bartender right out of the gate were like the poisoned cherry on top of a burnt cake. Foster approached the bar, dutifully presenting her badge. Lonergan, she noticed, kept his clipped to his belt.

"Detective Foster," she announced. She waited for Lonergan to introduce himself, but he didn't. He just stood there being big, so she finally jabbed a thumb in his direction. "And this is Detective Lonergan. Mind if we ask you a few questions?"

The sullen look on the man's face broadcast that he very much did mind. He leaned his elbows on the shiny bar top. "About?"

Lonergan flicked a look at the Riverwalk outside the front window. "Three guesses." He looked down at the plastic nameplate on the man's black button-down shirt. "Giles. Giles what?"

The two stared at each other for a time, Giles trying it on, finding he didn't have half the starch in his spine he would need to stand his ground with the big burly cop with the mean look and lousy disposition.

"Valentine."

Confident he'd won the face-off, Lonergan smiled. "*Mr. Valentine*, we're investigating the death of a young woman found across the river there." Foster held up Peggy's photo. Lonergan pointed to it. "You ever see her in here?"

Foster was aware that they'd caught the attention of the diners. You couldn't miss two cops walking into a bar. Through the south-facing windows, she found she had a clear view of the river and the spot where Birch had been found on the other side. She could just make out the small tree where the crime scene tape had been strung.

She turned her attention back to the prickly, trying-too-hard barkeep in his black shirt and red bow tie. He sported a well-groomed soul patch and a tilted fedora on his head, which made him look like a reject from a seventies Bob Fosse revue. And he smelled of cigarettes and peppermint, a combination she would think would be unappealing in such a high-contact job.

Valentine gave the photo only a passing glance; in fact, he actively avoided looking at it. "You're kidding, right? You know how many people we get in here a night?"

"A Sunday night? Here?" Lonergan glanced at the chalkboard behind Valentine's head that listed the drink prices. "With a Guinness going for eight dollars a pint?"

"What? People don't go out Sunday nights unless it's to church?" He grinned at Lonergan. "And, FYI, I don't price the stuff, I just pour it."

Foster kept the photo up, unconcerned with the price of the Guinness. "We get it. No one's ever glad to see us."

Valentine snorted. "Especially these days, am I right? You got some bad apples batting for your side, that's for sure." He glanced over at Lonergan and scowled. "And it only takes one."

Lonergan looked Valentine up and down slowly, like he wasn't at all impressed with what he saw either. "Nice bowtie, slick."

Foster held Peggy's photo up higher, no patience for the pissing match. "Mind looking again, a little closer, please? We could use your help."

Valentine pulled his eyes away from Lonergan's to face her. "This is a lot of heat for a mugging gone bad. All I'm saying."

"Who told you it was a muggin'?" Lonergan said.

"It was on the news. Possible mugging, they said. You people need to keep up. That's part of your problem, you ask me. You guys are Edsels in a Tesla world. Dinosaurs in a—"

"So you *don't* remember seeing her in here?" Lonergan said.

Valentine sighed, then snapped his fingers and wiggled them, beckoning for the photo to be handed over to him. "Lemme see it." He cocked his head toward Foster. "For her, not you. *She* said please."

Lonergan fumed at the snapping fingers. The gesture rankled Foster a bit, too, but she was the one in need of cooperation. "A *good* look this time, huh?" she said.

Foster set the photo on the bar. Valentine reached into his pocket and pulled out a pair of readers and slid them on. He peered at the photo for several moments, Foster watching closely as recognition dawned.

"You did see her," she said.

"How could you forget that hair? Aww, it was her you found over there? That's terrible. You know, this city really is going to the dogs. Maybe we'd get a little more police presence down here if we opened a couple of doughnut shops. What do you think?" He slid a look at Foster. "That was for him, not you."

"Tell us about the woman," Lonergan said through clenched teeth.

"She seemed like a good kid. She was really on last night too. The life of the party. Up. Laughing, center of attention. A good crowd came in after the march. She was one of them. Real popular with the boys."

"Any particular boy?"

"Nope. Equal-opportunity firebrand."

"You're sure?" Lonergan asked. "You can't see everybody who comes in here. Somebody coulda slipped past you, flown under the radar."

"They didn't."

"And you were on this bar all night yesterday?" Lonergan asked.

Valentine grinned. "Till the last light flicked off."

"Do you know what time she came in? How long she stayed?" Foster asked.

"It starts picking up in here about five. She came in maybe an hour later. She left just before eight. A bunch left around then, which gave me some breathing room, and I didn't see her after that. The place was hopping."

"What'd you serve her?" Lonergan asked. "Seeing as she was underage."

"Diet Coke. Two. Out of a bottle, not a glass. You know, you got no shot at winning Mr. Congeniality anywhere. Just saying."

Foster glanced around the bar, noting the security cameras. "We'd like to take a look at your cameras. That going to be a problem?"

Valentine's eyes stayed on Lonergan's. "You'll have to talk to the manager. Like I said, I just pour. Cameras aren't my deal."

"He here?" Lonergan asked.

"*She's* in her office."

The three stood quietly for a half moment.

"Want me to call her?" Valentine asked.

Foster offered a patient smile. "Please."

———

The manager was Maureen Pike, or Mo, as Valentine called her. Foster pegged her to be in her mid- to late sixties. Her auburn hair, dyed to an unnatural tone, was scooped up into a top bun, and cat-eye glasses hung from a chain around her neck, hitting her ample bosom dead center. The back room looked like it served as office, locker room, and break room, smelling of old coats, boiled soup, and long-ago-eaten ham sandwiches. Pike, like Valentine, didn't look happy to see them.

"We didn't serve her," Pike said right out of the gate. "Giles knows to check ID. And we're not just a bar, right? We're a bar *and* restaurant. We serve burgers and fries, fish and chips. We have a full menu. So if you're thinking she left out of here half in the bag, you'd be wrong."

"Sounds like you remember her too," Lonergan said.

"I saw her."

"At the bar," Lonergan said. "Her being nineteen."

"No law against pouring the kid a pop. Look, I get it. I've got grandkids. I can guarantee you she didn't get served here. I'd stake my life on it."

"Right," Lonergan said. "You got footage of last night or not?"

Pike keyed up the playback on the security footage and then slid her chair back for the cops to gather in to get a better look.

Hoping not to see Keith Ainsley anywhere, Foster watched the screen as smoky images of the front of the house ran past, starting at around four the previous day. The camera faced the door, focusing on the south side of the bar and a few tables, mostly those closer to the window. There was Valentine working the bar, paying particular attention to the female clientele. The bar was crowded, everyone appearing to be in a good mood.

"Busy for a Sunday," Pike offered, "thanks to the march. That meant dollars for us and every other place around here. Poor kid. How was she killed?"

Foster shook her head. "Sorry. Can't discuss that."

"The news said mugging," Pike said. "We get a lot of that down here. Tourists mostly. They forget where they are and put their guards down. They call the police, of course, but it's not like you people bust a sweat looking for anybody. But every incident impacts us, you know? People don't feel safe, they don't come out. They don't come out, we don't make money. We don't make money, I end up living in a box under a bridge, and I don't get to help my grandkids get to college. See how it goes? Last year, some idiot tossed a brick through my car window. Cops wouldn't even come out to take the report."

Lonergan turned from the screen to stare at Pike. "You file a complaint?"

"Get real. We both know what happens with complaints. The old File Thirteen, am I right? I feel sick about the kid, though. She was all smiles yesterday; now she's dead. Sucks. This area gets its fair share of drunken idiots who end up floating face down in the river. Not from here, though. I got no problem cutting people off. But like I said, she never got served an ounce in here."

Lonergan's eyes narrowed. "File Thirteen. You ex-military?"

Pike nodded, then gave him a sly grin. "You see me, I see you. Jarhead, right? Most humorless bunch of jokers I ever met. Me? Army. Fifteen years. So when I say I run a tight team, I run a tight fucking team."

Lonergan looked at Pike as though she'd passed a test, then turned back to the screen, his eyes focused on the footage as Pike forwarded the playback up to 6:00 p.m., when Valentine had put her in the bar.

Foster pointed at the screen. "There's Birch. At the bar. Pink backpack."

The young woman was alive, laughing, talking, a bottle of Diet Coke in her hand, a gang of revelers crowded around her. She had no idea that her life would soon be cut short. "There's Valentine. Busy, like he said." He was wearing the fedora, tilted, and appeared to be in the swing of things, pouring drinks, engaging with patrons, leaning across the bar to flirt with a middle-aged woman in a tight black dress.

"Valentine always flirt while he's working?" Foster asked.

"He fancies himself a Casanova type," Pike said. "He's a popular guy with a certain kind of gal."

Lonergan grumbled, "The kind being married but pretendin' they aren't?"

Pike chuckled. "You got it. The ones looking for a one-off. But he'll take the young and stupid ones, too, if he can move fast enough to catch one of them."

"And you let him get away with that?" Lonergan asked.

Pike shrugged. "Flirting's not a crime, and what he, or whoever, does once he clocks out is their business, not mine."

Foster watched Valentine work his magic, first with Black Dress, but then he moved down the bar and chatted with Peggy Birch. He slid her the bottle of pop, then leaned on the bar, smiling, flirting, fiddling with his tie. "He said he was here until closing; is that right?"

"He was. We had to shoo a couple out the door at cutoff time. Then he cashed out. Why?"

"He take any long breaks?" Lonergan asked, following Foster's lead.

Pike harrumphed. "And miss one single hottie? No way. Maybe to take a quick leak or something, but that bar is his seat of power. He leaves it for nothing. I hope you're not thinking Giles had something to do with this." She leaned forward in her chair, her eyes wide. "Because I'm telling you, he's not your guy. He's hot air. He's cotton candy. I'm not saying he couldn't kill anybody—anybody could—but I'm telling you he's not the kind of guy who could pull it off. He'd melt like an ice cube in the sun. He sure as hell wouldn't be out there now minding that bar cool as anything."

The footage advanced to the moment Birch walked out of the door behind a handful of others. Through the windows, it was clear that the group went left while Birch went right toward the stairs leading up to Michigan Avenue. Not together. So where had Peggy gone after that?

"Is this the only angle your cameras capture?" Foster asked. "What about the back of the restaurant or the tables outside of this tight arc? The ones against the east wall."

"We got that, too, but you asked for the bar."

Foster turned to face her. "I'd like everything. Would you mind making a copy? We'll take it all with us."

Pike rolled her chair forward. "You got it. Give me a couple minutes." Foster and Lonergan stepped back to let her work. After a time, the woman stood and handed Foster a copy of the footage on a thumb drive. "Here it is."

Foster took the drive, slipped it into her bag. "Thanks."

She and Lonergan wove back through the restaurant, past the bar, and out the front door. Foster stood there for a moment as Lonergan said something she didn't tune in to, watching the city do what it did: breathe, move, live. People rushed by. Sirens blared. Cars honked, and the brakes squeaked and hissed on the buses. She glanced across the river at "the spot." The skyscrapers didn't care, and neither did the river, but she did. She needed to know why, who. Had Peggy Birch's fate been sealed here at Teddy's? Foster glanced back and spied through the window the wolfish Valentine standing at the bar watching them. He'd noticed Birch enough to say when she'd walked into the bar and when she'd left. What else did he know?

CHAPTER 16

It was nearly 7:00 p.m. when Foster walked into her house, put her bag down, unclipped her holster from her belt, and plunked it on a side table. She'd made it through her first day back, and she'd done okay, sort of. Muscle memory, wasn't it? Like riding a bike or falling off a log. And after a long, frustrating day, it felt now like she'd never been away for even a second.

Back at the office, she and Lonergan had rerun the footage from Teddy's frame by frame for two hours, watching again as Peggy came in and commanded attention at the bar, watching as Valentine served her a Coke and hovered more than he should have. She'd paid special attention also to Teddy's front window to see if anyone stood outside looking in at Peggy, but there was no one. They hadn't yet started on the alternate angles, but they were both beat—her eyes were gritty from the strain of squinting at tiny images on a tiny screen. There was nothing else they could do tonight. Tomorrow, after the autopsy, they'd try again.

Foster peeled off her blazer, unbuttoned her blouse at the neck, and padded over to the bowl of colorful marbles on her dining room table. She plucked out a blue-green one and dropped it into a tall ceramic vase about the height of an average four-year-old. It was halfway full. Only then did she exhale; only then did she allow herself to stand down. Padding into the kitchen, she grabbed a cold bottle of water from the fridge. The dog barking outside she knew would go on for at least a few more hours before her neighbor next door finally let him in for the night. No concern for the neighbors, of course, who had to endure the incessant yips and barks and growls until then. Add to that the banger cars that roared up and down the block at all hours, their noisy engines revving and rap music thumping out of huge speakers at earsplitting decibels. There was no such thing as a quiet night in this neighborhood, but this was where she had to be. Besides, what would she do with a quiet night except fight against it? Foster's mind worked overtime when the world was too quiet and still. Ghosts visited in the night when time refused to budge, the hands on the clock unwilling to bring the relief of a welcome sunrise.

There wasn't much to the place. It was a two-bedroom house purchased after the divorce, after there was nothing left but her. The place wasn't anything, really, except for a roof and four walls and things she didn't care about or even half notice. Shelter. Bare necessity. A house, not a home. But it was here, and from her living room window, it had a view of the maple tree out front.

She took her bottle of water to the living room and sat in the easy chair facing the window, the lights out, waiting for the revving engines, listening to the dog bark. There would be the sound of gunshots later, random, followed close behind by the sound of police sirens and ambulances. She'd had the other things: home, peace. At one time, she'd thought she would always have them, but then there had been a thief and a gun, then a funeral and a parting, and now this.

She had work, which kept her from . . . what? It was funny, she thought, how the mind worked or wouldn't. Interesting what it held fast to and what it chose to let go. She could almost forget how low she'd gotten, how little she'd cared if the sun rose or set, if she breathed or stopped breathing. Why should she breathe when Reggie couldn't? How did she get to wake up and walk and eat and be when her son, her baby, was buried six feet under earth in a box, in his Easter suit, with his autographed ball of the '68 Cubs and his favorite Bulls jersey lying next to him? Number 23. It was a cosmic joke, a curse, a nightmare. A mother wasn't meant to survive her children. But she had work, and she'd rediscovered a pocket of resilience. And then it rained one morning eight weeks ago, and her partner, her friend, was gone.

Sometimes life had no mercy.

The tree outside was almost bare now, a carpet of autumn leaves at its feet. Foster watched as a slight breeze blew more and more of them away from the branches to land on the ground in all their crimson, golden glory. Why would the killer bury Peggy Birch under leaves? Did it mean something, or was it simply a quick way to try to conceal her? If so, he hadn't done such a good job of it. Her foot was visible, and he'd left her close to the pedestrian path. Was it significant that Birch was hidden, yet not hidden well? And now that Foster had a quiet moment to think about it, where *had* all the leaves come from?

She got up and walked into the kitchen to pop a frozen dinner into the microwave and await the dings. When she heard the familiar mewling at her back door, she poured a bowl of milk and walked it back as she'd done countless times. She knew she would find the raggedy tabby there when she opened the door. He'd latched on to her the first day she'd moved in four years ago. There were no tags around his neck, no collar. Just a stray, feral, unattached to anyone, like herself. She'd named him Lost, and it seemed to fit.

"You never miss dinnertime, do you?" she said, squatting down to place the bowl on the porch.

Lost didn't stop for conversation—never did; that wasn't what he came for. She watched as he lapped up the milk, ignoring her. This wasn't a love match. Their relationship, such as it was, was based purely on mutual need. Lost needed food to stay alive and knew it could be found at her door. She needed someone to care for, even if it only took the form of a bowl of milk and scraps given to a cat that came and went as he saw fit.

"Lost," Foster muttered, watching the cat lap away. "I don't think you are, though, are you? You know exactly where you are." The microwave dinged. Foster stood watching the cat finish. When he did, she leaned down and picked up the bowl and watched as he trotted away. "Bye, then," she said.

She ate her dinner at the small kitchen table with her notes and a few photos she'd taken on her phone of the Birch crime scene. Once they'd found her backpack floating in the river, the divers from the marine unit had been called out, but they hadn't found her phone or anything that might have been her clothing. Peggy's roommate said that she never went anywhere without her laptop, but divers hadn't found one of those in the river either. Not a robbery. Her wallet had been in the bag with money in it—not much, but a thief would steal a nickel if given the chance. Rape? The autopsy would tell. She wondered how the Birches were doing, especially Peggy's mother. She thought about the Ainsleys too. The Birches had lost everything. The Ainsleys had everything to lose.

Foster startled at the sound of her doorbell. She didn't know her neighbors and didn't often get visitors, especially not after the sun went down. It was almost seven thirty. This wasn't a neighborhood where people took evening strolls or where you freely opened your door at night. For a moment she didn't move, hoping whoever it was would go away, but then the bell rang a second time. She slid her gun out of her holster, tucked it into the back of her waistband, and went to the door. She was relieved when she squinted through the peephole to find her brother, Felix, standing there. But relief quickly turned to suspicion, and her guard went up, knowing his presence meant she'd have to be normal. It was a thing to know you were a worry to those who cared about you. There was guilt attached to it. Yet no amount of assurance that she could give seemed to satisfy Felix or her mother that she was okay, that she was fine.

She opened the door and smiled brightly. "You're out late." He followed her into the kitchen, where her plastic meal had gone cold in its microwavable tray. She slipped her gun back into its holster, then slid the weapon down the table away from Felix, who she knew didn't like guns. "You usually call first. Hungry?"

Felix hadn't missed the slip or the slide but let both go without comment. Instead, he shook his head, eyed her poor excuse for dinner, and made a face. "You seriously have to start eating better."

"Want something to drink, then?" She glanced down at the car keys in his hand. "Water?"

He walked over to the fridge and grabbed a bottled water, then turned to study the plastic tray her pathetic dinner was in, then her. He was graying rapidly, Foster noticed, like their father had. Felix looked a lot like him now: warm dark skin, thin nose, full lips, middle age settling in. She saw him take a quick scan of the house and knew it saddened him. There was very little furniture—a small sofa, a chair, a coffee table, a lamp. Not a single thing hung on the walls. He'd said it before countless times, that the place felt cold, lifeless, a stopgap, as though she didn't intend to stay long, as if she deliberately kept her home this way so that it would take her less than a minute to break everything down and go. "How you doing?"

It was time for the smile again. "Fine. You? How're the kids? Tamara?"

"All good. Everybody misses you. It's been a minute."

"Sorry. Tell them I'll stop by soon."

His eyes held. They'd danced this dance many times over the past five years. He always asked how she was doing, and she always answered the same way. He'd learned not to push it, usually.

"First day back. How was it? Don't say fine." The last bit came out in a rush before she had a chance to give her standard answer.

She picked at her dinner. "It was long. My new partner is . . . well, he's a lot. It felt like the first day of school, only I had a little more to worry about than finding my locker."

Felix finished his bottle, then tossed it into the trash can beside him. "Like?"

"Today, I had to tell parents their daughter was dead," she said. "I've had to do it before, of course . . . but it was different this time. It's me that's different, I guess." She could tell he was listening. She knew that he'd heard every word she said but had also picked up on the things she hadn't. "And since you're *a* psychologist but not *my* psychologist, *and* you're my big brother, that's all I'm going to say." She forked a morsel of microwaved chicken something into her mouth and even managed a playful grin. "So we good?"

Foster knew he wasn't going to let it go that easily. "Your partner," he said, the words slow and easy. "What's his story?"

She put the fork down, pushed the tray away. "He's an old-school cop. His words, not mine. He's a rock to paper. Like in the kids' game? He's . . ."

"Not G," he finished for her.

"I'm not an idiot, Fee. I knew I'd have to work with someone else. Adjust." She looked up, watching him peer at her through their father's brown eyes. "I can do hard."

Felix glanced over at the vase, the bowl of marbles on the table. "Who knows that better than me?"

He looked worried, though, as she watched him look around her place again. Was he remembering how things used to be when she'd had more, when she'd been happy and a different person? The big glass vase was a calendar of sorts. She'd dropped the first marble in the day Reggie was killed—absently, not really thinking about it—but then she'd dropped a marble in every day since. She also marked the days with coins and buttons and little found things slipped into a pocket. Every marble, every pin, was another day, another hour, forward.

Felix leaned over and pushed her dinner back toward her. "Eat that. It's crap, but it's better than nothing."

She flicked him a look. "You're not the boss of me."

"Am too." They smiled at the brief reversion to childish ways; then he got serious. "Really. Harriet." Their eyes locked. He really looked, and she let him. "Okay. I believe you," he said. He fished his keys out of his pocket and opened the door, pausing halfway out to take another look over her shoulder at the vase of marbles.

"How many now?"

"Eighteen hundred and twenty-five." The finality in her voice signaled there would be no discussion about it.

"The day's coming up. We're all going to the cemetery, release some balloons. I realize the ritual helps some people but not everybody." He stared at her. "I promised Ma I'd let you know anyway. No pressure."

Balloons? Even the thought made her anxious, angry. What was there to celebrate? Her kid was lying dead in a hole. "Don't look for me."

He leaned down and gave her a peck on the cheek. "I won't. But you know when I'll know you're *really* fine? When that vase goes and you move out of this house. You have people, Harriet. You know that, right?"

She straightened, pulled herself in. She strengthened the face, put fake sunshine in the practiced smile. "I know. You don't have to worry, Felix."

He let a moment pass, then nodded. "I'll always worry." He gave her a wink. "Call me. Come by and see the kids."

She watched him trot down the steps and away, then shut the door and double locked it. She eased down again in the chair facing the front window. It was just a maple tree. The police report, which she'd memorized, said that Reggie had been accosted on the street, this street. A seventeen-year-old thug pointed a gun at him and demanded his new bike.

A witness saw Reggie hand the bike over and raise his arms in surrender, right before he heard the gunshot and saw him fall to the ground. Her son, her baby, somehow managed to crawl to the tree, bleeding, dying. Foster had been there when her son took his first breath. It haunted her that she hadn't been there to protect him or cradle him when he'd taken his last. Here. Outside her front window. On the block where the neighbor's dog howled and she fed a feral cat. Eighteen hundred and twenty-five days ago.

CHAPTER 17

Bodie walked around Amelia's loft, just not getting it. How could Am live like this, surrounded by pieces of art that were supposed to serve as furniture? To him, furniture was functional, useful, something you needed but didn't give too much thought to. A couch was a couch, a chair a chair. The TV remote went on the coffee table. A lamp or two somewhere else. But Amelia's place was like an Andy Warhol painting somebody had vomited up. He eyed the yellow canvas spread over thin wires that was supposed to be a chair and the tall coatrack-like thing in the corner with bulbs all over it that was supposed to take the place of a good old-fashioned lamp. Amelia didn't even have drapes for the high, wide windows overlooking the condo building across the street, the illuminated Chicago skyline twinkling behind it.

Looking around at all the avant-garde pretentiousness—the exposed brick, the fancy furniture, the arty accent pieces—he was afraid to sit or touch anything for fear of breaking something that cost more than he did. Curtains, of course, would be too pedestrian, too normal. Amelia had dimmable glass, manipulated from light to dark by the touch of a button. He shook his head and smiled.

"Bodie, sit," Am called from behind him. "Dinner's ready."

He joined her at the table she'd set, or at least he thought it was a table. He'd never been able to pin it down. Was it a custom-made slab table or a polished plank from an old pirate ship? Were the chairs meant to be chairs? They looked to him like wine barrels someone had refashioned and plopped cushions on.

He laughed. "I've been here loads of times, but I still can't get over all this weird stuff. How can you kick back in a place like this? It feels like an art museum. There should be velvet ropes along the walls."

Amelia set the bowl of salad on the table, grinned, then looked around the space to see what he saw. "Color, lines, form . . ." She pointed at him, a playful scolding. "Life is art. Food is art. Art is everywhere. It's all in the presentation. Now sit down. I'm starving."

"What kind of art are we eating?" Bodie said, taking a seat on the wine-barrel-chair.

Amelia chuckled. "Lamb chops." She went back to the kitchen for the bread, veggies, and quinoa. "You know, I could help you spruce up your place, if you want? Take some of the first-apartment decor out of there, make it look nice."

Bodie reached over and snagged a leaf of lettuce from the bowl. "No thanks. I like being able to identify my furniture."

"Your loss," she said, placing everything on the table and sitting across from him. "Dig in."

They caught up while they ate, Bodie with Westhaven still souring on his tongue and Am with her studio and her ideas for new art pieces. Am lit up and came alive when she talked about her work.

"Late dinner," Bodie said, spreading his napkin across his lap. "I feel so cosmopolitan. At Westhaven, dinner was served promptly at six. Thought I'd try something new."

Amelia stopped to stare at him. "Was it really horrible?"

Bodie picked up his fork, eyed the lamb chop. "Horrible's relative, isn't it?" He drew his finger to his lips to shush her. "But we're Morgans, Am, and Morgans don't talk about . . . you-know-what."

"Why do you torture yourself?" Amelia asked.

Bodie cut through his meat, took the first bite. "Million-dollar question. How was the shopping?"

Amelia took a sip of wine. "What?"

"Shopping," he said. "Remember? You called me while you were shopping."

"I didn't find anything. I spent the afternoon in the studio instead. So what have you got planned for work?"

Bodie took another bite of lamb chop. "Still considering my options. I could go back to limo driving. The suit still fits."

"The craft beer thing I thought was interesting. Morgan's Amber Ale?"

He shrugged. "Good idea. Crowded market. I'll come up with something else. Don't worry. You won't have to spot me forever."

"I'm not worried, Bodie. I know you will."

"Meanwhile, I've just been walking around, taking everything in," he said. "I could walk around the grounds at you-know-where, but it's not the same as being able to go wherever you want." He saw her face, the concern on it. "Relax."

"Bod . . ."

He interrupted her, a lightness in his voice he put there to ward off the pity. "I walked all the time before I went in. At night. It's quiet, not too many people out. I walk to clear my head. For miles without even realizing it. The sky's so clear then. I'm telling you, night is where it's at. You'd probably think up a dozen painting ideas if you walked at night."

Amelia's silence made him angry. It meant his walking at night worried her, and she was trying to figure out a way to say so. He could see in her eyes that she was thinking about those women and how he'd climbed to the roof of his apartment building and stood with his toes over the edge. And though they'd decided not to talk about past things, he at least couldn't help but pay heed to the ripples they made in his life, the remnants of shock that reverberated and echoed now, like the rings a skipped rock made on a still lake.

"I'm solid, Am," he said, his eyes meeting hers. There it was. The doubt. He hated it, didn't need it. "There's nothing wrong with walking."

"Where do you go?"

"Everywhere. Nowhere in particular. I walk. I think. Then I go home. You have your painting, your weird furniture. I have that. All the same, isn't it?"

Amelia leaned back in her chair and for a moment just stared at him. "Meet anyone along the way?"

His fork and knife clattered to the plate. "I said alone. What would be the point of meeting someone along the way? And who? Anyone in particular you think I'd meet? I don't need mothering, Am."

"Just trying to help. Why're you so defensive?"

He hated how she could stay so calm when he was so upset. Look at her, Bodie thought, staring at him, judging him, her eyes as still as glass. He ran his hands through his hair, then stood. "Yeah, I'm gonna go. Thanks for dinner. I'll talk to you soon, okay?"

Amelia stood. "C'mon, Bod, don't leave like this. We don't have to talk if you don't want to."

He grabbed his jacket slung over the yellow thing. He cut his eyes her way. "You're just like Silva and those other doctors. Handling me like I'm crazy or something, like . . . like . . ." He glared at her. "I'm him."

"You're not him, Bod," Amelia said. "You never could be."

He softened, then reached over and kissed her on the top of her head, giving her a smile. "Thanks. I'm okay. We're good. I'll call you, huh?"

"Bodie . . ."

He turned and gave her one last look, seeing his own face reflected back. They were a pair. Twins. Two halves of a messed-up whole. God, what humans could endure . . . and what they couldn't. "Next time, my place. I'll order in."

CHAPTER 18

She cleared the plates, loaded the dishwasher, then stood at her window watching the night watch her back. It was an impulsive decision, partly, but she grabbed her jacket and keys and went out. She also walked for miles, like Bodie did, though she had never told him that it was yet another thing they shared. How strange was it that they both favored the same stress reliever, wanting to experience the city at the same time at night when the streets were practically theirs alone?

Not every thought of hers was of Bodie. Amelia had other things to think about, many things, and most of them pinballed around in her head without order or priority. It was why she could never sit still in school or concentrate on one task at a time, unless, of course, she was painting, creating. Her father had called them her sparks of genius.

She walked, her hands plunged deep in her pockets, her collar up, protection against the night. She liked the autumn, the bite in the air, the colors, the rustle of leaves, the smell of wood smoke from chimneys. The changing seasons were one of the great things about living in the Midwest, and Amelia loved them all, but particularly this one, a time of stark transition from the fullness of summer to a kind of sleep—a time of stasis—until life returned in the spring.

She eventually found herself standing at the corner of Rush Street at midnight, staring down the block at the trendy bars. She wasn't choosing, not really. It didn't matter to her which one. It wasn't as though she found herself here by coincidence, either; her route, her walk, had been purposeful. She needed a drink and she needed company and she needed not to have to think about her brother. There was no sin in wanting company, human contact, and it was ladies' choice. She picked the Rusty Anvil—a dark, brooding little place she'd been to before—and slipped inside to see what the night had to offer. Hopefully, she'd find someone she wanted. Barring that, she hoped to find someone who would do.

CHAPTER 19

Peggy Birch's murder was all over the news as Foster and Lonergan pulled into the medical examiner's lot on West Harrison Tuesday morning. The squat, sand-colored building took up almost the entire block, and if one didn't know its purpose, they could easily peg it for an art museum or a modernist courthouse. But she knew better. This was the place where they closed the file on lives that had been cut down by bullet or knife, rope or fist, or simply fate. Foster focused on her phone as the news of Peggy Birch's killing played out for morning commuters. The local reporter stood on the bridge, cameras rolling, as she detailed the violent death of a young woman, now identified as Margaret Ann Birch. There was a shot of the Riverwalk, the spot where crime scene tape had been strung and Birch found. The killing was one of six that had taken place over the weekend in a city where violence appeared to have no remedy. "No suspects are in custody connected to this latest incident," the reporter said before tossing things back to the anchor.

"Margaret Ann Birch," Lonergan groused. "They even flashed her picture. Why do they make it sound like she's the one did somethin' wrong?"

Foster got out of the car. It wasn't a discussion she wanted to have with him. Instead, she stood with her back to the ME's office, needing a bit more time. "The longer we take, the bigger the story will get," she said. "That's when people will get scared, and scared people do stupid things."

It didn't help that the department leaked like a sieve or that Birch's killing was front page worthy—*Young White Woman Butchered on Riverwalk.* The city would attribute the death to a maniac, a fiend, and if Ainsley was eventually charged and named, they'd go for the prurient, the base. Race would be dragged in, as it always was when bad things happened to those usually insulated from crime. Keith Ainsley would be eaten alive.

She stopped at the door, her heart pounding. The last time she'd passed through these doors, she'd done so at a run—her world spinning—to find her partner lying on the ME's table, a bullet in her brain. She had stayed with Glynnis until her family could get there so that she wouldn't be alone, as Glynnis had done for her when it had been Reggie lying there.

"Scared of dead bodies, Foster?" Lonergan quipped as he passed her up and strolled inside. "Some murder cop you are."

She glanced up at the sky, at the clouds, a breeze drying beads of sweat on her forehead, and then she walked inside to catch up. It wasn't the dead she feared but the memories they left in their wake.

Lonergan smirked. "Need a drink . . . or a paramedic?"

She could feel the heat rising in her face, her cheeks flushing. There was a lot to say, but not here or now. Foster had hoped that after yesterday Lonergan would have settled in and mellowed some. He hadn't. "Don't worry," Foster said, her body shaking with an impulse to smack the smug look off his face. "I know how to keep my powder dry."

CHAPTER 20

The house looked worse from the street. Nothing about it felt right. For one thing, the homes on either side were far too close, which would likely encourage neighborly conversations over the garden hedge. The symmetry of the two-story colonial was appealing—three windows with shutters across the top, two shuttered windows, and a blue door with a wreath of fall flowers below. Inside, the ad said, there were ten rooms, a full basement, and an attic. There was also a huge yard and a two-car garage out back. It would be ideal if not for the sneer of contempt the house appeared to give, as if it were human and discerning and rejected out of hand the person standing alone by the neglected bushes. As if that lonely figure were contemplating an attack or had stolen its wallet at gunpoint.

Maybe it was the peeling aluminum siding, which in itself was a turnoff. Who put siding on a classic colonial? It was like encasing a living, breathing thing inside a tin can. The ad hadn't mentioned the siding. If it had, this trip would have been unnecessary. There was no use going in. The house would never do.

Not like the others—not like Naperville or Saint Paul, not like Bloomington—where the houses had been perfect. On quiet streets offering plenty of room to work. Houses in places where the seasons changed, summer sun to autumn chill, autumn chill to blankets of pure, white snow. But not this house. It didn't feel right at all.

When the morning's paper was grabbed out of a deep pocket, the front page told the story of a young woman found dead downtown. Margaret Ann Birch. Nineteen. Pretty. Details were scarce, unfortunately. Early times yet. This was only the first. The fear and panic would come after the next, when the pattern formed. Pretty young things, all the same. The police had no idea what was coming.

Not sad. That was life. Sometimes the young grew old; sometimes they didn't. Every living thing died, and the jump from here to gone often wasn't such a grand leap at all.

But to be left out in the cold alone, well, that just wouldn't do. There should be a house. Not this one but one that felt right. A home. Margaret Ann Birch wouldn't see the winter. She'd miss how perfect the imperfect world looked when it was blanketed in fresh snow. The next would miss it too. And the next.

Things were what they were. Hopefully, the next house would be more suitable.

CHAPTER 21

It was cold in the autopsy room, and hard rock music—frenetic, incomprehensible—blasted out of Dr. Olivia Grant's stereo speakers like a thousand rabid bats out of Hades, as if the violent clash of notes was a defensive screech that had the power to beat back death, giving it no dominion over the living. As unappealing as the music was to Foster, the noise felt alive, and it took her mind off the cold and the bleak tiled walls that were the color of the ME's green hospital scrubs and the metal table and the body lying on it with the striking Y incision, which always drew the eye no matter how hard you tried not to let it.

The detectives hung back out of the field, watching as Grant stood at the table over what was left of Margaret Ann Birch. Though the autopsy had been scheduled for nine, Grant had started without them.

"I hate it when you bring me young ones," Grant said. "I really hate it."

Grant covered Birch's body with a white sheet, then faced the cops who'd come for information. She slid off her surgical cap to reveal cropped platinum hair, which set off her smooth caramel skin and big hazel eyes. Grant grabbed the small remote that worked the stereo and clicked off the music, plunging the room into an eerie, hollow silence. Death was back. It *did* hold dominion over the living.

"Didn't you say nine?" Lonergan held up a wrist with an old analog watch fastened to it. "It's just that now."

"Detective Lonergan. *You* again," Grant said, not sounding at all happy about the reunion. She then glanced over at Foster, who stood beside him. "Only this time you brought the A-Team. Good for you, not so good for her." She winked at Foster, then peeled her gloves off, padded over to the sink, and scrubbed her hands with harsh soap—hands, wrists, forearms. "I got to it sooner. I didn't want that child to lie on my table any longer than she had to. I didn't think I needed to wait for a quorum. Besides, you're the main one always ragging on me to speed things up. Now you're complaining. Typical."

Foster knew Lonergan was in no position to complain too loudly. This was Grant's world, and she ran it like she knew it. Grant turned and looked over at Foster standing stoically, her eyes on the sheet under which Beth Birch's child lay cold, having just endured Grant's meticulous probing. Foster had been here so many times doing exactly this. Grant had conducted Glynnis's autopsy, though there'd been no question as to the cause of death. She'd also conducted Reg's, and she had been kind, caring. Neither of them, Foster knew, would ever mention it.

Grant plucked up her paperwork from the desk. "Immediate cause of death, exsanguination, but . . . well, you could have guessed. Twenty-two stab wounds to the chest and abdomen, some deeper than others. Two missed the heart by millimeters. One got it right on the money."

She stepped away from the desk and arched her back to work the stiffness out of it. Too many hours leaning over the table, Foster deduced. "No evidence of sexual assault. Nothing significant under the nails, and by 'significant' I mean skin, blood, hair, saliva, semen. DNA. Perfectly healthy nineteen-year-old. All parts working as they should. Preliminary toxicology: No drugs. No alcohol. She wasn't impaired in any way at time of death."

"You're sure?" Lonergan again.

Grant lasered in on Lonergan with those big, steady eyes. "Can you think of any reason why I wouldn't be?"

"Just asking the questions, Doc."

"Wrong ones," Grant shot back. "If the words come out of my mouth, I'm sure."

His eyes bore into Grant's. "You're readin' too much into it, I'd say." He jabbed a thumb Foster's way. "Lot of that goin' around. Must be a woman thing . . . or somethin' else. Either way, they don't pay me for dealin' with it. We got witnesses that put her in a bar before she was killed."

Grant said nothing. The silence was for Lonergan, and judging by the scowl on his face, he was bothered by it.

"Stomach contents?" Foster asked.

"She consumed Thai hours before she died. Pad thai would be my educated guess. I found noodles, peanuts, peas, the whole nine. And cola. Coke. Pepsi. That variety. That might help you retrace her steps, but without prints or DNA, you don't have much of a jump start."

Lonergan shifted his weight. "Did you check the—" He stopped himself. "What about the wounds? Rosales says we're lookin' for a hunting knife. You got anything more specific?"

"Rosales was correct. The wounds appear to have been made with a large, serrated knife. A blade at least thirty centimeters, judging by the cuts. That's a little over eleven inches for the layman. A hunting knife would fit. If you find it, I might be able to match it to some of the nicks on her bones. Like I said, some of the cuts went deep."

"What about the blood on the jacket?" Lonergan asked.

"Not Birch's," Grant said.

"You're jokin'!" Lonergan's eyes widened.

"Now I'm a clown?"

He stared at Grant as though she had just grown two heads, as though what she'd said didn't make a lick of sense. "That's impossible."

"No, Lonergan, that's science—and all I can comment on. The blood on that jacket is not a match to Birch's. One last injury. A superficial scalp hematoma, right at the base of the skull. No distinctive marks from a foreign object. No evidence that she had been struck."

"Maybe she hit her head when she fell back after the first strike?" Foster said.

"The wound would be consistent with that."

Lonergan looked like he didn't know which way to go, what to think. His instincts had been wrong. None of the physical evidence tied Keith Ainsley to Peggy Birch. "Tests can be wrong," he said.

"Not when I run them," Grant said. "Unless I completely blew med school hematology, which I absolutely did not, there's no way to mistake the inconsistency in blood types. Birch was O-positive. Common. The spot on the jacket, B-positive, also common. And it was old blood, not fresh, as you'd expect. Several major arteries were either nicked or sliced clean through, which flooded her chest and abdominal cavities with blood. But your killer didn't stop there. He dug down and sliced through the abdominal wall, opening her up, and, well, you saw her intestines. All her organs are accounted for. Whoever did this didn't take souvenirs, at least not anatomical ones. Bottom line: your killer left quite a mess behind."

"What about the lipstick around her ankles and wrists?" Foster asked.

"I can confirm it's lipstick. And strange. But it's unspectacular, except for its placement. Not only strange but a little creepy, though I can't offer an explanation. Did you find a tube of lipstick at the scene?" Foster and Lonergan shook their heads. "Then you've got another mystery to solve. I have a bad feeling about this one. No prints. No DNA. What's that say to both of you?"

"Gloves," Foster said. "He was careful."

Grant turned to Lonergan. "And what's *that* say?"

Lonergan didn't answer. They both knew what it said. Peggy Birch had likely been picked out, targeted, and lured to the Riverwalk, and that would mean that in addition to the gloves, the killer had likely worn something to cover their clothing. They could hardly move through the streets covered in blood, even at that hour. They'd need a kit, an exit route. And they'd need to be very precise about where they stepped.

"His shoes?" Foster asked.

"Clean," Grant said. "Your email said you wanted to know if there was mud on them? There wasn't. They were also dry, so he didn't take them off, rinse them off in the river, and put them back on." She stared at Lonergan when she relayed the last part. "That's all I've got preliminarily. You'll get a more detailed report by end of day. Good luck."

Foster said nothing to Lonergan as they walked back to the car. Ainsley wasn't their killer. She was both relieved and anxious about next steps.

"You win, Foster," Lonergan said. "Guess your kid's off the hook."

Her kid. It was an odd thing to say, even odder for Lonergan to boil it all down to a game of wins and losses. She walked heavily, as though her body were buried beneath a wall of bricks, her mind racing. Thai food consumed hours before Peggy's death, no foreign prints, no DNA. Two blood types, lipstick. She turned to Lonergan.

"If it isn't Peggy's blood, whose is it?"

CHAPTER 22

She flew through the doors back at Area 1. Alone. Lonergan had dropped her at the lot and taken off. Downtime, he'd said. Back in an hour. They had a body attached to no physical evidence and physical evidence that didn't match any victim they knew of. Downtime? Where was Lonergan going that was more important than getting to the bottom of any of this?

She threw her bag on the desk, eyed Griffin's closed door. The boss had done this to her, but she wasn't about to go running back to cry about it. She was stuck with Lonergan. The office was busy, cops doing what cops did; Peggy Birch wasn't the only murder that needed solving. Next moves. What could they be? Did Lonergan expect her to wait here like a doll on a shelf until he got back and made the moves for them?

Shimmying out of her jacket, she sat at the grimy desk and pulled out her notebook. Timeline. Peggy's. She'd track her back from Teddy's, the last spot anyone could place her. Street-camera access was in the works. The Riverwalk was covered. That was where she'd start. And if she was being hopeful, the blood on Keith's jacket didn't have to mean anyone else was dead. There could be a thousand explanations for it, and the fact that no one had stumbled on another dead girl kind of proved it.

She needed to see the case spread out in front of her. If she saw it mapped, she might be able to figure out the why that would lead to the who. Looking around the office, she spotted a small whiteboard leaning against the wall. She commandeered it and propped it up at her desk, then went hunting for markers. When she had the board set up and had acquired the markers from the shelf of office supplies near the printer, she started to quietly transfer her notes from her book to the board: witness statements, times, a list of Peggy's closest associates, lines drawn under their names—Rimmer, Dean, Stroman. She even added Giles Valentine, the bartender at Teddy's. Next, she taped up photos of Birch and Ainsley along with a crudely drawn map she'd made of the crime scene, noting the position of the body in relation to the bridge, to the marina, to the stairs. Blood. It wasn't Birch's. God forbid someone stumbled on another pile of leaves. The blood wasn't Keith Ainsley's either. He hadn't had a nick or cut on him when he'd been found, for one thing, and the blood was old, for another, but just to be sure, on her way back, she had checked with Dr. Santos by phone from the car. Keith was AB-positive. That revelation had done little to alter Lonergan's spiteful mood.

Stepping back, Foster studied what she'd done, satisfied that it was a good start. She would add to it as she discovered more, but for now the order helped her breathe a little easier.

"Foster." She turned to see Griffin standing at the door to her office, arms crossed, glancing at the board but making no comment. "Lonergan?"

All heads turned her way, everyone quieting. "Following a lead. Should be back any second."

She could tell Griffin knew she was lying. The boss knew Lonergan better than Foster knew him, but she didn't challenge the statement. And from the looks she got from the cops in the room, she'd passed a test. She'd covered for her partner, even if it was Lonergan, and their nods and winks of approval signaled to her that she had earned their respect and fraternity. She'd take it, but a little white lie was as far as she would ever bend. They didn't know that about her yet.

The board set, Foster checked her watch, then switched to the security footage from the bar. Two sets of eyes would have been better, but it looked like Lonergan was going to leave it all to her.

She went through the main footage again, finding just a bar filled with happy, drinking people. Peggy Birch, the life of the party, as Giles Valentine had told them. Foster then moved to the other angles, the ones that covered the back end of the bar and along the wall. She checked her watch. It was just after eleven.

"What's all this?"

Foster looked up to find Detective Vera Li holding a white grease-stained bag that smelled like Wrigley Field on a hot summer day. "Excuse me?"

Li flicked the bag toward the screen. "That a lead?"

"It's footage from the bar Birch was in the night she was killed. We're looking for . . . anything, I guess. So far nothing. I'm just about to look at the rest of it."

Li scanned the room. "We? Where's Lonergan?"

Foster gave Li a slight smile. "Somewhere readjusting."

"Want another set of eyes?" She held the bag up. "And a hot dog?"

Foster's stomach growled as if on cue, despite her reluctance to accept the assist on principle.

Li chuckled, then pulled over Lonergan's empty chair and sat next to her. "Sure you do." She drew the dogs out of the bag and set one in front of Foster, taking the other for herself.

"What about whatever you're working on?" Foster asked.

"Kelley's at a dentist appointment. I'm taking lunch while he's at it. No sense wasting all this detectiveness. I figure we eat a little, cop a little." She nodded toward the computer. "Cue it up. Let's see what we got."

Foster stared at Li for a moment, watching as she bit into her hot dog with great enthusiasm and speed. Cops learned early to eat fast and often. You never knew how long your break would be or how long a meal would have to last you before you had the chance to eat again.

"No chips?" Foster asked.

Li grinned and stuck a hand back in the bag, grabbing two small bags of Jays potato chips, original flavor. She tossed one to Foster. "What do you take me for?"

They ran through angle two for about forty minutes before Foster spotted him. He came in minutes after Birch entered and sat well away from the bar at a small table in the corner, his eyes never leaving Birch as she stood at the bar with Valentine and the others.

"He's staring at her," Foster said.

Li leaned closer to the screen. "And he looks pissed."

They watched him glare at Birch from the table, then advanced the footage frame by frame until the blonde woman in the black dress who Valentine had paid close attention to approached him, talked him up, flipping her hair around, and then sat down with him. Twenty minutes later, the two left together. Foster rolled back to before the woman approached, zoomed in a little to get more of his face.

"That's who you were looking for?" Li asked. Foster nodded. "Who is he?"

Foster froze the frame, leaned back in her chair to think. "Her ex. Joe Rimmer, who told us he hadn't seen Birch in weeks."

"What about the blonde?" Li asked.

"A pickup would be my guess."

"She could also be his alibi," Li said. "Depending on how long it all took."

"Looks like we've got a new person of interest." Foster ran it all again.

———

They stuck Rimmer in the smallest, smelliest interview room available and then let him sit there for a time, letting the funk sink in and the fear rise enough to rattle his bones. Foster watched him through the two-way mirror from the next room as Rimmer shook, his glassy eyes darting around the depressing space. He repeatedly checked his pockets as if trying to remind himself that he wasn't holding anything they could ding him for.

Lonergan was back and took up the spot beside her. "Heard the boss was lookin' for me. I was followin' a lead . . . thought it'd be better if I took it solo."

She didn't bother turning to look at him. She'd seen enough, heard enough, endured enough. "What lead?"

"Doesn't matter. Didn't pan out."

She knew there was no lead. She'd asked around the office when he hadn't come back for almost two hours. It seemed Lonergan often disappeared when the going got tough. There were conflicting theories as to where he went, whether he cooled his heels in a bar or met a mistress in a hotel. It didn't really matter to her which it was. Lonergan, she'd decided, was a goldbricker. Griffin had said as much, and she had no time for it. If she couldn't work with him, she'd work around him.

"What's *he* doing here?" Lonergan asked.

"We found him on the footage from Teddy's."

"That lyin' piece of shit was followin' her?"

"He was in the same bar she was in," Foster corrected pointedly.

His eyes lasered in on Rimmer fidgeting in the other room. "On the very night she comes up dead."

"I've asked Li to sit in," she said.

He turned. "Li?"

"She helped get through the footage while you were . . . out. I needed another set of eyes. Yours weren't here. She sits in."

"Two days in and you're already calling the shots?"

"Just working the case, Lonergan."

"Which you're supposed to be doin' with me."

"That's right. But you flaked off and left the hard part to me. And I covered your ass with Griffin. So here we are."

He studied her. "Look, if you've got beef—"

She brushed past him. Sniping with the man was a waste of time and energy, and she lacked both. The sooner they got something out of Rimmer, the sooner they could move on. "I don't have beef. What I have is a dead girl. You coming or not?"

———

Three detectives, one liar. Lonergan, Foster, and Li stared down at Rimmer sitting at the table, sweating, smelling of weed. No one spoke for a good minute.

"What's this about?" There was a tremor to his voice, his tone as thin as a reed. He looked from one to another. "Seriously?"

Foster laid a copy of the freeze-frame from the bar on the table and waited until Rimmer looked at it, registered what it was, and seemed to short-circuit. He started to stammer; his eyes danced around the room. Lonergan took a seat across from him. Foster too. Li leaned against the wall, her arms crossed in front of her, eyes on the trembling man-child with the heavy metal tats up and down his puny arms.

"Joseph Thomas Rimmer." Lonergan leaned forward, smiling. "You're a dirty rotten liar."

Rimmer tried laughing off the formality. "You sound like my mother. When I was in trouble as a kid." He eyed the cops, all three, who gave him nothing back. "So I was at a bar. That's not a crime."

Foster pointed to Birch. "You see what I see?"

"I didn't know she was there. How could I?"

"A coincidence, then?" Foster said. "Chance."

Rimmer jumped on it with both feet. "Sure. Yeah. That's exactly what it was. I was there; she came in. What was I supposed to do, get up and leave? She doesn't own the city. I have just as much right to—"

Foster consulted her notebook. "She came in first, actually. At five fifty-two p.m. Sunday. You came in at five fifty-five."

"Start talking," Lonergan said. "Do not, I repeat, *do not* waste my time."

Rimmer swallowed hard, then swiped sweat from his brows with the back of a hand. "I don't—"

Lonergan held up a hand. "Nope."

He started again. "That's not—"

Lonergan slammed his fist down on the table, rattling it, rattling Rimmer. "Try again."

Foster said nothing and neither did Li, watchful against the wall. Rimmer wouldn't be the first jilted boyfriend to take the news of his dumping hard and do something about it. As she watched him now, closely, she wondered if he possessed a switch she couldn't see, a level of mania well hidden beneath a guise of a mellow music man who let things slide, who took things easy. All the while his wild, cornered eyes flitted around the cop room. He looked like he wanted to say something.

"What is it?" Foster asked, her voice calm, patient. "You were following her, isn't that right? Was it the entire day? It would almost have to be. You'd have had to be at the march, to be tracking her, or how else would you know she walked into Teddy's?"

Rimmer scooted his chair back and made like he was about to stand. Both Lonergan and Foster braced themselves. Li lifted off the wall. Rimmer froze, then eased back down.

"Whoa. Okay. Everybody calm the hell down," he said. "Look, I don't know what you think I did here, but I didn't kill her. I broke up with her, that's all."

Foster shook her head. "No, you didn't."

"She dumped *you*," Lonergan said. "She's in college. You're a do-nothin' who thinks he's gonna be the next Elvis. She had no use for ya."

Foster slid Lonergan a quizzical look. Elvis? But she saw what Lonergan was doing. He was testing Rimmer, wanting to see how long or short a fuse he had. She sat and watched him work.

Lonergan pushed the photo closer to Rimmer. "Start talking."

After a glance, Rimmer pushed it back. "So I was there. Big deal. But you see I have an alibi." He stabbed the image of the available blonde. "Right there. You can see her as clearly as you obviously see me, right? I left with her, and when I did, Peg was still there." Neither Lonergan nor Foster said anything. "You can see that. You've got eyes."

"The blonde have a name?" Foster asked.

"Didn't get it, or if I did, I can't remember it now." He uttered the words as though that were all the explanation they needed.

"What'd you think followin' Peggy was gonna do for you?" Lonergan asked.

"I went to the march. Okay? That's my constitutional right. I never saw Peggy there." He lowered his chin to his chest, lowering his voice too. "I caught sight of her after it was breaking up and everybody was heading in a million directions. I wanted to see where she went, so I followed her." His head popped up. "But that's *all* I did. You got the tape. Run it. You know already she was alive when I left."

"You coulda dumped the blonde and waited for her outside," Lonergan said.

"Well, I didn't. I was with what's-her-face."

"All night?" Foster asked.

"Absolutely. Look, can I go now?"

"Not even close," Lonergan said. "We're going to toss you into a holding cell and rummage through your life until we find something we can ding you for. That means tracking down your weed-selling buddies and their buddies and *their* buddies . . . I don't think that's going to make you too popular."

"Your lying to us puts you in a different category now, Mr. Rimmer," Foster said. "We'll need to take a closer look."

"All right. All right." Rimmer held his head in his hands, ruffling his hair in desperation. "I followed . . . all day. I knew she'd probably be there. She was into the whole activist thing. I thought if I could just talk to her, you know? In a neutral spot, away from her friends, we could, you know, smooth things out. A rock star's got to have a lady, and we looked hot together. I figured if I just . . . but I never got the chance. She was in the middle of shit all day. Then when she headed to the bar, I just . . . that blonde was a revenge hookup. That's all I did. *I swear.*"

Rimmer flipped the photo over so he wouldn't have to see it. "I never got an opening. And yeah, it steamed me. There she was living it up. It was like she wasn't bothered at all about us not being together or about missing out on being with somebody who was about to be famous."

Lonergan laughed. *"What?"*

Foster pushed on. "The woman you left with?"

"I told you . . . no idea. Maybe Casey or Cassidy or . . . it was something with a *C*, I'm pretty sure. But I was with *her*, not Peg. She's my witness, so I couldn't have killed anybody, even if I'd wanted to." He suddenly realized what he'd said. "Um, not that I did. Want to. I didn't. Besides, you see what the cameras did. I left first and didn't double back." He jabbed the photo with an angry finger. His face registered a spark of remembrance. "And the woman. She told me Teddy's was her place, so me not remembering her name's no big deal. You want her, ask around there. Somebody's bound to know who the hell she is. I'm telling you the God's honest truth here." He fixed pleading eyes on all three cops. "Ask her; she'll tell you I was with her. *Ask her.*"

At her desk, Foster called downstairs to the desk sergeant. No sign of Ashley Tighe, Stella Dean's study partner. Foster had obviously been stood up. When she hung up, she pulled up Tighe's driver's license and ran her address and number.

"What're you doin'?" Lonergan was watching her from his chair, his fingers laced across his belly.

"Stella Dean's whereabouts are still unconfirmed. Ashley Tighe was the name she gave us. Her study partner? While you were out, I called her. She agreed to come in and talk." She looked over at him. "She didn't show."

"Dean? You really think she could stab somebody over twenty times?"

Foster stood. "Anybody could, if properly motivated. You coming?"

"Where to?"

"To Teddy's for the blonde, then Tighe's for Dean."

Lonergan sneered at her. "What? You're not bringing Li along?"

Foster was already halfway to the door. "Grow up."

CHAPTER 23

Amelia had a sense that the other side of her bed was occupied but hadn't for the life of her any idea who was doing the occupying. She rolled over, saw the naked man there. Black. Lean. He took up most of the length of the queen-size platform bed. Amelia rose up on one elbow and just stared at him, enjoying the view, despite the pounding headache, which was courtesy of a fading high. She had a faint recollection of a night of cosmos or Thunderbird or something that would need to come back to her gradually after time, along with the naked man's name. Something with a *T*. Tony? Tommy? She gave up. It wasn't that important anyway, was it? This was a one-off. She'd never see him again.

She shook him, then took a lascivious peek under the rumpled top sheet. It all came back to her then—the night, the guy. A pickup in a bar at almost closing. She peered at the clock on the bedside table, almost twelve hours ago now. She shook Mr. Handsome again, harder this time—fun time was over. Half the day was gone already, and she had things to do. Preparations.

"Hey, good looking. Rise and shine. Time to go."

He groaned awake, turned groggily, blinked bleary eyed a few times, trying to focus. It didn't appear that he recalled the night any better than she did. It was definitely Thunderbird, now that she thought about it. She had the faint taste of it, akin to cheap gasoline, coating her tongue.

She rolled out of bed and found a pair of sweats and a T-shirt slung over a chair and put them on. "Gotta go, lover boy."

He sat up on the side of the bed and searched the floor for his pants. "Some night, huh?"

Amelia flicked on the television to the midday news while she watched Mr. T dress and hunt for his shoes. She spotted them kicked under a chair and pointed the remote to guide him to them. "There."

She turned back to the TV, hoping there was something new on the body they'd found on the Riverwalk. Nothing on that so far, but plenty on the overnight body count. Fourteen shot around the city, three fatally. What a violent town. Who knew how many bodies lay scattered around unclaimed, tossed away like trash, moldering in abandoned buildings or buried in a forest preserve? The possibilities were too dark to even imagine.

"I'm out," her date announced on his way to the door.

"Hey," she said. "What's your name again?"

"What's it matter?"

He had a point. "You're right."

"It's been real," he said as he walked out the door.

She locked the door behind him. "I might agree if I could remember it." She stretched, then padded back to the news. Seriously, she thought, what a violent town.

CHAPTER 24

They were back at Teddy's with Giles Valentine before noon, looking for information on the blonde. A lunch crowd was beginning to form, mostly tourists who'd wandered off the Riverwalk looking for a place to sit and eat before hitting the Mag Mile to get their pockets picked, legally, at the high-end stores there.

Lonergan held up the photo from the security footage and pointed to the blonde. "Who's this, and before you get cute and start dancin' around playin' with us, this shows you straight up talkin' to her when you shoulda been workin'. And on top of that, we've got a dead girl across the river, so this isn't some game."

Foster cleared her throat to let what Lonergan had said die down a bit. "We're hoping she's in here often enough that you may know who she is?"

"Since you never forget a face and talk up all the ladies who come in here." Lonergan sat the photo on the bar, tapped it with a finger. "We need a name and where we can find her. Now."

Valentine reached up and adjusted his tie. "What'd she do?"

Lonergan shook his head. "That's a question. Want to try again?"

Valentine's face colored. He really didn't like Lonergan. "Or?"

Lonergan stepped forward, glancing up at Valentine's hat and then down at the bow tie. He didn't answer the question, but the look he gave the man had him backing away from the bar.

"I hate cops," Valentine mumbled.

"Neither here nor there, pal," Lonergan groused.

For a moment Valentine said nothing; then he turned his attention from Lonergan to Foster. "Her name's Kate. She's a bit of a regular. She lives in the area. We've been out a couple times."

"That's all you know about her?" Foster asked.

Valentine's brows lifted. "How much do I need to know?"

Lonergan grimaced. "She have a last name, Casanova?"

Valentine wouldn't even look at him. He addressed Foster instead. "I got better than a name, but only for you, because a woman's dead, and I want him out of here."

The man pulled out his wallet and slid out a business card, handing it to her. Foster eyed the card. There was a name on it and a telephone number. She flipped it over, but there was nothing on the back. Foster read aloud. "Katherine Samuels-Key. She's married?"

Valentine's face lit up, his tongue wetting his lips proudly. "I didn't ask. She didn't tell." He slid a contemptuous look at Lonergan, who was staring daggers back at him. "That's how it's done this century, Pops."

Lonergan took a step forward to apparently show Valentine just how much of an old man he was, but Foster broke in with another question. "So she works the bar, goes with anyone here. You watch as she picks up whoever; still you keep her card in your wallet?"

He stared at her, confused, like he didn't get why she found that strange. "We're not dating or anything."

Lonergan leaned forward, his jaw straining. "Dumbass, is she or is she not a pro?"

Valentine backed up to the shelves, the contact rattling the bottles on the ledge behind him. He couldn't put any more distance between himself and Lonergan, but it sure looked like he wanted to. Valentine was all mouth. Lonergan knew it. Foster knew it too. She suspected that even Pike, his boss, knew it, but if Pike found out he'd been letting professionals work the bar on an odd night, Foster was sure his days were numbered here at Teddy's. That might have accounted for the sweat on his forehead and the attention to his tie.

"I don't know, okay? Her business is her business," Valentine said.

Foster suspected that the name on the card was as bogus as a three-dollar bill, but the number was good, otherwise Valentine wouldn't be carrying it around in his wallet. She waited to see if Lonergan had anything more to ask, but it looked like he was going to let the conversation die there, which, for him, was probably for the best. They had a number and an unreliable name. It was something.

"Anything else?" Foster asked Valentine.

He picked up his bar rag, wound it around his hands. "What more do you need?"

Outside the bar, Foster slid her notebook back into her bag and looked up at Lonergan next to her. "Why do you terrorize people like that?"

Lonergan sniggered. "I was right takin' you for a bleedin' heart. Look, you want to make an omelet, you got to break some eggs. A little in-their-face cuts the bullshit by half."

She glanced out over the river at the pedestrians strolling along the path on the other side. The flags along the bridge waved in the breeze. The water was calm. And standing next to her was a lummox of a partner working her last nerve.

"The problem I have is that I don't trust you." Her eyes met his.

"Your problem, not mine," he said.

She exhaled. "Like I said."

———

They met Ashley Tighe outside her residence hall sitting cross-legged on a bench, a philosophy textbook in her lap. She seemed nervous and sneaked furtive glances at the doors when anyone went in or out. Tighe, petite and barely five feet tall, with blinky black eyes and a mess of brunette curls, didn't look like she ate enough to keep a bird alive. Foster wondered if it was Stella she was worried about.

"I expected you to come in, like you agreed," Foster said.

There was another glance toward the door, a shift of body weight. "I changed my mind. I really don't want to get in the middle of anything. I don't know anything about what happened to Peggy."

"It's Stella Dean I want to ask you about," Foster said. "She says she was studying with you Sunday. Is that true?"

Lonergan stood by. He hadn't said much since the bar. Foster was fine with that. Tighe checked the doors again. Students passed, paying them little attention, too focused on their own thing, lugging heavy backpacks or riding bikes or talking on their phones.

"Yeah, we studied Sunday."

"Studied what?" Lonergan asked, his voice a little softer than Foster was used to hearing it.

"Econ. I get As. Stella's lucky if she pulls a D." She looked up at Foster. "Stella's why I didn't come. She's been burning up my phone. She wants me to say she was with me all day, but she wasn't. We met up at noon, and I was back in my room a little after two. It wasn't my idea to study with her, but Stella . . . she insinuated herself. She makes it almost impossible to say no to her about anything."

"Some friend," Lonergan said.

"Stella doesn't have friends," Tighe said. "She has . . . hostages. I thought I'd left mean-girl cliques behind in high school, but they're here, too, and Stella's their supreme leader, at least here in Barnwell."

"So you can only vouch for her between noon and two," Foster said. "You have any idea what she was doing before or after that?"

Tighe shook her head. "I try not to think too much about Stella." She clasped her hands in her lap, squeezing them tightly, then checked the door again. "She's probably watching us right now."

"Did she threaten you?" Lonergan's jaw clenched, and it looked like his eyes had shrunk down to two steely blue marbles.

"Stella never comes right out and says stuff, but she made it real clear she wanted me to lie and say we were studying longer than we were. What happens when she finds out I didn't? You don't know how she can get."

Foster could feel her entire body coil at the thought of Tighe, Stroman, and others tiptoeing around campus trying to stay out of Stella Dean's orbit. Had Peggy Birch done the same? Had she gotten on Dean's bad side somehow? Had Stella done something about that, and things had gone wrong?

"I wouldn't worry about that," Foster said. She hated bullies. Always had. She had a little something for Stella Dean. Foster scribbled her number in her notepad, then tore the page off and handed it to Tighe. "If you can think of anything else we should know, call me, please?"

Tighe took the number and stood. One last look at the door. No Stella. Tighe rushed off.

"Well, Dean's a liar," Lonergan said.

"Twelve to two," Foster said. "And then in bed by nine, so she said."

Lonergan slid his sunglasses on. "First part's a lie, the second part's gonna be a lie too. That leaves a lot of holes in her day."

"So let's plug some of them up," Foster said.

CHAPTER 25

Stella Dean wasn't so tough, Foster thought, as she stared at her across the table in the interview room. Detective Li sat beside her, her dark eyes holding Stella's without expression. Foster knew they made a formidable-looking pair, and from the guarded look on Stella's face, she could tell the intimidating effect was working.

The team was outside in the office making calls, checking Dean's background, diving deep looking for arrests, reports of disturbances . . . anything related to Peggy Birch that might indicate she had a motive for killing her.

Right now, though, Foster wanted Stella here at the table with the silence. She placed her notebook in front of her, then folded her hands on top of it and waited for the girl to get uncomfortable. There'd been no pizza from Zippy's Sunday night; that had been easy to check. The place had no receipt, no video, no employee with any recollection of Stella walking into the place that day. It was a campus spot. Faces were remembered easily, and no one had seen Stella's on Sunday. There'd also been no deliveries made to her dorm that night, so pizza from Zippy's and then an early turn-in had been a lie. So now Stella was here, and Foster and Li sat waiting, watching to find out what else she'd lied about.

"Look, I told you, I wasn't with Peggy Sunday. I never saw her. I don't know what happened." Stella glanced around the smelly, tight, depressing room. "God, this room is fucking awful."

Foster knew the room didn't impress. It wasn't meant to. The space was the last stop before a locked cell for some and where others received the worst news of their lives. It was a holding pen, a sweatbox, a swift and jarring reality check.

Stella's eyes widened. "Or did you bring me here to tell me you found out who killed her? Is that it?"

How odd, Foster thought, that Stella would think she'd be their first call when Peggy's killer was found. Odd and curious, but she said nothing, just watched, letting time stretch out while the team worked and Stella worried.

Lonergan was back on campus to talk to as many of Dean and Birch's dormmates as he could, and he hadn't been happy about it. Griffin, though, had made the assignment, and frankly Foster was glad to have the time apart from him, if only for a few hours. The boss was why Li was here in the room, which was fine, she supposed, though she couldn't help but feel that the pairing was some kind of test.

Stella looked to Li, then back to Foster. "Nobody's going to say anything, really?"

The picture they had gotten so far of Stella Dean hadn't been favorable. She was manipulative, bossy, intimidating, and volatile. Foster wondered why she'd been allowed to run roughshod over her classmates. Why had no one stopped her? Had Peggy defied Stella's attempts to intimidate her as she'd so obviously intimidated Stroman, Tighe, and the rest of their circle? Had Stella lost that temper of hers?

"It's like I'm a criminal or something." Stella tittered, but Foster could see the worry building and the anger that was coming up right behind it, all showing in the young woman's eyes.

Foster would know the right time to break the silence. She would hear it in Stella's voice the moment her confidence gave way to uncertainty, the very second she realized that her tricks and schemes and cunning ways weren't going to work with them and that she had no power here.

There had been nicer interview rooms Foster could have used to have this conversation, but she wanted Stella to sit in this one. She wanted her to smell the funk left behind by unwashed bangers and pushers in handcuffs. She wanted her to settle into the grime, sit where they sat. Stella had tried to squeeze an alibi out of Ashley Tighe, and now Foster was going to squeeze her so she'd know how it felt.

Suddenly there it was. The shift. Foster had waited patiently for Stella to move from confident to frightened. The cycle, like a second hand sweeping a clock face, had taken a little over an hour. Scared was where she wanted her. Now she could start.

Foster set an enlarged copy of Peggy's driver's license photo on the table, followed by a crime scene photo of the dead woman, her body covered by a bloodstained sheet, her empty, lifeless face and that red hair the only things showing. Foster put them down one after the other like a Vegas blackjack dealer.

"Let's talk about Sunday," Foster said. "You didn't go to Zippy's. You called Peggy all day, half the night, but she never returned your calls. Why were you harassing her?"

Stella sat mesmerized by the photos, then pushed them away, back across the table toward her. Foster waited for the grandiose emotional show she was sure was coming. Stella's eyes began to water. There it was.

"I wasn't harassing her," the girl responded. "Since when do you need a reason to talk to a friend?"

"More than fifteen times in just a few hours?" Foster asked. "Where'd you go?"

Stella tilted her head back and tried squeezing tears out of her eyes. The performance was coming. "I was in my room. Alone."

Foster had come prepared; she always did. She pulled out another photo, set it down. It was an image of Stella leaving her dorm at 3:14 p.m. After she and Lonergan had talked to Tighe, they'd hit the college's security office and caught a break—a retired cop working part time there. "You went out," Foster said. She laid down another photo.

142

"Here's you coming back. Monday morning. Eight minutes after seven. So let's try again. Where were you?"

Stella stopped working the tears and gaped at the photographs as if they were of her robbing a bank. She was cooked and seemed to forget all about the crocodile tears. "Where'd you get that?"

Foster didn't answer. This wasn't a conversation. "Stella?"

"I stayed with a friend, all right? No big deal. I only said Zippy's because who or where had nothing to do with whatever happened to Peg."

Foster picked up her pen. "What's your friend's name?"

Stella hesitated. "I don't know if I want to get people involved in all this."

"Not people," Foster said. "One person. Because I suspect that you were calling Peggy because you needed to know where she was. So that she wouldn't catch you stepping out behind her back." The look on Stella's face told her she was right. Stella wasn't only possessive, controlling, and obnoxious, she was also unfaithful. Foster's fingers pressed tightly around the pen. "Name. Address. Phone number." Their eyes locked. "Now."

"I should call my parents," Stella said. "They should be here, right?"

"How old are you, Stella?" Foster asked, but she already knew the answer. Stella was twenty-one, a senior graduating in June. Legally an adult. Foster didn't need her parents' consent to talk to her. Stella looked like she might be sick. Twenty-one had its benefits, but it had its curses too. "Welcome to the real world."

"A lawyer, then," Stella said, her eyes darting around the room. For a moment, they landed on Li, maybe for a little assistance, but Li wasn't giving any. "This doesn't seem fair."

Foster sat back. "You're not under arrest, Stella, but you can call your parents if you'd like. We'll sit them downstairs. They can wait for you while we talk. Maybe they'll be able to convince you to level with us. Or you can cooperate with us now and then go home. Up to you."

"If I don't answer, then what?"

"Then Detective Li and I will wonder why, and then you become our new pet project. You're not well liked at school, Stella. You won't get a lot of support there, I don't think. People will talk. We won't be discreet when we go back."

Their eyes held. Stella was the first to break the stalemate. "All right. Fine. It doesn't matter now anyway. Gina. Gina Carr. I was with her." Foster wrote down Carr's address and number as Stella recited them to her, then listened as Li got up and slipped out of the room, knowing she was on it.

"Now can I go?" Stella folded her arms across her chest, her lower lip protruding in a petulant pout. "I shouldn't even be here. I didn't do anything."

Foster gathered up the photos and closed her notebook. "Sit tight." Stella began to work up another cry, her face scrunching up. Foster got up and stared down at her, unmoved. "The act's not working. Not on me, anyway." Stella looked up, and her mouth opened to answer back. Foster held up a hand to stop the flow. "The problem for bullies, Stella, is that eventually they get back everything they've been giving out. It's called karma." She thought of Ashley Tighe and how Stella had twisted her arm to give her an alibi, how fear had her jumping at the sight of an opening door. Foster had Stella's full attention. "Eventually, there comes a time when weak little bullies come up against someone tougher." Foster strolled over to the door, opened it, but didn't leave right away. She took another long look at Stella. "For you, that's today."

CHAPTER 26

Li was sitting at her desk swiveling when Foster returned. Everyone hovering around her, including Lonergan, looked fit to be tied. "Okay, gang's all here. I just spoke to Gina Carr," Li announced. "She's twenty-nine. Fitness trainer. She confirms Stella was with her Sunday night, all night. She even went so far as to show me her Ring video that clearly catches Ms. Two-Timer getting to her place around five and tiptoeing out first thing the following morning. Skeezy but not illegal. Stella's not our killer."

"How'd she show you?" Foster asked.

Li grinned. "Over FaceTime. Fastest way."

"That's two possibles we've had to cut loose, by the by," Kelley groused. "Guess Lonergan beating the campus bushes was a waste of shoe leather."

Lonergan glanced over at Griffin's door and snarled, "Wild-goose chase was what it was."

"Twenty-nine?" Kelley said. "What the hell's she doing with a twenty-one-year-old?"

"Stella's legal," Li said, "but if she were my kid, Carr and me would have a serious talk."

Kelley chuckled. "Oh, is that what they're calling beatdowns these days?"

"I have a call into Rimmer's bar pickup, Samuels-Key," Foster said. "I left a detailed message. No callback yet."

"If she's married and stepping out," Symansky said, "she's not going to be all het up about getting in touch."

Foster nodded. "Then we pay her a visit."

"So nobody's thinkin' the blood on Ainsley's jacket's important here?" Lonergan said.

Kelley rolled his eyes. "What's with you and this Ainsley kid?"

Lonergan bristled. "Blood that wasn't *his*? C'mon."

Bigelow glanced around the cop huddle. "I thought we moved on from the kid?"

"We did," Li shot back, watching Lonergan out of the corner of her eye. "At least some of us."

"The blood wasn't Peggy Birch's either," Foster said. The look she gave her partner was dark, hard, like coal. "He could have picked it up anywhere. Someone could have brushed against him at that march. Someone with a bloody finger could have handled his jacket when he wasn't in it. At school. At a coffee shop. It was a spot of blood. He wasn't bathed in it."

The team quieted, and Foster turned to see Griffin step out of her office and watch them from across the room. Suddenly, their little bull session felt like an exam. Foster looked over at Lonergan, who, despite seething with anger, kept his mouth shut. Nobody deliberately torpedoed their career by showing out in front of the boss.

"So we stick a pin in the blood for now," Li said. "If we find something to match it to, then we circle back."

"Until then," Foster said, "we keep moving."

"Now that Stella Dean is out," Bigelow said, "my money's on Rimmer. We got him stalking Birch. It would have been easy for him to waltz out of that bar with the blonde, dump her, and then wait for Birch. Things go bad; he loses it. He's got motive; he's got opportunity. It's not too hard hiding a knife."

Foster nodded. "All that's true, but we're forgetting about the lipstick around her ankles and wrists. That means something." She turned back to the group. "We have to get in touch with Samuels-Key."

"I know we're looking at everybody who knew Birch. Standard op," Symansky said, "but there's nothing that says this can't be some random guy. He sees Birch coming out of the bar, spots her, takes the opportunity."

"And he's carrying lipstick?" Bigelow asked. "My wife doesn't even carry lipstick. My mother does, though."

"Where was your mother Sunday, Bigelow?" Symansky said, trying to lighten the mood. The relief was much needed.

"So we're lookin' for an unknown sicko," Lonergan said. "Wonderful."

Griffin stepped forward. "Good ideas. Gives us places to go. So go."

Foster watched as everybody packed up to clear out, but she took time to make one more call, leaving another message for Samuels-Key.

"She's avoiding me," she said when she hung up the phone.

Lonergan slid into his blazer and grabbed his keys. "News flash, Foster. Hookers usually avoid cops. Now let's go and spin some more wheels."

Foster picked up her coat and bag. "We don't know she was working Teddy's."

"You heard Valentine? She's a regular. She works the spot like it was a nine-to-five."

Foster slung her bag over her shoulder. "I heard regular. That doesn't mean hooker."

"She's married, she oughta be home, not pickin' up guys in some high-and-mighty bar. That's what I think."

She didn't care what he thought. Foster felt for the aspirin bottle in her bag and found it. Now she was ready to go.

"Nothin' to say to that?" Lonergan asked. "No namby-pamby explanations for her trollin' the bars?"

"I'll meet you at the car," Foster said, moving past him.

She stopped, though, when the phone on her desk rang. She walked back and picked it up. It was the desk sergeant downstairs. Samuels-Key was there. "Send her up. Thanks." Foster put her bag down and slipped her jacket off. "Trip canceled. She came to us."

Lonergan had apparently heard the brief conversation and was already moving. "Ten bucks she's a pro," he said.

CHAPTER 27

When they walked into the interview, Foster saw a middle-aged white woman pacing around the room, her hands busy working the gold bracelets on her wrists. Samuels-Key. The woman stopped and stared at them, real fear and a slight panic in her gray eyes. Foster didn't have to be a cop to see she was in a tight spot, that she was worried about being here and what that could mean for her marriage, maybe her livelihood, likely her everything.

Foster stood at the table. "Mrs. Samuels-Key?"

The woman nodded, her eyes wide, her look wary. She'd overdressed for the occasion in a camel-colored turtleneck, black pants, and black suede mules with chunky three-inch heels. A Burberry trench was slung over the back of a chair. It wasn't the kind of ensemble often worn in this room, Foster noted. Samuels-Key looked as though she were on her way to lunch at RL, the Gold Coast restaurant where celebrities went to be seen, and burgers were thirty dollars a pop.

Samuels-Key brushed a strand of blonde hair away from her angular face. Foster noticed the wedding ring—the diamonds, the white gold. What was a woman pulled together so tightly as she appeared to be doing fishing around a downtown bar for random hookups?

Foster pointed at the chair. "Sit. Please." She watched as the nervous blonde took a seat and draped her coat over her shoulders, Foster suspected not for warmth but for protection, like armor. "Katherine or Kate?" The woman ignored the question.

Samuels-Key held her head high. "Your messages said this was to do with a Joe Rimmer? I don't know who that is."

"You must know somethin'," Lonergan said. "You're here."

The withering look she gave him broadcast her scorn. "I'm here because I didn't want police knocking on my door as though I'm some common criminal." Her chin lifted. "I have neighbors. And whatever that person has done, it's got nothing to do with me."

Foster laid down the photo from Teddy's with her and Rimmer in it. She pointed at him. "That's Rimmer. You picked him up, or he picked you up, on Sunday night."

"You left with him," Lonergan said, seemingly unfazed by the woman's derisive sneer. "He's not draggin' you out the door."

"We'd like to ask you about that." Foster glanced over at Lonergan, who seemed to be champing at the bit to break Samuels-Key down. "And only that."

Foster could tell the woman was thinking through her options. It took almost a minute before she made her decision, punctuating it with a resigned, deep exhale. "Let's get this over with," she said.

"First, let's start with your name. I found nothing under Kate or Katherine Samuels-Key. Who am I talking to?" She could tell she'd surprised Lonergan, but had he stuck around for the grunt work, he'd have been there when she'd discovered the inconsistency. Things moved fast. She didn't have time to spoon-feed him.

The woman drew her coat tighter around her shoulders as though she were freezing, but Foster knew her discomfort had nothing to do with the temperature of the room. "This could ruin me," she said. "My husband is a hard man. Unforgiving."

"Sorry, but I need your name," Foster said gently.

"He won't have to know I've been here?"

Foster watched her. "All I can promise is that we'll be discreet."

Samuels-Key lowered her head, clasped her hands in her lap. "Melissa Cooke. What has he done?" She looked to her, to Lonergan, but got only impassive looks back. "Right. You won't say. I'm supposed to lay myself bare, but you get to keep all your little secrets."

Foster scribbled down Cooke's name, then consulted her earlier notes. "You met Rimmer at Teddy's. He told us he was with you all of Sunday night."

"He's lying. I barely stayed two hours. My husband was due home from a business trip early Monday."

"Where did you . . . hook up?" Foster asked.

"His place. North Side. We Ubered there. I Ubered back not long after. I have the receipt that proves I'm telling the truth."

Foster held out a hand. "Please."

Cooke shook her head, frowned, but opened her bag for her cell phone, then held it up for them to see the Uber confirmation. "Date and time of pickup and drop-off."

"Doesn't prove it was you in the car," Lonergan said.

Cooke gripped the phone. "Don't you have to prove I wasn't? Look, the details of my failed marriage are none of your business. I go to Teddy's for . . . a diversion, to forget for a while how miserable it all is. I met Rimmer. We left together, spent some time. That's the extent of our connection. I haven't seen him since and don't intend to. I can't help you beyond what I've already said. Now do the phone calls stop?"

"You also spent time with the bartender, Valentine," Lonergan said. "Anybody else?"

Cooke glared up at him, getting, as well as Foster did, the accusation in the question. "Sex wasn't a crime last time I checked, Detective."

He harrumphed. "It is if you're chargin' and settin' up shop at Teddy's."

Cooke turned red with fury. "I was not."

Foster's jaw clenched as she watched the unhappy woman fold in on herself, shame, anger, and guilt washing over her face. "I apologize for that," she said. She heard Lonergan grumble and felt him shift uneasily beside her. "Let's please continue. You left the bar around eight; the

Uber receipt has you being picked up at his place at ten thirty. It took you maybe twenty minutes to get home, then?"

Cooke avoided looking at Lonergan. "I walked in my door a little before eleven. When I said my husband was due back from a business trip, I should have said his latest mistress. It's a game we play. I pretend to believe him when he says he's working, and he couldn't care less whether I believe him or not. So I go to Teddy's. I could have stayed with Rimmer. No one would have missed me. But I wasn't having any fun, so I didn't. He was . . . unspectacular. And I was bored. Plus, he was distant. It was clear it wasn't me he wanted, but I knew that beforehand."

"What do you mean?" Foster asked.

"I had watched him at Teddy's. I could see he had eyes for the young redhead at the bar. I approached him to see if I could turn his head. Like it was a game. He admitted later that the girl he'd been watching was his ex. He was determined, he said, to win her back. I was okay with the revenge sex but underwhelmed all the same."

"He say anything else about his ex?" Lonergan asked.

Cooke looked up at him but wouldn't answer.

"Anything at all?" Foster asked. "Maybe *how* he intended to get her back?"

"Nothing about that. He never even mentioned her by name, but I knew he was hung up on her. He kept stroking my hair, touching it, winding it around his fingers. Then it dawned on me it wasn't *my* hair he was seeing but hers. He would have taken anyone home that night. I'm blonde, clearly, but he wanted my hair to be red, like hers. He kept saying, 'You'd be so beautiful with red hair.' I didn't expect any real feelings to be involved, I tucked those away a long time ago, but you'd like to think the man you're sleeping with is seeing you and not someone else."

Lonergan frowned. "You could always try sleeping with your husband."

Cooke let Lonergan's words sit, and then she stared up at him as though he were a dead thing stuck to the bottom of her designer shoes. "I could, but there'd always be three in the bed—me, him, and . . . whoever catches his eye. A secretary. A waitress. His best friend's wife." She glanced at Foster. "Is that all you need? Can I go now?"

Foster stood. "Thanks for coming in, Mrs. Cooke. We appreciate your time."

Cooke rose, pushed her chair in roughly, the legs scraping against the floor. She smiled in a nice-nasty way aimed mostly at Foster's partner. "*Mrs.* Cooke. I used to love being called that." The smile disappeared. "Now the words burn in my throat whenever I utter them."

Foster watched her leave the room, drawn in by Cooke's sadness, her emptiness. She got it, the woman's desolation, but then she pushed the feeling away and locked it out. Joe Rimmer had lied about his one-night stand. It was more like a two-hour stand, which gave him plenty of time to encounter Peggy Birch on that Riverwalk. Maybe he'd called her and they'd agreed to meet. Maybe she'd left Teddy's and then sat out on the Riverwalk to watch the water by herself, and maybe Rimmer had doubled back and found her there. All plausible.

"We need to bring that weirdo Rimmer back in," Lonergan said.

She pushed past him, furious, her fists clenched, her body tense. It was enough. He was enough. An oaf, a narrow-minded, boorish clod. At her desk, she slammed her notebook and files down and started yanking open drawers, slamming them shut again, looking for nothing but needing the noise, the slam, to keep from exploding.

Two days, that was all it had been.

"What the hell's wrong with you?" Lonergan asked.

"Don't talk to me," she said. She found her backup bottle of aspirin in the middle drawer, grabbed it, and slammed the drawer closed, the metal-on-metal contact echoing through the office. Heads turned; conversations stopped. "Do. Not. Talk. To. Me."

He smirked. "Look, Foster, if you expect me to coddle every cheap—"

She shot him a warning look. "Don't finish that sentence." She swallowed two tablets dry, her entire body shaking, the equilibrium she'd managed to maintain the last couple of days slipping. She couldn't work with this man. She'd thought she could find a way, a work-around, but she couldn't bear now to look at him with that smug, pretentious demeanor.

They weren't alone. The office was full of cops who were now watching them. She knew this. She could feel the eyes at her back. She had to think about career and impressions and reputation as well as fight to quiet the volcano simmering inside her. "You disrespected that woman," she managed, lowering her voice, burning, *burning*. "You judged her, and you were nasty about it." Her eyes moved from his face all the way down to his dusty shoes and back again. "Who died and made you arbiter of everyone else's morals? Her life is her life. How she lives it is none of your concern. We needed the timeline. That's all. Just that."

"It's people like her makin' the world such a shit show, you ask me."

"Nobody asked you. *Nobody*. Ever. You're a cop, not her judge. What's wrong with you?" She really needed to know because whatever it was didn't look like anything she or Griffin or the job or the world, for that matter, would be able to fix. Had he worked this way his entire career? How? she wondered.

"Look, Foster, I'm tryin' to get a killer off the streets. I got kids, you don't, which means I, unlike you, got skin in the game. I'm gonna do whatever I have to do, whether it comes out pretty or not is what I'm sayin'. You want all touchy feely, you need to partner with somebody else." He cocked a thumb toward the team. "Li, for instance, since you two seem to get on so well together."

Lonergan's eyes left hers and focused on something over her shoulder that straightened him up. She turned and saw Griffin standing at her door, her hands on her hips. She'd watched their exchange. "Great," he muttered. "Happy now?"

For a split second she thought of picking up her stuff and leaving. She needed a break, fresh air, peace, only she didn't have time for any of that. It felt as though she were locked in a tiny box and the box kept getting smaller. She had to fight to breathe evenly. Rimmer was a liar who was obsessed with Peggy, and he had several unaccounted hours to answer for. That was her next step. Slowly, the din in the office resumed as everyone went back to what they'd been doing. The "blowup" was over.

Skin in the game.

The words echoed in her ears. He had no idea how much skin she had. Damn him.

CHAPTER 28

The traffic light at Lower Wacker and Michigan changed from red to green without a single car or truck to pay heed or care. The canopy of steel and concrete above shut out the sky, giving the street a cavernous, otherworldly feel, as though it were some forsaken underworld or forbidden place where only devils roamed. At 2:00 a.m., there was just gloom and emptiness and the stench of sour milk, steam, and diesel. Yellow-tinted streetlights worked but did little to dispel the shadows. Not much would change when the city woke in a few hours, except for the rush of traffic clogging the street.

But now, down below, red-eyed rats darted about, foraging for left-behinds. Homeless encamped along the fringes, their makeshift tents and lean-tos huddled together against the filthy steam vents of the luxury hotels they couldn't afford to stay in. City workers, cops, routinely swept the homeless up and along so that the city wouldn't look bad to visitors who didn't know its failings. Out of sight, out of mind, the unfortunates, the troubled, as vexing to those in high places as the rats that shimmied through their sewer pipes.

This was the spot. It was the cover of half light that made it appealing. The old car slowed, then hopped the curb, pulling onto the gravel, the crunch of the tiny pebbles the only thing to disturb the stillness here. Once the trunk was popped, it was an easy pull and drag as the army-green tarp was drawn out, a pale arm escaping, red lipstick around the slender wrist. Quickly. That was how it needed to be done. As easy as emptying a trash pail or scraping mud off a shoe.

Not the ideal circumstances, not the way it would have been preferred, but in a pinch, stopgap, the improvised method would suffice. The tarp would be found in the morning. The rats would find it sooner. They'd smell the blood and the promise of a bountiful feast. It was a cycle—life, death. Everything that died got eaten.

The car drove away and left the rats their prize.

CHAPTER 29

She didn't hear Lonergan come in the next morning. She'd been at her desk for hours before her shift going over her notes, probing for inconsistencies, looking for a way forward. It wasn't until she heard his chair squeak that she looked up and saw him standing there, peeling off his overcoat. No exchange of pleasantries. They were beyond that now.

"Anything new?" he asked, taking his chair, rolling up the sleeves on his button-down shirt. All business, like nothing had happened between them the day before. They'd gone by Rimmer's apartment before clocking out last night, but there had been no sign of him. His stoned-out neighbor had no clue when he'd seen him last.

"Still on Rimmer. He's got family ties in Rensselaer," Foster replied curtly. "Maybe we won't have to go that far to track a lie."

"Well, he's not at his job," Lonergan said. "I swung by on my way in. The little twerp's AWOL. His runnin' kinda proves he's a lyin' little Zappa weasel."

"It doesn't *prove* anything," Foster said.

Lonergan stared at Foster. "We gonna talk about what went down yesterday or not? I figure you'd want to clear the air or somethin'."

If she'd thought talking would do any good, she might have gone for it, but she didn't see Lonergan changing, and she certainly didn't see herself changing to accommodate him. "We find Rimmer," she said. "We keep things moving."

Lonergan stood. "All right, then let's go run this prick to ground. He's startin' to piss me off."

Griffin's door flew open, and she came barreling out of her office. "Body!" Her angry eyes scanned the office. "Foster. Lonergan. Lower Michigan. Move it! We got another one."

Foster quickly gathered up her things, Lonergan grabbed his coat, and they were off.

Another one.

———

Just forty-eight hours from Peggy Birch's discovery, and Foster was squatting over another body, another white female. Rosales stepped back and waited for her to take a closer look while Lonergan walked gingerly around the body lying naked on a tarp, his face grim, his jaw set. The young woman had been stabbed repeatedly, like Peggy, but much worse. There were more wounds. They looked deeper; the tarp was a bloody mess. The musty smell of death was no longer a shock to Foster's system. She had long ago inured herself to that, and if she lived to be a hundred, she would never forget it.

Two patrol officers stood close while the evidence techs did what they were supposed to.

"Dumped here," Lonergan said. "Not killed here. No drag marks. The tarp doesn't look beat up."

Foster stared into the still eyes. They were half-open, fixed, no light or life in them. Blue eyes. "Who found her?"

The shorter of the two POs took a step forward but not too close. He looked a little green but made an effort to keep his eyes on Foster, not on the tarp. "Officer Perez." He pointed to his partner. "Officer Malcolm and I were passing around zero eight hundred. Traffic was just starting to pick up. We thought it could be one of the homeless sleeping rough, so we stopped to move him along." His eyes darted to the dead woman, then away. "It wasn't. We called it in."

"Thanks," she said, watching as Perez stepped back, clearly relieved to be doing so. The woman looked to be in her late twenties, thin, naked, and she was wearing a red wig. Not a clownish, Halloween red but a sedate, natural-looking red. In fact, anyone would likely take her for a natural redhead were it not for the wisps of brown hair sticking out around her ears and forehead.

Foster stood, stepped back, eyed Rosales. "Time of death?"

"I'd put it at around one a.m., but she's been laying here about six, seven hours. Lividity tells the tale. The timing gave the rats a chance to get at her a bit, as you can see. You see the lipstick rings? Same as the first body. Might even be the same shade, but I'm no expert."

"More damage this time," Foster said. "More anger played out."

Rosales gently lifted the woman's right arm and turned her hand palm up. "We have an ID on her already."

"You found a bag?" Lonergan asked.

"No. What you see is what we found, but we got prints, and hers are in the system. She's Mallory Rea, twenty-eight. Arrested twice in 2017 for trespassing and damage to private property. A lab that experimented on animals. She was part of an animal activist group."

Foster stared down at Rea, the activist, at the wig. It bothered her. Manner of death similar to Birch's, only more violent, more inhumane. Type of victim similar, both young white women. Both activists—Birch for police reform, Rea for animal rights. Could that be the connection? Was some twisted killer out here murdering women with a social conscience? Even the location of Rea's body dump was close to where Birch had been found. And something else, something immediately noticeable. The red hair, though Rea wore a wig and Birch's hair was natural. Foster got a queasy feeling as she noted the pattern forming. "Right. Okay. Let's get her out of this tarp and back to her people as quickly as we can."

"Oh, great," Lonergan grumbled. "The circus has arrived."

Foster turned to see at least a half dozen news vans parked outside the yellow tape. Reporters—some she recognized, some she didn't—getting ready with mics and cell phones, cameras and lights. She motioned to Perez and Malcolm. "Move them back out of camera range, please. Keep them there. I don't want them getting anything they can splash all over the morning news."

"Good luck with that," Lonergan sniped. "Two bodies? They're gonna be all over us like ants at a picnic."

"An odd thing," Rosales said, leaning over to expose the woman's thigh. "A spot of dried blood about the size of a dime. It's not splatter or contact residue. It looks deliberately placed." The photographer eased in, snapping away at every angle. Rosales stood and scanned worried eyes around the scene. The tarp held mysteries for all of them. "As always, we'll know more later."

"A spot," Lonergan said, glaring at Foster, "like on Ainsley's jacket." He paused to let the implication sit. "And he and Rimmer, who's got a thing for red hair and whose ex is one of our victims, they're both free as birds."

"I've got no problem circling back to him," Foster said. "He may be able to tell us more now."

Lonergan pulled his eyes away from Foster's to stare at Rea. "Let's cover her up. Give her some dignity, huh?"

His sudden show of sensitivity surprised her.

"Don't look so shocked, Foster." Lonergan scowled, then turned and walked off, pulling his phone out of his pocket to make a call.

Rosales's brows lifted. "Shocked me too."

Foster stood by for quite a while watching the crime scene photographer record the scene. Two victims now. When the techs were through, when they'd done all they could for Mallory Rea, she stepped back and looked around for Lonergan. They needed to get moving. "Quick as you can, huh, Rosales? Thanks."

———

The Ainsleys weren't too happy to find the detectives on their doorstep.

"Oh, so now the harassment starts?" George Ainsley said as he stood in the doorway dressed for the office in an expensive suit, a designer watch the size of an old Kennedy half dollar on his wrist, looking every bit the successful lawyer paid thousands by billable hour.

He matched the neighborhood and the block, where the houses were big and quaint, where there were trees instead of gangways, family homes instead of drug dens.

"We'd like to speak with Keith," Foster said.

"Better here than . . . you know," Lonergan added.

George Ainsley smiled. It was a lawyer smile. The kind that oozed confidence, the kind that gave them reputations for being sharks and the devourers of imbeciles. It broadcast disdain without the man having to say a word. The elder Ainsley opened his mouth to tell Lonergan where to go, but Foster warded off what she imagined would have been a blistering retort.

"Just a short conversation," she said. "You'll be there. A few minutes and we're out. There've been developments."

They stood for almost a full minute before George stood back and let them in. "Ten minutes. Starting now."

Keith Ainsley looked years older than the last time she'd seen him, wearier. His shoulders drooped, his skin looked dull, rough, and there were dark circles under his eyes. He obviously had not been sleeping. Or eating much, Foster assumed, as he stood before her with hollow cheeks, his eyes averted. It'd only been a couple of days since the Riverwalk. But it was a lot being handcuffed, questioned, and suspected of murder, even when you had lawyers for parents.

"Where were you last night, Keith? Around one a.m., specifically," Foster asked when they were all assembled in the well-turned-out living room. The room smelled of oranges and flowers, and everything was light, bright, and expensive looking—the sofa, end chairs, coffee table, and lamps—all in the traditional style. There was also a shiny baby grand piano near a large wood-burning fireplace, and Foster wondered which of the Ainsleys played it. She stared at Keith, tucked between his parents, on the couch opposite her and Lonergan.

"Don't answer that," George said. "What developments?"

"A woman was found murdered this morning," Foster said. "Stabbed like Peggy Birch. Her body discovered not far from the Riverwalk."

"Keith was here all night," Carole Ainsley blurted out, knowing full well where this was all going.

"Yeah, we're kinda gonna have to hear that from him," Lonergan said in his nice-nasty way, which Foster knew would put the Ainsleys off. It took less than three seconds to have that confirmed.

"You're hearing it from us," George hissed. "He was home. He's been home since he was released. You have another murder?" He cocked his head toward his son. "He's not your guy."

Foster scooted forward on the sofa, cleared her throat. "There's the matter of blood. There was a spot found on Keith's jacket. It turned out not to be Peggy Birch's or his."

"Which is why you can't connect him to any crime," Carole said, anger building. "So why are you *here*?"

Foster waited a second to see if Lonergan weighed in. He did not. "There was a similar spot of blood on our second victim. It hints at a connection. If Keith remembers a little more about Sunday, maybe he can help us figure out where the blood came from." Her eyes locked onto Carole Ainsley's. Foster could see the fear in the woman's eyes. She was fighting for her kid's life. The outrage was just the part the world saw.

Foster sat quietly as the three Ainsleys conferred, their heads close together, their voices reduced to gruff whispers. Two murders ramped things up. The unanswered question of the unidentified blood on Keith's jacket, its similarity to the blood found on Rea's thigh, kept him in the frame. Though inwardly she felt for Keith and could see the toll all of this had taken on him, she had two killings to contend with. If there was even a possibility that he held the key to understanding it all, she needed him to tell her.

The conferring stopped. The Ainsleys' heads separated, and all three glared at Foster and Lonergan. A united front. Keith flicked a look at his parents and got dual nods back. Foster's heart raced.

"I can't tell you anything else about Sunday," Keith said. "But for the other time you're talking about, I was playing *Mortal Kombat.*"

Lonergan laughed. "You what? By yourself? All night?"

"Online with a friend. Jean-Pierre. He's in Paris. Maybe we played a few hours, not all night. But I never left my house."

Foster let a beat go. *Mortal Kombat.* Reggie used to play it. "Did you record your game?" she asked. He nodded. "Show us?"

Keith checked with his parents, then got up and left the room, and the temperature, already frigid, dropped another thousand degrees, the contemptuous looks from the Ainsleys as corrosive as acid tossed on a marshmallow. Foster was sure they got Lonergan. He wasn't a deep well. Foster was the one they looked at as though she'd ratted them out to slave catchers. But she didn't wither under their stares. She hadn't a single ax to grind. On the contrary, she was making sure Keith got the same benefit of the doubt everybody else got.

"You know, we didn't come lookin' for your son just for kicks," Lonergan said. "He was *there.* We're just supposed to ignore that?"

George Ainsley sat as cold as death itself. "This is probably the first place you came when you found the second woman, isn't it? Keith's name was the one and only that popped into your head, despite the fact you've got nothing on him."

"We're pursuin' all avenues," Lonergan said. "*You* explain the blood."

"You know what's at stake," Carole said, and she said it directly to Foster.

Foster didn't answer because she didn't have to. Carole Ainsley hadn't asked a question; she'd made a statement. And she knew full well Foster knew exactly what the stakes were.

Keith returned moments later carrying a laptop with a caduceus on the lid. Seated between his parents again, he cued up the recording, let it play, and then swiveled the laptop around so Foster and Lonergan could see it. Foster leaned closer. The game was a noisy clash of chains and crossbows, swords, and weirdly dressed alien-like characters hurling fireballs and jumping all over the place, the action fast and loud and incomprehensible to the average adult. She asked Keith to run it through to the end so that she could see how long he'd played, then pause it there so she could note the elapsed time. She didn't know how the whole thing worked, but she could clearly see that Keith had been playing the game with someone.

"And your opponent in this is Jean-Pierre?" she asked.

"Yeah," Keith said.

She underlined the time the game ended. Twelve thirty-nine a.m. Local. It didn't matter what that translated to in Paris. Jean-Pierre wasn't her concern, but to be thorough, she asked, "Last name?"

"Bernard. We started about nine thirty last night and played for about three hours. JP's got insomnia. I haven't been sleeping that much either lately."

"Would you mind running it again?" Foster asked.

As the game replayed, Foster focused on the time in the right-hand corner, watching as the digital numbers advanced seconds at a time. The game had lasted two hours and forty-seven minutes precisely, followed by a two-minute sign-off, taking place at the very time Mallory Rea was thought to have been killed.

"Nothing says that laptop was in this house," Lonergan said.

George Ainsley stood. "Keith never left the house; neither did that laptop. You have his statement. You have your proof. You need anything more, we'll do it officially and by the numbers. You come back again, you'd better have a warrant for his arrest and a lot more than you have now."

The door slamming behind them was as definitive as a rough toss-out could be, but there was no time to feel any way about it. "It's not him," Foster said, sliding into the passenger seat of their unmarked car. She braced for the argument.

Lonergan started the car. "I agree. That nerd video thing . . . hard to play that and kill a person at the same time."

He pulled away from the curb. Foster clicked her seat belt and settled back. "And finally, there is light."

CHAPTER 30

Rimmer was on the run, and every cop in the city was on the lookout for him. Foster didn't think he was smart enough to evade them for long, though. It was only a matter of time. She wasn't sure he was a killer, but he was definitely a liar. That was what they needed to talk about.

Meanwhile, they finally had the footage of the Riverwalk from Sunday night. The camera dump from Lower Wacker where Rea had been thrown away would take a bit more time, though less than it would have normally, given that they now had two deaths to solve. Nothing got city wheels turning faster than the threat of bad press and the possibility that someone would sue the city for allowing a murderer to run free. The boss's office was busier than usual with brass racing in and out looking for assurances that CPD was making progress. The visits, the jumpiness, no doubt prompted by threatening calls from the fifth floor of city hall. What she and the team didn't need was for the trickle-down heat, the hot potato, to get passed off to them, though she knew full well it would.

Lonergan had disappeared again.

"He left you to do the hard work again, I see?"

Foster looked up to find Li standing there. "At this point, I'm thankful for the alone time."

Li glanced at the screen. "That's from the Riverwalk?" She slid over the empty chair from the next desk over.

"Yes, I'm running through it looking for . . . anything," Foster said. "These murders. They're out of the norm and obviously linked. Ainsley's accounted for. He's clear. Rimmer's still a question mark, but if the breakup with Birch was his motive, how's that explain Mallory Rea? Did he break up with her too? The color of both women's hair might be something. Rimmer was hung up on Peggy's, according to Cooke. But Rea's hair was fake."

Li scooted her chair closer to the desk and Foster's screen. "So we're looking for someone else. Roll it. Let's see. Or would you rather wait for Lonergan?"

She slid Li a look. "Like that would ever be a thing."

Foster started the playback. Two hours went by. Slowly, they advanced through the frames, freezing the image when a person strolled into camera view. Though the footage was black and white and bathed in shadows, they could clearly see that none matched Birch. There was also no sign of Rimmer or Ainsley. Foster kept tabs on the elapsed time in the lower right corner as Sunday night crept closer to Monday morning. At 11:00 p.m. she found herself leaning in closer to the screen. Li did the same. "Here we go," Foster said.

Frame by frame, one fuzzy image after another. Until there it was, at three minutes after 11:00 p.m., a weaving figure entered from the left. Male. Dark. Unsteady on his feet, as if drunk. "From the direction of the marina," Foster muttered. "Where he said he was. Same clothes. The jacket."

"That's Ainsley, all right," Li said.

They watched as the figure they presumed to be Keith Ainsley flumped down at the base of the bridge. After a few seconds, his head fell to his chest and stayed there. "He's out," Foster said.

"Keep it rolling," Li said.

Foster kept her eyes on Ainsley, on the stairs, on the path, on the time as it ticked off on the counter. At four minutes after midnight, two dark figures descended the stairs from Michigan Avenue onto the

Riverwalk, one with a backpack and long hair, one dressed in dark clothing, a large duffel slung over their shoulder.

Li pointed at the screen. "There's Birch."

Foster's eyes were glued to the screen. Keith hadn't moved. "That could be Rimmer. This person has a slim build. Five eight, five nine?" Foster stopped the footage to get a good look at the bag. "The bag worries me."

"You know who walks around with a duffel at midnight?" Li said.

"Killers," Foster answered glumly. "Could be his kit."

Li looked up. "She doesn't look like she's being forced."

"Killers can be disarming." Foster started the tape again, but the pair was out of view. She quickly cued up the footage from a different camera mounted farther east, clicking through, not finding Birch and the stranger. "We lose them somewhere between the first camera and this one," she said.

"In-between's where she was found," Li said.

Foster advanced the tape slowly until the dark figure showed up again forty minutes later with the duffel, heading toward Keith Ainsley. Alone.

Li shot up from her chair. "Holy shit!"

The talk and bustle of the squad stopped, and cops gathered around them, including, she noted, Griffin. Foster rewound the footage, started back at the critical moment, and narrated for everyone, her heart beating so loudly she would swear cops in the next room could hear it.

"Ainsley, first," Foster said, "then Birch with someone else. This camera picks him up at a little after eleven. There." She stopped the image, pointed at the time, then played it again. "From the marina." She started again. "And there. He weaves by. Stops. Watch his head fall."

"No knife visible," Li noted. "That's a good shot of him under the lights." Everyone drew in closer. "He's unsteady on his feet."

"Now wait." Foster started the footage again, and everyone watched as it picked up the two dark figures, one with a backpack, one with the duffel, as they moved into the frame. "They walk toward the marina. Nothing changes for a time. Then forty minutes later, one figure walks back, not Birch, and stops at Ainsley. He squats down, and—" Foster freezes the footage at the point it captures the figure's arm outstretched toward Keith. "He touches his jacket." She turned to the team. "And what'd we find on Ainsley's jacket? Blood."

"We don't see a knife, but it doesn't mean he didn't have one," Kelley said. "He's got pockets."

"They tested his jacket six ways from Sunday," Foster said. "No blood trace in the pockets. Only that one spot." She turned back to the screen. "Put there by that guy."

"Aww man," Symansky said. "The scumbag framed the kid?"

"If it was supposed to be a frame," Foster said, "it would've been Peggy's blood. Something else is going on. But this proves Ainsley was in no condition to kill Birch. Someone unknown made direct contact with him, presumably Birch's killer."

"Then what the hell?" Kelley said. "Whose blood are we looking at?"

Li slumped down in her chair. "Honestly, I'm almost afraid to find out."

"This could be Rimmer," Foster said. "Birch wouldn't have been afraid to walk with him along the Riverwalk in the middle of the night, I don't think."

"Hey, what's up?"

The team turned to find Lonergan standing at the fringes of the huddle.

"Where've you been?" Griffin asked, none too gently.

Lonergan had the good sense to squirm a little under Griffin's glare. "Tryin' to track down Rimmer. What's all this?"

Griffin wasn't letting it go. The team stood holding its collective breath as the boss stared into Lonergan's eyes and gave him time to absorb the heat. "I didn't get a heads-up you were going out solo.

Neither did your partner, I suspect. You do know we're up against it here? That we've got two dead women?"

"I figured divide and conquer. Foster's on the tape. I thought I'd try and get a line on him."

"And did you?" Griffin's eyes held his. "Get a line."

"One of the coffee shop kids had a name of one of Rimmer's band-mates. I tracked him down. He didn't know where Rimmer was, but he did tell me the band cut ties with him the day we talked to him. He was too much of a showboat, apparently. Hogging all the limelight. I got a name of a pal he might be crashing with to keep off our radar. Foster and I can run it down."

"Nuh-uh," Griffin cut him off. She turned to Foster and Li, pointed at the screen. "Have you two gotten through all that?"

"Not yet," Foster said. "We've just made it a bit past midnight. I think if we roll it back a couple hours before and a couple hours after we—"

Griffin interrupted her. "Finish it. But first, Foster, my office. Li, keep looking." She turned and walked away on angry heels.

Foster walked into Griffin's office on a high. They were making progress, finally. So why was she in Griffin's office losing momentum? "Boss?"

Griffin sat down at her messy desk. "I'm teaming you with Li. I want you working full force, and Lonergan's a burr under my saddle."

"What? Boss, I can deal with Lonergan," Foster said. "We're not children."

Griffin looked up at her through narrowed eyes. "As a team, you're inefficient. I can't have inefficient right now with brass breathing down my neck. That's all."

The elation Foster had felt just seconds ago was gone, popped like a balloon at a three-year-old's birthday party. She turned for the door, her feet not wanting to get there.

"Li isn't Thompson, Foster," Griffin said to her back as she opened the door. "Send Lonergan in."

How quickly lows followed highs, Foster thought as she made her way back to her desk. A step forward, one back. A climb to a steep summit, only to have someone knock you off it. Two partners in less than a week. The start of another climb. A new record for her, one she hoped she wouldn't have to break. Li was still at it. "Anything?"

"Not yet," Li said, not bothering to look up.

Foster looked over at Lonergan, glowering at his desk. "Boss wants to see you."

He bristled, stood, adjusted his belt. "Goin' to the woodshed."

When he walked away, Foster watched him go, feeling oddly sympathetic.

"So it's you and me," Li said, sliding Foster a look and a sly grin. She held out a hand for Foster to shake. "Formally. Detective Vera Li." To Foster's confused look, she added, "Griffin might have hinted a shuffle was coming. Back at the hot dog. I was testing the waters." Li jabbed a thumb toward Griffin's door. "She sees all, knows all. We good?"

Lonergan stormed out of Griffin's office in a cloud of invisible steam and glared at Foster from across the room. "Kelley, it's you and me," he shouted. "We got Rimmer's buddy. A lead *I* dug up." Kelley's face fell as he grabbed his jacket. "Meet you in the car," Lonergan barked. "I'm drivin'."

Foster turned back to Li. "We finish the footage. Grant's expediting the Rea autopsy, so we have that in the morning. Hopefully we find something there. That work for you?"

Li was already sitting. "Way ahead of you, partner."

But after more than an hour, there was nothing else of significance on the footage. Whoever had walked with Peggy carrying that duffel bag had been smart and careful and cunning. That didn't sound like Joe Rimmer, but he couldn't be counted out yet.

Foster flipped through her notebook. "I found a family address for Rimmer in Indiana. His parents and a younger brother are there. Maybe he—"

Symansky yelled from across the office. "Foster. Li. Your lucky day. Unis found Rimmer. They're bringing him in now. I should call Lonergan back in . . . but I'm not gonna. Let him work up a sweat for once."

Foster looked over at Li, who was smiling from ear to ear. "What?"

"You don't know this yet," Li said, "but I'm a bit of a good-luck charm. You're welcome."

"Anything else I should know about you?"

"Absolutely, but I'd rather surprise you."

CHAPTER 31

Rimmer sat nervously across the table from them, his clownish attempts to conceal his identity laughable. The man bun was gone, his greasy hair cut short and dyed white, and he'd shaved his face as smooth as a baby's bottom. He looked about twelve. But his eyes were still glassy. He obviously hadn't given up his affinity for herbals.

"Headed to Minneapolis. By train. That's a new one on us," Li said, not bothering to hide the sarcasm. "Spur-of-the-moment decision, was it?"

"I have a gig up there, okay?"

"Where exactly?" Foster asked.

"A bar. Small space. But it's a hot spot. Some cool bands play there."

Foster picked up her pen, held it over her notebook. "Which bar?"

"And which band?" Li asked. "Because your old one cut you loose."

"So I go solo. I don't need those guys. They're small time, anyway. The point I need to make here is that I did nothing to hurt Peg in any way, all right? I don't get why I'm here."

"You lied to us," Foster said. "Your pickup from Teddy's can only vouch for you until about ten thirty Sunday night. What'd you do after she left? Where'd you go? And if you don't have anything to hide, why are we looking at you with dyed hair, a shaved chin, and a train ticket in your pocket?"

Rimmer's eyes rabbited around the room. He began to bounce in his chair like he had to pee. "Okay, look, I lied about the woman, but

I didn't want you thinking I did something when I didn't. I know how it looks, me breaking up with Peg, her ending up dead, but you got the wrong guy. I figured I'd head out of town and give you cops a chance to do some work for once and find that out for yourselves." He looked over at Li, whose face gave nothing away. Foster watched as his Adam's apple slid up and down on his throat. "No offense," he added.

"That's the dumbest move I've ever heard of," Li said.

Rimmer dropped his head to the table, his forehead to the metal top. "I know this looks bad. You don't think I know it's bad?" He lifted his head up. "But it's not me. It looks like it could be me, but I swear, I left that bar and never went back. You got a Bible? Bring it in here. I'll swear up and down on it all day."

Li laid a photo array of young women on the table, Mallory Rea's driver's license photo included. "You recognize any of these women?"

Rimmer took a look. "I have never laid eyes on any of them in my life." He gave them the three-fingered scout sign. "Swear to all the gods—Buddha, Jehovah, Raijin—"

"Where did you go after your date left?" Li asked. "And before you lie, know that we've got video of you walking out of your place right after she ditched you. Street cameras." Foster slid Li a look. She knew of no such video.

Rimmer let out a frustrated growl. He was cornered, caught. He bounced more. "Weed. All right? I was selling weed. I've got a side hustle, okay? After what's-her-name left, I got on it. And it wasn't like I could cop to that, could I? I don't exactly look like a dispensary, do I?"

"Where were you selling?" Foster asked.

He shook his head emphatically. "No way. Far as I go on that."

"Would you rather get dinged for the weed or as a possible suspect in a homicide?" Foster asked.

Li leaned forward, whispering across the table. "Be smart. Go for the weed."

"Another reason I was skipping town. Exactly this. You guys get a sniff of something and latch on like leeches. I figured the train station was safe; I mean, who hangs out at the train station?" He rolled his eyes. "The one time one of you is not somewhere eating a cruller."

"We're going to need the name of your weed guy," Foster said. "And anyone else who can place you."

"Or?" Rimmer asked, his eyes moving from Li's to Foster's.

Foster flipped the page in her notebook. "Your date said you made an interesting comment about her hair. She said you twisted it, caressed it, and remarked that you wished it were red instead of blonde. Red, like Peggy's. Odd thing to say."

"Really odd," Li said.

"I sold a couple of bags to Monk in the cemetery on Irving Park Road," he blurted out. "Around eleven. Then I went back home. When I heard about the second girl, I knew I'd be the one you guys would be looking for, so I knew I had to bounce. My buddy Blake cut my hair, his girl Caroline helped me dye it, and I made for the station. I figured you guys would be too busy to check, right? Bigger fish and all that?"

Foster slid over a legal pad and pen for Rimmer. "Write down their full names, addresses, and phone numbers, please."

"Even Monk's?"

Foster let a beat pass. "*Especially* Monk's."

Li sat stone faced, watching Rimmer sweat and wrestle with his predicament. Rimmer flicked her a look every second or two. "What's wrong with *her*?" he asked Foster.

Foster looked over at Li, then turned to smile at Rimmer. "Nothing. Names, addresses, and telephone numbers."

———

They needed the rest of the afternoon to confirm it all, but the info checked out—the haircut, the dyeing, even the Sunday-night weed selling. Joe Rimmer was an infant in a man's body, a weed pusher, a lousy boyfriend, a disappointing lay, but he couldn't have killed Peggy, and they didn't yet know enough about Rea to push him on that. As Foster suspected, Li's mention of the video had been a ruse to get Rimmer talking. He'd also agreed to a DNA swab before they let him go, so at least they had that if they needed to match it to any physical evidence left behind on Rea. It was the best they could do.

Li looked up from her computer at 9:00 p.m., well past end of shift. "That's it. My eyes are crossing. I'm going home to kiss my baby." She stood, stretched. "Before he forgets what I look like and starts calling someone else Mama."

Foster checked her watch. She hadn't realized it was so late. She'd eaten nothing but frustration and a McDonald's side salad all evening. "See you in the morning."

Li slipped on her jacket. "What about you? There's nothing else we can do tonight."

"I won't be much longer," Foster said.

Li hesitated. "Okay, then. *Mañana.*"

Foster watched her go. "Right."

CHAPTER 32

The lights were on in the loft apartment. The windows were hers. It was late but not too late. A little after ten. Why were all the lights on? Why wasn't she asleep in bed? She was an adult, of course, no longer a child, so bedtimes were long ago a thing of the past. Still. The trees across the street provided good cover, though the bench was hard and cold on a cool, crisp night. It was easy enough to sit and wait and watch her pass back and forth in front of the windows, not knowing anyone was watching. Maybe she was expecting company? That would be interesting. Maybe she was worrying a problem and couldn't sleep, pacing the floor hoping to find a solution.

How alive she was, how striking. An artist. Of course. The creative mind was truly a marvel. To have in one's nature and in one's very bones the conjurer's art of transformation, the ability to cobble beauty from nothing or turn light to dark or the reverse.

Art was humanity in reflection. It was invention and God spark, both expression and divination. Was she thinking about these things now? Had she ever thought about the origins of her strength? About how deep the power to transform ran and how far it could go? There was an indomitability in sea change and mightiness in a creator's hand. Did she know this yet? Sense it?

The lights flicked off. The windows went dark. Bed, or . . . ? No. Amelia emerged from the building moments later dressed in a leather moto jacket and tight jeans. Art in motion. She slid into a sleek silver convertible parked at the curb. It suited her. Like a modern-day *Argo* sailing off toward adventure and glory. Pleasing. Truly. She revved the engine, checked herself in the rearview, and sped away. Where was she off to, this goddess, this Diana, this originator? This learner, this tyro.

A slow whistling started, unhurried, unfazed. It echoed in the still night. *Someone to watch over me.* Fitting. An inside joke. There was time yet. All the pieces weren't yet assembled but soon would be. Everything had its season. Turn, turn, turn. No need to rush.

CHAPTER 33

She'd meant to only drive around, get some air, feed her soul, but she'd somehow ended up in front of Bodie's apartment watching the sleeping block as though it were a job she was being paid for, as though she alone were responsible for all the messed-up lives sleeping in the city, not just her brother's. As though she alone were the sentinel, the one who kept the brakes on.

When she went out, it was to cleanse her palate, to invigorate her mind, to stimulate her so that she could paint and, by painting, move the world around. Despite what Bodie had told her, she knew that peace and quiet were not what brought him out at night. Bodie didn't get things right. He was like a pair of mismatched shoes or a wrong-way driver on the interstate. Odd. Out of sync.

Amelia parked across the street and waited without a single guarantee that Bodie would venture out. She could just go up and ring his bell, and they could talk, but she knew Bodie would lie, and she knew she would let him because Bodie needed those lies to live.

Eleven thirty p.m. That was when he walked out of the building and turned east toward Lincoln Park. It would be empty this time of night, Amelia knew, which she supposed was why Bodie chose it. She slipped out of the car and followed at a distance, across the street, head down, collar up, with an itch of eagerness and a fair share of apprehension coursing through her.

She'd followed Bodie before. Bodie had been her job for as long as she could remember, even when he ventured far away and bounced back again, and now, after the girls, the roof, and Westhaven. After the death of that young woman on the Riverwalk.

He always headed toward the park. Some nights he stayed in, but there weren't too many of those. Bodie was a creature of habit. He liked routine, predictability, structure, which she'd always thought made him a prime candidate for institutionalization, though once there, he rebelled against the confinement. Odd. He was like a restless cat, always caught on the wrong side of a door. Amelia chalked it up to a wide streak of Morgan disquiet, inherited from their father, a complicated man—an unsolved puzzle, she suspected, even to himself. And as far as inheritances were concerned, well, disquiet was the lesser of evils.

She lasered in on Bodie's back as he turned onto Cannon Drive and passed under the stone arch of the Grant Monument, good old Ulysses sitting atop his horse, the moon shining down on the weathered bronze. A few late-night dog walkers passed, pulling scrawny rescues along behind them, their phones in hand, texting or watching videos, oblivious to everyone around them.

The monument was as far as she knew she could safely go. If she followed him onto the pedestrian path, he'd surely look back and see her. But she knew his route and knew he'd be back this way, so she picked a bench off the path, behind a tree, and she waited, burrowed into her jacket. The temperature was dropping, and the lake nearby smelled like a wet dog, but the gentle whoosh of the water, a dark, undulating void from where she sat, lulled her into an almost Zen-like state. Forty minutes. That was how long Bodie would take. It wasn't the walk that worried her so much; it was what came after.

She drew back when she heard footsteps approaching from the path. It was Bodie, and it was too soon, barely a half hour since he'd disappeared down the path. She watched from behind the tree as he moved past her, then watched as he stopped in his tracks a good distance from her and just stood there, his hands in his pockets, his chin up, face toward the moon. What was he doing? It wasn't until he began walking again that she allowed herself to breathe. Discovered? Did he somehow know she was there?

She gave him an extra-long lead, then crossed the street and followed him back, tracking him all the way to the bars along Lincoln Avenue, watching as he slipped into one under blinking neon lights. He chose a different one each night. This one was just a block north of his apartment. This was how he had gotten into trouble before. Amelia knew that he would emerge near closing with a woman on his arm. A last-call consolation who'd walk back to his place on liquored-up legs. It shouldn't have been her business, but it was. Amelia was in no position even to judge, seeing as she and Bodie shared the same predilection.

But her brother always took things too far.

She waited across the street, keeping an eye on the door of the bar for Bodie and his date, watching the street as hip bar hoppers in their messy twenties strolled the sidewalk or swayed at the curb waiting for Ubers. Why had Bodie stopped back there on the path? He'd never done that before.

She had an hour to think about it, tucked into the littered doorway of a closed shoe-repair shop, before Bodie reappeared with a young woman, far younger, she noted, than he was. Thin, tipsy, not drunk. She flitted around him like a firefly kissing the flames of a campfire. She appeared up for a good time. A pink feather boa fluttered in the night air as she pulled her coat tight and her floppy hat down, very Janis Joplin–esque.

They started walking toward Bodie's place. Amelia followed. She followed them all the way back and waited until they went inside, then hung around until the lights flicked on in his apartment, then went out in the bedroom. A glance at her watch. Just a little after one.

She was cold, damp, and so she called it, confident that Bodie would stay put for a while. There was a bar she knew, one that was open until 4:00 a.m., so she headed there. She wasn't seeking company, though she wouldn't turn it away if she found it. Amelia needed inspiration to feed her artistic nature. She needed life.

CHAPTER 34

Dr. Mariana Silva couldn't sleep. She hadn't slept a single night through since Bodie Morgan had walked out of Westhaven and away from her three days ago. Truthfully, she hadn't had an untortured night for years, her mind too busy to shut off, vengefulness and a sense of urgency feeding the fire in her belly. How dare they? She had been the best in her field, the leading authority. Years of study, years of sacrifice and dedication, and it was gone, important doors closed in her face, like she was no one.

She paced the floors of her home office, her curtains opened to the middle of the night, an entire city beyond her windows, not caring if she lived or died. She was the best. Her research on psychopathy, her findings, were being taught in medical schools all over the world, but here she was. Stuck at insignificant Westhaven, a hellhole far beneath her, unworthy of her talents. They said she'd breached protocol, overstepped her bounds, gone way too far. They were wrong. She hadn't gone far enough. She'd been on the brink, the very precipice of a breakthrough, only to have everything blow up in her face. Colleagues she respected suddenly refused to acknowledge her, and she discovered that she had no friends. She'd given everything to the advancement of science, and it had given her destruction in return.

But she had a plan. A book. Something to prove that Dr. Mariana Silva was still a force to be reckoned with. Her book on antisocial personality disorders with case studies highlighted to prove her theories would transform the psychiatric field and return her to her rightful place. And when she got there, when she was back, there would be hell to pay for those who'd cast her out.

The book was where Bodie Morgan came in. She had known him the moment he'd sat down across from her in their first session at Westhaven. She was enthralled by his brokenness and hungry to plumb its depths. He sought out women, coveted them, yet feared them. Silva found the broken a complex wonder, an intriguing excavation project, one she'd chosen over a personal life of her own. What could a husband and children give her that picking through a twisted mind could not?

Stravinsky wafted out of her stereo speakers as she stared out her window at the Chicago skyline and the desolate ribbon of Lake Shore Drive lit up below. Even this city didn't deserve her. She was languishing here, dying on the vine, treating mild depressives and bipolars when she was made for much, much more. But the book and Bodie Morgan were her ticket out. All she needed was a plan, a way forward.

She could think of little else but that bogus childhood he'd tried to sell her. He an only child growing up with doting, loving parents on a quiet farm somewhere in Indiana. The two long years at university before striking out on his own. She chuckled unpleasantly now as she recalled it. Oh, it was stress, he'd said, that had driven him to the roof of his building, loneliness that led him to follow those women. Who did he think he was talking to? She sipped her wine, drew the curtains. He thought her a fool, just some hack at an insignificant hospital who couldn't see what was right in front of her. That's why she'd authorized that day pass. It was an experiment. She wanted to see how angry he got, how frustrated, at having a taste of freedom, only to have it yanked away and then quickly restored. Delayed gratification. Stress. Manipulation.

She turned from the window, set her glass on her desk, and pulled back the panels that covered a wide, tall corkboard. Quietly, she lifted a pair of scissors from her desk, picked up the morning's paper, and cut out the article on Mallory Rea's murder. Carefully, she cut around the photo of the lovely young woman who'd been found on Lower Wacker, not far from the first woman, Peggy Birch, the one with the pretty red hair.

How their mothers must be suffering, she thought as she worked the scissors around the two-column piece on the front page. Two deaths. Two young women. Few details, but she didn't really need them. The moment she'd seen Peggy Birch's photograph, she'd known. Such a pretty girl. The kind Bodie was drawn to, the type he preferred. The second woman didn't fit. Silva stared at her photo, the brown hair, the blue eyes. What had drawn him to her? It was likely even he didn't know. She would get the answer, though, when she had him back.

She used pushpins to tack the article on Rea up on the corkboard. The photo she'd secretly taken of Bodie Morgan was pinned next to it, along with an index card with his address. That would be her next move, an in-person appeal, an earnest offer of help. When she had him, she would study him, use him, help him, for science and for herself.

Stepping back to study the board, she took it all in, the drama shaping up before her. The articles on Birch and Rea were pinned by red pushpins. The locations where they'd been found were pinned by blue pins. Cop blue. She thought it fitting. Her head angled as she stared at the black-and-white photo of the female detective caught sweeping past the cameras and reporters at one of the murder scenes. Identified as Detective Harriet Foster, she was one of the lead investigators on the cases. Was she up to it? Silva wondered. She looked serious enough, determined, but she was up against a predator, and that required an extra gear. She searched for signs, tells, that Foster had that extra gear, but she wouldn't know until she looked directly into her eyes, until she could see what she was made of. That was Silva's talent, her calling.

"Detective Harriet Foster," she muttered, "I can't wait to meet you."

CHAPTER 35

It was close to 2:00 a.m., and Foster should have gone home, but instead she walked along the Riverwalk listening to the city breathe and groan, whistle and sigh. Down here by the water, now that the frenzy of tourists and joggers and lookie-loos had gone, the quiet canyon of glass and steel was peaceful, the buildings and skyscrapers ringed around it steady watchers, lighted guardians as imposing as any rock formation.

She could see Teddy's across the water, with its exterior lights on but closed for business. There was no one walking with her, no one else on the Riverwalk. She doubted it would have been any different at the same time on Sunday night as Peggy Birch had lain slaughtered and Keith Ainsley had slept. Peggy had come down here with someone. She'd walked down those steps of her own volition. It wasn't Rimmer or Stroman, Dean or Keith Ainsley. On the video, she hadn't appeared distressed; that dark figure hadn't clutched her by the arm. Foster stopped and turned slowly in a circle. "Why here?"

Foster glanced at the decorative trees and the puny bushes where Peggy had been discovered. No clothes. Her backpack floating. No cell phone. Leaves. The sound of Foster's hard-sole shoes echoed on the path as she made her way east toward the marina, smelling of wet earth and algae, the hint of rotten eggs more pungent here than it would be at street level. The lake.

Nothing at the marina but boats and more paths heading south. Plenty of places for Keith and his friends to party, though, on the lawn, at tables by the outdoor café, on benches. She wondered how often patrols came through. Had anyone rousted the group from the spot Sunday night? She'd have to check. She'd also check the marina cameras. Thai food. Peggy's last meal. That needed a follow-up.

The dark figure. She was tired of referring to him that way. He'd been careful, hadn't he? His head was always turned away from the cameras as though he knew where they were and how much they would capture. It also looked as though he'd made every attempt possible to stay just out of the full light of the streetlamps. They had approximate height and body type. And the duffel. Did it contain a change of clothes? The knife? Would it have been used to carry Peggy's clothes, phone, and laptop away? Yet he'd thrown away the backpack with her ID in it. He hadn't cared if she was identified or not.

A chilled breeze rolled off the river, and Foster burrowed into her jacket. She stood for a moment looking out over the water, watching the undulating blackness, imagining it went on and on and that there was nothing on the other side, that the spot she stood on was the end of the world. She had no use for killers, especially those who killed children. They were the worst of thieves. One last look at the boats, the water, the moon, and she turned back, retracing her steps along the path, back toward the Riverwalk and the bridge.

She should be home, getting ignored by Lost, getting a good half night's sleep, getting ready for Rea's autopsy, and yet here she was . . . hunting. Back at the bushes, she trained her small flashlight behind them, running the cone of light slowly along the wrought-iron fence, Lower Wacker just beyond it. A few yards from the bushes there was a gap in the fence, a gap that provided easier access from the Riverwalk to the service road. She walked through, stood for a time on the other side, then trained her light up and found the cameras. Rea had been found in that tarp maybe only a few yards away. The gap had to be significant, the cavernous quality here a contributing factor. Tossing bodies away, she thought, as though he were putting out the trash. Birch killed on the other side of the gap, Rea killed elsewhere but dumped here. Elsewhere . . . where?

She thought of H. H. Holmes—a man so sick, so twisted, that he'd made murder his vocation—and his house of horrors. Considered America's first serial killer, Holmes had built his house of torture right here in Chicago. Having a place, a building, had given him the privacy to do as he wished for as long as it took. She prayed they weren't going to have to start looking for a place. They didn't have the resources or the manpower to check every building in the city.

She walked back and stepped through the gap, back onto the Riverwalk. Under leaves, under a tarp, under the street. Under. Hidden, but not well. She stopped, turned toward the fence again, slow enough that she didn't dislodge the thought but quick enough to make the connection. *Lower* Wacker. The Riverwalk. Under the street. Under the feet of passersby. In the dark, out of the way, closer to hell.

"Hiding them," she muttered. "But he wants them found, or why not just bury them in a ditch?" There had been Birch's foot sticking out of the pile of leaves and Rea's arm poking out of that tarp. The lipstick. "Presentation. Display. Proud of it." She made another full circle, taking in the Riverwalk, the river, the bars, the bridge, the fence, the gap, the path, the bushes. A chill ran through her. "Oh my God."

CHAPTER 36

At eight Thursday morning, Detective Li plopped her bag on her desk, startling Foster from what looked like yet another close examination of security footage. Since Foster and she were teaming up now, Kelley had moved to sit across from Lonergan, taking his Sammy Sosa bobblehead, leaving his tiny potted cactus. Griffin had a penchant for moving them all around like chess pieces on a board—no desk was sacrosanct, no spot wholly one's own. This desk, that desk, it was all the same. Li eyed the plastic cube next to her bag that held photos of her son. Two seconds. That's all it would take to pick it up and move it to another desk.

"More footage?" Li asked, peeling out of her jacket. Foster looked up, momentarily confused, like she was seeing Li for the first time or like she had lost track of the time, the day, or even the year. "You can't have been here all night," Li said, looking her new partner over. "You're wearing different clothes." Li checked her watch. She'd come in early, expecting to get a jump on things, only to find Foster already here, as if she'd been here for hours.

Foster stood, reached for her coffee cup, finding it bone dry. "I went home." Li's eyes held hers. "For a shower and fresh clothes." Li's brows lifted. "Then I came back," Foster said. She glanced over at the clock on the wall. "About five hours ago."

Li glanced over at Foster's monitor, the footage freeze framed. "That the Birch crime scene?"

"Yes, but from an alternate angle. We should have Rea's in a few hours. The person we saw with Birch didn't go back up the stairs, right? And none of the cameras picked him up heading toward the marina. We know he circled back to Ainsley, touched him, and then he's gone. He had to go somewhere. Walking, maybe, but it'd make more sense if he had a car parked along Wacker, right? Look at Rea—he wouldn't have carried a body in a tarp for any great distance. So I went back last night to the Riverwalk. There's a gap in the fence that separates the Riverwalk from the road. There are cameras, of course, but a few dead spots. If he parked in one of those spots, he could have easily slipped through the fence and driven away after killing Birch. That time of night, there wouldn't be a lot of traffic going through. Maybe, if we can pick up footage along Columbus, north and south, around the time we're looking at, we could get some plates to track down, then . . ." Foster stopped when she saw the look on Li's face.

"You're Lonergan-ing me," Li said. She checked her cell phone, scrolling through it. "Nope. I didn't get a call or text saying that's what was going down." She held the phone up so Foster could see it. Li could tell by the blank look on Foster's face that she hadn't even thought of calling.

"I couldn't sleep," Foster said. "I figured I'd take another look. Did you really want to walk the river at two a.m.?"

"That's my job, isn't it?" Li said flatly, not tempering the chilliness one bit.

Li had been in bed at 2:00 a.m., her baby son asleep in his crib, her husband working his thirty-third hour straight in the ER. And if she was being truthful, had she the choice between sleeping in a warm bed and walking the Riverwalk in the dead of night, she would have chosen the bed hands down, but she was a cop. Sometimes quiet nights didn't happen. Sometimes cases bled into your homelife, and you had to spend 2:00 a.m. down by the river's edge.

"You're right," Foster said. "I should have read you in."

191

Li let it sit for a moment. "That kind of goes without saying though, doesn't it?"

"My mistake," Foster said. "Next time you'll get a call."

Li's eyes widened. "There's going to be a next time?"

Foster smiled. "I get hunches. I follow them."

"All righty then. Next late-night prowl, count me in."

"Deal," Foster replied. "Buy you a coffee? A real one, not from the cop pot. As a peace offering."

Li stood for a moment, studying Foster. If her new partner kept up the pace she was on, she was going to be a prime candidate for burnout. Li could see it in the lines around her eyes, the strain in her neck. Foster was tightly wound and forcing her way through her days. Li had noticed her secreting clips and pins and little things into her pockets. Now she couldn't sleep, she said. Foster had no idea that Li knew why. Griffin had given her a heads-up about her son's murder, and of course everyone knew about her former partner. But Foster didn't talk about any of that. She hadn't shared a single personal thing about herself, and it didn't look like she ever would. Li, though, had other plans. She had no intention of working with a stranger.

"You cannot buy me with coffee, Harriet Foster," she offered lightly. "I want chocolate. Lots of it. But for now, show me what we're looking at so I can catch up."

With the smoke cleared, the two went over everything again. Foster took the Riverwalk, paying close attention to the fence gap. Li took the captures from Michigan Avenue the afternoon of the march and running all the way up to the time of Birch's murder. Rea's autopsy had been pushed back until noon, which gave them more time to be careful and deliberate.

Li finally disengaged after hours of searching, rolling her chair away from the monitor, running her hands through her hair. "Oh my God, if I have to look at another frame, I'm going to beat somebody down."

Foster faced her. "So I *should* have called you in last night, then?"

"Yes, but also hell no. You do you, Foster." She stood, stretched. "I'm going for shit coffee. Want another one?"

"No thanks." Her eyes went back to the monitor. "I'm wired enough already."

Li walked away on leaden legs. "Good call."

She was back in minutes with a fresh mug of scorched coffee that literally twisted her lips when she took a sip. Li tucked back in front of her computer to pick up where she'd left off. "We have less than an hour till the ME." Foster nodded but didn't answer.

"I'm married," Li said. Out of nowhere, not related to anything. No time like the present, she figured. "With a son. Two years old." Foster looked up. Li grinned. It was time to ease into knowing each other. "You didn't ask, I know. But we should know a little about each other. Will, my husband, is an ER doctor at Rush. Very smart, *very* handsome. Very not Chinese. Also, very busy, rarely home. My mother moved in about a year ago to help with the baby. Walter." She saw the perplexed look on Foster's face. "After Will's grandfather. Don't ask. My mother wasn't happy. Still isn't, but what can she do, right? We call him Wally. It still sounds like an old man's name. I go by my maiden name for the job. Otherwise, I would have had to do all kinds of paperwork and switch out that strip of masking tape off my locker."

"Two's a fun age," Foster said.

Li snorted. "Is it? When? Because right now it's a lot, and it's constant. And my mother, my dear, wonderful, beautiful Chinese mother, is driving us nuts."

Foster smiled and turned back to her screen. "An ER doctor. Wow. The scheduling alone."

"Freaking tell me about it." Li grinned over the rim of her cup. It was a start. *Slow and easy wins the race.* She tucked in to resume her search. "I'm seeing tons of pink backpacks from this march. Trying to pick out Peggy, even with that red hair, is like looking for a needle in a hundred haystacks."

Foster was only half listening as the deserted Riverwalk played on her monitor, frames blinking as the moon shifted position or the streetlights above changed color. "I'm not having much luck here either. All I . . ." She stopped, leaned in, her eyes glued to the images. "Wait."

Li rose and walked over to stand behind Foster. "See something?"

Foster pointed at a shadowy figure slipping through the gap. She froze the frame. "There. It's him." She checked the time stamp. Twelve thirty-nine, Sunday night. Foster consulted her notebook. "We have him with Ainsley at twelve thirty-six. Three minutes later he's slipping through that fence." She started the tape again, and they watched the figure move through the gap and disappear into the night. "Three minutes to walk back to Birch, maybe take one last look, and then vanish."

"It sure looks like the same guy who came down the stairs with her," Li said. "He's carrying the duffel. Only it looks empty, doesn't it? Like it weighs nothing."

"Still no shot of his face," Foster said. "His head's down and turned from the cameras. He knows where they are. I'm not seeing a car. It has to be parked out of camera range, otherwise where's he going?" Foster reached for her phone, dialed. "We need footage from Columbus and Michigan, Randolph and the Lake Shore feeders going east-west. His car will be on one of them." While she made her call, Li sounded it out.

"Two people come down those steps, one of them Birch with her pink backpack. Ainsley's there passed out. The one that's not Birch checks him. They move on, out of the shot." She leaned forward, focusing on the screen. "He's back forty minutes later, bends down, touches Ainsley's jacket, I guess, putting the spot of blood on it, and then, poof."

Foster hung up and sat down again. "Through the fence and away."

"You heard all that while you were on the phone?" Li asked, impressed.

"I can chew and talk at the same time."

"Good to know," Li said. "And we know this guy stepping through the gap in the wee hours of the morning's probably not just some rando nightwalker because . . ."

"Most decent people, like Elyse Pratt, would raise the alarm when they stumble on a dead body, call the police. No 911 call came in on Birch until hours later from the bridge. So either Mr. Rando's completely oblivious and didn't see Birch lying there, which is highly unlikely . . ."

"Or he put her there," Li broke in, "and was legging it, slow and easy. And he used the same escape route for Mallory Rea . . . skirting the cameras."

"We need to find that car," Foster said.

Li was already on it, sliding up to her desk again to begin the search. "And one cold SOB."

CHAPTER 37

Dr. Silva stood at Bodie Morgan's apartment door, her fist poised for a knock. She took a bracing breath and then rapped lightly, going over her pitch as she waited for the shuffling inside to get closer to the door. How she hated being in such a vulnerable position, having to literally beg, her very future dependent on someone like him. Protocol? Ethics? Boundaries? She was breaching them all, but she didn't care. One way or another, she was going to get the hell out of Westhaven.

There was a peephole, but in a split-second decision she reached up and covered it with a finger. If Bodie knew she was at the door, he'd never open it. She could feel him on the other side, hear him breathing as he peeked through the hole to find it blocked. For a moment there was a groundswell of anticipation, hesitancy; then she heard the chain disengage and the door unlock and swing open. Bodie stood there. For a moment there was a look of irritation on his face, replaced smoothly by the well-practiced smile she remembered, followed by the disguise of the quiet, affable man she would stake her career on being as fake as fool's gold.

"Dr. Silva," he said. "Since when do shrinks make house calls?"

"You wouldn't come to me, so . . ." She left the sentence unfinished, her eyes meeting his, a dance, a circling of minds commencing. "I wanted to make sure you were getting along all right. Coping. Can we talk?" Bodie's eyes went hard as that something, that thing, flickered across them. Silva felt him pull in, close off, push her away without physically doing it.

"I appreciate the trouble," he said, "but I'm fine."

Silva glanced past him, hoping to get a glimpse of his apartment, but Bodie shifted to block her view. "Mind if I come in?"

He pulled the door in. "Actually, yeah. I'm kind of busy." He angled his head, shooting her an amused look. "And since you're technically not my doctor anymore, I'm a little confused. Why are you here? Isn't this against some kind of rule or something?"

"Truthfully, yes," Silva said. "I am going a bit above and beyond. But I want to help you. Get you back into sessions. I can see you're struggling, and I'm worried that you might do harm to yourself . . . or others."

For a second, she didn't think he'd respond, but slowly a smile appeared. "So you've said. Every session. Like I'm some ticking bomb. This is about those women they found murdered, isn't it? You think that's me?" He laughed. "That's the problem with psychiatrists. They see mental dysfunction everywhere they go. You've wasted a trip, Dr. Silva. I'm not your golden goose. You probed me so many times; well, I probed you right back. I know you want out of Westhaven. I don't know what landed you there, but you hate it just as much as I hated it. And now you want me for . . . what? Am I your ticket out? Your prized pig? No dice."

"Perceptive," she said. But she wasn't surprised. Most sociopaths were quite perceptive and more than capable of turning the tables. She had no leverage, but she couldn't just let things go. "But that doesn't change my willingness to counsel you, to help you work through issues that are holding you back and keeping you from moving forward. You have to admit that . . ."

Bodie stepped back, ready to close the door in Silva's face. His smile died. "It's you that needs the help, apparently. You got my address and tracked me to my place on some trumped-up wellness check. Let me count the infractions." He lowered his voice to a whisper. "For your peace of mind, I have no intention of harming myself." He backed up to close the door. "Now leave me alone. Don't come here again."

The door closed in Silva's face, and she stood there as the lock engaged on the other side. She could feel Bodie staring at her through the peephole, and she stared at it as though they were still standing face to face.

Don't come here again.

He'd uttered those words to frighten her, the threat implied. But he didn't know her. He didn't know her at all.

CHAPTER 38

Foster and Li stood by the autopsy table, masked, watching as Dr. Grant stood over Mallory Rea, her skin almost translucent under the bright lights. Rea hadn't been married; she hadn't yet had kids. She worked in PR at a downtown firm and was an activist. There would be friends, presumably, who would mourn her loss, and her family, of course. Her parents had been notified and were flying in from Phoenix anytime now. It wasn't much to know about a person.

"Same kind of knife, I'd say," Grant said. "Serrated. Pretty significant in size. We'd need it to compare these wounds to Birch's, but this looks pretty similar." Grant looked over at Foster and Li. "No luck on that yet?" Foster and Li shook their heads. "All body parts present and accounted for, though most are in pieces. I'd say this attack was much worse than the first victim. Frenzied, if I had to say. Angrier. The wounds are more numerous and a lot deeper. She wasn't impaired in any way. All her labs came back normal. All systems functioning as they should have, until they weren't. And there's the lipstick around the ankles and wrists." Grant moved away from the table, over to the sink, where she pulled off her gloves, tossed them into a biohazard bin, and washed her hands.

"Angrier with Rea than he was with Birch," Foster said. "Why?" She hadn't expected an answer. She was talking to herself, but Li offered one anyway.

"Because he didn't get what he wanted," she said. "Maybe he was rushed or had to settle for Rea when he couldn't find anyone else."

Grant dried her hands and came back to the table. "Her death would have been painful. She would have known she was dying."

Foster stared at Rea. Her hair was wet, slicked back, light brown. The wig she'd been wearing when she'd been found popped into Foster's head. "Anything from the wig she was wearing?"

Grant padded over to the counter and held up the wig in a plastic evidence bag. "Nothing on this that can help us. Like Birch, I found no DNA, no prints, no hairs, no fibers. So this is unnaturally and exasperatingly useless to any of us."

Li sighed. "Great, and by *great,* I mean *fuck.*"

"He's not pinging on age," Foster mused. "Birch was nineteen; Rea was almost thirty. Both white. Both female. Birch was last seen in a bar. Rea? We don't know yet. There's nothing else." Foster looked over at Li, hoping she had something.

"Both activists," Li said. "Birch was out marching the day she was killed. Rea got arrested breaking into a lab to free rats or monkeys or whatever. Maybe it's that?"

Grant blew out a weary breath. "I saved the best for last. The dried blood on Rea's thigh?" Grant lifted the sheet to expose Rea's upper leg. "It's human. But it's not hers; it's Birch's. How's that for a connector?"

CHAPTER 39

"For the love of God, Manny. Drag that can out back, will ya? It's full and reeks like the county dump," the cook bellowed.

The kid grabbed the heavy metal can, his music blasting through bootleg AirPods, his phone tucked in his back pocket. Half an hour until quitting time, and he couldn't wait. That gave him just enough time to get home, shower, and change. He and his girl, Imelda, were hitting the clubs tonight for her birthday. Thursday was ladies' night, half price. But first the can and a thorough mop of the kitchen floor. Carmello's Italian Ristorante was closing early today, no dinner service, in honor of Mama Carmello's ninetieth birthday. Manny wasn't complaining. All the best to Mama Carmello, but a night off was a night off. "All right, Earl, cool your jets, homey."

"I'll cool my jets when you're dead. Now get that can outa here."

Manny flipped Earl off when his back was turned, then dragged the can out the back door to the dumpsters lined up along Lower Michigan. He hated coming out here, the stench of sour milk, funk, rotten food, and all an assault to his senses. He hated this job, too, but for now it was what he had, and it was better than nothing. Imelda didn't come cheap. Holding his breath, he dragged the can of kitchen scraps and old grease to the first dumpster. He was ready to toss his load when something caught his eye. For a moment, he thought *rat*, but the thing didn't move, and now that his eyes had adjusted to the dark, whatever he was looking at was much bigger than a rat. His first thought was that it was some homeless guy sleeping one off or taking a break from dumpster diving at dusk.

"Hey, buddy, you can't flop here," he yelled. No movement. "Dude, c'mon, you're killing me here."

The guy was sitting with his back to the restaurant wall, a blanket covering him head to toe, only the soles of his shoes showing. "Yo, brah. You got to move it along, *comprende*? Why you pick out here anyway? It's funky as shit back here."

He looked around, his nose crinkled in disgust. He had Imelda waiting, a night of boom chicka boom planned; he didn't have time for some homeless guy taking a nap by Carmello's smelly cans. The shoes looked pretty new. Small feet for a guy. Pink laces. There was a purse next to him, some of its contents spilled out on the greasy ground—a compact, spare change, a pair of eyeglasses. A purse? A *woman*? "Ah, that's just sad, man." Manny nudged the foot with his foot. "Lady. Lady, you gotta get up, okay? You gotta get yourself to a shelter. You can't lay out here like this. It ain't safe."

When he got no response, he tugged on the blanket, and it slipped down to the woman's waist. Manny stumbled back, his heart in his throat beating a mile a minute. The scream that flew out of his mouth brought Earl running out the back door, cleaver in hand.

"What the fuck?" Earl said. "They're just rats, you big chicken."

Manny pointed at the woman, her eyes open, her slender throat cut ear to ear, blood staining the front of her shirt. Earl screamed, dropping the cleaver. Manny had never stopped. Two desperate voices echoed off the metal cans. Imelda and the club, the boom chicka boom, no longer at the forefront of Manny's mind.

CHAPTER 40

The next morning, Griffin stood at the whiteboard, grim of face and in a lousy mood. Chicago had more or less become inured to overnight gang shootings, carjackings, and violent deaths and assaults, but when the bodies of three white woman showed up on the city's front doorstep, the race to keep up shifted from a marathon to an all-out sprint. Media was going nuts. Some goon even equated their killer to a modern-day Jack the Ripper. None of it was helpful. All of it was added pressure CPD didn't need.

The room was tight, warm; the odor of sweaty cops who'd been working through the night was strong. Griffin turned to her detectives, all assembled. They looked like a battle-worn battalion who'd just had their asses handed to them.

"Another female victim," Griffin said. "But not like the first two. Differences?" No one spoke. "What are we, in ninth-grade algebra class? *Differences.* Somebody."

"She was fully clothed," Symansky said. "And the bastard only slit her throat."

Kelley raised his hand, but when Griffin glared at him, he slowly put it down. "He left her wallet with her ID in it. Money's gone, though. No cell phone, so he probably took that too. Her camera looked pretty banged up. It was found close to her."

"Evelyn Wicks," Lonergan said. "Thirty-one. Tourist. There was a hotel key card in her front pocket from the InterContinental. She's in town with a friend—Susan Fahey. They're a couple of Brits."

Griffin gave Lonergan her full attention. Lonergan wasn't out of the doghouse yet. "Why wasn't Fahey with her?"

"I got that." Bigelow slid his glasses down off his head to read his notes. "Fahey says Evelyn went out to snap some pictures around two yesterday. She begged off. They'd been out sightseeing most of the day."

Lonergan nodded. "Then Fahey falls asleep, and when she wakes up, it's almost seven, and she sees Wicks isn't back. She starts callin' her phone but gets no answer. That's when she buzzes the front desk and they called us. But by then, Wicks had been found behind Carmello's."

"Fahey's coming in," Bigelow said, "so we'll see what else she can tell us."

"Tourists. Jesus," Griffin muttered, turning back to the board. "So a robbery gone sideways?"

"Or a murder and an opportunist who's got no problem robbing a corpse," Symansky said. "May the son of a bitch rot in hell."

"Why didn't he take her camera, then?" Kelley asked. "It's scuffed up—maybe she fought for it before he slashed her—but it's still worth something, right? A run-of-the-mill mugger, a crime of opportunity like we're saying, they would've taken the camera and either sold it at the nearest CTA station or handed it off for someone else to sell it."

"The camera's SD card was missing," Foster said. The room quieted. Everyone turned to face her. "I assume the camera had one when she left her hotel." She looked around at the detectives and could almost see the wheels turning in their heads, though no one volunteered a response right away.

"She took a picture of something she wasn't meant to," Li said, breaking the silence. "Or of *someone*." She rose, padded over to the board, where a map pinpointing the body dumps was pinned. "The hotel's here. She was found a block west. Here. She could have taken the stairs on Michigan. Maybe looking for the Billy Goat. Tourists get turned around looking for that all the time. Maybe she snaps a couple of photos there, then starts walking around. Snaps the wrong thing." She turned toward the team. "Absolutely plausible."

Lonergan grumbled. "Or the thing fell out of the camera when it got busted? Then got twisted around underfoot when the scene ramped up. Nobody was lookin' out for an SD card. Or maybe she took the card out herself to have it developed somewhere."

Symansky laughed. "Developed? Lonergan, what century are you from?"

Lonergan's face colored, his mouth twisted into a snarl. "Shove it, Symansky."

"All right, cut it out," Griffin barked. "What else?" She clapped her hands impatiently. "C'mon. So far we have a lot of theories, no definitives. Give me definitives. Our dance card's full, people; I don't have to tell you that. In addition to Wicks, three other homicides came in overnight." Groans went up around the room. "Welcome to paradise. Wicks's autopsy's number one priority. It looks like she connects by age, by race, but she's obviously not a redhead, and she wasn't hacked to pieces and left naked by that dumpster. The missing SD card's curious? Let's look for it in case it did get trampled on. Maybe it was in her pocket; maybe she swallowed it—I don't know. I'm grasping here. Talk to me." Griffin scanned the room. *"Now!"*

"Bigelow and I can take the autopsy," Lonergan said.

"No. I'm shaking things up. Foster and Li take the autopsy. You and Bigs talk to the friend, Fahey? Symansky, Kelley, you take the guy who found the body, and you're on cameras this time. I'm spreading the pain around. Start around the Billy Goat. I can't think of anything else down there she'd want to take pictures of. And I don't think I have to impress upon anybody here how quickly we need to do all of this. Now get out."

The phone in Griffin's office rang, and her face fell. Then the phone in her pocket started up, her ringtone the theme to the TV show *Cops*—"*Bad boys, bad boys, whatcha gonna do, whatcha gonna do when they come for you . . .*" "All of you, get out there and get me something before they peck me to death." She rushed back to her office and slammed the door shut.

"Wow, I wouldn't take her job on a bet," Kelley said.

Symansky smirked. "I'd take it for the pay jump. I got two kids using me like an ATM."

Foster watched as Bigelow and an unhappy Lonergan walked back to their desks, Lonergan working up a mad she had no remedy for.

"Grant is so not going to be happy to see us again," Li said as she grabbed her bag out of her bottom drawer. "This makes three in less than a week." She wiggled into her jacket, grabbed her cell phone. "The pattern idea doesn't look like it's holding. This guy's all over the place. Maybe Wicks is just a down-and-dirty mugging? Unrelated."

Foster grabbed her things. "What kind of mugger carries a blanket around with him?"

Li groaned. "I really hate the weird ones."

CHAPTER 41

Dr. Grant glared at Foster and Li over her autopsy table. What remained of Evelyn Wicks lay there, small and still, her slender neck gaping open, her eyelids at half-mast. There was no music blasting out of the speakers this time, their second indication, after Grant's daggerlike glower, that things weren't going to go well. It took less than five seconds for that to be confirmed.

"Nuh-uh. Don't bother taking your coats off," Grant said, her eyes as hard as Satan's ore. Nothing made her angrier than violent, senseless death, Foster knew, especially when it involved the young. "The slaughter of innocents is an abomination," Grant had once whispered to her as they'd stood over her son here. Foster had agreed with her then and now. And she hated this room, hated being back here, hated standing over bodies, young or old. Grant pointed to the gaping gash at Wicks's throat. "Cause of death. Exsanguination."

Li cleared her throat, lifted her eyes off her shoes to hold Grant's. "Any physical evidence worthy of note?"

The beat Grant let pass was long, fraught with danger, and dripping with reproach. "Wouldn't all of it be *worthy of note*?"

"Yes. Absolutely," Li said. "I just meant—"

Grant cut her off, her eyes sliding to Foster. "Are you any closer to finding this fool?"

"Depends on your report," Foster said. "On whether it helps or hurts us."

Grant stared at her, then moved away from the table and plucked a folder off the counter. "Preliminary report. Still waiting for full tox, but I don't think we'll find anything there. Nothing under the fingernails. Like the others, no prints, no semen, no hairs, no saliva, no signs of habitual drug use, no needle marks. Also, no lipstick, but there was a dainty rose tattoo on the left ankle. Years old. This theft of life is not like the others, but it's equally egregious."

"And . . . the blood," Foster said.

"No signs of Rea's or Birch's blood anywhere on her body or clothes. Clean cut, approached from the back. Quick and dirty."

"Anything else?" Foster shoved her notebook into her pocket.

"You're looking for a lefty," Grant said. "The knife traveled right to left, leaving jagged edges."

"No way of confirming that for Birch or Rea, though," Li said.

"Gold star for you, Li. Anything else?"

Neither of them had another word to say.

Grant stood over Wicks. "Three's your limit, ladies. Get out of my autopsy room."

Li pushed through the front door and took a deep breath, Foster walking right behind her, fishing for the car keys. She had a headache, three bodies, and a mountain to climb. And it felt like a thousand-mile walk back to the car. She wondered if Li felt as defeated as she did, though she certainly didn't look it. Foster slid into the car behind the wheel as Li eased in beside her.

"My God, she's scary as hell," Li said as she reached over to engage her seat belt. "I'd rather face off against a dozen bangers than walk into that woman's autopsy room." She ran a hand across the back of her neck and then presented her palm to Foster. "Look. Flop sweat. I am literally sweating like I just got caught swiping mascara off the shelf at CVS. Is it me, or is she literally blaming the two of us personally for these deaths?"

"I don't think it's us," Foster said. "She's as frustrated as we are."

"You say." Li slipped on her sunglasses, then glanced over at Foster. "I got definite hostility." She reached over and turned on the heater. "And now I'm freezing. And it's fifty degrees outside." Li rubbed her hands together in front of the vents. "Did you know that about ninety percent of people are right handed? I am. I noticed you are. In the dark times, they thought lefties were witches or hexed by the devil. Might be on the mark in this case."

"Where do you suggest we look for witches?"

Li settled in, flipping down the visor. "You don't look for witches, Foster. They find you."

CHAPTER 42

Amelia sat across the table from the good-looking stranger, smiling. Speed dating. Did people really do this? She sure as hell didn't, yet here she was, intrigued by the novelty of it and not so much her prospects for a "magical" match. It had been a spur-of-the-moment decision to come. Something new to do in a bar at night. Her eyes trailed down to the name tag on his chest. Jason. It was likely fake, but she didn't care.

"Not your scene?" Jason asked. Amelia looked at him, the hint of an appraisal in the glance. He wasn't bad looking. Nice green eyes, sandy hair, and the dimple in his right cheek was cute.

"It's . . . new," she said, taking a sip from her wineglass, watching him over the rim. "Certainly, a way to get out and meet people. Mingle, as they like to say."

"You don't usually get out and meet people?"

"I do, but in the wild. The old-fashioned way. Like a person. This?" She scanned the room. Mostly women, a few brave average-looking men. The bar just a bar, not the least bit quaint or elegant. The owners had gone for publican snug. Not her style. "Seems a little forced."

"I agree. What do you do, Amelia?"

There were those dimples again. "I'm an artist." There was no reason for her to lie.

He sat back, sipped his ale from the bottle. "That's impressive. What medium?"

"I'm a painter, primarily. But I also find beautiful things and transform them into things that are more beautiful."

"You any good?" He was joking. She liked that. It showed confidence.

She stared at him with just a hint of amusement in her smile. "Very."

"I'll bet. You know, my cousin used to find old pieces of driftwood on the beach and whittle them into all kinds of things. He was pretty good at it too. You do stuff like that?"

"I have done, though it's been ages since I've been to the beach. Anyway, enough about me. What do you do?"

"I'm an architect. I live in a suit and build things that will last a thousand years, barring nuclear Armageddon."

Amelia's eyes wandered just for a second to the other tables. Everyone looked like they were having fun, getting into the groove of things. At the next table sat a balding man in his forties who kept adjusting his blazer cuffs to make sure his Rolex showed. Amelia could tell the watch wasn't working on the woman across from him. But she forced a smile, nodded a lot, and sipped her Manhattan. It was clear she'd done this before. When the bell rang, marking the five minutes, Mr. Rolex would be Amelia's problem, and five minutes would feel like forever.

"I'd consider that interesting. Without architects, we'd all be living in caves, right?"

He lifted his bottle. "And without painters, we'd be deprived of beauty. Renoir, Matisse, Vermeer, you. Can you imagine a world without beauty?"

She could, but this was not the time or place to discuss it. There was a timer sitting between them, the tick of seconds winding down. Their five minutes had dwindled down to less than two. Five minutes was just enough to meet, just enough to pique an interest, not long enough for a true connection. It was just long enough to begin to feel trapped if things weren't going well but still short enough so that the agony had an end point. She glanced over at Mr. Rolex talking a mile a minute, blowing hot air around.

"Not many people could," she said. "A world without art or creativity or beauty isn't a world I could live in."

"Okay, speed round," Jason said, rubbing his hands together. "Favorite color."

"Green," Amelia said as she looked into his clear green eyes. It wasn't the truth.

She leaned her elbows on the table, getting into the rhythm of the thing. Just for kicks. Just to see. "Your dream city?"

"Easy. Florence."

She chuckled. "I assume *not* Missouri?"

He laughed. "Definitely Italy. Vanilla or chocolate?"

Her eyes danced. "Are we talking ice cream or . . ."

The timer sounded. She shrugged playfully. "Time's up."

Jason stood, held out a hand. "It was nice meeting you, Amelia the artist."

Out of the corner of her eye she saw Mr. Rolex get up, grab his glass, and wait to sit across from her. Amelia rose and squeezed Jason's hand, telegraphing a message. Soft skin. A megawatt smile impossible to resist. "Would you like to see my studio?"

His brows lifted in surprise. "Will you paint me?"

"If you'd like."

He leaned in to whisper in her ear. "Then I'd love to see your studio, Amelia."

She took her hand back. "Then let's get out of here." She followed behind him, admiring the view. She could hear Mr. Rolex behind them complaining about the disruption in the order, but his frustration wasn't her problem. He'd just have to flash his watch at someone else.

As she and Jason passed the long table where they had placed their calling cards, Amelia stopped. There were rows and rows of cards with names and professions written on them, no numbers, no addresses. If you found a match, those were details you could relay yourself. She quickly found hers, plucked it up, and slid it into her bag. Poof. Like she'd never been here, except for Jason.

"Ready, Mr. Builder of Buildings?" she asked when they stepped outside onto busy Rush Street.

"This is a first," he said, "a woman inviting me up to look at her sketches."

She gave him a long look. She didn't choose just anyone. "If you live long enough, Jason, you see everything at least once."

CHAPTER 43

What a mess, Silva thought as she pushed her way through the crowd holding up the sidewalk the next morning. Barely 10:00 a.m. and there were at least a hundred people standing around, pushing, jockeying for position in front of the District One police station.

This was her next move. The police had a problem, three dead women, and they were about to learn that Dr. Mariana Silva was their solution. She was bringing them a prime suspect, a threat to himself and to public safety. That fell within her bounds, her responsibility, as a mental health clinician, or so she would argue. Extraordinary measures had to be taken when lives were at stake. Her proof that Bodie Morgan was a real and present danger? Her instinct and experience. Hadn't the first victim been found just a few short hours after Bodie Morgan walked out of Westhaven? She didn't have all the details of the case, of course, but Bodie had twenty-four hours to roam the city on that day pass. And Silva didn't believe in coincidences.

The crowd pushed forward, banners and protesters, reporters and cameras, pedestrians stopping to watch the chaos. The entire thing felt apocalyptic, end-of-world-ish, as though a deadly pathogen had wormed its way into the population and there wasn't enough lifesaving vaccine for everyone. They needed to put a face to the maniac prowling their streets. They needed order restored, and it didn't look to Silva like they cared much how they got it. A woman with a large sign shouted for a total city lockdown, another for an 8:00 p.m. curfew and a callout to the National Guard. *SAVE OUR CHILDREN,* one sign read. *DOWN WITH CLUELESS COPS,* read another. They had no idea the dour, humorless woman with the sharp dark eyes studying them held the key to everything.

It took Silva longer than it should have to convince the sergeant at the desk that she wasn't some attention-seeking crackpot and that she had information vital to the murder investigation. She was forced to show her Westhaven credentials, meaningless to her and embarrassing to present but official enough to get the sergeant's attention.

"I'm Dr. Mariana Silva," she finally had to say in an authoritative tone that had heads turning at the front desk. "Do you want to stop these murders or not? I need to see Detective Harriet Foster."

Quickly deposited into a small, stuffy, smelly interview room with no windows, she waited for Foster to come in, knowing discussions about her were going on outside the closed door, feeling that eyes were on her, maybe, through the two-way mirror. They would look her up to see if she was who she claimed to be, but they wouldn't find everything. This made her smile. Pride. She had a lot of it.

The door opened, and she watched two women enter. Foster and a lean Asian woman, their badges clipped to their belts, stern looks on their faces. All business. No time for grandstanding. They pulled out chairs across the table and sat facing her. It was Foster she wanted to see, up close, and here she was, as straight as a ship's mast. But she was meeting only the cop, the job, not the woman underneath. That woman, she could clearly see, had been stowed away. How fascinating, Silva thought. She stared into Foster's sharp eyes, searching for private truths as she always did whenever she encountered anyone, only this time the eyes probed back, searching for Silva's secrets as intensely as Silva was searching for hers.

"I'm Detective Foster. This is Detective Li. You say you have something for us?"

All business. Task at hand. "I do," Silva said, pleased with herself.

215

A beat passed. Li was impatient. Three bodies on the ME's slab. There was zero time for a meandering conversation with a strange walk-in. "Well, then?"

"You were partnered with a man before," Silva said, addressing Foster. "I saw your pictures in the paper." She gave Li half a smile. "But I like this pairing better. I've found that women are far more intuitive than men."

"You're a psychiatrist." Foster consulted her notes. "At Westhaven Psychiatric Hospital. And you're here because . . ."

Silva flinched at the mention of Westhaven. God, she hated the place. But she knew Foster and Li weren't going to give her much time. "I specialize in antisocial personality disorders. To the layman, sociopaths, psychopaths, though we eschew the terms. That's what you're dealing with. The papers weren't explicit, but were the murders unusually violent? Were the victims found naked? Was there something distinctive left behind, like a mark or a symbol?"

Neither Foster nor Li said a thing, but Silva could tell she'd just become more interesting to them both. She decided to make good use of the moment. "Young women of a certain type. Concealed, especially their faces."

"Who is he?" Foster asked.

Li added, "And where can we find him?"

Satisfied she'd broken through, moved from quack to serious contender, Silva took a moment to collect her thoughts and choose her words carefully. "He's a former patient, a man I believe to be very unstable. His name is Bodie Morgan, and I believe he is a danger to himself and others."

"You're turning in your patient?" Foster said.

Silva's eyes held hers. "I'd like to think I'm helping him. That's how strongly I take this. Mr. Morgan had been arrested for stalking two young women several months ago. That much he told me, though, of course, he maintained it was all a misunderstanding. Apparently,

Morgan's lawyer suggested Westhaven, and he resented having to take the suggestion. He isn't the first person to flee to a psychiatric facility to avoid jail time or demonstrate good faith to a judge. Thirty days. I listened to him tell me about himself. He wasn't truthful."

"Go on," Foster said.

"I couldn't break through," Silva said. "The sessions ended in stalemate. I can help him. There's a course of therapy. But he has to be willing. And though I suspect him, believe him to be dangerous, I have no proof that he killed anyone."

"You come forward now? After *three* deaths," Foster said. "Why not after the first or the second?"

"You're angry at the loss of life. You also feel some personal responsibility for the victims, for not catching him in time to save them." Silva wasn't talking to Foster directly, just running through ideas aloud, confident she'd read Foster correctly.

"Can we skip the parlor tricks?" Foster asked. "Tell us more about this Bodie Morgan."

"He's deeply damaged. Trauma literally oozes out of him. I've spent my entire career working to understand the mentally ill."

Silva folded her hands on the table, enjoying being the center of attention, maybe a little too much. She was in no hurry to wind it all out for them. "He's suffering from a disconnect. A short circuit in the wiring. I would say brought on by childhood distress, maybe even abuse. There's active abuse, you see—slaps, beatings, kicks—and passive: emotional manipulation, neglect, the use of fear or persuasion. Bodie Morgan has experienced some or all of this and is likely acting it out with the women to which he's drawn."

"Not all abused children become murderers," Foster said.

"True. But you'd be hard pressed to find a murderer who hasn't been abused in some way. If I had to guess, and I rarely do, I would say whatever happened to Bodie changed him in profound ways. Unfortunately, I can't tell you more. I can only bring him to your attention. I would be willing to be of assistance if you decide to look at him further. He might feel more comfortable speaking with someone familiar." Silva slid her business card across the table. "I'm available day or night."

"His address?" Li asked.

Silva recited it, then sat back and waited. "I've been completely truthful here."

Li flicked Foster a look, got up, and left the room.

"More checking?" Silva asked.

"Yes," Foster said.

Silva had expected an easier time and a lot more deference. She got neither. "You don't trust me," she said.

Foster paged through her notebook, waiting on Li. "I'm not in the trust business."

"No, I can see that."

Li returned. Silva tracked her as she sat down and slid a file toward her partner. Everyone waited in silence until Foster read the contents.

"The officers who arrested Bodie Morgan found him on the roof of his building ready to jump," Foster said. "So he's suicidal on top of being a psychopathic killer?"

Silva shook her head. "He wasn't going to jump."

"You sound sure of that," Li said.

"I am. If he was found on the edge of that roof, it was for some other reason."

The room grew so quiet that Silva could hear warm air blowing out of the vents. Foster closed the file and stood up. Li stood too. "Thanks for coming in, Dr. Silva."

The meeting was over. She was being dismissed. Would they consult her when they spoke to Bodie? She needed the guarantee. "He'll shut down," Silva said. "I should be here when you talk to him. In fact, I believe, given the choice between talking to me and talking to you, he'll choose me."

Foster smiled, but there was something in it that Silva couldn't quite make out. "We won't give him that choice. An officer will see you out."

Silva was guided to the exit. As the police escort walked her down the hall, she could feel Foster and Li watching her, judging her. She grew angrier with every step she took. What right did they have to question her motives? They were going to freeze her out; she knew it. She pushed through the front doors, leaving her escort behind.

"Damn them," she said under her breath.

CHAPTER 44

At her desk, Foster pored over the record of Bodie Morgan's stalking arrest. She looked up at Li sitting across from her, pulling up ID records on the women who'd pressed charges against him. "He does seem to have some serious issues," she said.

Li stared at her monitor. "Listen to this—the two women who reported Morgan for stalking them say he really freaked them out. It wasn't just him showing up at the same places, a bar, coffee shop, whatever." She shoved a copy of a driver's license across the desks. "This one, Katherine Wright, filed her complaint first. Morgan wouldn't let up. I really hate a creepy guy."

"She met him where?"

"Both complainants say they remember meeting him in a bar. Not the same bar. But both bars aren't far from Morgan's apartment or theirs. And meet him, apparently, is all they did. He approached, tried to pick them up, and I guess they smelled the weird on him and froze him out."

"But he kept coming back?"

Li nodded. "Nearly every time they walked into a bar, he'd be there. Again, different bars, different nights, he's there and starts up again. What'd they both do? They complain to the owners. He gets tossed."

"And they choose different bars the next time," Foster said.

"Right. Logical. Only he shows up there too. He gets tossed again, and for a while it's all good, and then, bam, he's back. Then the second victim swears she sees Morgan in her backyard, just standing there looking up at her windows. That would have done it for me."

"There was a chase," Foster said, referring to the report in front of her. "A Detective Tynan caught him?"

Li leaned back, smiled. "Oh, this is rich. The second victim's Reese Tynan, whose brother, Detective *Ciaran* Tynan, just happens to work out of the Sixteenth District. Reese tells Ciaran all about the bar creep; bro cop moves into her place, staking it out. Morgan shows up doing his creepy loser thing, and Ciaran comes barreling out the door to grab him, only Morgan runs off. The chase ends on the roof of Morgan's place. Tynan put in the report later that it looked like Morgan was getting ready to jump when he finally cornered him, but he snatched him back before he could. Morgan's sporting a fat lip and a shiner in his mug shot. Tynan swears Morgan tripped on the stairs on the way down. I say he had the trip coming. Silva was right. It being his first offense, he got probation instead of time. His walking voluntarily into Westhaven, I guess, was his attempt at proving he wasn't a complete scumbag?"

"Both women don't live far from Morgan," Foster said. "He didn't go far."

"And he doesn't live that far from Birch's campus either," Li said.

"If it's Morgan," Foster said, "maybe Tynan caught him just as he was about to graduate from stalking to murder." Li slid the copy of Reese Tynan's driver's license across to her. The copies were in black and white, but her eyes went right to the information she wanted to confirm.

"They're both redheads," Foster said.

Li nodded. "Like Silva told us. He has a type."

CHAPTER 45

There was a knock at his door at the ungodly hour of 10:45 a.m. If it was Dr. Silva again, she was going to regret it. Bodie squinted through the peephole, certain that he would see her standing there like a harbinger of doom, a vulture waiting to pick his bones clean. But it wasn't her. Instead, he gazed upon two serious-looking women. Police.

He knew they were police by the tight set of their jaws, the way they stood, the way they checked the hallway and braced for the opening of the door, ready for anything. Instantly his mood darkened. He wasn't frightened or intimidated, just annoyed. He wanted to be left alone to figure things out. How could he do that if there were cops at his door? Even the knock sounded authoritative, demanding. Like they had a right. Why was it always women sweating him, pushing him, ignoring him, running him?

He opened the door, and immediately two badges went up in front of his face. He stared at the silver stars, then at the women holding them. He could tell from their expressions and body language that this wasn't a wellness check or some random canvass unrelated to him. This was about him.

"Bodie Morgan? I'm Detective Foster. This is Detective Li. Mind if we come in? Ask you a few questions?"

Bodie stood in the doorway, his hand on the door. This was as far as he wanted cops to go. He didn't want them in his home around his things, looking, sizing him up, finding him lacking. His home was his space. He decided who came and went.

"What's this about?"

"Your name came up during an inquiry into a case we're working," Foster said. "We think you might be able to shed some light." She let a beat pass. "I'm being intentionally vague here, Mr. Morgan, seeing as we're standing in the hallway, and I'm sure at least a few of your neighbors clocked us from the elevator and now have their ears pressed to their doors, listening to every word we say."

Li turned when she heard a door down the hall gently shut. She turned back to Bodie, smiling. "See?"

Bodie didn't care about cops at his door. He didn't care about his neighbors. He didn't know half of them, and the other half wouldn't piss on him if his pants were on fire. Snobbish, standoffish, rude, thinking everything was always about them. "What case? And how did my name just happen to come up?" He was no fool. He knew how cops worked. They lied. Like that girl's brother who'd told his pals Bodie had tripped down the stairs when he was dragged and punched and kicked all the way down. They'd pretended not to see afterward when the bruises formed, when his lip swelled.

It looked to Bodie like the Black cop was weighing something in her head. The other stood beside her doing the same. Maybe the protracted silence, the no-give in their expressions, was a little intimidating, he decided. But he had every intention of standing his ground. He narrowed the crack in the door when he saw Detective Li glance past him. His space. His right to keep them out.

"We're investigating the murders of three women. I'm sure you've heard or read about them," Foster said. "We'd like to talk to you about where you were this week, specifically Sunday night, Tuesday night, and yesterday." She gave him a smile, but it was a smile with edge. Foster put him in mind of a jungle cat—stealthy, calculating, still, until she pounced on her prey and tore it to shreds.

And he was the prey.

"If there's anything else you'd like your neighbors to know, we'll continue . . . here . . . in the hall, or we can talk inside or down at our place, where most folks don't like to be. Up to you."

"But we *will* have the conversation, Mr. Morgan," Li added just as coldly.

He stuck his head out, looked up and down the hall. He could just imagine what the neighbors were thinking, that he was some crazed killer, some sicko maniac. *It's always the quiet ones,* they'd say later down in the laundry room or on the elevator. He could just hear them . . . *I always knew something was off with him.* "Fine. I'll come in tomorrow. Leave your card."

Neither cop moved. It didn't even look like they were breathing. He was being accommodating. What was their problem? The door across the hall opened, and a middle-aged white woman came out with a small laundry bag. The cops turned to watch as she locked her door, smiled, took in the scene, sneered at Bodie, and then headed for the elevator. Laura Avers. That was who the woman was, the snootiest, most high-handed busybody he'd ever met. News of this would be all over the building by lunchtime. If he could spot a cop a mile away, she likely could too. The detectives turned back to face him.

"Now," Foster said. "Here or there."

He took a second to weigh the options he'd been given. He didn't want to open up his place, but he didn't want to be hauled down to a police station either. He was done with being confined, locked in. Resigned, he chose the lesser of the two evils and stepped back and let them in. "You've got five minutes, and if there's anything I don't want to answer, I won't."

Right inside the door their eyes got busy. That was what Bodie didn't like about cops. They looked at everything, saw everything, then ran it through their cop brains and came up with something that always meant bad news for you. You were guilty or innocent, telling the truth or lying, the decisions made in a flash. They'd already arrested him, beaten him, put him through changes. He had a police file now that was his scarlet letter, a devil's mark to match the one he was born with.

Five minutes. That was all he'd give them. Just five, and then his neighbors, the ones who shunned him and avoided him for no good reason, could go to hell and back.

The Black cop, Foster, spoke first, but as her lips moved, Bodie half hearing her, he worried about what she'd learned about him in just the short time she'd been here. "Where were you Sunday night?" she asked. "Late. Around eleven or twelve?"

Bodie moved to act as buffer between them and his things. If they peered into the kitchen, they wouldn't see much. Bodie didn't require much. He never filled the space he occupied. Unlike Amelia, he didn't have the patience for showy things like art and cars. "Here."

"Just out of . . . confinement," Li said, "and you stayed in?"

His heart raced, his mind too. They knew about Westhaven. How? "Yes. And what's that got to do with anything?"

"What did you do . . . ?" Foster padded around the room. "Here."

"I had dinner, watched some television. I was beat and wanted to sleep in my own bed." Despite the roiling going inside him, he was surprised by how calm he sounded. He hadn't cared about the bed. Bodie reasoned he could take a torch to the whole apartment and not mourn a single item lost. He'd walked the night away, free, but he wasn't about to tell them that.

"Can anyone confirm that's what you did?" Foster asked.

"It's just me here, as you can see."

"What about Tuesday or yesterday? Still home alone?" Li asked.

He'd been out walking both nights, and then he'd gone to a bar. Also, not their business. His hands gripped the back of his couch, his eyes on the cops. He was mindful of the time he'd given them. "Yes. That's not a crime. Why are you here?"

"We found two reports filed accusing you of stalking," Li said. "Women."

His entire body burned. "They misunderstood. I was walking. I got turned around." He looked from one to the other.

"Reese Tynan found you in her yard," Li said, "peeking through her windows."

Bodie gripped the couch tighter, his throat as dry as a Saharan sirocco. "It was a mistake, and I paid for it. You know one of yours tried to beat the crap out of me? *I* should have pressed charges."

Li angled her head. "Why didn't you?"

"I know how the city works," Bodie snarled. "And your time's almost up. You asked; I answered. I have a lawyer, so don't think you can intimidate me."

"Did you know Peggy Birch?" Foster asked. "Mallory Rea or Evelyn Wicks? Meet them somewhere?"

The names from the paper. The women. "No."

"You're sure?" Li asked.

"Who sent you here? Someone had to. Why are you harassing me like this?"

"Do you have family nearby, Mr. Morgan?" Foster asked. "Friends? A place of employment?"

"None of your business," he said. "Your five minutes are up. I want you to leave." He let go of the couch and walked them to the door. When they eased back into the hall, he stood in the doorway again to claim his space. "Who told you to come here?"

Foster buttoned her jacket but didn't answer. "Thanks for your time, Mr. Morgan. We'll be in touch."

Li slipped on her sunglasses and smiled. "Have a nice day."

Bodie shut the door, locked it, and took a moment to breathe. He darted over to the phone and dialed Amelia's number. Waiting, his body shaking, for her to pick up. "Answer, damn it." He paced his living room, running his free hand through his hair.

Amelia picked up on the fourth ring. "Hey, Bod. What's up."

"The police were just here. At my place. They think I killed those women." He turned around to survey his apartment, feeling violated. "They saw all my stuff. I know they don't believe me. They'll be back. They always come back."

He left no space for Am to respond, he knew, but he was rattled, afraid. He couldn't take another locked room. It took a while for him to calm down and realize that Amelia hadn't tried to break in or ask a question or anything, that he'd only gotten silence from the other end all this time.

"Are you there?" he asked.

"Aren't I always?"

"You heard what I said?"

"Every word. It's ridiculous. You couldn't kill anyone."

She was calm. He hated that Amelia never rattled and he always did. He hated being the weak one, again. And he hated that he read a subtle condemnation in her words, which he knew she'd intended to be reassuring. Why couldn't *he* kill anyone?

He pounded his fist on the wall, furious at her, at himself. "Damn it, Am."

"What? I just said—"

"Skip it. The point is they don't believe me. They know about my case. They know what happened, and they don't believe me."

"What I'd like to know is what brought them to your door," Amelia said. "You were charged with trespassing, given probation. There was no violence. Out of all the people in the city, out of all the trespassers, why'd they come to you?"

Bodie had no answer. His head was a muddle, too many thoughts, all at once, all different directions.

"Think," Amelia said. "Someone led them to your door."

"Someone? Someone like who? I don't know anyone who would—" Bodie froze, and then a rage he could barely contain began to scorch him from the inside. "Dr. Silva. It was her. She was here, wheedling, trying to get me back in sessions."

"Why does she want *you*?"

Again, Bodie could swear he heard subtle derision in Am's voice. Why wouldn't Silva want him? Why wouldn't anyone? His brain raced a mile a minute. Police meant trouble. Police meant a locked cell. "It was her. That evil . . ."

"Bod? You're fine. Everything's going to be fine."

As she spoke, he could feel himself calming down. Amelia always helped with that. "You're right. Everything's fine. I'm okay. I didn't tell her anything but lies, so she has nothing. I'm good. I see that now."

After a moment of silence between them, Amelia said, "Bod? Maybe no walking tonight?"

He nodded in agreement, though Am couldn't see it. "You're right. Not tonight."

"Good. Now, tell me again about Dr. Silva?"

"What do you want to know?"

"Everything."

CHAPTER 46

Amelia slid her phone into her pocket and went back to her canvas with Bodie on her mind. He was in trouble again, which meant she had trouble to resolve. She could have used a cuddle from Winston, but Joie wasn't in, her work in progress, her work space, deserted this morning. Amelia raised a brush and stood there evaluating, deciding where to start. The first stroke was always the most important for her, setting the tone for the entire session. She twirled the brush in her hand, a fresh dab of crimson paint on the tip, waiting for her muse to tell her where to apply it; then she stepped up to the canvas, said hello, and painted a dot. Her first strike.

"Bodie . . . a killer." She laughed, then stopped. She stepped back from her work and thought about what Bodie had told her about his persistent psychiatrist. Why was she so invested in her brother? What had she seen in him? What had he said?

The basement flashed in her mind with its stench of death. She remembered how otherworldly the silence had been. After their gruesome discovery, she never saw her father go down to the basement again, but she knew he did. She could feel it, sense it, though not a single sound had ever breached the padlocked door.

She would lie in bed at night and imagine what might be happening floors below her and who might be on the table. The abnormal had a way of becoming normal. All it took was the will to let it. Amelia knew at twelve that it was her father this way or no way, and so she adapted, accepted, and ignored. She'd made a choice that Bodie hadn't been equipped to make. No, Bodie had no stomach for killing. He had no stomach for life either. Bodie was a broken train, a damaged birdhouse, a casualty of blackhearted blood. Now Amelia needed a plan.

She let out a long exhale, then picked up another brush, a smaller one, and dipped it in white, then approached the canvas again. Art. Her art. Art from her mind, her soul, her essence. Her life. Her blood and sweat, her gift. Smiling, contented, she expertly painted a tiny rose. She thought of secrets and how they took on a life of their own after a time. Everyone had secrets.

She stepped back to admire the rose with a critical eye. "Dr. Mariana Silva."

Amelia stepped forward again, grabbing another brush, looking for a good spot on the canvas. "Ah. There."

She painted a door, a padlock, a tree, and the still face of a woman with the bluest eyes.

CHAPTER 47

Foster had requested a couple of hours of personal time. There were things she needed to do, things she'd neglected, things she had to be there for. She slid her car to the curb in front of Glynnis's house and sat for a while watching kids play on the front lawn, birthday streamers festooned along the front door of the neat Georgian home. Balloons. It was Glynnis's son's birthday. Todd was ten today.

She didn't see him roughhousing on the lawn with the other boys but didn't have to wonder why. Glynnis's death had hit them hard. She doubted Todd would be in much of a party mood. Leaning over to the back seat, she grabbed the brightly wrapped gift from the seat and got out. She'd bought him a model airplane, hopefully one he didn't already have. She would have promised Glynnis that she would stay close to her family, be there for them, if she'd had the chance.

After weaving through the kids, she rang the doorbell and waited, the box in her hands, feeling a little self-conscious about being here, feeling like an outsider in a place that, until two months ago, had felt like a second home. There'd been backyard barbecues and dinners, cocktail hours where she'd find that Glynnis had invited an unattached man she thought Foster would hit it off with. Glynnis's husband, Mike, had been a pallbearer at Reg's funeral. He'd helped keep her upright at the grave site, she remembered, as the world had spun around and all she could see through tear-filled eyes was a silver casket with a

Superman decal plastered on it, the casket holding all that she was or ever would be.

Mike smiled, happy to see her. "Hey there, stranger." He opened the door to let her in, then gave her a hug that threatened to crush the box. "Glad you could make it."

"Like I'd miss Toddie's birthday."

"Thanks. Here. Let me take that." He reached over and took the box, setting it on a side table of gifts piled high. "He's in the back, I think. They're tossing the football around. C'mon."

She followed him back, past a few adults—parents of the kids outside, she figured—offering nods and smiles as she passed through the front room and the hall, past Glynnis's perfect sunny kitchen, to the open back door. Through the screen she could see Todd sitting on a swing, languidly moving back and forth, watching three boys about his age scramble over a dusty football on the patchy grass, their party clothes in disarray, grass stains at the knees. He looked so small and so much like Glynnis—a mess of brown curly hair, thin, eyes the color of a cherished teddy bear.

"Oh crap," Mike said, taking in the scene. "He was playing with them a second ago. One minute it looks like he's okay, the next . . ."

"He and Jamie aren't doing well?"

Mike turned to her, true heartbreak on his face. "They're not doing great. It's just . . . how do you get past it? I have no idea what to say to help them process what happened."

"Having your mom here's got to help."

"I couldn't do this without her, that's for sure. But it doesn't take the place of their mother, does it? I've put us all in therapy. I need my boys to come out of this whole. I want that for myself too."

She gave his arm a comforting squeeze but said nothing. He was right. Nothing could ever take the place of their mother, and therapy was good. Glynnis would approve. She stepped out onto the patio. "Let me wish him a happy birthday. I can't stay long. I've got to get back. I'll come find you on my way out. Say goodbye."

"Wait, you haven't said how you're doing. You two were besties. Hell, I think she liked you more than she liked me half the time. Now you've got this monster case. *Three* women? How're you holding up?"

Foster thought for a moment. There was so much she could say, so much she didn't want to. She settled on the latter, giving the standard response. "I'm good. We'll find him." She could see the worry settle on Mike's face, but she looked past it.

"I have no doubt," he said. "Hey, when you come back through, I'll introduce you to those half-soused parents up front." He leaned in. "In fact, there's a single dad in there who . . ."

She chuckled, then punched him lightly on the arm. "Get away from me."

He gave her a playful wink. "Glynnie would have."

"I know."

As she stepped off the patio onto the grass, she could hear him still laughing as she approached the swing.

"Hey, Toddie."

The boy looked up, his long face brightening. "Aunt Harri. You came."

She sat down on the other swing. "Sure I did. You're one of my favorite people. And ten's a big birthday. Double digits." She looked over at the boys running in the yard. "Why aren't you over there?"

"I was. It was stupid, so I stopped."

The two swung at the same lazy pace for a while, watching the boys play and squeal and gleefully run amok. She wouldn't push him.

"I don't see Jamie. Where is he?"

"In his room. He's always in his room now. Because he's thirteen . . . and weird."

She took comfort in the fact that the family was getting help. Mike was doing the right thing. "I'll stop and say hello before I leave. So how have you been doing? How's school?"

He stopped swinging, twisted around to face her, the chains criss-crossing. "I don't want to talk about school."

"Okay."

"Do *you* know why she did it?"

Foster felt the air leave her lungs, rapidly, all in a rush. The earnest ten-year-old's eyes stared at her without blinking, nailing her to the spot. He didn't have to say who "she" was or what "it" was. "She" and "it" would be all they'd ever have to say to have everyone affected understand. But what did you say to a kid about the loss of a mother who'd taken her own life and left him behind?

Maybe this wasn't her place. In fact, she was sure it wasn't. She glanced over at the back door, hoping Mike was close by and she could signal him over, but he wasn't there. "The question" was hers to grapple with here on the swings with Glynnis's boy.

"Sometimes you don't know why," she said. "Sometimes you find out too late that people are suffering in some way." Her eyes held his, those light-brown eyes filled with hurt and uncertainty. "Sometimes they can't talk about it, so there's nothing you can do to help them."

"So I'll never know why?"

"You might not. That's the hard part."

"You didn't know?"

She tried taking a breath, but there was nothing there. She shook her head.

Todd twisted back. "Maybe it was me and Jamie? We fight a lot over stupid stuff. Like when he swiped my mitt and then hid it in the basement behind the washer. Maybe if we didn't do stuff like that, she—"

Foster reached over and stopped him from swinging, turning him around to face her. "Listen to me. Toddie? *Listen.* Nothing. *Nothing* you did or said caused your mother pain, you hear me? She loved you both so much, every hair on your heads, inside and out. *That's* the truth. What happened was not your fault. It was just a tragedy, a very sad thing that happened."

"Like with Reggie," he said.

For a moment, the mention of her son's name stunned her. "Yes. Life is hard sometimes, Toddie; it just is. Terrible things happen, but good things happen too. All we can do sometimes is hold on for the good things and reach out to the people who love us."

"Like you?"

She held his sharp chin gently between thumb and index finger. "Like me and your dad, Jamie, your grandmother, your friends. All of us are here for you. Always. Your mom would want you to be so, so happy, especially today. She'd want you to be okay. So will you try? Just a little?" She got a tentative nod. She smiled. "I'll try too. But if you ever need to talk, if it all gets too big, you can always call me. Promise you will?"

"I will. Your number's in my phone."

"Good." She tousled his hair. They went back to swinging in silence. The boys on the grass had given up on the football and were just rolling around on the ground.

"What if there aren't any good things?" Todd asked.

"There are," she said. "There'll be lots of good things."

The chains on the swings squeaked as they swung back and forth. There was the smell of the grass, the cleanness in the autumn air. Inside adults laughed and joked around, the sound of it breaching the screen door. The entire world moved, went on with what it was doing as a little boy who'd lost his mother came to terms with it on a squeaky swing in a backyard on his birthday.

"She hurt too much to stay for my birthday," he whispered. "It was nothing I did."

Foster could feel her eyes begin to fill but fought it back. "No, Toddie. I promise you it was nothing you did."

"I'm still not playing any dumb football or rolling around in the grass like an idiot. I'm ten now."

Her eyes narrowed at the wrestling boys. "I feel you, bud."

CHAPTER 48

Another dead girl, another article cut out and tacked to the board. Silva stood at her board studying the photos, noting the similarities between the victims. The police weren't going to use her. She hadn't made an impression on Foster or Li. Now what? How could she get close to the investigation? She needed to be in a consulting position with access to Bodie Morgan.

She walked over to her desk and booted up her laptop to the first two chapters of her book in progress. She needed more, a lot more, but she couldn't finish without her jewel in the crown. Books needed to be sensational, provocative, sexy. They had to have a hook, a draw. Three young women murdered in the streets? A predator on the loose? And her so close and yet so far from the center of the action? Infuriating.

Silva slammed the laptop closed, grabbed her coat, and left her apartment, ending up a short time later in front of Bodie Morgan's apartment. It was after ten and the street was empty. She noticed an unmarked police car sitting outside his building. They were watching him. So they'd taken her seriously, after all. What lies had he told when they'd questioned him? Could they now see what she saw so clearly?

She wanted desperately to go in and try again to get Bodie to come back to Westhaven, to her, but she hung back, hesitant to try again, at least this way. He would know by now that she had brought him to the police department's attention. Approaching him now would not be wise. No, she had to outthink him, maneuver him into a position that left him few options. Silva drew her collar up against the cold, then walked away.

Soon, she thought. Soon.

CHAPTER 49

Li was at her desk when Foster came in a little before eight the next morning. The office was still relatively sedate. It was even quieter outside for a change, the protests not yet started up for the day. Someone had already burned the office coffee, though, the scorched smell of scalded beans floating overhead like a cloud of slow-moving acid rain. Same old, same old.

Something about Dr. Mariana Silva worried Li. How many psychiatrists hovered over their patients after they'd been released from their care? Was the woman neglecting her other patients as she ran after Bodie Morgan? Did the woman really believe her former patient was a killer and that more lives were at risk?

Foster stood at her desk, smiling slightly. "I know you went home. You're wearing a different shirt." It was an echo of Li's words to her when she'd beaten her partner in by hours the other day.

Li looked up, grinned. "Touché, *partenaire*. I've pulled up everything I could find on Silva. There's something there. Did you get that feeling?"

Foster sat in her chair, stowed her bag in the bottom drawer. "Yeah. She seemed almost eager to throw Morgan under the bus. I get that she believes he's dangerous, but from what she told us, she couldn't have that much information on him to base that opinion on. We can't take her belief in his guilt to court."

"He *was* jittery," Li said.

"Most people we talk to are jittery," Foster said.

"Well, I get suspicious when people are too helpful," Li said. "It's unnatural. I'm going to find out what Silva's deal is." She leaned back in her chair, eyed Foster across the desk. "You sure interested her, though."

Foster grabbed her coffee mug and prepared to hit the coffeepot. "What?"

"You didn't see how she stared at you? She was trying *real* hard to figure you out, and you were doing the same with her. Me? I've nailed her already. She's got a screw loose. She's worked so long in antisocial personality disorders that some of it probably rubbed off." Li slid a legal pad across the desk filled with her scribbled notations. "But like we found out yesterday, she's who she says she is. Leading psychiatrist, flying all over the world giving speeches, research, writing books, lecturing, tops in her field, head of a prestigious program at Johns Hopkins. A real star . . . until three years ago."

Foster scanned Li's notes. "What happened three years ago?"

"No idea. I can't find a single thing. Just one day she's the 'it girl'; then she's nowhere. She shows up at Westhaven a year later, and she's been there since. So now I'm wondering, what happened to the missing year?"

"Maybe she got tired of the grind, burned out, and took time off," Foster said.

Li wasn't buying it. "Does she look like the kind of person to take time off? She's wound tighter than steel wire rope. She was practically climbing our walls."

"I'm playing devil's advocate here," Foster said. "Maybe the decision was personal. Is she married? Have kids?"

Li shook her head. "Her career's her life. Looking at her career trajectory, if anything, she should be running Westhaven. Instead, she's one of four psychiatrists on staff. On Westhaven's website, Silva's not even listed as a senior staff member, and she's got more on her CV than the guy running the place."

"That's strange." Foster handed the pad back. "So, we find out what knocked Silva off her perch three years ago and what she was doing for a year."

"And Morgan?"

"We keep close tabs on him," Foster said. "Until we're sure he's not who we're looking for."

Li paused. "He could have been that dark figure with Birch. I don't believe he was home alone that night. If it were me, after a month in a psychiatric hospital I'd be all over the place, stuffing myself with hot dogs and drinking myself under the nearest table."

"Then we push back on his alibi and find those missing years." Foster glanced over at Li's mug and found it half-full. "Freshen that up for you?"

Li winced. "I can barely get this down. No thanks. I say we double team her," she said. "She's champing at the bit to get an inside track, so we use that. One of us checks her out at Westhaven, and to make sure she's not there when we do it, the other calls her in here to 'consult.'"

"Who does what?" Foster asked.

Li clasped her fingers behind her head and gave Foster a devious smirk. "I want a shot at knocking her off her high horse."

"Then I'll take Westhaven."

They shook on the deal; then Li dialed Westhaven's number, anticipating her next encounter with the slippery Silva. "It takes one to know one. Funny, isn't it, how something gets stuck in your head? *It takes one to know one* has been rattling around in mine since she was in here. Wouldn't it be funny if—" There was pickup on the other end of the line. "Yes, Dr. Silva? This is Detective Li. Would you have time to come in and talk to us again this morning? We could really use your help." She rolled her eyes, then listened for a response. "That's great. In an hour? Good. See you then." She hung up, holding her arms wide. "Masterful. She almost leaped through the phone wires."

Foster gave Li a thumbs-up, then headed for the coffeepot. "It takes one to know one."

CHAPTER 50

Li walked into the room and sat across from the doctor at the table. "Dr. Silva, thanks so much for coming in."

"No Detective Foster?"

"Not today. She's working on something else." Li could swear she saw disappointment in Silva's eyes.

"Have you arrested him?"

Li set her phone on the table, along with a legal pad and a pen. "Not yet. But we wanted to double back and ask you a few more questions. Can I get you anything? Coffee, water?"

Silva crossed her legs and adjusted her neat, severe suit, a silk paisley scarf tied at her neck for a splash of femininity, well appointed, professional. She brushed aside the offer. "If you don't have him, why am I here?"

"We went by Mr. Morgan's apartment yesterday."

"Did he let you in?"

"He did, actually. The badges helped. I wanted to hear more about your suspicions and your work. You must have encountered a lot of patients like Morgan."

"A few. Each one different, of course, but in terms of their sickness, their diagnoses, familiar in a lot of ways."

"Any at Mayo or Johns Hopkins?"

Silva hesitated. "You've done your homework, I see."

"I love homework," Li boasted. "Always have."

Silva twirled the topaz ring on her finger, turning it around and around at an even, steady pace. Li watched the move with interest, wondering if Silva was nervous or anxious.

"I've lectured, taught, all over the world, but yes, I was affiliated for a time with Mayo and Johns."

"Mayo. Let's talk about that. Why'd you leave there three years ago?" Silva tensed slightly. Li could see the woman's shoulders bunch up.

"To pursue other challenges. As a matter of fact, I'm writing a book based on my research. I've worked with patients many would consider the worst of the worst. It's vital that we learn what compels them to do the things they are called to do."

"Called to do?"

"By their illness."

"And your opinion is that Morgan is ill."

"It's a little more than opinion, Detective."

"You've been with Westhaven two years. You were last on staff at Mayo three years ago. Before that a year at Johns. There's a year missing. What'd you do in the gap?"

"Research," Silva said. "For my book, as I mentioned."

"Fascinating. Here?"

"Detective, with all due respect, you're wasting my time. I thought I was coming here to talk to Bodie Morgan." She stood to go. "When you have him, call me."

Silva reached for the doorknob. "But in the interim, when he kills again . . . the blood will be on your hands, not mine."

Li needed to keep Silva here to give Foster enough time at Westhaven. "He's hiding his victims," she said. She knew her words would draw Silva back to the table, and they did. Silva slowly returned and sat down again, her eyes practically dancing with delight. "Any idea why he'd do that . . . in your professional opinion?" Just a small piece of information, a morsel, a crumb, but it seemed to excite Silva to no end. "It's not a detail released to the press."

"Hiding them," Silva said. "How?"

"That I can't say."

"Then all I would be able to offer would be general ideas."

"I'll take those," Li said, sneaking a look at her watch, hoping Silva took her time.

"He'd want to conceal what he'd done, distance himself from the act of killing. There normally aren't feelings of remorse or guilt attached to people like him. That's part of the malfunction, but perhaps he's still struggling with what he is, still battling his impulses. There will come a point when he won't be able to. To give you more, I'd need more to go on."

"The person we're looking for is meticulous, selective, smart," Li said. "After reading Morgan's arrest report, he comes off as being kind of a mess. He doesn't seem to fit the profile you're giving me. I'm no psychiatrist, Doctor, but I would expect more Hannibal Lecter, less Walter Mitty."

"That's just it—you can't expect anyone to be what they appear to be, can you? Those like him are accomplished actors, talented mimics. They learn to simulate emotion; they learn to blend in. It's only when you begin to pull back the layers that you can clearly see they're not like any of us."

"So they walk among us, and we have no way of knowing," Li said. "That's a little frightening."

"Yes, it can be. Did you know that fifteen percent of our population has a personality disorder?" Silva's eyes bore into Li's. "To varying degrees."

Li stared over at the woman, creeped out by her intensity. "So . . . the missing year. You were working on your book. Where?"

"A tiny place. In the woods. There were few distractions. What more can you tell me?"

Li was calling it. She'd given Foster as much time as she was going to. Silva was giving her the willies. She got up from the table, walked over to the door, and opened it, the noise of the cops moving around outside a welcome reassurance. "Thank you for your time, Doctor."

Silva was upset. "Wasting it, you mean." She gathered her things and met Li at the door. "He's hiding them now," she said, "but soon he won't bother."

"We'll stop this long before that happens," Li said.

Silva lingered for a moment. "You sound confident." The insult in her tone was impossible to miss. Li opened the door wider and stepped back for Silva to walk through it. "One more thing," Li said. "Did Morgan ever mention lipstick?"

It was information, another detail that seemed to feed Silva, as expected. "Lipstick," Silva repeated. "I need context."

"On the bodies," Li said. "Sorry, I can't get any more specific."

"You're being deliberately vague, Detective. You think you have time for games, but I assure you, you don't. This very minute, he's out there choosing his next victim. This is time you've wasted, time you've forced *me* to waste. How can I possibly help you if you won't trust me?"

"You've helped us already, Dr. Silva. You've given us a lead we didn't have before. We appreciate that." Li nodded to a uniform to walk her out and watched as Silva left. Then she went to get her phone to call Foster and let her know Silva was on the move.

CHAPTER 51

Foster's cell phone buzzed in her pocket, and she slid it out to see who was calling. A text from Li. Silva had just left her. Time was short. She slipped the phone back and smiled at Dr. Emil Gershon, Westhaven's director, who stared at her with ferret eyes, his thin fingers laced together and resting on his executive desk. He seemed a little stuffy, rigid, not someone prone to flights of fancy. The herringbone suit with a vest and a stiff brown bow tie hinted as much. It was as though he'd stepped out of another era and staunchly refused to update himself to this one.

Coming in, she'd noticed that Westhaven was a lot smaller than she'd envisioned, though it stood resolute, cold, and imposing from the street, like a gray stone fortress, minus moat, keep, and turrets, a place no doubt easier to get into than out of. It was only as she drove through the gate and parked in the side lot that she noticed the cracks in the facade, the chipped front steps. The serene grounds, though, looked inviting enough, well suited to self-reflection. It had been the bars at the ground-floor windows that pulled her up short. The locked gate with the guard stationed in his small guard box didn't help assuage fears of being confined, even voluntarily.

"Sorry about that," she said to Gershon. Foster did the math in her head. From the station to the hospital's front gate, if Silva was on her way back, she had maybe forty-five minutes, no more, to get what she needed.

His dark, beady eyes scanned the room as if looking for a safe place to land. "The police. I don't understand. What has Dr. Silva done to come to your attention? Westhaven has an unblemished reputation; our staff and clinicians are . . ."

She stopped the sales pitch with a raised hand. "I'd just appreciate a little background, Dr. Gershon. As much as you can tell me. Please."

"You said homicide. What could Dr. Silva possibly have to do with a homicide?"

"Actually, we were hoping to enlist Dr. Silva's help. We have a very difficult situation at the moment. You've watched the news. We're dealing with a disturbed individual. Dr. Silva has the experience, and Westhaven has an excellent reputation."

Most people responded to a little ego stroking; Gershon appeared not to be an exception. "How did you hear of us . . . I mean, of her?"

Foster held his look, then told a lie. "I don't know, Dr. Gershon. I go where I'm assigned to go. My task is to find out if Dr. Silva can assist us in running this dangerous person to ground."

"You've come to the right place, then. We may be a smaller facility, but we employ only the best. Dr. Mariana Silva is highly regarded and has quite an impressive history with decades of clinical work under her belt. I should know; I vetted her myself."

"Westhaven is lucky to have her," Foster said.

A pompous smirk joined the beady-eyed stare. "I see it the other way around. *She's* lucky to be here."

"You vetted her yourself, and you obviously found nothing untoward. But Westhaven isn't Johns Hopkins or the lecture circuit in Lucerne. So with all due respect, sir, either you punched up and won the lottery, or there's some reason Silva punched down and landed here. Which is it?"

"Blunt," Gershon said with a sneer. "Painfully."

"No offense, Doctor, but things are moving fast. We need to know what we need to know, and we need to know it now."

"All right. Standard procedure. We needed another staff psychiatrist and put the call out, and Dr. Silva expressed an interest. I could hardly believe our good fortune. I conducted my research, contacted her previous employers, thoroughly reviewed her resume. I knew her by reputation, of course. She's authored numerous articles in all the top medical journals and magazines, consulted everywhere. Now we have her, and as a result, Westhaven has a deeper bench."

"And the patients Silva treats?" Foster asked.

"They're often classified as apex predators. Lions in the jungle, the top of the food chain. Though their disorder cannot be cured, per se—and there is no magic pill or long-term course of treatment—they can be taught skills to help manage their toxic tendencies. Here, though, we mostly treat depressives, mild personality disorders, PTSD. Actually, I had a fear that Dr. Silva would find us rather boring compared to the more dramatic cases she's encountered over her long career, but she has tucked right in."

"What was Dr. Silva doing just prior to joining Westhaven?"

"Why is that important?" he replied.

"Just getting a complete picture, Dr. Gershon."

"She was on sabbatical, I believe. Working on a personal project. A book. She's written several. We all step away on occasion to publish or teach. Psychoanalysis is a constantly evolving field. I'll save you some time here, Detective. Shall I? Dr. Silva is the best there is. Period."

Foster checked her watch, stood, and placed her card on Gershon's desk. "Thanks for your time. I hope we can double back if there are other questions?"

Gershon beamed, a Cheshire Cat in herringbone. "Please do."

The hall outside his office was empty except for her, but she could hear activity somewhere—murmured voices, feet shuffling along the floor, doors slamming shut. The soft soap PR pitch from Gershon felt a little suspicious. She'd met the woman. She'd sat across from her and looked into her eyes. She wasn't as she seemed. There was something there, and she needed to know what that *something* was. Next move? A deeper dive. That missing year.

Maybe Li had already found it. Foster sent her a quick text for an update on her way to the car. As she passed the entrance to the out-patient clinic, she stopped and turned back, giving her watch a quick glance to check for time. If she hurried, if she got in and out, she would miss Silva.

The stout blonde woman sitting at the front desk paled when Foster presented her badge and identified herself; then she slowly rolled her chair away from the counter a few inches, as though Foster might lunge over and slap on cuffs. She read the nameplate on the desk. Ellen Vosk.

"Is there someone I can talk to about Dr. Silva, Ms. Vosk?"

"Dr. Silva?" Her brown eyes widened in surprise. "Is it about an appointment? Never mind. No, it wouldn't be, would it? Or it could; I don't know. I'm rambling. Sorry. It's the badge and . . ." Vosk's eyes landed on the gun at Foster's side. "Not every day we get a visit from the police."

Suddenly self-conscious, Foster readjusted her jacket to conceal her service weapon, hoping to put Vosk at ease. "It's not a raid. I just need some information."

"Right. Yes. Information. You'd have to talk to Dr. Norton, then. He's in charge of the clinic. But unfortunately, he's with a patient right now. Would you like to wait? I don't think I can interrupt him. Sometimes sessions can get intense, and he—"

"How long?"

"He just started, so it'd be fifty minutes."

Foster looked over the waiting area, finding three people sitting in cushioned chairs, a television mounted to the wall tuned to a game show with wheels and buzzers and excited contestants jumping up and down. No one was paying her the least bit of attention. She turned back to the receptionist and lowered her voice. "How's Dr. Silva to work with? You like her?"

The questions seemed to catch Vosk off guard. "*My* impressions? Oh, um. Fine, I guess? She's very serious. She doesn't spend a lot of time out here in reception. Any, as a matter of fact."

"Meaning not friendly, standoffish?"

The woman cast a look toward the hall presumably leading to the office area. "She's . . . efficient. But you really need to talk with Dr. Norton. I don't think I should discuss staff members to . . . you know."

"Understood." Foster plucked one of Dr. Norton's business cards from the card holder on the counter. She eyed Silva's there, too, and took one of hers as well. "Email and direct line. Great." She smiled. "All right. I'll call back and talk to Dr. Norton. Thanks."

Vosk nodded, her eyes burning with curiosity. "She hasn't done anything . . . illegal, has she?"

"Would it surprise you if she had?"

The woman took a moment to think about it. "I'm not sure. Maybe?"

Foster stepped closer to the counter, lowering her voice even more. "You're not sure if it would surprise you?"

"Well, she hasn't been here that long." Vosk bit her lower lip. "But she hasn't made things easy."

Foster waited for more, but that was all there was. Vosk busied herself with the papers on her desk, moving them nervously from one side of the desk to the other. There was more she could say, Foster was sure, but she was also sure she wouldn't get anything else. It wasn't a crime to be difficult or unliked, even if she had found Silva a bit off putting and arrogant. And still the same questions rattled around in her head. Why had Silva come *here*? Why was she so tied up with Bodie Morgan? Why had she fallen off the map for a year?

"Have a nice day," Foster said, moving away.

Vosk rolled her chair forward now that she was going. "Sorry. I'm so afraid of guns. I can't imagine carrying one around all day. How do you do it?"

Foster pulled the jacket closed again, this time buttoning it. "You get used to it." She rapped her knuckles on the counter once. "Thanks again."

Out front she stood on the stairs, checking her phone again. Nothing from Li. She felt around in her pocket, working the odd assortment of paper clips, pushpins, and thumbtacks around in her fingers, counting them absently, feeling them, pricking her fingers a little. Each tiny thing represented a small victory, a move forward. When she felt that strength move through her again, she pulled her hand away.

Foster was about to push off the stairs when a white man, about thirty, walked up and stood by her, rocking on a pair of battered white running shoes, a Westhaven staff ID pinned to his blue polo shirt. "Heard you asking about Dr. Silva," he said. She took a step back, turned her gun side away. His ID read *John Aarons*. "They're never going to tell you anything in there. They cover for each other." His grin revealed a set of uneven teeth stained by nicotine. "Kinda like cops, right?"

Another cop basher. Now on alert but also pissed off, Foster took a full assessment that started at Aarons's greasy widow's peak and ended at his frayed pant cuffs. Threat? Low. Irritation factor? High. She slid her sunglasses on, turned away from him. There was work to do. "Good day."

"I mean, they're never going to tell you no one here likes Silva. She's a witch. Maybe a real one, for all I know. What do they call them? Wickers?" Aarons slipped a pack of cigarettes out of his back pocket, lit one, and then offered another to her, which she rejected with a headshake and scowl. "She thinks she's too good for the place—that's the deal," he continued. "She treats everybody like they're servants, like we're all here to make her life easier. Like I said, witch. But they're not going to lose their jobs ratting her out. Not even that gasbag Norton. If you didn't get anything out of Gershon, the head gasbag, you won't get anything out of him either. Codependent. That's what they are."

"But losing your job's not a concern for you?"

"Nah, I hate this job and this whole place. Too many locked doors."

"What *is* your job?"

"Clinic assistant. Glorified bouncer, more like. The lithium wears off and they lose it, I help the staff get them in a chair and calmed back down. But I'm already halfway out the door." He cocked his head, his eyes narrowing. "You like being a cop? I hear you guys get a decent benefits package. Vision and everything. I've been thinking lately I might try to get on." A man with a briefcase passed between them, heading inside, giving them only a passing glance. Aarons didn't appear to notice.

"Tell me more about Dr. Silva," Foster said, "since you appear to know a lot."

"She's been here a year or so, and nobody's had a moment's peace since. She barks orders, throws her weight around. The doctors don't even like her, but I think it's mostly because she tries to snag all the hard-core cases. She goes through the files picking the ones she wants, like she's filling her stable with champion horses or something. Prima donna, that's what she is. And there's gossip." Aarons grinned, seemingly proud of himself for having the inside scoop. "Something happened with her in Baltimore. Don't bother asking me what, because I don't know. Somebody heard Gershon say that if it wasn't for this place, she'd be no place, you know what I mean? They're thicker than thieves, those two."

Aarons took a drag on his cigarette, blew the smoke out slow. "Scuttlebutt is all. For sure nobody's got the balls to ask Silva about it to her face. She's not the kind of person you want to be on the bad side of."

Foster glanced out over the grounds, the lot, her car parked in it. Could Baltimore account for the missing year, the unexplainable exit from Mayo? "Anything else, Mr. Aarons?"

"Well, about me signing on with you guys. Maybe you got an in?"

Foster looked at him without an ounce of enthusiasm or encouragement. "Go online. Find out when the next test is scheduled. Sign up to take it."

He looked disappointed. "Test? You gotta take a test? Why? I'm, like, ready-made for the work. Look at this." He lifted up his short sleeve, flexed. "The guns alone, I mean, c'mon. No knock on you gals, but guy cops with guns like these have it over whatever it is you all bring to the table, no offense."

"The man who passed us a minute ago. Describe him to me."

Aarons's face went blank. "What man?"

"White guy. Midforties. He got out of that gray Nissan over there." Aarons turned toward the lot and spotted the Nissan—nothing about it seeming to ring a bell from the look on his face. "He's wearing a blue suit—white shirt, blue tie—under a tan raincoat with a plaid lining," Foster said. "He's carrying a brown leather sample case about the size of a businessman's special in his right hand, slightly worn at the seams. Dark eyes, dark-brown hair cut short, thinning on top. Thin nose. Thin lips. Approximately six foot one, no wedding ring. Black shoes. He doesn't work here, or else he would have acknowledged you in some way when he passed by, or you him. Pharmaceutical rep?"

Aarons's cigarette dangled from his slightly parted lips. "What the fuck?"

"It's not about the biceps. Thanks for the information, Mr. Aarons."

She slowed on her way to the lot to send Li a text. Short, sweet. **Re: Silva. Let's check Baltimore for that missing year. Some trouble there.**

Before sliding into the car, she gave the hospital entrance a final look. Aarons had gone back inside, likely to track down the man she'd described. Just what the department needed, another Lonergan. She shook her head and started the car.

"Biceps."

CHAPTER 52

The studio was in an old factory building in the West Loop. Redbrick, solid, built to last, though the businesses that had built them, that had carved the names of their entrepreneurial founders into the stone over the entrances, had gone bust long ago. Times had changed and found them lacking. There were now cheaper, more efficient ways to manufacture pickles, bread, steel cans, and shirt buttons. But the buildings still stood occupied, now by quaint antique shops and chic art galleries, frilly bridal boutiques, and artisanal cafés. There was no signage out front, but there was nothing much you couldn't find by a simple internet search. This was Amelia's place.

She wasn't inside. He knew when she came and went. It was the Black woman with the strange hair and the squat bulldog who he watched through the window. She was sculpting something, the dog by her side. He didn't like dogs, and they didn't like him. But he wanted to see what Amelia had built. He wanted to get a sense of who she'd become. And he wanted her to know that good things, glorious things, were coming. That there would be a house like before, projects like before, and family.

The smell of turpentine and plaster were the first things to register as he pushed his way inside to stand in the center of the long, wide room. Nothing surprising about the interior; he'd expected no less. The factory dinge had been replaced by exposed brick, high ceilings scored by track lighting, and white walls. Artsy, like the cafés and galleries down the street. Not a single remnant of the indentured factory workers who eked out difficult lives for dimes a day remained. His eyes drifted to the large painting anchored to the wall, unfinished, its colors and complexity and genius pinning him to where he stood, flooding his senses, filling him with pride, awe, and envy.

"Help you?"

Reluctantly, he turned from the canvas to address the young woman with the purple streak in her curly hair. She peeked from behind a plaster statue that made no sense to him, something with wings, something esoteric and frustratingly ambiguous. The dog leaped off its pad and trotted toward him, halting halfway there. The low growl started deep in its belly and rumbled up, gaining momentum, until it turned into a round of wild, frenzied barking, the noise of it as painful as a red-hot spike through his head. He took a step forward but stopped himself. He needed the barking to stop. He couldn't be held responsible if it didn't stop.

"Winston, relax. What's the matter with you?" She grabbed the dog by his collar and held him back. The dog glared at him as if he could see his soul, as if he knew what he'd done and what he'd keep on doing.

He smiled, and the rage passed; the burning in his brain cooled. "Sorry. I didn't mean to upset him."

The growl was back, low but growing. "He's usually cool with people. I don't know what's the matter with him."

The man ventured forward, closer to the silly plaster block. He could tell the woman was worried about her dog's reaction. It was out of character, and now she was suspicious of him. Searching his memory bank, he ratcheted up the smile, adding warmth and a playful twinkle to his brown eyes. He became a person.

"This is beautiful." He stared at the statue in progress. "What's it called?"

"Not sure yet. It'll tell me when I'm done, or at least I hope it will." Winston retreated to his pad, but his dark eyes followed his every move. "I'm Joie, by the way."

"Pleasure to meet you, Joie. I was looking for Amelia? I thought she might be in."

He could feel the woman's guard drop, though he made sure not to get too close, not to invade her personal space. Easy to do. She held no interest for him. Neither did the dog.

She dusted her hands off on the plaster-splotched apron she wore. "Oh, she hasn't been in today. We don't keep regular hours. Was she expecting you?"

"No, I'm just passing through. Unplanned stop." He turned back to the canvas, letting the lie sit. Amelia's painting really was magnificent. "Did she paint this?"

"Yeah. It's her masterpiece, for sure. She's obsessed with it, but I suppose all artists get wrapped up in their work, right? Otherwise, why bother in the first place. Eh, how do you know Amelia?"

He moved closer to the canvas, taking the work in, every inch, every line. Reaching out, he lightly touched it with his index finger, feeling the tracks in the paint left behind by the artist's brush. "We're old friends."

He could almost feel Joie working it out. Old friends, yet he was considerably older and unspectacular, average in every outward way. The grin on his face when he turned away from the canvas was self-deprecating, shy, not the truth. "You could say I knew her when."

"If you leave your name, I'll let her know you stopped by."

The woman looked down at Winston, who was on full alert, watching him, ready to go at him if he made even the slightest of wrong moves. Protecting his owner, of course, but the dog's vigilance was making Joie uneasy. He watched as she stepped back and put the block of plaster between them, sneakily slipping her chisel out of her apron pocket. It was a subtle move, one that told him she wasn't comfortable.

The chisel would not have been enough. "Or your number," she said. "I'm sure she'd like to get in touch."

"That's okay," he said. "I'll come back. Surprise her. You can tell her for me, though, that she's a wonderful artist. Will you?"

"Sure. She'll love to hear that." Joie flicked a look at her block of whatever. He could tell she was relieved he was going.

He turned for the door, giving the canvas one last look, but stopped and turned back. "Tell her also that it's still all for one and one for all."

Joie's brow wrinkled. "Like from *The Three Musketeers*?"

He brightened. "You know the story?"

"Doesn't everybody? We read it in like seventh grade."

He considered her reaction for a moment. "I suppose you're right." He looked down at her pet. "Sorry for upsetting Winston." The dog's ears perked up as he lifted half off the pad, the growl starting again. "Enjoy your day."

Stepping out onto the street, he stood on the sidewalk, watching the street. Pleased with himself, he was. He'd made first contact after so many years of lurking in shadows, planning, perfecting. Behind him the studio door locked. He didn't have to turn around to know that it was Joie locking herself in and him out. Didn't matter. He'd done what he'd come to do.

"Her masterpiece."

He smiled, a real one this time, then walked away whistling. Something light, jaunty. There were good things coming. This was the start.

"What a wonderful day, Amelia."

CHAPTER 53

Joie practically tackled Amelia when she came through the door an hour later. "We have to call the police."

"Why? What happened?"

Joie's eyes were wild, jumpy. Not like her. Winston, too, looked wired, ready for a fight. Amelia quickly turned to her canvas, relieved to find it as she'd left it. Then she scanned the room, but nothing seemed to be out of order there either, so not a burglary.

"This strange man came in looking for you," Joie said. "He just wandered in off the street and said he was here to see you. That you were old friends."

"That's all? I thought something serious had happened." Amelia broke away from Joie's grip and slipped out of her jacket, moving over to check her brushes and her paint. "What old friend?" She didn't have any old friends—or new ones for that matter. She had herself, her art, and Bodie.

"You don't know him?"

Amelia chuckled. "How could I? You haven't told me anything."

Joie dug into her apron pocket for her phone, her hands shaking. "White guy. Fifties. Kinda average all around. Brown eyes but deep set. I'll never forget them. And the coldest motherfucking smile you'd ever want to see. It sent shivers down my spine. But the worst part was that Winston took an instant dislike to him. He growled, barked, wouldn't go anywhere near him. He never does that. He's a love bug; you know that. But this guy? Not on your life. Dogs know."

As Joie recited the man's particulars, Amelia knew. The eyes, the smile. "Who are you calling?"

"The police, of course. I should have done it an hour ago, but I wanted to check with you first in case he was actually legit."

"Wait," Amelia said. "He just came in and looked around? He didn't say anything?"

"Nothing important. Something about you being a good artist." Her fingers trembled on the keypad. She missed the final digit in 911 and had to start again. "Damn it. He liked your canvas, I mean, *really* liked it. He could barely keep his eyes off it. Then he talked about *The Three Musketeers* for some stupid reason. Some 'all for one, one for all' bullshit. He's obviously some loon. The second he walked out, I locked the door on him. No way he was getting back in here."

Amelia placed a hand on Joie's, stopping the call. "Then it's over." Though she sounded calm, every neuron in her body fired, excitement crackling through her like sparks off a roaring fire. "And I know exactly who that was."

"Well, who?"

"My Uncle Frank. Not actually my uncle but an old friend of my father's. He's practically part of the family. A bit odd, but he's okay." She saw the skepticism in Joie's eyes. "Really."

Joie held the phone in her hand. "*Uncle* Frank."

"Yep. He scared you, huh?" She chuckled. "You were perfectly safe. Winston too. But what's with the 'one for all' business?" Keeping it light, keeping it normal, but she knew. She knew who and why, and the moment was suddenly as bright as a Christmas morning. The day. It was here. Now.

"Not funny. You weren't around. You didn't feel the temperature of the room drop when he walked in, and you didn't see Winston freak out. He went off."

Amelia glanced down at Winston. He was watching her, but it didn't look like she was going to get her customary rush or cuddle. Something had changed between them. He growled at her, then backed away, drawing closer to Joie. Amelia gave him a sympathetic pout. "Poor Winston."

Joie exhaled, relief flooding her. "Wow. Okay. Uncle Frank. Tell me something. I'm telling you, old dude needs to work on his people skills." She slid the phone into her pocket and padded back to her side of the studio, Winston trotting along beside her.

"He's all right once you get to know him." Amelia stepped up to her canvas, her back to Joie, physically incapable of getting the smile off her face. "He said I was a good artist, huh? That's wild. He say anything else?"

"Loved your painting. Didn't say squat about my shit. But the real creepy part was after he left, he just stood out front looking around; then he walked off whistling like he didn't have a care in the world. I mean, who whistles? And who doesn't have a care in the world? The world's sinking like a rock, and he's just living the dream, apparently, and in a mood to whistle? Think about it. When's the last time you even heard someone whistle?"

Amelia turned, a brush in her hand. "Nothing wrong with whistling."

"When you're a creepy old dude who scares the Milk-Bones out of an innocent dog? Yeah, there is. That's elevating the creep factor by like a million." Winston stood up, moved off his doggy pad, and eased in beside Joie.

Amelia squatted down and called for Winston. "C'mere, boy. Where's my hug?"

Winston growled, refusing to move. Joie reached down to comfort him. "See? He's still not right. He's even growling at you now."

Amelia stood watching Winston for a moment, and then she turned back to her work. It was too momentous a day to worry about dog cuddles and growls. She felt too good, too light. She began to hum.

"I'm telling you," Joie said as she began to chisel, "you say he's harmless, fine. But the hairs rose up on the back of my neck. He felt dangerous, like he was cold all the way through. There's something off with that guy, family friend or no family friend."

Amelia felt Joie's eyes on her back but didn't turn around. She had work to do. He'd seen her painting and admired it, but had he really *seen* it? Did he fully appreciate her vision? "Was there anything else he said, Joie?"

"I don't think so, but . . . you're humming."

"Oh, sorry. I didn't mean to disturb you. I'll stop."

"No, you're humming the same song he was whistling."

Amelia smiled and squeezed her eyes shut for one blissful moment. "How weird is that, huh?"

CHAPTER 54

"I've found it!" Li shot up from her chair, signaling to the entire team. "Yep. You heard it right. Detective Vera Li has cracked the code." Everyone gathered in to hear as Li read from her notebook, holding court. "Silva's missing year. She was last on staff at Mayo. Before that, Johns Hopkins. That's all squared away, no problems; then she drops a year before she comes here."

"Her sabbatical," Foster said, "according to Gershon."

Li shook her head. "Stillman-Gates, the Westhaven of Baltimore or maybe a half step up. But the question, my friends, is not how she got to Stillman but why she left Mayo." Li waited. All the tired cop eyes in the place were on her; no one was in the mood for a magic show.

"Consider the question asked?" Symansky said, the bags under his eyes large enough to carry a week's worth of groceries.

Griffin, who'd come out of her office for the details, stood with her arms crossed, looking at least a year older than she had the day before. "Li, do not make me come over there."

"Buzzkills, all of you. Turns out Silva got into a little trouble," Li said. "She was censured and then outright fired by Mayo for reportedly getting 'too close' to a patient. But not just any patient, a killer infamously dubbed the Beltway Slasher. Silva, being a big cheese psychoanalyst affiliated with an elite institution, had been brought in to get inside the Slasher's head."

"Did she try busting him out?" Kelley asked. "Because that would make one helluva movie."

"Not sure," Li said. "I don't think so. Anyway, whatever went down, Mayo kept it close to the vest and cut ties with her as fast as they could, but enough got out so that some people knew about it and talked about it, at least in Baltimore. Quite the stain. Anyway, Silva's locked out, and literally everything dries up for her. The fall is steep and humiliating as hell."

"Betcha it's sex," Symansky said. "It's always sex."

Kelley frowned. "She's in her *sixties*."

Symansky sat up and glared at the younger man. "News flash, buckaroo: sex don't stop when the AARP card shows up in the mailbox."

"So she landed at Stillman, then at Westhaven," Foster said, hoping to get back on track. "Where Gershon didn't care about the 'too close' thing? Where she then glommed on to Morgan?"

"Maybe she wanted to get 'too close' to him, too, and he wasn't having it," Symansky said.

Kelley tossed a grungy-looking hacky sack up in the air, caught it, and repeated the toss. "That might explain her shoving him under the bus. A woman scorned."

Foster scribbled notes, thinking about the connection, wondering what it said about Silva's motives or her game plan. She looked up and over at her partner. "How'd you find Stillman-Gates?"

"I started at Westhaven and worked backward," Li said. "It seemed odd to me that she would jump from hospital to hospital, especially at her level, so I checked, found the gap, and made a list of other psychiatric facilities in Baltimore and started calling. I also had an old boyfriend in the city. He's a psychologist now, married with kids, but we had a cordial conversation. His move to Baltimore broke us up, but I harbor no hard feelings." The room quieted. "Right. Not important about the breakup. I get it.

"So Caleb, my ex, told me the whole thing never made the papers because everybody involved, especially Silva, clamped down on it super hard. The Slasher case was huge there, so you can imagine the heat Mayo would have gotten. If their donors and benefactors got a whiff of the scandal, there's a good chance a lot of the hospital center's funding would have dried up, so they dropped Silva like she weighed a million pounds, locked the castle up tight, and raised all the drawbridges so she couldn't get back in." Li snapped her fingers. "It was like she was never there."

Foster turned back to her computer, her fingers tapping away. "The Beltway Slasher, a.k.a. Alvin Keyes. He killed eight women. Slashed them from ear to ear. He copped to eight murders. They only found five bodies. He got more than two hundred years in prison. Obviously, he's still there."

"Till he shrivels up and blows away," Li said. "Wicks was slashed from ear to ear."

Lonergan laughed. "You think Silva did that?" He stood up from his chair. "What are we doin', writin' a screenplay? Look, she's a quack lookin' for her fifteen minutes, right? She was high, now she's low, and she can't deal with it, so whatever attention she can get, she'll take. This Morgan's an odd duck, so she throws him at us, we take a dive down the rabbit hole, or Li does, and then she gets to play savior."

"Or some Slasher rubbed off on her," Kelley said. "Her and Morgan can be tag teaming. He does his; she does hers. The lovers' spat could be an act to mess with our heads."

Lonergan threw up his hands. "And it gets worse."

"Check them both, but do it fast," Griffin said, turning for her office. "Good work, Li. Keep it up, everybody. Kelley? You're a twisty SOB. Keep that up too."

The team waited for Griffin's door to close before they continued. Foster asked about Lonergan and Bigelow's conversation with Wicks's friend Fahey.

"She had nothing more to add," Bigelow said. "She's a mess, though. This was supposed to be a fun girls' trip; now Wicks is going home in a box. The whole thing doesn't make us—or the city—look too good, that's for damn sure."

"So we look closer at Silva and Morgan? See if there's more there than what they're saying?" Foster asked.

"We hit Morgan's neighbors," Symansky said. "Somebody knows all his business, his comings and goings."

"Same for Silva," Bigelow said. "There's nothing that says she couldn't have worked a knife or dragged a body in a tarp."

"Seriously, what is she?" Kelley said. "Sixty-one, sixty-two?"

Symansky reeled on him. "God damn it, Kelley. *I'm* sixty-one. Do I look dead yet?" Symansky was two years shy of mandatory retirement age, but it didn't appear to Foster that Kelley wanted to mention that or respond to the direct question. Instead, he went back to tossing the hacky sack.

"And why not Silva?" Li said. "Women kill all the time. Half the people we bring in here in cuffs are female. I'm sure at one point your wives have thought about doing you all in, especially you, Lonergan." She winked at him playfully as he grumbled back.

Symansky raised his hand. "I know mine has. She told me so straight to my face."

Li cocked a thumb toward Lonergan. "See?"

Foster was getting used to the team's banter, though not comfortable enough yet to join in. She was still the new kid and had to ease in, make a place for herself. "So Silva's at the top of our list along with Morgan."

"You get anything on him so far," Bigelow asked, "besides the brush-off?"

"Only what Silva says he told her, and she's sure it's all lies," Foster said.

Li raised her hand. "Me again. We had DOB, SSN, and address. He told Silva he spent a year at the University of Michigan, so I called the school. Unfortunately, I hit their privacy firewall. I can't get his records, but I did get a few details from the young guy answering the phone in the registrar's office, who didn't know that he wasn't supposed to tell me squat. I pulled out my sincerest voice, sounded helpless. Guys fall for that every time, doesn't matter what age they are."

"Hey, that's sexist," Kelley said.

"Also true," Li said.

"I'm offended," Symansky said.

Li lobbed a balled-up piece of paper at his head. "Tough. Anyway, I told the kid I was Morgan's aunt, who'd lost touch with the family, and that I was desperate to find them to tell them Grandpa Victor passed away."

Bigelow frowned. "Grandpa Victor?"

"It worked. I got a home address at the time of his registration, the names of his parents and—wait for it—his sister, Amelia. Morgan told Silva he was an only child. He's not. Parents Tom and Priscilla Morgan, sister Amelia, who also registered at UM and actually graduated. It's a start."

Kelley glanced over at Griffin's closed door to make sure the boss wasn't within earshot. "A little skeezy there, Li. I'm impressed. Until Griffin gets wind—then I never met you."

"Why would he lie about being an only child?" Bigelow asked. "What difference would it make to Silva or anyone else?"

"According to her, patients like him lie about everything," Foster said. She looked over at Li with newfound respect. She'd moved the needle for all of them.

"So Morgan's got family," Foster said. "I wonder where they are."

"Well, I did skim death records," Li said. "Nothing for Tom, Amelia, or Priscilla, so if they're not dead, they've got to be someplace."

There was no clear road map here, she thought. Silva or Morgan. It was a coin toss, a gamble, time wasted or time well spent. If Morgan wasn't the one, then focusing on him would give the real killer the leeway to strike again. If he was their man or Silva their woman, then Detective Vera Li had just saved them all.

"Let's see if we can find his people, then," Foster said. "Morgan or Silva or whoever . . . they don't get to take anybody else."

CHAPTER 55

Fruitless. That was what the night had been. The entire team pored over everything; uniforms were on the streets, their eyes open for body dumps; everybody else was locked up tight in their homes, protection from a killer they were convinced the police couldn't catch. Foster pulled up in front of her house for a small break, a few hours' sleep, though she knew already from behind the wheel that there was no chance of that. Something wasn't right. She had a feeling that, despite Silva's assessment of Morgan and his lies, they could be looking at the wrong man. Morgan had seemed weak to her when she'd encountered him in his apartment, unsure of himself. Could that have been an act?

Before she got out of the car, she glanced at the clock on the dashboard. Nine fifteen p.m. God, it felt like the middle of the night. Her back ached from hunching over her computer, her stomach growled, and she was expected to refuel, sleep, and come back in the morning fresh and ready to go. But there was that feeling, that fear, that the cover of night wouldn't work in their favor. That someone was out there hunting, and someone else would die.

She stood for a moment at Reggie's tree. Her hand traced along the hard ridges of the bark, her fingers registering every gnarly crack. A few hours to rest and worry and not sleep, then back at it. Down the block the neighbor's dog barked, and Foster stopped to scan the raggedy street. She felt something, had a sense that someone was there, and stood still listening for sounds beneath the canine's racket, like the crunching of dried leaves underfoot, clothes rustling, murmured voices. But there was nothing but the strange feeling of being watched. Later there would be the sounds of sirens, gunshots, and loud, profanity-laced arguments down the block. Brushing off her uneasiness, she turned and went inside to another microwaved dinner, another marble in the vase. She could feel time racing. That was why there would be no sleep, only her notes. She'd go over everything again and again. And tomorrow she'd go back.

CHAPTER 56

Why had the Black cop, Foster, stopped at that tree? Was she some tree freak? A tough cop who talked to trees. How funny. The lights flicked on inside her house, and she moved around the place, unaware or unconcerned that the night had eyes and that it hid things.

What a dump of a neighborhood. Why live here on a cop's salary? It made no sense. She'd been distracted on her way home, obviously, or she would have known she was being followed. Reconnaissance. That was what this was. It was better to know your adversary, to see what they were made of, what they valued, what they didn't. This place? No answers, only questions. This cop, this Foster, was an unknown element, a potential problem. She and her partner were making the right moves. They were a threat, but now wasn't the right time. It was enough for now knowing where. Other things would come soon enough.

The car started, pulled away, the night still young . . . for some.

CHAPTER 57

He had no idea what her name was. Something with an *R*, but it was 1:00 a.m., and the who didn't matter; it was the why that did. She was okay looking enough, not as young as he liked, but at the end of a bar night, his choices were limited.

"I don't usually do this," she cooed, leaning all over him, smelling like beer and despair. "You're special."

Bodie smirked, pushed her upright, and led her into the lobby of his building. "Sure. I know. We're all special."

The sloppy ascent to his door ended at his doorstep, where a box sat wrapped in brown paper, tied with string. Bodie hadn't a clue what it might be. He didn't order things online; he didn't shop for anything but necessities.

"It's your birthday, hon?" R. asked.

Bodie bent down, opened the box. Maybe it was from Am. A peace offering for the tense exchange they'd had. She was like that often. Judgy, then thoughtful. He opened the box, looked inside, then dropped it at his feet.

"Oops." R. giggled. "Didn't break it, did you?"

"Go away," Bodie muttered.

"What?"

"I said go away. This isn't happening tonight." He reached into his pocket, peeled off two twenties, and shoved them into the woman's hands, pushing her toward the elevator. "Get a cab."

The string of profanities that followed didn't faze him. All he saw was the box. All he felt was the years peeling away. All he heard was himself whimpering like a coward in a closet in Am's room in a different world than the one he'd woken up in today. Surprisingly, his hands didn't shake when he picked the box up again and looked inside. The small wooden train was still there, feeling like death in his hands.

"Son of a bitch."

———

He pounded on Am's door, frantic, not caring a whit about her neighbors or the lateness of the hour. In his defense, he'd tried calling first, but she hadn't picked up. Am could be such a bitch sometimes. He kept the pounding up. "Am. Am!"

A door across the hall swung open, a man with bedhead and sleepy eyes poking his head out. "What the hell? Do you have any idea what time it is?"

Bodie reeled, their eyes meeting. Bodie's transmitted something that forced the man back a step and drove him to narrow the crack in his door. "Shut your door," he ordered, "and mind your business." He watched as the man shrank back and quietly eased the door closed. Bodie waited for the lock to click before he turned back to Am's door. He was about to pound again when the door opened. Am stood there in a short robe, her hair mussed.

"What the hell?" she whispered. "Do you know what time it is?"

Bodie pushed past her, the box with the train in his hands. He shoved the box at her. "Look."

She looked down at the box but didn't take it. "Bod, it's two in the morning and . . . what's this?"

He pressed the box into her hands. "Look!"

A half-naked, half-drunk man shuffled out of the bedroom, struggling into a shirt as he came. He was leaving on tiptoe, like he was embarrassed, like Bodie cared what Am did in her bed. "Later," the creeper said to Am, giving her an unenthusiastic thumbs-up she didn't bother to acknowledge or return. Bodie waited impatiently for the idiot to get out and close the door behind him.

"Now look what you've done," Am said, but he could tell she didn't mean it. The man, like R., was a port in a storm. Temporary. Not meant to be anything.

"Am," he barked.

"All right. All right." She took the box and then shuffled into the kitchen and dropped it on the table. Bodie expected a shocked expression, a gasp, something, when she opened it, but he didn't get any of that. Am stared at the train, then at him. "It's a train. I don't remember asking for one. It's not our birthday."

"Not funny. You know what you're looking at. *He* made it. He's not dead or somewhere else. He's here, and he knows where I live. And if he knows where I live, he knows where you live too."

Am pushed the box away. "Calm down."

She didn't look surprised. There was no fear.

This wasn't a revelation.

"You know, don't you?" he said, seething. "I can see it in your eyes. You know he's alive. You know he's here."

She closed the box carefully. "Look, Bod—"

"How long?"

She opened the fridge and took out a bottled water and twisted off the cap. "I don't think this—"

He wasn't about to let her turn this around. "How. Long."

Amelia took a sip of water first. "Remember the letters he wrote us? There was something extra in mine. A number where we could reach him . . . if we needed to. So it wasn't a complete abandonment, more of a stepping back."

"For you. There was nothing in *my* letter, and there's been nothing since. You've seen him? Talked to him?"

"I dialed the number a few times over the years. Sometimes I just needed to hear his voice, to know we still had family." She put the bottle down and crossed her arms against her chest, staring at the kitchen linoleum. "Family's important." Amelia looked up into his eyes. "I haven't seen him. I don't know where he is."

He searched her face. "You're lying."

She shook her head. "Both things are true."

"When were you going to tell me?"

Her eyes swept over him. "Why would I? Look at you. You're all over the place over a dumb train. It was enough that I knew where to go if we needed anything."

He bristled. "You mean if *you* did."

"I said 'we.'"

"Did you call him when I was arrested? Or when I was in Westhaven?"

"He couldn't have helped with that," she said.

"So you didn't?"

"No, I didn't."

Bodie watched her, not believing what he was hearing.

"He's killing," he said. "You know he is, and all the time you knew it. And you know the police are looking at me."

"It's not him," she said.

"It *is*." Bodie felt himself go. Anger, fear, frustration, all of it taking hold, turning him around and over. He grabbed the box off the table and threw it to the floor. Am didn't flinch. She never did. He was the

275

one who jumped at shadows and led a wrecked life. "It's him, and I don't want any part of it. Hasn't he done enough?"

"I'm sorry you feel that way," she said, bending down to pick up the box. She lifted the lid to find the train with most of its wheels broken off. "You ruined it." She fiddled with the wheels, trying to reattach them, but it was no use. "You can't choose your family, Bod. He loves us."

"Stop." He took the box from her, helping her up. "Just stop. He doesn't know what love is. He's sick, evil. And he's here to do it all again. He's why Silva's gotten it into her head—"

"I told you she's nothing to worry about."

"Easy for you to say. Easier for him."

"Trust me," Amelia said. "All of this will work out."

He glared at her. "Trust you." He glanced down at the box, the sight of it repugnant to him. "I'm not some scared little kid this time, Am. I'll turn him in like it's nothing if it means I'd be rid of him for good. And I won't forget you lied to me."

He walked out, leaving her at the door. Maybe this was the break; maybe it would be clean, like this, him simply walking away, but even as he left, he doubted it. The hooks were in and buried deep, the tether to Am too tight to easily sever.

As the sun prepared to rise a while later, he stepped out onto the rooftop of his building as he'd done countless times before. He walked over to the edge and stood there, his heels firmly planted, his toes cupping the rim. He tilted his head up to smell the impending dawn— clean, fresh, new. It promised to be a beautiful day.

The last time he'd stood here, the police had grabbed him away, branding him some suicidal freak. He hadn't been. He wasn't now. But this was a good place to think and choose. One decision, one spark of a notion, made the difference between being here and not being anywhere anyone could reach. He liked having the choice and actively affirming the former by simply stepping back. It was a test he always passed. He was stronger than Am or their father gave him credit for, smarter than they knew.

This rooftop was far above the filth and screech of the street. He could pass the test here. The demon that had raised them was alive. He was killing. Bodie now had to wrestle with the mother of all moral dilemmas. It was fortuitous that his aerie perch gave him a clear view of the building across the street. Third floor. Corner window. Where the redheaded girl lived.

CHAPTER 58

At eight on the dot Sunday morning, Foster barely had time to slip out of her jacket at her desk before she was called into Griffin's office. When she entered, she found Dr. Silva there, as well as Li. The determined, gung-ho feeling she'd had when dawn had come and there had been no reports of a new kill quickly left her.

"What's this?" As she said the words, her optimism faded, and her body coiled for battle.

Silva smiled. "You came to my camp. I thought it only fitting that I return to yours."

Foster looked to Griffin, to Li, and then back to Silva, her disposition hardening. Silva wanted to play, was that it? Some demented game of human chess? A game Foster and the others didn't have time for, let alone the energy. She'd gotten just six hours' sleep the night before. It was better than nothing, more than she'd thought she'd get, but less than she needed to wrestle with the doctor's mind games.

"Right," Griffin said, unamused. She stood, grabbed her coffee cup off her desk. "We're not doing this. Foster. Li. Handle it. *Quickly.* Then get on with it." Griffin walked out of her office. Foster figured they had five, six minutes before she got back from hanging around the coffee machine intimidating everybody.

"Well, I see you're all alike," Silva said. "Rude. Crass. I want to file a complaint for harassment. If I have to go higher up, I will."

Li sat quietly, her legs crossed, watching Silva. She looked about as happy as a hangman on execution day. All the chairs in the office taken, Foster moved over and leaned on the windowsill. Silva looked pleased with herself, confident that she had the upper hand.

Foster let a beat go. "Alvin Keyes." Suddenly, Silva's face blanched and the smugness went. Foster watched as Silva's breathing got faster, shallower. She was scared.

"And Stillman-Gates," Li added. "You left behind ripples. They remember. People talk. You're tainted goods. That's why you're here."

"I don't know what—"

Foster shook her head. "Wrong beginning, Doctor. How'd you ever get hired at Westhaven? What deal did you work up with Gershon? How have you kept your license to practice? Or have you? We haven't checked yet, but we will."

"Is Bodie Morgan your new Beltway Slasher?" Li asked. "Another notch on your belt? What do you have to do with these murders? Where were you the nights Birch, Rea, and Wicks were killed? What the hell are you doing in the middle of our case?"

Silva bolted up. "No wonder you can't stop him. None of you have any idea what you're doing."

"We'll be looking at you from all angles," Foster said.

Li stood. "We'll lock it all down."

Foster reached over and plucked a pen off Griffin's desk. She held it out for Silva.

"What's that?" the woman asked.

"It's for the complaint you came to file," Foster said.

Silva flew out of the office, flinging the door open so hard it banged against the wall and swung back. Foster, Li, and the newly returned Griffin gave the woman a minute or two and then eased over to the window to watch her as she pushed past the media cameras and protesters and legged it to her Beemer across the street.

"Why's she running?" Griffin asked, taking a sip from her mug. "You two threaten her with a rubber hose or something?"

"No hose. Foster broke her with a look." Li grinned.

"You got all up in her personal space," Foster said.

They moved away from the window, Griffin easing into her chair, a satisfied smile on her face. "Check her. Check everybody. If the mayor looks dicey, check her too. Now get out of my office and close the door. I don't need any more crazy walk-ins today."

———

Two days without a new body. No new pushpins for the board. No grieving parents, no Dr. Grant. Maybe he'd moved on? Foster thought. Maybe the heightened police coverage around the city had boxed him in? She hoped so. It didn't have to be pretty. She'd take the win any way she could get it.

But it didn't feel like a win. It didn't feel to her that he had moved on. The welcome respite felt like a pause, not an end: stasis rather than cessation. That was what had them all jumpy—the overhanging threat, the dread of the next call.

"I think I have something," Foster said, swiveling her monitor around so Li could see it from where she sat. "You couldn't find a Priscilla or Tom Morgan connected to Bodie, but now I think I know why. I put in for his expedited birth certificate. It's in. The names of his parents don't match. But there's something else."

Li got up, came around, squinting at Foster's screen. "Who the hell are Priscilla and Niles Jensen?" Her eyes scrolled down, widened. "Multiple birth? Twins? Get the fudge out."

"Boy and a girl," Foster said. "Boden and Anika Jensen. I'm putting in for Anika's certificate, too, but the info's going to be the same, right? And you didn't find a death record for Priscilla Morgan because she's not Priscilla Morgan . . . but there's a record for Niles." Foster pulled up another screen. "He died in a car accident two years after his twins were born."

"So where's Priscilla Jensen?" Li asked. "And who's Tom Morgan?"

"Good questions."

Li went back to her desk. "Well, let's see. You go high, I'll go low?" Foster sat confused. "What?"

"You take official channels; I'll google," Li said. "High. Low. First one to get something wins an Italian beef from Al's. That'll be me. I like it dipped. With peppers. No fries. I don't need the cholesterol."

———

It took more than an hour before Foster's head popped up. "Uh-oh."

Li froze. "I don't like the sound of that. Am I out of a beef sandwich?" Foster turned her monitor around. "Missing person report?" They both read the screen, reaching the end at about the same time.

"Priscilla Jensen, twenty-eight. Left to go shopping with her babies and never came back. The kids were three months old," Li said. "That's messed up. Did it get any press? Is there more?"

Foster keyed through. "Yes." A front-page story from a suburban paper included a photo of a young, smiling woman and, inset beside it, a photo of the babies swaddled in blankets. *Young Family Missing* read the headline. "Look at her. Red hair. Blue eyes."

Li rifled through the mess of papers, notes, and files on her desk, finding what she needed. "Neither Bodie nor Amelia—Anika, I guess— are on social media, but I did find a tiny mention of Amelia on the school's website. On a list of past winners of some art award? Amelia Morgan won it the year she graduated with a BA." Li sifted through the desk junk again and pulled up a sheet. "Even found a photo, but nothing pops up from a simple name search."

"They're fraternal." Foster turned back to her keyboard and typed in *Amelia Morgan, artist*, getting nothing. She did the same with *Anika*

Jensen, artist and got the same. The awards angle gave her an idea, though, and she typed in variations of names hitched to awards in the art world. It took a bit, but the return was worth it. "Here," she said. "The Brinberg Grant, last year, awarded to Amelia *Davies*."

Li held the old photo she had from her search up to Foster's monitor. Years had passed, obviously, from graduation day to last year, but the women in both pictures were the same person. "Bingo. If she changed her name, why's the name change not showing up?"

"Maybe a glitch? But Anika Jensen is Amelia Morgan, and Amelia Morgan is Amelia Davies." Foster's fingers flew along the keyboard. "Found a driver's license linked to Amelia Davies. We have an address." The tapping was loud, furious. "She's got a studio. North Side." She sat back. "We found her."

Li was already reaching for her jacket. "Road trip?"

Foster grabbed her stuff. "Yep."

CHAPTER 59

Amelia's guard went up the moment she turned to see the two female detectives walk into her studio. It wasn't a surprise; she'd expected them to eventually connect her to Bodie, and she was ready. She was glad it was now, when Joie and her mangy mutt were out of the studio, and she had the place to herself. She stepped away from her canvas, a paintbrush in her hands, her T-shirt and baggy pants splattered with blues and yellows and reds.

"Hello, can I help you?" she asked brightly.

"Amelia Davies." The Black cop didn't pose it as a question. She recognized them both from Bodie's description. She didn't need the badges and the intros, but she got them anyway.

"That's me." She took them in and kept the friendly smile on her face, ratcheting up the openness in her expression, making sure her eyes matched. Helpful. Interested. These were the things she hoped to convey. "What can I do for you, Detectives?"

Foster eyed the massive painting on the wall. It was intricate, crowded. "We'd like to ask you some questions about your brother," she said.

Amelia paused for a moment, weighing, then deciding. "What's Bodie done now?" She padded over to a table with paint-smudged towels and rags and wiped her hands a bit. "Has he been hurt? Arrested?"

"Not that we're aware," Foster said. "When's the last time you spoke to him?"

"A few nights ago. He was fine." She looked from one to the other. "Or as fine as he gets. I know you think he killed those women. He told me. But he didn't. Bodie looks, but he doesn't touch."

"We didn't get much from him," Li said. "At least anything that sounded like the truth."

Amelia put her brush down and tossed the towel aside. "The truth is what Bodie thinks it is. Look, my brother has issues, I'll be the first to admit it, but he's harmless. He's awkward, a step behind, that's all. I know he scared those women, but like I said, he looks but doesn't touch. He's not your guy. Believe me."

"How would you know what he does when you're not with him?" Foster asked.

Amelia sighed. "I know what he's capable of and what he's not. You're right, I can't be there every minute, but I'm there often enough that I'd know if he went off the rails."

"Davies," Li said. "Not Morgan. Is there a Mr. Davies?"

Amelia chuckled. "No husband, past or present. I changed my name. Davies has a better feel. Chalk it up to the artist in me."

"Any other family who might be keeping tabs on your brother? Parents?" Foster knew the answer but wanted Davies's response.

She kept smiling. Open, but not at all. "Just me. We lost our mother when we were quite young. Cancer, I think. We have no memory of her. Our father died when we were eighteen and off to college. He was an accountant, good with money, so we were well provided for. It's not great being orphaned before you're twenty, but you learn to deal with it. Bodie had a harder time finding his way."

"You lived here? In the city growing up?" Li asked.

Amelia shook her head. "Portage Park." The lie was quick, firm, sounding truthful. Foster and Li could check, but they would find no traces of Amelia there. "Does Bodie need a lawyer? Are you going to arrest him? I really have been keeping an eye on him. In fact, I have a witness for the night you're talking about."

"Who?" Li asked.

"A date. A hookup. He went out when Bodie came in. It was late—or early. Two a.m. I can't remember his name, but if it's important, I'll try a little harder to recall it. Maybe if you leave your cards?" Amelia read the cards offered, then looked up to see Foster wander over to the canvas behind her for a closer look. The closer she got, the more uncomfortable Amelia became.

"Impressive," Foster said, "though I don't know a lot about art."

No, no, no, no. It was a drumbeat pounding away in Amelia's head. She wanted the cops away and out, away from her art, away from her. She stepped between Foster and the canvas, the smile back but strained. "It's not officially art yet, but it's getting there. If that's all, I really should get back to it."

Foster stepped back. "Thanks for your time."

She and Li turned for the door, but Li stopped, turned back. "Ms. Davies, you have a passport?"

It was a strange question, Amelia thought. Why ask about a passport? "I don't need one. I hate to travel. Why?"

"Does your brother have one?" Foster asked.

Amelia shook her head. "Nope, and I would know."

"Thanks, then," Li said.

Foster took a last look at the painting, smiled, and followed her partner out.

CHAPTER 60

He watched the car pull away with the detectives inside. They walked right by and didn't notice him. No one ever did. He looked like no one special. A favorite uncle. Your dad. The friendly guy at the hardware store. People trusted him. They let him get close. All it took was a smile and a twinkle, a dip of the head. That tourist hadn't a clue. He'd been standing in front of the Billy Goat deciding whether to go in when he saw her snap the picture of the sign. He couldn't say for sure if she'd gotten him, too, but he couldn't take the chance. He'd meant it to be a simple robbery. It was the photos he needed, but she'd foolishly resisted when his charm wore off.

His eyes followed the car with the cops in it all the way to the corner until it turned off onto the next street. They'd been oh so close yet completely oblivious. He didn't attract attention. He was normal and unspectacular to everyone in all ways but one. Not being seen until he wanted to be seen was his power, his strength. It was the perfect trap. He dug into his pocket and pulled out the tiny SD card. Such a small thing. It wasn't like him, the rush job. He was a man who liked to plan and set things up. She'd forced his hand. The best thing to do, he decided, was just to forget about it, wipe his memory clean. With both hands, he snapped the memory card in half, then stepped off the curb and dropped both pieces down the sewer grate. If he knew this city, and he knew this city, no one would ever find it buried in decades of muck and stench and rat waste.

Waiting for a break in the traffic so he could cross, he worried not about the girl but about the police making connections. If they were good, and it looked like they were, the steps they were taking would lead away from Bodie and Am and eventually to him.

He wasn't worried about Amelia. She was smart and could handle herself. The open question was Bodie. Maybe the toy train had been the wrong way to play it. He'd meant it as a subtle reentry announcement, but the look on Bodie's face when he'd raced out of his building with the box in his hand told him that he'd made a mistake. Bodie feared him, and that fear, he could tell, had turned to hate.

He strolled into the studio on a high to find Amelia standing in the center of the wide, deep space, facing the door, as if she'd sensed he was coming. Her face held no expression, not anger or love. There was no welcoming smile, no scowl, no frown.

"Dad," she said.

What a beauty she'd turned out to be, he thought. Like her mother. "Quite a place you've got here, Am."

She said nothing. He walked around and studied the canvas, proud of what he'd created. It had been a test, a spur-of-the-moment thing. Could he love? Could he *pretend* to love? "Police. What did they want to know?"

"They think it's Bodie."

He chuckled at the absurdity. Bodie couldn't kill a flea. "How did he like the train?"

"It scared him."

"The world scares him." He stood in front of the canvas, greedy eyes sweeping over it, not wanting to miss a single brushstroke. "Excellent." He turned slightly to catch her out of the corner of his eye. "I'm proud of you. Quite a chip off the old block, huh?"

Amelia angled her head and smiled. "In some ways. In some ways not."

"I never had the police knocking at my door," he said, his back to her. "Not once. Subtlety, not savagery, is the key. Precision. Artistry, which I'm sure you can appreciate, but artistry takes time, experience. The mind has to be uncluttered, singularly engaged. One thought. One goal."

"If they search in the right places, they may find you there."

"They'll find Tom Morgan." His hands clasped behind his back, he wandered over to the sculpture he'd seen his first visit. It still made no sense to him. "I'm not surprised you became this. You could always see what your brother couldn't."

"About that," Am said.

He faced her. "Yes?"

"I have no idea where to start," she said.

She was charming. Beautiful. "We have time." He walked toward the door. "Good to see you, Am."

He knew she watched him as he walked out the door. He could feel her eyes on his back. She would remember everything he did, everything he said. The song he whistled had an upbeat, happy rhythm to it, which was how he felt. He was complete, his life having come full circle. Like everything was his for the taking.

CHAPTER 61

Amelia couldn't sleep. She was too excited about her father's return and what it meant, what it could mean, so at eleven she went out to where people gathered and lights were bright. The grocery store she ended up in fit the bill, though there weren't that many late-night shoppers in the place. Restless and unable to order herself, she wandered the aisles. She didn't crave crowds normally, but tonight she needed something, something she couldn't name, but she'd know it when she saw it. What had he said? *Singularly engaged. One goal.*

She picked up a bag of rice, tossed it into her basket alongside a bottle of cheap wine, a prepared salad, and a half gallon of vanilla ice cream. It was activity, mindless, robotic. Amelia noticed the young woman pushing a cart ahead of her in the aisle. She was on her cell phone, a Bluetooth in her ear. Her side of the conversation sounded lively. Amelia followed her out of the aisle, into the next. Canned goods. The young woman hadn't noticed. Why was she shopping so late? Why was she in the canned-goods aisle when her cart held greens, oat milk, a loaf of whole-grain bread, and a pack of chia seeds? Amelia pretended to search the shelf for something in a can while the young woman talked to Seth. They were planning to meet. Maybe a club? A rave? That was what young people did, wasn't it?

Amelia picked up a can of baked beans she would never eat and put it in her cart, watching. Next aisle. Careful not to get too close. Seth and the pretty woman. Around frozen foods, the call ended, and Amelia watched as the woman grabbed a bag of broccoli from the freezer and made her way toward the front of the store, ending up in the fifteen-items-or-less line. Amelia eased in behind her, bumping her cart on purpose.

"Sorry," Amelia was quick to say in a deeply apologetic voice. "I'm a total menace with these things."

The woman smiled back. "Don't worry about it." Blue eyes. "I see you're a late shopper too, huh?"

"Best time to get in and out," Amelia replied. She looked at the woman's items as they hit the belt. "You eat really healthy."

"Have to. You eat good, you feel good, right?" As she said it, she clocked the half gallon of ice cream in Amelia's basket, along with the wine and the rice and the beans she never ate.

"Guess you're right. The ice cream is for a friend, by the way." The woman laughed. Amelia laughed too.

That was it. The cashier rang the woman up, and then she waved goodbye, heading for the exit as Amelia tracked her every step.

"Twenty-eight fifty," the bored cashier said.

Amelia slid her card into the reader, waited for the approval and receipt, then grabbed her bag and followed the woman out. She found her standing at the curb, texting. Amelia squared her shoulders, preparing to make another attempt at small talk, but before she could approach, a green compact rolled up. A grungy man got out, pecked the woman on the cheek, took her bag, and put it in the trunk while she got in the car. Seth?

Amelia watched the car pull away and stood there with the bag of things she had no use for, feeling the miss. As she swiped for an Uber, she went over how she'd played the encounter, the bump, the apology. Not too much. Not enough for it to be weird or to raise alarm bells. Just enough. There was no accounting for Seth or the pickup. Not a miscalculation on her part, just factors she couldn't foresee.

She waited eight minutes for the white Prius driven by Tammy. When Amelia got in, the woman turned around to greet her, wide smile, dirty blonde hair kissing her shoulders.

Amelia eased back, the evening saved, good fortune returned. "Nice night, isn't it, Tammy?"

CHAPTER 62

Foster looked out her back door at the bowl of food she had set out for Lost earlier, only it remained untouched; he was nowhere around. It wasn't like him, but she wasn't overly worried. He'd likely found another supplier along the chain of houses on the block. She would have let it go, turned off the lights, and gone to bed were it not for a sinking feeling that something was about to come to a head. She stepped off the back porch to stand in the yard and glanced up at the moon. Was Lost lost? Why the hell was she worried about a feral cat who only gave her the time of day because she fed him? She was sure Lost held no great affection for her. Given half a chance, he would likely walk over her dead body if he found it in the street, yet here she was, worried he'd gotten run over by a truck or mauled by that crazy dog down the street.

She turned to watch her house. It didn't spark joy. The house looked just as sad and lifeless out here as it felt inside. That was a problem, but even recognizing it as such was a huge step forward for her. She lived in a sad house. She led a sad life. These were hard-fought-for declarations, emerging from a well of pain that hadn't diminished but that had been tempered some with perspective and time. Progress.

In the center of her yard, she took a moment just to breathe, eyes up, arms out. She was here, alive, damaged, but coming back. She slid her hands into her pockets and looked around the postage stamp of a yard, its scraggly grass littered with leaves from the one crooked tree planted at the foot of it. The snow would come in a month or so, but next spring, maybe she'd do something with the grass. Sod it or whatever. Life. Full of maybes.

A shiver swept over her, and she flipped her collar up. The night felt different. This was the second time she'd had the feeling that someone was watching her, and she turned three sixty, slowly peering into the shadows, watching for unexpected movement, but finding nothing. Paranoia. It was the case getting inside her bones.

A large truck rattled down the street out front, and the dog took its cue, barking itself hoarse. Somewhere close, the steady beat of rap music blasted out of a window. That sealed it. She headed inside for the quiet but caught sight of something she hadn't noticed before on the grass. Cigarette butts. About a half dozen of them clustered maybe ten feet from her back door. Too many to have just blown in on the wind. Too close together to be by chance.

Squatting down, she noted the slight indentations in the lawn. Shoe prints. Too big to be hers. She shot up, turned in a circle, listening again to the night, feeling eyes she couldn't see. The calm she'd had a moment ago was gone, and so was the hopeful outlook she'd managed to conjure up.

Someone had been in her yard, watching her house, watching her. They had stood where she was standing now. She stared at the house to see what her intruder might have seen. Her kitchen window, the curtains partly open. Her refrigerator, her kitchen sink. Her eyes trailed up to the second floor, to her bedroom window. It was a violation, theft of her privacy.

An angry fire started deep and bubbled up to lodge in her throat. Maybe fear should have been the prevailing emotion, but she wasn't afraid. She was hyperalert—eyes, ears, all senses on point—and she was pissed. Her first thought: Bodie Morgan, the twitchy stalker who'd stood in Reese Tynan's yard watching *her* windows. That thought made her even angrier.

She stomped up her back steps, flung her door open, and barreled into the kitchen, where she yanked open the catchall drawer, pulled out a flashlight, and slammed the drawer shut. From the pantry shelf, she pulled down a small Ziploc bag and stuffed it into her pocket on the way through the house and out the front door. She stood on her front stoop and scanned the street, daring someone to show themselves.

Her car sat where she'd parked it. Nothing looked out of place, no busted windows, no flat tires. She walked around the vehicle, shining her flash along the chassis. She got down on all fours and checked underneath: clean. On her second pass, the flash hit a spot on the back end of her muffler, and the metal lit up like Christmas. A circle the size of a tennis ball, reflective, bright. Down on her back, she scooted her way under the rear of the car and ran a finger over it. Dry. She sniffed her finger. Whatever it was had a metallic odor, pungent. Some kind of spray?

After wiggling out from underneath, she stood, dusted herself off, looking up and down the block, fuming, unsettled. Reflective spray, the kind cyclists used at night so cars could see them in the dark. Someone had tagged her car. They wouldn't have had to follow close. Anyone could have trailed her from more than a block away and not lost her. She'd led them right to her place.

Foster walked up and down the block, checking parked cars for skulking occupants. She walked both sides of the block, listening for running engines. No one was there. Back at her front door, she called Li from the porch.

"Whaddup, pard?" she answered.

Foster let a beat go, not sure how to say it, fighting the vulnerable position she found herself in. "Are you alone?" She moved away from the porch light into the shadows and kept her head on a swivel. "Is your mother or your husband in the room with you now?"

Foster could sense Li clock in over the phone. "It's after ten. He's at the hospital. She's in bed. What's going on?"

Foster went inside, locking the door behind her, then passed through the kitchen to the yard, plucking the baggie out of her pocket as she went. The butts were still there. Reaching down, she plucked them up and secured them in the bag. "Someone followed me home. I found reflective spray on the back of my car the size of a satellite dish. He couldn't have lost me if he tried. Someone's also been in my yard. Could be unrelated, but I don't think it is. I'm hoping it's just me he chose to tag, but you need to go out and check your car right now."

"Already moving," Li said. Foster could feel the tension in Li's voice and hear the rustle of her clothing, her breathing, and the opening and closing of a door. "You say 'he'? You mean Morgan?"

Foster didn't move a single muscle while she waited for Li's report. "I hope so," she said. "If it isn't, we've got a bigger problem." She listened to Li's end of the line. For a time, she heard nothing but Li walking and breathing, and then . . .

"Son of a bitch."

"He knows where you live too," Foster said.

"Son of a *bitch*!"

It sounded like Li was running. Her breathing was heavier now, panicked, short. "I'm moving my family. They can stay with my brother. Then I'm coming in. Meet you there."

The line went dead. Foster slipped her phone back in her pocket, then decided to take another look around the yard, reclaiming it as hers. Standard search pattern, though there wasn't much ground to cover. He'd elevated the game. Morgan, or whoever. And made a mistake.

She didn't scream when she found the cat's body lying against her back fence. His eyes were bugged, his tongue hanging out of his mouth. From where she stood, the flashlight shaking in her hand, she could see his neck had been broken. She flicked the light off and stood there in the dark. She barely registered the sound of the dog barking down the street. Lost wasn't her cat. Neither of them had claimed the other, but she cried anyway.

CHAPTER 63

He walked around the old house, a small flashlight pointed downward, not wanting to draw attention to his presence this late at night. He knocked on walls, flexed the floorboards, getting a feel for the place. It wasn't much. Not like the perfect house they'd had before, but it would do for now. He'd made sure of the basement. It was wide and deep with thick concrete walls. There was a separate entrance and sturdy stairs, room enough for a table and plenty of wall space for his tools, for crafting and creating. He was satisfied. For now.

He eased open the basement door and peered down the stairs before slowly making his way down in the dark, his feet thudding decisively on the wooden planks. There was a stale reek of dust and damp and long-ago sewage, but he could air things out when he moved his things in. Mornings, there would be natural light flooding in below from glass block windows that ran all along the basement's length. They would have to go. He'd block them out or cover them up, in the meantime. Easy job. When he pulled the string attached to the single light bulb overhead, the dull light didn't reach far into cobwebby corners, though there was nothing much to see yet, only a few discarded rags, a junked bed frame covered in years of dust, and an old rusty bucket someone had left behind.

How much better it would be this time without having to padlock the door. Everything was out in the open, and he felt liberated, like he'd been freed from a tomb. Only this time, he had someone to share in his creative process, his art of transformation. He'd never worked with anyone else. He'd have to learn how. But the house was here, ready and waiting. That was something.

His reconnaissance had been a success. Foster was easy. She lived alone. No one visited, and her neighborhood was not one the police put a lot of effort into. But she was dangerous. He'd have to remember that. Li was different. There was an old lady in her house—he assumed she was her mother—a husband who dressed in scrubs and was rarely there, and a baby, a boy. Nice little family. They lived north. Wrigleyville. The police responded faster up there. The decision as to who he would go after first had already been made. Foster. She appeared to be the one leading the charge, the first up the hill. It was always wise to cut off the head of the snake first. But not yet. Timing was everything in things like this. Far better to let the enemy come to you instead of running out to meet them. Patience.

He pulled the string again and cut the light. Yes, this house would do just fine.

CHAPTER 64

Dr. Silva walked out of Westhaven late. Almost midnight. But what did the hour matter, she thought, when she had plans to make. The cops were being obstinate, freezing her out, and Bodie Morgan was proving just as uncooperative. Who did he think he was? Didn't he know who he was toying with? Still, she wasn't that worried, not yet; Silva had strategies upon strategies to put into action. It was only a matter of time before she got what she wanted. Now, though, what she needed was home, a shower, and a quick meal before bed. Tomorrow she'd set about turning things around.

Norman was not on the gate; the new guy was in the guardhouse. Silva couldn't recall his name, but she waved at him as she drove past and turned onto the narrow road leading to the main thoroughfare a quarter mile up.

As she drove away, she glared at Westhaven's facade and pulled a face. Substandard. Embarrassing. She was much too good for the place. Alvin Keyes, the Beltway Slasher. They could say what they wanted about her, but she'd been the one to get him to reveal where he'd buried three of his victims. The damage to his mind, the psychotic break he'd experienced, had been a risk worth taking, at least for her. Where was the gratitude? The recognition? It was a clear case of the ends justifying the means, and in return she'd been banished.

"But like the phoenix," she muttered to herself, "I will rise."

Silva punched the buttons on her radio, and the car flooded with orchestral music. She'd be home in forty minutes.

CHAPTER 65

She'd watched Silva's car turn out of the gate and head for the main road, and she'd smiled, knowing she'd never get there. She imagined Silva anticipating getting home, getting ready for bed safe in the knowledge that she was secure, tucked in, and in charge. Maybe she was thinking about pouring herself a nice scotch or a bourbon, slipping out of her heels.

Amelia started her car and crept it forward at five miles per hour, lights out, her eyes on Silva's taillights. Silva would stop soon. She'd be forced to. This Amelia was doing for Bodie. For family. Silva wanted him locked up like an animal for the rest of his life, babbling like an idiot, zonked out on drugs, tarred and feathered like some madman. She couldn't have that. Bodie might not appreciate the efforts Amelia took to keep him out of trouble, but that didn't mean she didn't have to make the effort. Now that their father was back, it was even possible that Bodie might overcome his aversion to him, and they could all be together again, but better this time.

"Just a little further," she muttered, watching Silva's car up ahead. "Just a little." Her eyes narrowed as Silva approached the spot. She stopped her car yards away and cut the engine. When she heard the loud pop of the tires and saw Silva brake to a sudden stop, taillights blazing red, she smiled. "Game time."

Amelia watched as Silva got out of her car, leaving the driver's door open, the car dinging, a frenzy of bassoons, flutes, French horns, and cymbals firing out of the radio. Silva checked her left front tire. Amelia knew it was flat. She'd scattered the small tire spikes across the road. Silva thought she knew Bodie, but Bodie knew her too. He knew this road was sparsely traveled at night. He knew Silva often worked very late and drove home alone in a black BMW. He knew which way she turned when she passed through the gate. And Amelia had checked. There were only cameras near the hospital entrance, trained on the guardhouse.

The worried look on Silva's face excited her, and she could almost see the old woman work it through in her head. This was a major inconvenience. She'd have to call someone for a tow or a tire change. Her after-work scotch or bourbon or shower would be pleasures delayed. When Silva reached inside her car and came out with her cell phone, Amelia got out and walked up looking innocent, helpful. "Everything okay there?"

Silva tensed, but when she saw it was a woman, she appeared to relax. "I must have run over something in the road," she said. "I've got a flat."

"Oh no." Amelia sounded sympathetic, worried even for the woman's safety. She checked the tire, kicked it. "It's flat, all right. I could change it for you. Pop your trunk. I'll get the spare."

"That's not necessary. I've got AAA."

"It's no trouble," Amelia said. "I could have you going in fifteen minutes. It's so late. You don't want to be out here any longer than you have to be."

"I didn't see you on the road behind me," Silva said.

Amelia could tell Silva was getting nervous, suspicious. The woman took a step away from her. "You weren't paying attention," Amelia said. "So, the spare?"

Silva glanced behind her at the stretch of empty road. She was too far away from Westhaven's gate and the guardhouse. "Thank you, but

I've got service." She clutched her phone to her chest like it would protect her. "I'm a doctor. I work at the hospital there. I'll be fine."

Amelia stepped forward and lazily kicked at the road, brushing the spikes away with the toe of her boot. "I know who you are, Dr. Silva."

Silva flicked a look at the driver's door. It stood open. The steering wheel just inches away. Amelia could tell she wanted to run for the safety of her front seat but didn't dare move. "What do you want?"

"I'm a Good Samaritan," Amelia said. "You're in a bind. I've stopped to help."

Silva slid a look at the spikes, then read the smiling face. "You're no such thing."

Amelia slid the knife out of her pocket. She couldn't stand here all night out in the open. It was then that Silva broke and lunged for the open door. Amelia caught her by the back of her coat and shoved her inside.

"Don't," Silva pleaded. "You don't have to do this."

"I know," Amelia said. "I want to."

The first plunge of the knife hit Silva right below her rib cage, the better for suffering, Amelia decided. Blood quickly flooded her silk blouse as she let out a sorrowful whimper. Amelia so enjoyed the sound of pain. The second strike hit right above Silva's collarbone, Amelia striking before the good doctor panicked and laid on the car horn in a desperate attempt to sound the alarm. Silva made no sound as blood ran like a river down her torso. Amelia leaned over and whispered in the dying woman's ear, "Night-night, Doc."

She lifted the knife for one last go but stopped when something reflected off her knife blade. It was the glare of headlights coming up the road. Out of time. Silva's head had fallen back against the headrest, her mouth slack, tears trickling down her cheeks. Amelia longed for one more strike but didn't dare. The headlights were coming. She looked down at Silva, bereft that she wouldn't be able to watch her breathe her last.

"Die well," she whispered before pulling a red wig from inside her jacket and placing it on Silva's head. The wig was a big *F U* to the cops, one she hoped would have them spinning their wheels to explain. She slammed the door shut, kicked the rest of the spikes to the side of the road, ran back to her car, and sped away. When she hit the main road, she turned left toward the highway. Pumped but denied her payoff.

"No, no, no."

Each "no" was punctuated by a bang to the steering wheel. She'd planned it so carefully, the time, the method, and she'd meant for it to go so differently, had anticipated it taking hours, not minutes. But her thoughts quickly turned toward self-preservation. Had she brushed every last spike away? Had the driver in the approaching car noticed her fleeing taillights? Though she'd made sure not to touch a thing inside Silva's car, had she left behind even a single strand of hair? She glued worried eyes on her rearview mirror and drove well below the speed limit. She slowly caught her breath, convincing herself she'd done well enough, that she was sure none of this would be tied back to Bodie or her. Dr. Mariana Silva was dead, and the Morgans would be okay.

By the time she got home, she'd almost convinced herself that they would be. The kill hadn't been as clean as she would've liked or as her father would've expected, but it was done. She poured herself a glass of white wine but barely tasted it as it slid down her throat. So she poured another, then another.

Bodie was safe.

She'd done her job.

But it had all happened too quickly.

Angry, she hurled the empty glass against the wall and watched as it shattered into a trillion jagged little pieces. "Now what am I supposed to do with the rest of my fuckin' night?"

CHAPTER 66

Bodie stared at the detectives looming over him. They'd just shown up at his door in the middle of the night and dragged him out. One cop was a big white guy with a buzz cut, the other a human version of a Ken doll. It was those dead girls. Amelia had told him not to worry, but he did. He didn't do well under pressure. He shut his eyes to the grim faces and clenched jaws and scornful looks. They stared at him like he was nothing. Defective scum. He hated himself for wishing Am were here to help him.

He'd been in this cramped room for hours now. It was now 6:00 a.m. They were trying to wear him down, confuse him, scare him into incriminating himself. He knew how they worked. Cops were all the same. It should be his father sitting here, anyway, not him, but as angry as he was at the man, however much he blamed him for the shithole his life had become, he couldn't bring himself to give up his family's secret. He should have asked for a lawyer hours ago, but then he'd have had to talk and tell things, and Morgans didn't do that. "For the thousandth time, you've got the wrong guy," he said. "And you can't just bring me down here and lock me in a room whenever you feel like it. I'm a citizen. I have rights."

The detectives who'd identified themselves as Lonergan and Kelley said nothing.

"Look, you're barking up the wrong tree, all right? I just want to be left the hell alone."

The door burst open, and the female detectives he remembered from his apartment came in, looking just as grim as the two in front of him. Foster and Li. How could he ever forget their names?

"Account for your time," Foster said.

His breath caught. Did they know about the girl in the other building? Had she seen him, turned him in? "When?"

"Let's start with yesterday," Li said, "all the way up until we brought you in here early this morning."

Bodie stared up at Li, then Foster, then at the two cops holding the wall up. He knew exactly what he'd been doing most of that time, but he couldn't tell them. If they knew he'd been on his roof, if they knew he'd been watching the girl, he'd be done. "Why?"

Li banged on the table, her eyes wild. "Wrong answer. Account for your time. We'll tell you when to stop."

Foster tossed a photo of the reflective paint on the back of her car and one from Li's. In both, the zoom-in on the glowing circles was prominent. "Someone marked our cars." She tossed another photo of the cigarette butts lying in the grass. "Someone was in my yard."

Bodie got it now. His father was hunting again, only this time he wasn't hunting pretty young women; he was hunting cops. The man was insane. "Not me." It was all he could think to say. Foster and Li were in trouble, and so was he. "I didn't. I don't smoke." His pleading eyes watched the cops. All of them looked like they wanted to kill him. "I don't know where either of you live. I don't own a car." He stared at the photos. "I didn't do that." Even he could hear the desperation in his voice, the fear. He needed to man up. "I need to make a call."

"Your sister can't help you now," Li said.

It startled him. They knew about Am? How much did they know? He faced each cop down, feeling the heat, shaking inside but fighting for his life. Was everything unraveling? He'd thought he could get out of this on his own, but now he needed to talk to Am. "I *have* to make a call."

Li slammed her files down on her desk. "He wants to make a call? That sicko was outside my house with my baby sleeping inside. My mother."

"Someone was," Foster said calmly. "But look at him. Unless we're dealing with a Dr. Jekyll and Mr. Hyde situation, I can't see him getting it together well enough to coordinate all this. And he doesn't smell like a smoker. No telltale signs either—nicotine-stained teeth, yellowing at the fingertips."

"I know it sounds like it should be him," Symansky said. "He's done something like this before, but I'm with Foster. We can't even get him on killing the cat." He slid her a look of sympathy. "Condolences by the way."

"He wasn't mine," she said. She didn't want to talk about Lost. "We hold him for a while longer to make sure but get him what he asked for. Maybe we find a way to get him to give us a blood sample. Meanwhile, we get some coverage on Li's place."

"What about *your* place?" Symansky asked.

"I've got it covered," Foster said. "No one there but me." She quickly dismissed the topic. "Where are we? Tom Morgan?"

"There's not even a parking ticket for him," Kelley said. "He's a ghost."

Li plopped down into her chair, still livid, but she pulled out the pages of information she'd amassed. "This family's off. The different names on the birth certificate. Bodie in Westhaven, the sister changing her name for no good reason, the mother, Priscilla Jensen or Morgan? I can't find her. We've got Niles Jensen confirmed dead in a crash. That leaves Tom. Adopted father? Guardian? Amelia claims he died when they were in college, and Bodie told Silva the same thing. But I can't find a death certificate. Of course, I haven't checked all fifty states. Amelia told us their father was a CPA who was a wiz with money? Well, I found an old business ad for a CPA by the name of Thomas W.

Morgan. In Naperville. The ad's fifteen years old." Li handed a xeroxed copy of the ad to Foster, then dug into the pile again. "And an old record for a house sale in the same name. The time frame fits with Davies's account of when their father died. But no idea if *this* Morgan the CPA is their Morgan the CPA. I doubt Bodie in there would confirm, but I suppose we could try."

"I'm almost afraid to say this, but there've been no new bodies found since we've been pressuring Morgan," Kelley said. "We've been keeping tabs on him too."

"And we have no way of knowing how long that spray's been on either of your cars," Symansky added.

"But the butts were fresh," Foster said. She stood, checked her watch. It was almost 7:00 a.m. "Let's talk to Davies again. Maybe she'll be a little more forthcoming if she knows we have her brother on ice."

Li stood to grab her things, but before she could, Griffin stuck her head out of her office. "Foster. Li. Silva's been attacked."

"Dead?" Li asked.

"Almost. Somebody got her outside Westhaven last night. She's been transferred to Rush."

"Our MO?" Foster asked.

"No, but there was a red wig in the car." She snapped her fingers at the team. "Lonergan. Bigelow. You two. At the scene. Symansky, Kelley, you're on Westhaven."

"Boss," Foster said, "what time was Silva attacked?"

"The call came in a little before twelve a.m. I'm still looking into why it took so long for us to get tagged on it. Somebody somewhere didn't pull it together. Jesus, the blockheads I have to deal with." She slammed her office door behind her.

Foster and Li exchanged a look. "Morgan wasn't brought in until after one a.m.," Foster said. "He could have had time to attack Silva and get back home before Lonergan and Kelley showed up at his door."

"But we're watching him," Li said.

"That squad car's not in front of his place twenty-four seven. He's always been free to come and go." Foster pulled her bag out of her desk drawer. "He has motive, and he had opportunity." She slammed the drawer shut. "And I hate stalkers."

Li grabbed her coat. "Sometimes I hate this job."

CHAPTER 67

Sun streamed in through Amelia's bedroom window, warming her face, bringing calm after a restless night. She'd been worried over her messy kill. She expected more of herself. She had a lot to live up to. Her father was a master. Precise and artful, calm and selective, and ever since she'd discovered who he truly was, she had wanted to be just like him. She wasn't afraid of him like Bodie was. On the contrary, she loved him, craving his approval. Last night hadn't been artful. Still, the morning light put it all in perspective. She couldn't dwell on past mistakes; all she could do was learn from them and move on. Silva was no longer a threat. That was a win. She'd made it so she'd never speak to anyone ever again. Bodie would be safe because Bodie was innocent. Her family could be whole again.

She flicked on the news, anxious for the morning report. Would her father be proud despite her hasty retreat? As she pulled clothes out of her dresser, she turned to read the news crawl at the bottom of the TV screen. *TOP NEWS. DOCTOR ATTACKED. IN CRITICAL CONDITION.* She read it. It registered. The room began to spin and her thoughts with it. Critical condition. Not dead.

Easing slowly down on the side of the bed, Amelia stared at the set, listened while the perky anchor read the details of an attempted robbery gone bad, of a prominent doctor stabbed and left for dead, rescued by a motorist who'd happened upon the scene and called the police. No mention of the wig. Stunned. That was what she was. Just like that she was somewhere else, someone else. She'd failed. Silva was alive.

Amelia stood to pace the room, her hands clawing through her hair. Take the initiative; that was what her father would say. Make the move. What move? There was no move. Had he seen the news already? Of course he had, and he would know that she'd failed.

"I can fix this. I just need to think." She could feel it slipping, the normal. She'd held it in her entire life behind smiles and an easy spirit when really something else was going on underneath. Now the normal was tearing at the seams, and she could feel a shift. Like an earthquake rumbling under her feet, growing in intensity. "There's always a solution." She slapped her forehead violently to reboot her brain. "Find it. Find it."

She dressed quickly and drove to her studio. She needed her canvas. She needed to touch it, smell it, see it. There were no failures here. As though the images in front of her had a hypnotic effect, she could feel herself calm the moment she saw them. Running her hands over the canvas, she closed her eyes and listened to the paint tell her story through the tips of her fingers. This painting was her, everything she was or ever would be. Life and death and transformation, and only she knew the secrets it held.

Her paint stood ready. She picked up a brush and already could feel herself come back from a dangerous place. As if approaching a lover, she stepped forward and made her first brushstroke, then a second, then a third. She painted Silva, that look of terror on her face when she'd known she was going to die. And she painted tire spikes, scattered around like they'd been on the road. Stepping back to admire her work, she glanced over at the small pink backpack in the upper left-hand corner. Everywhere on the canvas were little red rings unnoticeable to anyone who looked, but not to her.

Birds fly. People die. She recalled the childhood chant she'd made up to cope with the quiet house after it had become clear what her father was, what she was by blood. People died all the time. Why hadn't Silva?

Lifting the brush, she painted Silva again, this time in black. Black like the night. Black like oblivion. Black like dead. Leaving the wig had been an error. She could see that now, but the fix was in her talented hands. She glanced down at them, steady now, smeared with paint. Capable hands. Genius hands.

"Red hair. Blue eyes."

Amelia searched her canvas for those things and found them many times over. The phone rang. She let it. She couldn't be disturbed now. Brush up.

"Birds fly, people die."

Simple words. True words.

CHAPTER 68

Silva was in ICU hooked up to machines, barely there, after a touch-and-go surgery that might not stick. Foster and Li talked to Silva's doctor, the attending on duty, who must have been up all night, like they had, but she exhibited no signs of fatigue. In her immaculately white lab coat, she ran through the damage that had been caused by the ferocious attack and how close Silva was to dying even now. Foster glanced down at the woman's ID. Dr. Kiara Varadkar.

"Her age," Dr. Varadkar began, "along with the severe injuries, combine to create a toxic brew, really. She's stable now, but not stable enough that I'm comfortable talking about outcomes. She's very lucky to have survived to this point. All we can do is monitor her and hope the internal bleeding does not restart. I'm simplifying things."

Foster glanced toward Silva's ICU bay, the curtains drawn. "Was she conscious when she was brought in? Did she say anything?"

"She was unconscious when she came into the ER. She was in and out on her way to surgery. She's mostly out now, incomprehensible when she's briefly in."

"We need to talk to her," Li said.

Varadkar shook her head. "Out of the question. I cannot allow that. She's dancing on the head of a pin as it is . . . the stress alone could . . ."

"We think the person who attacked her also killed three women," Foster said. "She might be able to give us a description. Five minutes."

"I'm sorry," Varadkar said, adamant. "My first responsibility is to my patient's well-being."

"Two then. In and out," Li said, pleading.

"I know what you're up against," Varadkar said, "but she's only hours out of surgery. She's not strong enough for questioning. I just can't do it."

"When then?" Foster pressed. "If she dies while we're waiting, we get nothing."

Foster could tell Varadkar wasn't unsympathetic, that she was weighing Silva's prognosis. "Not for another few hours, at least. Maybe then if she's stronger . . . if nothing else goes wrong . . ."

"Fine. I'll wait." Foster turned to Li. "I'll hang out here until she comes around enough to talk."

"While you're doing that," Li said, "I'll go back and see what I can turn up. This couldn't be some kind of copycat thing, could it? Or totally unrelated. Somebody from Westhaven? She's got no friends there."

It didn't feel like a copycat to Foster. Something about Silva's attack appeared desperate. "Maybe something else. She wasn't butchered like the others. Whoever did this had other intentions."

They both realized at the same moment that the doctor was still there.

"Did you say *butchered*?" Varadkar asked, her mouth hanging open.

Foster let her question sit. "Thank you, Dr. Varadkar. I'll be in the waiting room. I'd appreciate your letting me know when I can get in to see her."

Varadkar backed away from them. "Seriously? I wouldn't take your jobs if it came with a golden goose."

Foster took up residence in the ICU waiting room, a depressing place. It smelled of antiseptic and woe, the television bolted to the wall tuned to some idiotic morning show and a cooking segment on vegan lasagna. The volume was way too low to catch most of what was going on, but there was no way of turning it up, so Foster cooled her heels in one of the chairs and waited for Silva to rally, hoping she would, dreading how things would go otherwise.

She called Bigelow's cell for a report on the scene. "What's it looking like?" she asked when he answered.

"It's looking like a hit gone hinky. The guy got her as she left the hospital. Dark stretch of road. A good distance from the main street. Trees all over the place that would have made it even darker last night. Plenty of places to ambush her, which he did. Her car's got a flat. There's a tire spike embedded in the front left one, and the techs found a couple more in the street. Hold on." Foster heard muffled noises on Bigelow's end. "Okay. I just sent you a photo of the car. Blood all over the driver's seat. And the wig. The EMTs said it was on her head when they arrived. Someone put it there. The driver who found her came up close after it happened. He says he swears he saw two sets of taillights up ahead of him as he approached the main street. When he eased by, he saw that one of Silva's tires was flat. He got out, looked in the driver's window, and that's when he saw her inside bleeding to death. How's Silva?"

Foster peered over at the nurses' station. The medical staff were hard at work. "Still breathing . . . but that's about it."

"Well, whatever this was, it wasn't a robbery. Her bag's still on the seat. Wallet intact. We're not picking up any prints either. Lonergan's stomping around here like he's General Patton."

A slight smile. "Good luck. There was no weapon found?" she asked.

"Nada. It's looking like the guy planned this but then ran out of time with the car coming up on him. We'll keep you posted."

Foster ended the call and rose to walk the room, thinking of wigs and knives. She watched the clock, sweating every passing minute. When that got old, she went over her notes again, checked in with Li and Griffin, then walked the room again, then sat again. It took four hours before Varadkar popped her head into the space. Foster bolted up from her chair, holding her breath, hoping she wasn't there to give her bad news.

"Five minutes, no more," she said, waving for Foster to follow.

Foster slipped into the quiet bay to find a diminished Silva lying feeble in the bed, the steady beeping of the lifesaving machines an ominous reminder of how critical the woman was. Her eyes were closed, her mouth twisted in pain. Her middle was swathed in layers of compression bandages. Dr. Varadkar eased up to the bed, placing a gentle hand on Silva's wrist. Her eyes fluttered open, but only halfway.

"If you're still up for it?" she asked Silva when her eyes met hers. Silva nodded almost imperceptibly, then turned her head in Foster's direction, but even in her precarious state Foster could practically feel the heat of Silva's resentment toward her. The last time they'd met, they hadn't parted well.

"I won't take long," Foster said. "And I won't waste time. Your attacker. Can you tell me what he looked like?"

Silva wet her lips and swallowed hard as if mustering whatever strength she had to respond. She shook her head slightly, grimaced in pain, and emitted a whimper. "Not 'he.'" Her words came out in a foggy croak thickened by medication and blood loss.

Foster heard but didn't understand. She glanced over at the doctor but got nothing. "Say again?"

"Not. He. A woman. Waiting."

Varadkar kept her eyes on the numbers and squiggles on the monitors.

"A *woman*?" Foster asked.

"White. Cold eyes. I knew what she was. She knew my name."

"Tall? Short? Thin?"

"Yes. But something familiar."

She was fading, and Varadkar called it. "That's time."

Foster backed away from the bed, recalculating as she went. A woman, *not* Morgan. She was almost to the curtain when Silva spoke again.

"I smelled chemicals . . . oil? . . . and she whistled. After she . . . left me . . . she whistled."

Foster turned to leave, knowing she didn't have nearly enough.

"Not . . . oil," Silva managed. "Paint. She smelled of . . . paint."

Amelia Davies. She'd whistled when Foster and Li had talked to her in her studio. She had smelled of paint. There were no other women that they knew of connected to Bodie Morgan, besides Silva.

Paint.

Foster looked over at Varadkar for an okay to approach the bed again. She nodded back at her and held up one finger, letting Foster know she had sixty seconds, no more. Foster dug her phone out of her pocket, scrolling through, her fingers fast, sure. She pulled up the photo they had of Amelia Morgan, a.k.a. Davies, and walked back over to the bed and held the phone close so Silva could focus in on it.

"Have you seen her before?"

Silva fought against the medication but managed to get her eyes to focus. When her eyes widened in terror at the image in front of her and the beeping of the machines increased, Foster had her answer. Lights began to flash on the monitors; the fast beeping turned into a loud alarm. Silva was in some kind of distress and was struggling now to speak. "Yes. It's her," she croaked. "Who?"

"Out," Varadkar ordered as she lowered the bed rail to get to Silva. Foster backed away from the bed as two nurses rushed in to answer the alarm. "Who?" Silva asked again, weak but more insistent this time, her eyes finding Foster as she stood back.

"She's Bodie Morgan's twin," Foster said.

As the medical staff assessed her, Silva seemed to be in another world, her look changed. It wasn't fear Foster would swear she saw in Silva's eyes anymore but exhilaration.

"Out," Varadkar ordered again when she turned to see Foster still standing there. "Now."

Foster bolted out of the bay and rushed toward the elevator, dialing Li as she went. She stabbed the elevator button, impatiently waiting for Li to pick up. When she did, she blurted out, "She just ID'd Amelia Davies."

"No fucking way," Li said. "Why would she . . . her brother!"

"Silva said she smelled paint on her. That fits. Let's hit her studio."

"If it's her, wouldn't she be halfway to Timbuktu by now?"

"And leave him behind? No. And I don't think she'd go far, not with Silva still breathing."

"I'll fill Griffin in," Li said.

"And Li, we need to get someone on Silva's door. Amelia might just be scared enough to try again."

"Roger that. I'm heading into her office now. Meet you at the studio."

Foster stepped onto the elevator crowded with visitors. There really wasn't room, but she pushed her way on anyway, ignoring the put-upon sighs meant to chastise her.

When she got to Davies's studio, Li was already there with two squad cars out front for backup. "What'd you do, fly?" Foster asked.

Li eased through the door. "Where you go, I go."

Amelia wasn't working on her painting, and there was no one at the sculpture. But the door had been open. Someone was here.

"Police," Foster called out. "Amelia Davies?"

"Or Morgan or Jensen," Li muttered.

A shocked Black woman walked out from the back with her hands up in surrender, a stocky dog with drippy jowls trotting along behind her. "Oh my God. Oh my God. What's happening?" She noticed the squads outside. "Don't shoot. I'm Joie Lenk. I work here."

"We're not going to shoot. You think we just walk into places and light them up for no good reason? Put your hands down." Li was gruff, offended.

Slowly the woman complied. "Then what do you want?"

"We're looking for Amelia Davies," Foster said. "Is she here?"

Joie looked past them to the cop cars outside. "What the hell did she do?"

"Is she *here*?" Li asked.

Joie walked to her worktable, the dog following, eyeing them the entire time. "No. I haven't seen her in a couple days. Not since . . . never mind. What's happened? Why are you looking for her?"

"You were starting to say something. Not since? Not since what?" Foster approached the table. Li stayed put, still salty.

The woman wiped back a purple strand from her face. "Look, I don't want to get involved in anything. I just rent the space. I don't know her all that well. But the vibe's different lately; even Winston feels it. Both of us feed off energy, and it's gotten strange here. Suddenly, this place feels . . . tainted." She patted a hand against the plaster thing with wings. "How can I work here now? I need light, hope."

Foster stared down at the dog, who stared up at her. *"Not since what?"*

"I wanted to call the police when it happened, but Amelia talked me out of it. I mean, it was her uncle and all, so I didn't push it. But if he was going to be coming around, upsetting Winnie, well, I just can't have that."

"Ms. Lenk, do you want to tell us what happened?" Li was losing patience.

"I was working. Amelia wasn't here. A man came in looking for her. Right away Winston went nuts, barking, growling, baring his teeth. He didn't like this guy at all. He never does that."

"What'd this guy want?"

"He wanted her. Said he hadn't seen her in a while and was just passing through. He told me to tell her some hokey thing from *The Three Musketeers*? You know, the 'all for one, one for all' thing? Then he checked out Amelia's painting, gushed all over it, started this creepy whistling, and left. He freaked us both out. I swear the place went from frigid to warm the second he left. When Amelia got in, I told her what happened, and she said he was her Uncle Frank and that it was no big deal." Joie rubbed her arms as if she'd gotten a chill. "It sure felt like a big deal."

"Uncle Frank," Foster said, her eyes wandering over to the canvas, the one that had attracted her attention the last time she was here. The intricacy of it pulled her in. "What do you know about her other than this?" She pointed at Amelia's work.

"Not much, really. We get along okay. I know she has a sister who recently broke her leg. And that she always takes three pumps of hazelnut in her latte. She's moody, doesn't talk much, and isn't big on sharing confidences. Winston loves her, only—"

Foster turned when Joie stopped talking. "Only what?"

"Well, the last time she was in, after Uncle Frank frosted up the place, Winston wouldn't go anywhere near her. He gave her the same treatment he gave him. Usually, the two of them are cuddled up on the floor like a couple of pound puppies. I can't explain it."

Li pulled a photocopy of the CPA ad she'd found for Tom Morgan out of her pocket and showed it to Joie. "Does he look familiar?"

Foster stepped back from the painting but didn't take her eyes off it.

"Holy shit!" Joie said. "Put some years on him, gray his hair a little bit, and yeah, that's Uncle Frank. But wait, this says his name's Tom Morgan. So . . . wait, is he her uncle, or isn't he?"

Neither Foster nor Li answered. "Did you see if he was driving a car?"

"Yeah. When he left, I ran to the door and locked it so he couldn't get back in. I thought I saw him drive away in a dark car. I don't know models, so I don't know what kind, and I couldn't get a look at the plate from where I was standing. He headed east."

Li got her notepad out and drew a pen from her pocket. "Four doors or two doors? Black or blue, if you had to say?"

Joie thought it over. "Four doors, definitely. Maybe blue?"

Foster studied Amelia's canvas. It was frenzied in spots, calm and soothing in others. There seemed to be a weird sort of linear progression from a flowing serenity to strikes of violence. She moved closer, close enough to see the grooves in the brushstrokes. She lightly ran her fingers over the surface. As she moved down the length of it, as she listened to Li try to get more out of Joie Lenk, she suddenly recognized the face of a woman Davies had painted, a face she'd seen before on Dr. Grant's autopsy table.

"Li."

When her partner eased in beside her, Foster pointed to the face.

"Looks like Peggy Birch," Li said.

"And look there. And there." Foster pointed left, then right. "There. And there." Amelia had also painted Mallory Rea with her wig, and while one of the other faces belonged to someone she'd never seen before, the other belonged to Silva.

Li stepped back to get a panoramic view. "Holy crap." She searched the painting. "I don't see Wicks. Do you see Wicks?"

Wicks wasn't there. Foster ran her finger over Silva's face, painted all in black. "Still damp. She was here after the attack."

Li backed away to contact the team that had been sent to Amelia's loft. "Yeah, Al, anything?"

Foster looked over the canvas, finding little disparate things—musical notes, eyeglasses, toy trains, a child's dollhouse, an old SUV. None of it made sense to her. Amelia alone held the key. But the damp image of

Silva said a lot. Li rejoined her, but the look on her face wasn't encouraging. They stepped away from Lenk to confer.

"She's not at her loft," Li whispered. "Symansky says the neighbors haven't seen her since early yesterday, which apparently isn't unusual. She comes and goes. Holed up in her place for days, gone for days."

"Have they seen anybody who looks like an Uncle Frank?"

Li shook her head. "No one matching the description we just got has been seen hanging around her place." Foster gave the canvas another long sweep. "We've been looking at the wrong Morgan."

She and Li returned to Lenk, who stood in the center of the room looking extremely worried. Even the dog beside her seemed to be feeding off her anxiety. "Ms. Lenk, did this man smell of cigarette smoke?" Foster asked.

"I didn't get too close to him, but yeah, now that you mention it, when he left, the whole place smelled like tobacco. I had to spray the room. I can't stand the smell."

Foster didn't have to say it. Li didn't have to hear it. Tom Morgan was likely the man who'd followed them both home. The man who'd marked their cars and stood in Foster's yard staring up into her windows, leaving his spent butts behind. He'd killed Lost. And it was clear now that killing was the Morgan family business. She looked over at Li, dread blooming. "Uncle Frank."

"My ass," Li said.

CHAPTER 69

Tom watched Amelia pace around the empty living room, too gone to appreciate its charms, too scattered, too muddled, to care that he'd been very careful with the purchase, finding just the right kind of house, in just the right spot, with a basement that would work for both of them. It didn't appear that Amelia had slept much or eaten. Her clothes were disheveled, her look distant. He was witnessing her unraveling.

Amelia stopped. "She's alive. I messed up. I should have slit her throat instead, then plunged the knife into her. You would have known to do that. It was the headlights coming. I felt rushed. I don't do well when I'm rushed."

"You need to calm down," he said.

Her pacing resumed. "Can't calm down. Not until she's dead."

"Am." But she wasn't listening. Her hand skimmed the walls as she passed them, her head shaking. He'd never imagined that this was who she was beneath her confident exterior. All the time he'd watched her grow, he'd seen strength and resilience . . . intelligence, not this. He'd hoped to create a killer in his own image. He'd planned it, cultivated the entire thing.

"Amelia!" She stopped and turned to face him. "Breathe." There was no furniture in the house yet, or he would have told her to sit. Instead, he instructed her to lean against the windowsill, close her eyes, get ahold of herself. As his protégé, she was no good to him like this. How could she possibly carry the mantle of his genius in such a state? If she didn't rally, the house was useless, his plans gone to waste.

"All's not lost," he said.

"But . . ."

"Quiet. Think."

Even if Amelia was a scattered mess, he was not. The doctor was alive. That was a problem. Am had acted impulsively and had put them both at risk. The police had already linked her to Bodie, and he knew that Bodie would eventually break. And he knew the police, once on the scent, wouldn't be so easily distracted. Who had seen him? The woman in Amelia's studio, the one with the dog. Maybe someone in Bodie's building when he'd dropped off the train.

Amelia lifted off the sill. "I have to run. Close up the studio."

He despised impulsivity. It was a sign of weakness. He'd expected so much more of Amelia. As he watched her, there was an empty feeling inside him, as though he'd lost something precious that he prized above all else, something he would need to let go of. Maybe he could find another. It wasn't too late to try the experiment again. He'd been lucky when he'd crossed paths with that young mother with her two babies. That was when he'd decided to see if he could be normal, human, like everyone else. If he could hate, he'd reasoned, why couldn't he also love? But did he love, or did he only covet? Even now he wasn't sure.

Whatever the case, he had to deal with this cock-up. A cleanup on aisle eight, so to speak. Tom grinned at his own joke as Amelia slowly settled and appeared to come back to herself. But his respect, his *affection*, had waned. "Better?"

"I'm sorry. I've let you down."

She had, but maybe he could retrain and redeem her. "You haven't, kiddo." He moved around the room, checking Amelia, not seeing the promise he once had, letting the lie comfort her. The loving smile he had perfected, the one that worked so well with babies and children, brightened his face. "Every problem has a solution. Now this is what we're going to do."

CHAPTER 70

"Okay, this is what we're going to do," Foster said, with Li and the others huddled up in the office. "We still have Morgan here. Amelia's going to want to help him. That's what Silva was about, I think. Another attack while we still had eyes on him was supposed to make us believe we had the wrong guy."

"But she messed that up big time," Kelley said.

"Now she's got her own problems," Lonergan groused. "We got every cop in the city lookin' for her with that ID from the doc. We got her so far for attempted murder, and if Silva dies, the full ride. She's not gonna be hangin' around here."

"And we swept Morgan's place," Symansky said. "No reflective paint. The only thing's got us looking his way is Silva fingering him and the fact that he's the oddest damn duck I've ever encountered."

"I'm still looking for Priscilla," Li said. "And Tom."

Foster tacked photos of Amelia's canvas up on the board. "Meanwhile, this is the painting she's been working on. Li and I photographed the entire thing. It's huge."

"Good God, she's all over the place with that," Kelley said from his perch on Symansky's desk. "Where's the cohesiveness? The through line?"

"We're not critiquing the quality of her work," Lonergan bit back. "Head in the game, will ya?"

Kelley mouthed a rude comeback, then took a sip of coffee, glowering at Lonergan.

Foster pointed out the finer points. "A pink backpack. Silva's face, the paint still fresh. Spikes, which punctured her tire. And here, here, and here, doors and padlocks. And over here a house." Her finger bounced along the photo. "The house repeats several times. It has to be important. Look also at the little dots, some of them almost too light to pick up. Spots in red. Like blood."

"There's also a face there we haven't seen before," Li said. "Which means there's somebody we haven't found yet. Maybe the blood on Ainsley's jacket belongs to her?"

"Here," Foster said, pointing to a faint sketch of a face that hadn't yet been painted in. "No idea who this might be. It looks like she started but didn't finish. There's no telling how long she's been at this."

"There are no prints or DNA on the victims," Bigelow said. "So nothing connects her to anybody, even to Silva, as quiet as it's kept. And if Silva dies, we don't even have her shaky ID going for us. Davies could argue, and her lawyers will, that Silva was mistaken, hopped up on pain meds and out of her head wrong."

Lonergan readjusted in his squeaky chair. "And this painting looks like what a kid would do with movie posters. Maybe she's just one of those twisted people who're news junkies and lose their minds over high-profile cases. Instead of tackin' up newspaper clippings, she paints the details."

"I'd believe that," Li said. "Maybe, if it weren't for the spikes. Those never made the news reports, or if they did, I didn't see it. Davies wouldn't know about the spikes unless she put them there . . . or someone who was with her." She stepped up to the photo again, pointed at an image in the far corner. "A cell phone. We never found Birch's." She found another spot on the canvas. "And another. We never found Rea's either."

Lonergan frowned. "Wait. Back up. Someone like who?"

Foster faced him. "Tom Morgan."

Lonergan stood, the clearing of his throat loaded with pomposity and scorn. "You're takin' a wrong turn. A woman'll poison you, shoot you, but I don't see one guttin' you from stem to stern, then draggin' you under a bridge. That's a guy. That's a guy with issues."

"I can name at least five women right off the top of my head," Foster said, challenging him. "Including Davies. We have Silva's ID."

"Maybe," Bigelow said, "but I think Lonergan's kinda right. These women were hacked up. Women don't tend to do that."

"And maybe we're trying to shoehorn Silva's attack into the others," Symansky said. "They *could* be unrelated. Her ID could be wrong. The painting, not coincidence but Davies pinging off the same thing that's got the whole city wound up, with some weird additions."

Kelley nodded. "Right. I know we all want to wrap all this up and find the guy, but we can't make the mistake of making stuff into what it isn't. We've got a few threads here. We need to make sure we're not jumbling them up."

As much as Foster hated to admit it, she knew they were right. "First move then, find Davies. Second move?"

"The family," Li said. "Priscilla." She studied the photographs of Amelia's painting, pointed to it. "That house."

"So we let Morgan sit in there for a while and think," Lonergan said. "Maybe we tell him his sister's in trouble. See if he tries to do somethin' about it. Least that's how we used to do it before cops went all soft."

You could have heard a pin drop in the room. Finally, Kelley spoke. "You know, I don't see anything wrong with that plan."

Bigelow gave Lonergan a thumbs-up. "Score one for Lonergan-Bigelow."

"I'm going to follow up with Naperville PD," Li said.

"I'll start with Priscilla," Foster said.

"What about Davies?" Symansky asked. "We're not going to beat the bushes for her?"

"Her brother's had his phone calls," Foster said. "I think she'll come to us."

CHAPTER 71

There was only a brief moment of anxiety as Amelia Davies walked into the police station hours later with the lawyer she'd hired for Bodie and, if things went sideways, herself too. When she'd gotten back to her phone after meeting with her father, there had been five frantic messages from Bodie telling her where he was and what had happened. He had no idea she'd attacked Silva, and she didn't tell him, but he knew other things, things she didn't want the police getting out of him. She wondered the entire way there how difficult it would be to sneak into the ICU to finish what she'd started.

But the immediate problem now was Bodie. Again. Amelia didn't fear the police. She'd plunged that knife pretty deep. Silva couldn't possibly last too much longer, and Amelia doubted she was in any condition to talk to anyone, let alone Detectives Foster and Li. She got strange looks from the police when she announced herself at the desk and she and the lawyer she'd hired for Bodie, Edwin Bishop, were shown into the small interview room, but she did her best to ignore the stares. It was confidence she wished to convey.

"Remember, let me do the talking," Bishop said. "Follow my lead."

Amelia sat calmly at the table. She wasn't worried or tense, not anymore. She knew she was smarter than any detective. "I understand."

She liked that Bishop sat beside her in a ridiculously expensive-looking suit, graying at the temples, his face expertly shaved. He looked every bit the part of a high-priced attorney, which was what she'd needed. She wanted to make an impression, to strike fear into the detectives' hearts so they would know they were not going to have an easy time with Bodie.

The door opened, and Foster and Li walked in and sat at the table. Bishop spoke first. "Ms. Davies has retained counsel on behalf of her brother, Bodie Morgan. What are the charges, and when can I confer with him?"

"We let Mr. Morgan go about five minutes ago," Foster said. A cell phone rang. It wasn't hers or Li's or Bishop's. "That's probably him calling now to tell you all about it."

Amelia ignored the ringing. They'd made a move she hadn't anticipated.

Bishop looked confused. "What's happening?"

Li folded her hands on top of a file on the table but didn't answer. Foster cleared her throat. "Bodie Morgan's psychiatrist was attacked last night. We'd like to talk to Ms. Davies about that. Would you mind telling us, Ms. Davies, where you were around midnight last night?"

Amelia almost laughed. "You can't be serious."

"Are you accusing her of attacking this person?" Bishop asked.

"We're not accusing her of anything," Foster said. "We're just having a conversation."

Bishop started to get up. "Like hell you are. It's a fishing expedition."

"Not quite," Li said. "Silva ID'd Ms. Davies as being the woman who attacked her."

Bishop glared at them. "Physical evidence? Witnesses? No, or she'd be in cuffs already. Amelia, let's go."

Amelia cocked her head and studied Foster. She was the one Amelia was up against. Her father had always taught her that outthinking an adversary was only a victory if the adversary was a worthy opponent, that you could take no pride in besting an inferior. Foster had set a trap for her, and she'd taken the bait. Well played.

"Not yet." Amelia smiled sweetly, as if butter wouldn't melt. She wasn't a fool. She hadn't been raised by a fool either. Cue look of concern, soft eyes. Amelia remembered what was expected. "I saw it on the news this morning. I was so upset. Is she going to be okay?"

"Have you ever met Dr. Silva?" Foster asked.

Amelia ran through the choices in her head . . . no or yes, truth or lie. She went with the lie. "Early on in Bodie's stay. She had questions about our family and our childhood she hoped I could answer."

"And did you?" Li asked.

"Some. I gave her as much as I could. I wanted to help my brother."

"Why was she shocked then to hear he had a twin? You?" Foster asked. "She ID'd your photo as the woman who attacked her but didn't have your name."

"I assume Silva is in critical condition," Bishop said. "Heavily medicated after such a violent attack. She can't possibly be in her right mind. She could be confused, disoriented. This is clearly an unreliable victim account." He searched their faces. "But you know that already. A conversation, you say, but this is you trying to get us to do your work for you." He smiled. "No dice. Amelia." He gestured for Amelia to get up.

"But I want to help," she said. "I was at my studio last night. I stayed pretty late. Unfortunately, I have no one to vouch for me. I was alone."

Li laid a copy of the CPA ad on the table. "Let's talk about your father, or, as you called him, Uncle Frank?"

Amelia's heart began to race. She could feel the corners of her mind beginning to fray. She looked down at the ad but didn't reach for it. "My father is dead. You've obviously talked to Joie. I don't know who that man was. I only said he was my Uncle Frank so that she would calm down. She was practically hyperventilating."

"What about your mother?" Foster asked.

Bishop scraped his chair back from the table. "Why is any of this important? What are you two up to?"

"While looking into your brother, we found a few inconsistencies we'd like to clear up," Foster said. "We can't find Tom Morgan anywhere prior to opening up his business in Naperville years ago, and there's no death record for him now. Where did he die? And exactly when?" She waited for Amelia to answer, only she didn't. "And your mother, Priscilla Morgan? Same situation. No death record. No history."

"But we were looking under her real name," Li said. "Priscilla Jensen. Her married name. Her maiden name is Walsh. Your father was Niles Jensen. Here's your birth certificate." Li slid it across the table, then laid another down next to it. "And here's your brother's."

Amelia stared at the certificates, knowing everyone was watching her. She couldn't think. Jensen. Walsh. Not Morgan? It was a lie. Cops lied. The words on the paper appeared to dance as she focused so hard on them. *Niles Jensen.* "Is this your idea of a joke?" she said.

"We think we might know what happened to your mother, but we're still looking into it," Li said.

"Meanwhile," Foster said, "we stopped by your studio earlier today and had a chance to see your painting again." She opened her folder and slid photos of the painting out, fanning them out on the table. She pointed to Silva's face. "The paint was still wet on this one." She pointed to the others. "A backpack. Phones. I don't get the padlocks, but there are plenty of them. Can you tell me why your painting appears to corollate with the murders we're working on?" She pointed to the unidentified faces. "And can you tell us who these two women are?"

"Whoa," Bishop said. "Stop right there. Are you about to charge *her* with something?"

Amelia couldn't take her eyes off the names—Priscilla and Niles—and she felt herself fracture as the floor seemed to drop from beneath her feet.

Niles. Not Tom.

"Amelia? *Amelia.*"

She realized it was Foster talking. "Your painting. Can you explain it to us?"

Their eyes locked. "No, I don't care to."

Bishop stood. "That's it. We're gone." He opened the door, beckoned for his client to leave with him. "Not a shred of evidence. Silva met her before. The wonky ID was certainly fueled by pain meds. Then birth certificates and her own painting." He shook his head. "You'll have to try harder than that." He wiggled his fingers for her to come, but Amelia couldn't get her legs to move. She couldn't move, couldn't force herself to leave. The detectives were staring at her. Could they see?

"Your father died in a car accident two years after you and your brother were born," Foster said, as though sensing what Amelia so desperately wanted.

Li slid the accident report toward her, along with a copy of Niles Jensen's driver's license photo. "Quite a resemblance between you and him. Same eyes."

To Amelia it sounded like their voices were coming from far away. She couldn't take her eyes off the photograph. It was true. She could clearly see her eyes, Bodie's, staring back at her. She hadn't seen any of their features in the man who'd raised them, the man who'd groomed her to kill, but it hadn't mattered until now.

Foster leaned forward. "Priscilla Jensen went missing with her babies in 1990. She went out shopping and never came back home. Her twins—Anika and Boden Jensen—were never found. Your father searched for you. Filed a missing person report. I think the loss ruined him. The report on his accident says his blood alcohol level was three times the legal limit. He barreled into a tree."

"Your mother's disappearance is still open," Li said. "You and your brother, however, are a different story. We could confirm with DNA, but I think we know what we're looking at. Now, we're wondering who Tom Morgan is and why he chose to raise you as his own."

Amelia could feel herself floating further and further away from the person she'd thought she was just a few moments ago. Li placed a missing person flyer down next to the other things. *MISSING* stenciled across the top got her attention, but not as much as the photographs beneath it, one of a young red-haired woman and the other of two infants lying on a baby blanket.

Amelia drank in her mother's face—every line, every curve—seeing it for the first time that she could remember. Beautiful. Young. Happy. Big blue eyes. She reached down and ran her fingers across her mother's cheek as she felt herself disappear. The truth. Finally. It was in her mother's crooked smile, in the shape of her nose, the rise of her forehead.

Everything he'd ever told her was a lie.

She wanted to scream and weep and kill, but she couldn't. Everyone would see. Everyone would know.

"Tom Morgan isn't your father," Foster said. "We think he may be your kidnapper. And most likely your mother's killer." Foster gave it a moment. "You see it, don't you?"

Amelia did. She saw it clearly.

"We're done," Bishop said, pulling Amelia gently up by the arm. "We're not saying another word. Come at us again, and you'd better have something better than this little slideshow."

Amelia smiled. It was meant to show that they hadn't wrecked her, though they had. Following Bishop out, she was leaving behind the person she'd been. She thought about the beautiful woman with the blue eyes who once had babies she loved. She'd gone shopping a long time ago and never came home. And a dead man had Amelia's eyes. Dr. Mariana Silva was no longer important to her. Only one thing was.

CHAPTER 72

Foster hovered over the phone on speaker as Bigelow reported back every few minutes with updated details on Davies's movements. He and Lonergan were tailing Amelia at a normal pace in an unmarked car and were now headed north on Lake Shore Drive. Everyone hoped she was on her way to confront Tom Morgan. They didn't have enough to arrest her. Silva's ID wouldn't have been enough to build a case on or sway the state's attorney. They needed more.

"Well, she's not making a run for it, that's for sure," Li said. "She would have to go a lot faster than that. We stunned her, though. I almost felt sorry for her. Finding out your whole life's a lie?" Li looked up from her computer, where she'd been digging into the Morgans' time in Naperville. "I know we're hoping she's running to Daddy, but what if she never wants to see him again and she's running to tell Bodie the news?"

Foster looked over. "I don't think she's thinking about her brother right now."

Li smacked her monitor. "Squeaky clean in Naperville. Paid his bills. No complaints on record for his business. Coached Little League and everything. I ran a name check for the community paper and found a photo of him with the team." She slid the photo over to Foster. "Same guy as in the ad. Same guy Lenk ID'd as Davies's creepy whistling uncle." She leaned back. "So he's at least a dirty babynapper who passed the kids off as his own, but I think we're both thinking he killed Priscilla

Jensen first. And if he killed her and he's here now, I think he might have had something to do with Birch and the others. And if Silva's right and Davies tried killing her, he's got help. Which means . . ."

"We've got a family of killers," Foster said, completing Li's sentence. "All for one, one for all."

They sat patiently waiting for Bigelow to report in again through the open line.

"Damn it," he said. "Hold on." They heard a car horn blare and could hear the engine rev. "We lost her on Sheridan, right after the turn off the Drive. Don't see her anywhere. That's that."

Foster ended the call and sat for a time thinking. Li swiveled back to her computer. "Lonergan's driving."

Foster pulled out her desk drawer, searching for a pen that worked, but found a thumbtack lying amid the detritus and slipped it into her pocket. "Yes."

There was a moment's silence. "Could happen to anyone," Li said. "Happened to me once. Not a suspected homicidal maniac, though."

"I don't have anything against Lonergan," Foster said, hoping to cut off the discussion.

"Yeah, you do."

Foster shot up from her chair. "I don't." She stormed off toward the restroom.

Li called after her. "Yeah, you do."

When Lonergan and Bigelow made it back, they eased into the office quietly. The activity in the room didn't stop, and no one made a big production out of the tail that had gone wrong, but everybody knew about it, knew how important finding Tom Morgan was. Foster could feel Lonergan watching her from the other side of the room, but she avoided eye contact. Did he expect her to rub his nose in it? Gloat? Did he really think she was that petty?

After more than an hour, Foster sat back in her chair, running her hands over her face, tired, hungry. They'd all been sleeping too little, eating too sporadically, afraid to relax for fear of another body dump. And Foster couldn't forget the added worry, for herself, for Li. One of the Morgans, or maybe all of them, knew where they lived. They'd been to their homes, stood in their yards. In Li's case, they had gotten dangerously close to her family. Foster was tired of not knowing.

"We've been tracking similar homicides," Foster said. Li looked a question. "Bodies dumped. Young women of a type. Priscilla Jensen's officially missing. Her body hasn't been found. So . . ."

Li perked up. "We stop looking for bodies and look at missing person cases instead, especially those around Naperville and the University of Michigan campus." She was already tapping. Foster scooted closer to her computer and did the same. They needed a lucky break, or else no break at all would be of any use. It took hours before they figured out the pattern, and then they called the team together.

Foster tacked the photos on the board. "Six women missing from the time the Morgans moved into their house in Naperville till the time Tom sold it and the kids went off to college. Notice anything?" She turned back to the team, at the cops seated or leaning on desks, weary eyes on the crowded board.

"Just the obvious," Lonergan said. "They all look kinda like Birch."

"Uh-oh." It was Kelley right before he reached for a bottle of antacids on his desk. "I'm not going to like this."

Foster pointed to the last photo up. "The last one we could find was fourteen years ago. Susan Rafferty. Twenty-two. Went missing from the Sloppy Cup Café in Naperville on a Sunday afternoon."

"And you can connect Tom Morgan to her?" Symansky asked.

"Not yet," Li said.

Bigelow raised his hand. "If it's Tom, what's he been doing since he ran out of Naperville?"

"Better question is, Where's he been doing it?" Foster said. "We've got pings out all over the surrounding states. Killers don't stop killing.

We know that, so chances are good we're going to come up with more photos to put on that board."

"But now he's back here. Why?" Lonergan took off his blazer and rolled his sleeves up.

"I think he came back for Amelia," Foster said. Her statement quieted the room. "I think Tom Morgan's a killer and he raised her to be one too. Look at her painting, her attack on Silva. Nobody in the press knew about those lipstick rings. I didn't see any of them report on a pink backpack. I think Tom killed Wicks for the reason we thought. She took a photo of something she wasn't supposed to. Him. I believe that's true because I don't see any cameras painted up there, and Amelia didn't paint Wicks's face."

"A family of killers," Symansky groaned. "Damn it all to hell and back."

"We suspect we have at least two more victims because of the faces we can't put names to," Foster said. "That first spot of blood found on Ainsley has to belong to one of them. Either we find Tom Morgan and Amelia and they tell us where these women are, or we have to hope we find them ourselves or someone stumbles on another tarp." She scanned the team, each face. "We stop them."

CHAPTER 73

Bodie walked out of his building and turned sharply toward the lake. He needed to walk. He needed the quiet. He craved the darkness. He knew there were cops in a car watching from across the street. They'd been there off and on for days. Surveillance. Like he was too stupid to know. He'd heard about Silva, but he hadn't been able to work up a lot of sympathy. He knew it was his father's doing. And where was Am? He'd been calling her since the police had let him go, but she hadn't answered his calls or called him back. Was she with him? Had she always been?

Why couldn't he turn his father in? What prevented him from simply walking into the police station and telling Foster and Li and the others that his father killed women? He didn't know. That wasn't quite right. He did know. He had been taught to lie and cover, to repress and ignore, to normalize that which was abnormal.

He liked the sound of his footsteps on the path and also knowing that his were the only footfalls he could expect, but this night, when he turned toward the sound of lapping waves and walked a block, there was the sound of footsteps behind him. Am. He reeled, but it wasn't her; it was Detective Foster.

"What do you want?" It was harassment. The cops had no right to hound him this way.

Foster stood there, six feet away at best. "I'm looking for your sister. I thought maybe you'd know where she is."

That threw him. He thought it was him they were trying to break down; otherwise, what was the surveillance for? He scanned the park, looking for the other one, Li, but Foster appeared to be alone. "My sister? Why?"

Foster glanced around. "You always walk this late at night? Not the safest thing to do."

"I've got half the police department watching me," Bodie said. "Answer the question."

Foster let the distance between them stand. "Dr. Silva ID'd your sister as her attacker. And when she's strong enough to add more, if she ever is, we'll arrest Amelia. And also, because we think she can lead us to Tom Morgan."

Bodie pedaled back, just a couple of steps, just enough to put more air between them. The mention of his father's name elevated his unease. The police knew he was alive and back in the city. They knew that Amelia and Bodie were connected to him. Did they also know the worst of it? He opened his mouth to deny everything, but Foster stopped him with a warning look.

She slipped a hand into her pocket and pulled out an envelope and handed it to him. "We spoke to her earlier today. She came in with a lawyer to get you out, but you'd already gone. You haven't spoken to her since then, I take it?"

Bodie shook his head, still startled by the intrusion, not sure what to make of it. He stared down at the envelope in his hand. "What's this?"

Foster backed up. "Read it. Amelia likely ran to him, to confront him about everything. She seemed pretty upset. What's in there isn't anything you couldn't have found on your own, if you'd known to look for it, and it answers a few questions you might have had. We gave your sister the same information. My card's in there, too, in case you decide to get in touch."

Foster turned and walked away, and Bodie stood there clutching the envelope, then fast-walked down the path toward the lake. He wanted far away from Foster. He wanted to find a quiet place, someplace with no one around. He raced into the park, found a bench under a tree near a light. A woman passed him, a scraggly terrier trotting beside her. He needed them to pass before he opened the envelope.

He couldn't read fast enough—his eyes soaking in every word, every implication—sweat dripping down his back, even though it was fifty degrees. By the time he'd finished reading, his hands were trembling. "Oh my God." He read everything again, then a third time. Then he tried calling Amelia's number and got voice mail again. He'd left earlier messages, frantic ones, pleading for her to call back. This time, he had just one thing to say. He laid the envelope on his lap as though it were a precious thing, then waited for the beep. He had just two words for his twin, likely the last words he'd ever say to her.

"I'm free."

He walked fast back to his apartment, clutching the envelope, but the walking quickly morphed into a trot and then a full-out run. He was angry, angrier than he had ever remembered being. She had kept it all from him, knowing what it would mean for him. If he wasn't tainted, he could be anyone, do anything. He didn't need Amelia. For the first time in his life, he could be completely his own person. No Am to hide behind, to defer to. No Bodie Morgan bringing up the rear, disappointing everybody, including himself. No Tom Morgan. No sin.

"Boden Jensen." He whispered the name to himself, trying it on. "I'm Boden Jensen."

He could feel himself shedding his old skin as a weight lifted off his shoulders. He didn't have one drop of Tom Morgan in him. When he reached his apartment, he crumpled the envelope in his fist and tucked it inside his jacket, placing a hand over it as if to protect the truths that lay inside. He didn't need to talk to Amelia. She would only lie. He didn't need to talk to her ever again if he didn't want to. She didn't know it yet, but he was already gone.

"I'm Boden Jensen," he muttered to himself, finally clean. "And I'm free."

CHAPTER 74

"Tell me about my mother," Amelia said as she watched Tom Morgan stare out the window onto the backyard of his new house. She'd given it all night and half the morning to decide and now stared at the familiar stranger as though he were nothing, no one. "You always said you would tell Bodie and me about her when we got older." He didn't bother turning around. Was she not even important enough to face?

"I did, but now's not the time," he said. "We have a lot to do. There's the doctor and the detectives."

"The doctor. Right."

"I don't hold her against you."

"But you keep bringing her up."

It was true that you never really knew a person. She'd thought she knew exactly who and what she was, who'd made her, only she didn't. She hadn't a clue. She wondered if he could feel the change in her. She could feel it. He had always been so intuitive, so tuned in to the shifts in the air, sensing when things were off. Could he do that now? Could he sense that Amelia knew? She hadn't told him about the police station. It was no longer his business.

"I'd like to know now . . . about her."

He turned around. He wasn't smiling; neither was she. There was no longer a reason to lie. "When did she die?" Amelia asked. "How?"

"You're upset about the doctor," he said, ignoring her questions. "I've already forgiven you for that. I think we should start with Detective Li. She has a child. Her loss will be devastating, and it will hobble them long enough for everything to fall apart. I've done the advance work. I anticipated that things would likely come to this."

"You anticipated that I would *fail*."

"Your mother died of a rare blood disorder shortly after you and Bodie were born. She suffered horribly in those last days. You can see now why I kept it from you? To spare you both."

"Yes, I see now. And you loved her."

"Of course."

Clearly, now, she could see there was no real resemblance. Funny, how the mind worked, how conditioning happened over time, clouding things, forcing the eye not to see what the brain knew it did. If anyone would have asked her days ago, she would have sworn that she was this man's spitting image. But now she was Anika Jensen, not Amelia Morgan or Davies. She had parents who'd loved her, a different life. "About your plan . . . ," she said. He put warmth in his eyes when he looked back at her, but she knew better. It was a thing he did.

He wagged his finger at her. "*Our* plan."

"Right."

What could she have become if she hadn't been corrupted by this? she wondered. It was far too late to know. He'd lied to her, to Bodie. She knew she was looking at her mother's killer. She could feel something coming for her. It was like a train roaring down a track, its lights flashing a warning. Impact was inevitable.

"You seem distracted," he said. "You can't be. I need you at the top of your game. Are you?"

Amelia smiled sweetly. Her mother had been pretty. She and her father had made a handsome couple. She wondered what they were like together before this man came along. "Of course. Dad."

His face brightened. "Good. I haven't shown you the best part. The basement." He brushed past her, heading toward the kitchen. "Follow me."

Amelia turned to watch him, steel in her spine. Gone. Someone new in her place. "Right behind you."

CHAPTER 75

Foster peered into the car with the dead woman sitting in the driver's seat, the victim's head leaning back against the headrest, her throat cut, blood everywhere. It wasn't a fresh kill. It looked like the woman had been there for a while. The car wasn't disabled. It had been driven into the empty, scraggly lot under the L tracks at Lawrence Avenue. Li walked around the car on the passenger side, shining her flashlight into the back seat.

"Who found her?" Foster flicked a look at the PO's nameplate. "Mendoza."

"Security guard was walking through. Saw the car sitting here. He thought it might be stolen, so he looked inside and got the shock of his life." Mendoza angled her head toward the shell-shocked Black guy standing dazed in a cop huddle several feet away. "That's him. Wendall Price."

"Did he touch anything inside?" Li grimaced at the spray of blood on the inside of the windshield, on the dashboard, the steering wheel, all over the woman's T-shirt, painting it a dull, rusty crimson. The car smelled of metal and body stench, the woman's eyes half-open, her mouth frozen in a rictus grin that testified to the pain and surprise she must have experienced in her last moments.

"He says he didn't," Mendoza said. "I believe him. When we got here, he had his head between his legs. He says he faints at the sight of blood."

"He found her when?" Foster asked.

The uniform referred to her notes. "About an hour ago. We rolled up six minutes after. No telling how long the car's been sitting here without anybody paying it any attention. We've been on pins and needles waiting for another redhead dump, but when we got here and saw she was blonde . . ." She looked around at the busy crime scene. "This is out of the way, L tracks overhead. No idea what this is."

"ID?" Foster asked.

"Found her bag with her wallet inside. Money in it. Tammy Bergin, thirty-four. Lives over in Andersonville. Drives Uber. The decal is in the back window. The car's registered to her."

Li reached into the car, checking the seats, the floorboards, Bergin's bag. "No cell phone." She checked the console, the dashboard GPS and nav system, her nitrile gloves skimming lightly over the bloody touch screen. "Nav is wiped. We'll have to go through the company to get her last pickup." She backed out of the car. "That won't be a hassle." She said it facetiously. "But I don't think we'll learn anything we don't already know, do you?" Her eyes met Foster's.

"Bergin's face is on Amelia's wall," Foster said. "One of the unidentified is now identified."

———

Foster leaned against the windowsill in the women's bathroom, the lights off, her head down, eyes closed, listening to the rush and movement of the cops beyond the door. An Uber driver? That didn't seem planned. It hadn't been a clean kill either. Amelia was getting reckless, messy. She and her "father" were killing now just to kill. When would they stop? What could she do to make them stop? Li's voice from the doorway startled her eyes open.

"Found something," Li said. Foster looked up to see the worried look on Li's face. "What're you doing standing in the dark like an idiot? Um, I mean, sorry. Did I say that last part out loud?"

Foster lifted off the sill. She liked Li's bluntness. Her partner was growing on her. "Found what?"

"A house. It might be where they are." Foster followed Li back to her computer. "We know about the house in Naperville, so I kept thinking maybe that's his thing. He likes houses. So I ran a check of all new house purchases, cross-checking them against the names—Davies, Morgan, Jensen." Li plopped down into her chair and swiveled her monitor around for Foster to see. "Came up with nothing, of course. That would have been too easy. Then I started on the first names, cross-checking against what we knew of all three of them. Look."

Foster leaned over, her eyes on the screen. "Frank and Anika Morton."

Li stepped back, a satisfied look on her face. "Uncle Frank? Anika Jensen? They jumbled the names. Unoriginal, but whatever. But look down where it lists professions—accountant and art teacher. A bit of a stretch where she's concerned. These people don't exist. Nothing comes back on either of them that connects to who this paperwork says they are, but they fit with what we know about Davies and Tom. I googled the house. Check the photo."

Foster leaned back to the screen. "The new house and the old one look similar."

"Similar? They're practically clones. That's where he is, and where he is, *she* is."

"Where is it?"

Li rubbed her hands together like a fiend in an old silent movie. "You're going to love this. Mount Greenwood."

Foster was sure she'd misheard. Mount Greenwood was a neighborhood on the city's southwest side, populated in large part by city workers, firefighters, teachers, and cops. It was the farthest point away they could live from the worst of what the city offered up in terms of drive-by shootings and gang warfare and still be within city limits, which was required for city employment. "A family of murderers living in Mount Greenwood. They're cocky bastards, I'll give them that."

Li scribbled the address on the legal pad on her desk, then underlined it several times. "That's the place." She was already out of her chair, grabbing her jacket. "Won't hurt to drive by and take a quick look."

Foster glanced over at Griffin's office, but the door was closed. "We'll fill the boss in when we get back."

———

The house looked like it had been freshly painted and spruced up to sell, which it had; the for-sale sign staked into the front lawn sported a **SOLD** sticker on it. The block looked sedate—neat little homes, neat little lawns, lots of trees, Halloween decorations in every window right alongside FOP stickers and the city's official flag—three white stripes, two light blue ones, and four red stars in the middle.

"Nice, huh?" Li said as they got out of the car. "We were thinking of moving out here when the baby gets a little older. Maybe a nice swing set out back, a kiddie pool in the summer." She glanced up at the house. "Dormer windows. I love dormer windows."

"All I see is the commute," Foster said, "when the snow's five feet deep and you have to shovel out."

Li stopped. "Yeah. Didn't think of that."

The house looked empty. No car out front matched the one registered to Amelia Davies. There was no answer to their knock at the door.

Li peered in through the gap in the tacked-up newspaper at the window. "They could be in there."

"This is as far as we can go, though." Foster turned to scan the street and saw a burly white man cross over from a brick house on the other side. "Company." Li turned.

The white man stopped at the lawn, hard eyes looking up at them. He'd planted his feet, angled his body, and flicked his right hand over to reveal the badge he clasped in it. "Name's Nowak. Help you two with something?"

"Police," Li said.

The man gave them a sly smile. "Knew that when I saw you pull up in the unmarked. Need a hand?"

"No, we got it," Li said. "Thanks, though."

"Have you seen anyone going in and out of here?" Foster asked.

"The Realtor. The guy she sold the place to. Midfifties. Dark hair. Drives a late-model Honda Accord. Got the plate number inside if you need it. Also, there was an old Rover parked here earlier. Didn't see who got in or out."

Li pulled her phone out of her pocket, scrolled to the image she wanted. "This him?"

He came a little closer, sliding his star into his pocket. "Yeah. Older, though. More gray."

Li scrolled to the next photo. "How about her?"

He squinted. "No. Haven't seen her."

"Thanks. I'm Foster by the way."

Li waved. "I'm Li. Vera. Thanks for stepping up."

Nowak nodded, then turned and walked back across the street and into a beige house with an inflated ghost on the lawn.

"You know he's watching us from behind the drapes," Li muttered, keeping her lips from moving so Nowak couldn't read them from across the street.

"Of course." Foster tried the door. The knob turned freely. She pulled her hand away, letting that sink in. "Unlocked."

Li exhaled. "Okay, so we have an unlocked door and an audience."

"In Mount Greenwood," Foster said, "where there are probably ten cops on this block besides that one with the ghost."

"A neighborhood where you could probably leave your keys in your car overnight and nobody would steal it," Li added, "or so the legend goes."

Foster slid her a look. "We're still in the city."

Li pulled a face. "Um. Are we, though?" Li waved at the beige house across the street. "I'm thinking of the body count. If they're in there, we get to stop them here. Nobody else dies." She pushed the door open before Foster had a chance to argue the point, then stepped inside. "Police," Li called out, her voice echoing off the bare walls, the uncarpeted floors. No heat. No furniture. Just house. "Amelia? Tom? Frank? Bodie?" She turned to Foster. "Nobody home."

"You just breached the door," Foster said. "We're not going to talk about that?"

"Exigent circumstances," Li said.

"Fill me in?"

"You heard Nowak. The Rover parked out front? Remember the Rover in Davies's painting? She's a threat to public safety."

"Not even close," Foster said. "If Griffin finds out we went this far with so little, she'll bust us down to traffic."

"We're just looking, following a lead," Li said. "There's no one here. No rights to infringe upon. No harm, no foul. We don't even have to call for backup. He's across the street staring out his window."

Foster wasn't happy, but they were in it now. The best they could do was to get in and out as quickly as possible. "Why buy this house?" she asked. "Why not kill and move on?"

"I bet Silva could tell us." Li wandered into the kitchen. Foster went as far as the doorway. It was a wide, open space with an island and lots of large cabinets. The previous owners had apparently done a complete paint job on it. The entire room smelled like fresh paint. Eggshell, if Foster had to guess the color.

"Will you look at this cabinet space?" Li said, moving around the room. "C'mon." She ran her hand across the cabinets. "What I wouldn't give for this kind of setup. You cook, Foster?"

"I microwave."

Li studied her. "When we catch these assholes, you and I are going to have to talk."

"No thanks."

They spotted a door, and Li approached it. "Basement?"

"That'd be my guess," Foster said. "We're *not* going down there."

"Of course not. That'd be foolhardy. No harm in taking a peek, though." Li turned the knob, opened the door, and stopped to listen for any sounds from down below. "Smells like a basement. Hello?" Nothing came back but echo. "See? Nobody."

Foster turned toward the dining room. "We're either too late, too early, or completely wrong about everything. And I'm tired."

She looked out the back windows at the long yard. It was large enough for a kiddie pool and swing set. If no one was here, why was the front door unlocked? "Anything?"

"A pantry," Li called back.

Foster saw something out back, moved closer to the window, squinting to make it out.

"And another door," Li said.

Beyond the yard, on the alley side of a short, weathered fence. The top of a forest green truck.

"Might be a storage . . ."

Foster reeled. "Li!"

Foster heard Li scream, the scream followed by the sound of something falling down a flight of stairs and the slamming of a door. She ran for the kitchen, even before the echo of both had a chance to die away.

"Li!" There was no response. "Vera!"

She rounded the corner, coming face to face with Amelia standing at the basement door, a bloody knife raised, a vacant look in her eyes. "She's in the basement." Amelia angled her head. "Want to join her?"

CHAPTER 76

Li lay at the bottom of the steps, the back of her head throbbing, burning, a ringing in her ears, a rush of blood coursing through her system. She was too stunned to move, even if she could manage it. Stars floated behind her eyelids, and her head felt like a lead block. Amelia Davies. She'd bolted out from the pantry door and shoved her. It had taken Li only a split second to see the woman was out of her mind. The madness was in her eyes.

Li's entire body burned with a heat of a thousand suns, but her lower back and right ankle burned the most. She tried moving, but the pain knocked her back and stole her air. Taking a quick assessment, she could tell that her right knee was only jammed, not broken, but it was beginning to swell. Her ankle was another story. She could feel the break.

How the hell was she going to get out of here?

"Not good." Li squeezed her eyes shut as pain bolted its way up her back. "Not. Freaking. Good." Through narrowed eyes, she focused on the door at the top of the stairs. Had Amelia locked it? Why couldn't she hear Foster or Amelia talking above her? She had to get up. She had a kid and a family. She had a partner. Gathering one giant inhale that rattled every rib in her chest, she bit her lip and went for it, pushing past her body's protestations. Her screams, as loud as they seemed to her, were no match for her suffering. She could barely see through the tears.

CHAPTER 77

Foster moved back out of striking range of the knife, but Amelia charged, giving her no time to defend herself. The knife came at her fast, and Foster raised her arms to protect her face, the first strike slashing across her right forearm, cutting through her jacket sleeve, cutting into flesh. Amelia pushed in, knocking them both back against the wall, her frenzied face just inches from Foster's. Amelia was deranged, Foster thought, and in another place.

Foster could feel blood streaming down her arm, feel the sting and ache of the gash. "Stop." But Amelia didn't. It didn't even look like she had heard her. This wasn't the same woman she had interviewed at the station, the one poised and confident and so, so sure of herself; that woman was gone.

"Get out," Amelia growled. "It's *my* house now."

Amelia broke free from Foster's grasp, and the knife came down again, this time slicing across Foster's right hand. Foster yelled out like a wounded animal and tried backing away again, but Amelia barreled forward, and they both went down hard. Foster could smell her own blood as it colored her hand and began to pool beside her, a madwoman on top of her, intent, it seemed, on making another hole and then slitting her throat. Foster searched Amelia's face for even a tiny glimpse of sanity, something she could reason with, but there was only madness.

Foster gripped Amelia's wrists and held on to them, trying desperately to keep the knife away from her throat, but she could feel herself losing the struggle. Amelia was strong and bent on killing, and Foster's bloody grip was slipping.

"You're going to die today, Detective Harriet Foster," Amelia said, her voice low, menacing, her knife inching closer to Foster's throat.

For Foster, there was a flash of resignation, a moment in which she considered what dying here would mean. She could be with Reg. The pain of his loss would stop. She would no longer be a worry to her family. Good things. But as she held on to Amelia, struggled to fight her off, as she eyed the bloody knife as it got closer to her, wondering whose blood was already on the blade, she quickly dismissed the thoughts and her moment of weakness. She didn't have just herself to think about. Her partner was in the basement. Li had a husband and a baby, a life. If Amelia got by her, Li would surely be next.

"Amelia. Stop!" Foster screamed as she gathered what was left of her strength and pushed back.

Amelia leaned down, close to Foster's ear, and whispered, "You ruined everything. You and *her*. I'd barely begun to perfect my craft. But you just wouldn't stop coming."

The pain she was in was off the chain, but there was no way Foster wanted the last eyes she saw on this earth to be those of Amelia Davies. "Anika!"

Amelia startled at the mention of her birth name, and her focus broke. Suddenly, an agonizing wail from the basement pulled Amelia's attention away from killing. It was all the chance Foster needed. She pulled her hand off the knife and elbowed Amelia in the stomach, then followed up with a blow to her jaw. When Amelia flew back and rolled away, Foster scrabbled away on her knees, flinging herself into a corner across the room, leaving a trail of blood behind her. She needed to stand but couldn't yet. It looked like Amelia couldn't either. Facing off from their respective corners, the two were like spent boxers between rounds, waiting for the bell.

Amelia chuckled, though nothing at all was funny from where Foster sat. She watched as Amelia gleefully wiped her blood off the knife, then ran the blade along the leg of her jeans, back and forth, each slow pass cutting into her own skin. Blood quickly soaked the denim. Then Amelia held the knife up to the light from the window, admiring the blade. "This is his, you know. He gave it to me so that *I* could . . . follow. It's not big enough to sever hands or feet. I needed a saw but didn't have one . . . yet, so I had to symbolize the cuts with the lipstick—wrists and ankles. Hands and feet. Hands and feet." The slow singsong in her voice turned Foster's stomach. "And a spot of blood, one to the other. Like signing a painting. Genius, right?"

"Li!" Foster called out, but her partner didn't answer back. Where was Tom Morgan? Was he in the basement as well? Foster tried reaching for her gun, but her bloody fingers wouldn't work. She stared over at Amelia, but though Amelia stared back, Foster doubted she knew she was there. As she struggled with her holster, Foster stalled for time. "Amelia Davies, you're under arrest." The snap on her holster popped free. The gun, she knew, would be difficult to grasp when she got to it. How would she even lift the weapon, let alone aim it and shoot it?

Amelia snapped back from wherever she'd gone in her head, and Foster doubled her efforts with the gun—faster, more determined to get it loose—but no amount of hurry or level of necessity had any impact on her injured hand. Amelia worked her way up onto her feet. Foster got to hers too. If she was going to die, she'd do it standing. Foster slowly raised her arms in front of her, like a fighter, shielding her throat and chest, waiting for Amelia.

"You can't arrest me," Amelia said. She shook the knife. "I have this. I intend to make my mark with it." With the knife she traced a lazy pattern in the air. "I'll sign you. Like I signed all the others." She pointed the knife in the direction of the basement. "And then I'll sign her."

Foster took a quick inventory. Right forearm sliced, bleeding. Right hand slashed, the cut deep, bleeding, fingers swollen, nearly inoperable.

She was beginning to feel light headed. If she lost consciousness, she was dead. "Put the knife down and back away from it." She meant it as an order, but Amelia paid her no heed. Instead, she stood in Foster's way, a human blockade between her and the basement door.

"Maybe I kill her first, if she isn't dead already. Save *you* for last?" Amelia chuckled like a wicked child playing a dangerous game.

Foster stepped forward. The chuckling stopped. "It's not going down that way."

Amelia charged again.

CHAPTER 78

Li was sitting up. That was progress. Whenever she moved or shifted, there was a sharp punch to her spine, and when she ran her hand along the back of her head, she felt a giant goose egg right at her nape. And then there were the twisted knee and broken ankle.

"Sitting's good," she muttered. "Sitting's great." Li glanced up at the ceiling, at a network of cobwebs hanging off dusty rafters. She hated spiders. She hadn't hated basements before today, but now she hated them too. Sweat drenched the front of her shirt, she was covered in black, greasy grime from the basement floor, and every bone, every tendon, every bit of cartilage in her body cried out for a doctor and an emergency room. The sound of a violent struggle above her breached the basement door. Foster.

Li reached for the phone in her pocket to call for help, but her fingertips brushed up against only pieces of jagged plastic. The device had been smashed to bits when she fell. She thought of Nowak across the street. He might wander back over to see what was taking them so long, and then again, he might not.

Bodies fell and crashed upstairs. Foster was in trouble. Li pushed up and fought her way to her feet, using the bottom step to lean against. It took a few seconds before her vision cleared. "I'm up. All right. I got this." She felt for her gun at her side. Still there. Still in one piece. "In business."

Li looked around, hoping to orient herself. The dark room felt drafty and deep and smelled of sewage and mold, but a shaft of dull light coming from somewhere was just enough to help her make out a bare light bulb three feet from her. Hopping over, keeping her broken ankle off the floor, she pulled the cord, but the bulb was low watt, and the light it gave off was not enough to do much good.

Li turned back and hobbled toward the stairs. There were a lot of them, and they were steep. The struggle upstairs had stopped, but there was no way of knowing whether that was a good thing or a bad one. She grabbed hold of the railing and planted her left foot on the bottom step, ready to go. She'd have to pull herself the whole way up. She had braced for the climb and was about to shove off when something bathed in shadow propped behind the staircase caught her eye.

It looked like a person leaning against the wall. She let the railing go, drew her gun, teetered on one leg. She aimed, but she had absolutely no confidence in it. "Police. Step out." Her eyes narrowed. She could swear there was someone sitting there. She could just make out the outline. "I said step out. Now." She prayed she wouldn't have to shoot. She prayed even harder that whoever it was didn't come out fighting.

When nothing happened, she hobble-hopped forward, wincing, sweating, her eyes now adjusted to the half-light, the scraping sound of her right foot dragging across the concrete floor. She got just close enough to stare down into Tom Morgan's eyes. He was dead. His chest had been savaged and his throat cut. He was sitting in a pool of his own blood. Li moved back toward the stairs, holstered her gun, then grabbed the railing, and started up. No love lost for Morgan, she thought. In fact, it was better than he deserved.

CHAPTER 79

Foster shoved Amelia back, but not before the blade sliced along her side, nicking the skin along her ribcage. Foster slid her way along the wall, trying to get closer to the basement before Amelia clocked back in. It had been a few minutes since she'd heard any sound from that direction. What if Amelia had shoved her knife into Li's back before she'd pushed her down the stairs? What if she was bleeding to death? Amelia stood looking out on the backyard through the window, her father's knife at her side. Foster took a step. If she ran for the basement, could Amelia run her down before she got there?

"I see you," Amelia said.

"Where'd you get the leaves you covered Peggy Birch with?" Foster asked, hoping to distract Amelia.

"Details. Details. Just like you people." Amelia turned her head. "I found them in a bag in an alley. No one wanted them, so I took them. In my trunk. Until I needed them."

"In a duffel bag," Foster said. "With that Rover out back waiting."

Amelia shrugged. "Naturally."

Foster stole a look at the entry to the kitchen. It felt like it was miles away. "Since you're talking, where's Tom?" Foster asked.

"Up or down. I'd bet down."

She turned to face Foster, the knife behind her back now. "Why should I care? He's a kidnapper, a killer, a liar. Who are you really? You're hiding something."

"None of your business who I am," Foster said. "Put the knife down and move out of my way."

Amelia chuckled. "I bet Detective Li's not happy down there. There aren't any cabinets." She laughed. "He killed in our basement, you know. When we were kids? We saw one. I don't know how many more there were. We ignored it. He expected it." She pressed the knife tip to her chest. "I've only taken four. Red hair is rare. That's why I got so angry when that one girl lied. Wearing a wig isn't fair."

"We found Tammy Bergin," Foster said, sliding along.

The name confused Amelia. Her brows furrowed. "Bergin? Who's . . . ? Ah, the driver. She talked too much. She *was* a consolation prize. I couldn't get the one I wanted. Her boyfriend saved her. *Seth.*" She paced the floor. "He made me this way, you understand. I didn't start it. He made me believe I was something I wasn't. Bodie too. I've been thinking, in a way it's like I've been killing my mother—isn't that funny?"

"No, it isn't."

Amelia chuckled. "You're always so serious. You're also bleeding a lot." She took a step toward Foster. "You'll bleed more later."

Foster pushed up higher on the wall, tired of inching, tired of listening to Amelia deal with her fake-daddy issues and try to justify the unjustifiable. "No. I won't." She lifted her left hand, the gun in it. It shook, but the right end was pointed in the right direction. She didn't have to be that precise to put Amelia down. "Throw it down. Step away."

Amelia screeched like a wounded banshee and then came running. Foster fired.

CHAPTER 80

Foster missed, and Amelia plowed into her hard, knocking the gun out of her grip. With the last of everything, Foster grabbed hold of Amelia's shirt and flung her back and off her feet, then lunged for the gun that had hit the floor and landed beyond her reach. She clawed for it, on all fours, not wanting to die here. She could hear Amelia coming, feel her feet pounding on the bare floorboards. This was it. She'd live or die in the next few seconds.

Time slowed. Foster's hand found the gun, she flipped onto her back, and she fired once. Two shots rang out. Foster panicked at the sound of the second shot, until she saw Li sliding down the wall, her gun in her hand. Li looked like death warmed over, but she was alive. Amelia stumbled back, clutching her chest, a stricken look on her face. Blood began to pool on her shirt in two places. Two rounds. One objective. Amelia went down hard.

The entire house went quiet, except for the echo from the rounds. "You okay there, Li?"

"No." Li tried to reposition herself on the wall. It looked painful. "You?"

"I've been better." Foster worked her way to her feet and approached Amelia carefully.

Li tried straightening her right leg out but didn't get far. "Please tell me she's dead."

Foster leaned over and felt for a pulse. She found one but wasn't sure if she considered that good news or bad. "She's still breathing."

Li squeezed her eyes shut. "Fuck. I need to get back to the range. Tom Morgan's dead. In the basement . . . for real this time."

The front door swung open and Nowak burst in, gun drawn, eyes sweeping right to left. "Police!"

"Yep," Foster called out. "Mind calling it in?" She looked over at an unconscious Amelia. "And cuffing *that*."

But before Nowak could make the call, there was the urgent sound of approaching police sirens.

Li smiled, then grimaced. "Ah, the cavalry."

Foster took a good look at her bleeding arm and hand. "Griffin's going to kill us."

Li managed a grim smile. "I knew that the second I landed at the bottom of those stairs."

———

The house quickly flooded with cops and paramedics. Davies was rushed out on a stretcher; Foster and Li followed right behind on stretchers of their own. The techs came for Morgan. He'd been dead for hours. Obviously, Amelia had gotten over her "daddy worship" and had decided to make him pay for killing her mother and deceiving her.

Griffin wasn't happy when she walked into Foster's emergency room bay an hour later. She had been stitched up, bandaged up, her arm placed in a sling, but that didn't mean Foster would get an ounce of sympathy from the boss. Li was a couple bays down getting a cast put on her broken ankle. She'd gotten luckier with the knee. It was only sprained. None of it was good, except the part where they'd caught two maniac killers and hadn't died. Foster hoped that would temper Griffin's anger somewhat.

Griffin took one look. Foster saw her jaw clench. This was no courtesy visit. "Let's hear it."

Foster cleared her throat and ran it through again from the second she and Li had breached the door to the moment they'd shot Amelia. When she had finished, Griffin was almost the color of an heirloom tomato, and her eyes looked as inky as a snake's. "Are you a hot dog, Foster?"

"I am not, boss."

"Are you *trying* to get yourself killed?"

"We were following a lead . . ."

"No backup," Griffin said, cutting her off. "With nobody knowing where you were going. If it weren't for Lonergan finding the address to that house on Li's desk, we'd have had no idea." She stepped closer. "I could have lost two cops today. Two. In one day."

"Yes, boss."

Still, Griffin wouldn't let Foster's eyes go. "You want to play Russian roulette, you're going to have to do it somewhere else."

Foster shook her head. "This is not that." It didn't look like Griffin believed her. "It was a bad call."

"Which one of you made it?"

A beat went by. "I did."

Griffin glowered. "Li said it was her. I don't know whether to pat myself on the back for putting you two together or kick myself in the ass for doing it."

"I'll take the fallout," Foster said.

Griffin stood there, steaming, but Foster barely knew the woman, so it was difficult to work out what else was going through the woman's head. "Yeah, you will. Li will too." She yanked open the door. "I'm not sending either of you any damn flowers . . . friggin' Rambo bullcrap."

"Amelia?" Foster asked.

"Lucky for you two, she's too evil to die." Griffin stormed out and let the door ease closed behind her. Foster leaned back in bed and thought about how close she'd come to not being here, how she'd actually stopped for a moment midstruggle to work out whether she was okay with dying by Amelia's hand. That she'd chosen correctly was a positive. It confirmed that she was strong enough, invested enough, to stay. Why hadn't Glynnis been?

Foster stared down at her shoes, at the flecks of blood on the leather. Her blood, and Amelia's too, likely. She decided then that they'd meet the trash the second she could get them there. "The world keeps turning," she muttered absently. Spotting a paper clip on the instrument tray along with what was left of the bandages and gauze used to wrap her wounds, she picked it up and slid it into her pocket.

Habit. Necessity. Whichever it was, she was sure that she wasn't ready to stop marking time. She knew that wanting to live and knowing how to live on were different things.

Reg's memorial was approaching. There would be balloons, Felix had said. She would not be there. Foster knew another thing for sure— she was afraid to let Reg go, afraid of how little was left if she did. She ran her bandaged hand along the sling, feeling for the bandages beneath it. She'd come away with more than eighty stitches . . . and her life. She lifted off the bed, then pulled herself up straight. "Okay, Reg. Let's do this."

CHAPTER 81

Amelia stared up at the ceiling of her hospital room, finding patterns in the paint, lines that the paint roller had left behind, forming channels all along the surface. Her wrists were cuffed to the bed railings, a cop at her door day and night. How long she had been here, like this, she couldn't say—maybe weeks. It really didn't matter. She'd been shot; she remembered that. It had to be weeks because she didn't hurt as much as she had before, and the beeping machines and worried looks on the doctors and nurses who attended to her were gone, most of the bandages too. She heard something about her being transferred soon, but she had no idea where or when, and again, it really didn't matter.

"A caged bird with clipped wings," she muttered, watching the patterns. "A creator of beauty." She lifted her wrists off the bed, rattling the cuffs. "Captured." She sighed. There was nothing she could do in the state she was in but think and watch the swirls. She wanted her canvas but knew she'd never see it again. She'd never get to add Tom Morgan to it. Amelia began to chuckle, then laughed outright. "The look on his face. So shocked, so betrayed." The laughing stopped; anger replaced it. "The *liar*."

She squirmed, uncomfortable, fighting the cuffs. "Get me out of these. You have no right to treat me like this. Let me go." The cop peeked in from the hall, then turned away. "You hear me, you cop. Get these off me."

She tried to sit up, but the cuffs made that an uneasy thing. "You have no right."

A nurse rushed in with a syringe, approached the port in the IV bag, and sneered at her. "Don't you dare knock me out." The nurse paid no attention to the warning. Amelia watched the syringe empty and knew what was coming. "Damn you, you bitch, I'll get you next. I swear if it takes me a thousand years, I'll get . . . you . . . next." Her eyes blurred, but not before she captured the name on the nurse's badge hanging from a lanyard around her neck. "Gina Shields, RN . . ."

Shields backed away from the bed, shaking, then ran from the room as though the devil himself were chasing her.

CHAPTER 82

Bodie gave his building one last look, then jumped into the car he'd just bought himself. He was leaving. Starting fresh somewhere else. There was no moving van. There wasn't a chair or a plate or a rug he wanted to keep from his old life. He was going with the clothes on his back, headed . . . somewhere.

Amelia's mind was gone. She was locked away in a padded cell, a killer who would never see the light of day again. His father, or the man he'd thought was his father, was dead. He was alone for the first time in his life and at a crossroads. He was Boden Jensen. Clean slate. His own man.

He started the car, listening to the purr of the engine, breathing in the new-car smell. He was normal, not the son of a devil. He'd been corrupted, but he could change and grow and become new. Niles Jensen, his real father, had wanted him, looked for him. He'd missed out on knowing him, having that love, and he couldn't get that back, but maybe there was family somewhere? Cousins, a grandmother, connections? He'd start there. He'd find his family.

He put the car in gear and drove away without looking back.

CHAPTER 83

Silva walked down the hall of the prison's psychiatric wing on her way to room 333-A. Locked ward. The place for the hardened psychotics, the dangerous ones, the ones who, if given half a chance, would gouge your eyes out with a ballpoint pen and smile about it afterward. She wanted to see the woman who'd tried to kill her. For a moment, she stopped in the hall to press her fingers into the tender flesh at her side. It still hurt. She still had to turn a special way and breathe a little differently, or she'd feel the tug, the strain of what the knife had left behind. But after many months, she was healing. She had a reason to look on the bright side of things. Twins. Bodie and Amelia Morgan.

Silva stood in front of the metal door of 333-A and slid back the small door used for observation purposes. This wasn't Westhaven; Amelia was too sick, too dangerous, too unrepentant for that. It had taken Silva every ounce of pull she still possessed to gain access to her prize, here, behind locked doors. But she had needed to see Amelia again. Face her.

Inside the small, barren room sat Amelia dressed in a pink prison jumpsuit, her hair a mess of tangles. She sat on the narrow bed, rocking, staring out of the slit of a window at a piece of sky. Medication had stabilized her to some extent, Silva had been told, but her psychosis was severe, her mental injury profound and likely irreversible.

"Hello, Dr. Silva," Amelia said, though she hadn't turned when the little door opened. "I've been expecting you."

Silva smiled, a thrill of triumph snaking up her spine. "Hello, Amelia. We have so much to talk about."

ACKNOWLEDGMENTS

I am indebted to my village of lifter-uppers and kick-in-the pantsers who keep me pushing forward when the weeds get deep. That village includes my writing family in Crime Writers of Color, Mystery Writers of America, and Sisters in Crime who prove that though writers write alone, they don't have to struggle alone. Together we're better! A profound thanks to my agent, Evan Marshall, and to my new Thomas & Mercer peeps, editors Liz Pearsons and Clarence Haynes, as well as to the entire T&M team. I hope we'll do great things together. To the wonderful folks at Dana Kaye Publicity—Dana herself, awesome, and my fantastic publicist, Julia Borcherts—who are as passionate about my work as I am, thank you. For technical assistance, I give my thanks to Detective Gregory Auguste and retired Detective Keith Calloway, Chicago Police Department. I hope I got most of the police things right. I asked a lot of questions, but I'll likely ask more for the next book, too, so also thank you in advance.

The writing life is difficult. You're never really sure you're doing it right. Luckily, at every point along my journey there seemed to be someone there who kept me writing, kept my eyes on the prize. To all those angels who turned back and stuck a hand out or offered sage advice and words of wisdom, or even just an encouraging smile, thank you. I honor your kindness and your time by paying it forward.

And a special thank you to my mother for instilling in me the joy of reading. I wouldn't be here without that. And no one could have exhibited better humor at having to read *Green Eggs and Ham* more than a million times to me at bedtime. I think I absorbed the sound of sentences from Dr. Seuss. Rhythm. Symmetry. The flow of the words. Thanks, Mom! All my love.

ABOUT THE AUTHOR

Tracy Clark is the author of the highly acclaimed Cass Raines Chicago Mystery series, featuring Cassandra Raines, a hard-driving African American PI who works the mean streets of the Windy City dodging cops, cons, and killers. Clark received Anthony Award and Lefty Award nominations for her series debut, *Broken Places*, which was shortlisted for the American Library Association's RUSA Reading List and named a CrimeReads Best New PI Book of 2018, a Midwest Connections Pick, and a *Library Journal* Best Book of the Year. *Broken Places* has since been optioned by Sony Pictures Television. Tracy's short story "For Services Rendered" appears in the anthology *Shades of Black: Crime and Mystery Stories by African-American Authors*. She is the winner of the 2020 and 2022 G.P. Putnam's Sons Sue Grafton Memorial Award, also receiving a 2022 nomination for the Edgar Award for best short story for "Lucky Thirteen," which appears in the crime fiction anthology *Midnight Hour*. A Chicago native, she works as an editor in the challenging newspaper business and roots for all Chicago sports teams equally. She's a proud member of Crime Writers of Color, Mystery Writers of America, and Sisters in Crime, and she sits on the boards of Bouchercon National and the Midwest Mystery Conference. Find her on Facebook (https://facebook.com/tclarkbooks), Twitter (@tracypc6161), Instagram (@tpclark2000), or her website (https://tracyclarkbooks.com).